HUNTING SAVAGE

A PETER SAVAGE NOVEL

HUNTING
SAVAGE

A PETER SAVAGE NOVEL

DAVE EDLUND

Light Messages

Hunting Savage (Peter Savage, #4)
Dave Edlund
www.petersavagenovels.com
dedlund@lightmessages.com

Published 2017, by Light Messages
www.lightmessages.com
Durham, NC 27713

Paperback ISBN: 978-1-61153-209-8
Ebook ISBN: 978-1-61153-208-1
Library Control Number: 2016952719

This is a work of fiction. All characters, organizations, and events portrayed in this novel are either products of the author's imagination or are used fictitiously.

To Eileen, you are everything to me... and so much more.

ACKNOWLEDGEMENTS

THIS IS THE FOURTH BOOK in the Peter Savage series, and it would not exist without the support and encouragement of you, the readers. Thank you. It sounds trite as I write these two words, yet I mean this from my heart, for what is the point of writing a novel if no one reads it?

There are many persons to acknowledge and express my gratitude to. I'll begin with my publisher, Light Messages. It has been said that producing a book is a team effort, and I couldn't agree more. Thank you Betty and Wally for your unwavering support and hard work to expand distribution channels; not only domestically but also in other countries. I also want to acknowledge Kylee and express my appreciation for the amazing graphics she creates and the social media marketing work she puts in on my behalf. And a special thank you to my editor, Elizabeth. Your keen insight and candid feedback contribute immensely to making these stories better.

I also want to acknowledge the generous support from my beta readers for your comments and suggestions, as well as all those who have posted reviews. Thank you.

When it comes to issues of military tactics and technology, I have relied heavily on the expert knowledge of Joseph Linhart (Captain U.S. Army, Retired) and Sergeant Seth Lombardy (U.S. Army). These gentlemen were instrumental in supplementing my research on Army ordinance and especially artillery fuzes, to ensure accurate depiction in this novel.

Finally, two of my long-time mentors deserve special mention; Gary and Gordon. You have each been a driving force behind my writing adventure. If not for the encouragement and honest critical feedback from the both of you, I probably would not be here now, at the keyboard typing these words. Your influence goes beyond my capability to measure.

So, here we are—adventure number four. The plot is mostly set in Bend, Oregon, and the Cascade Mountains just west of Bend. The locations introduced in the novel are real. I've wanted to share more of my hometown, and this seemed to be the perfect opportunity. As for the settings along the slope of Broken Top and the edge of the Tam McArthur Rim, these places are very special to me. I've spent many wonderful weeks in these mountains hiking, camping, hunting, backpacking. Surrounded by pristine natural beauty, it is a grand location to sit and think—and dream about the next thrilling escapade of Peter Savage!

AUTHOR'S NOTE

BY THE TIME *HUNTING SAVAGE* IS RELEASED, the U.S. Presidential election will be done and over. However, I am writing these words on the eve of the first debate between the major party candidates, and at this point in time the outcome is far from certain. No worries, I'm not going to pontificate on what could have been or should have been. Rather, my objective is to draw attention to the dangers we face in this era of highly polarized politics and strained international relationships.

Although I am speaking without hard and accurate facts, it seems to me that in the years following the financial meltdown of '08, governance by politicians in Washington continues to set record levels of inaction and disapproval, year after year. At the same time, the bitter rhetoric is continuously ratcheting up. And it's not just U.S. politicians—we see similar challenges overseas.

The danger is that this bitter divide is a fertile breeding ground for ultra-nationalism. Using fear as a tool, too often politicians strive to drive a wedge between one's patriotism and common sense. Although fear takes many forms, in *Hunting*

Savage it is the fear of terrorism that is used as a means to justify violence on a very wide scale.

International terrorism has played a prominent role in global policy for several decades. Historically, terrorism has been almost the exclusive domain of marginalized groups fighting for political or religious ideology. Are we witnessing a shift to nations using terror as an overt (rather than covert) action? Is the Russian-backed invasion of Ukraine and resulting proxy war that much different from the actions of IS in the Middle East? And what are we to say of the bombing campaign by both Russia and the U.S. in Syria—with hundreds of thousands of civilians suffering daily from the brutality and death brought about over ideology and politics?

It is easy to prey on one's fear of violence to win a political election. But what if such tactics are not only used by the candidates? What if such tactics were to be employed by other countries? Outrageous? Perhaps not. With unresolved allegations of Russian hackers trying to gain confidential information in order to influence the U.S. Presidential election, unfriendly nations may already be trying to influence the selection of our leaders.

And what of our allies? We know that the U.S. has not always behaved in a friendly fashion toward its closest allies—getting caught spying on Angela Merkel was bad form to say the least. It's reasonable to think that some of our closest friends may have agendas not necessarily in line with evolving U.S. foreign or domestic policy. Maybe, just maybe, some of those close allies are willing to play their own version of "dirty tricks" to influence our elections in their favor.

That is the question posed herein.

In a complex world, the truth doesn't always fit neatly into 15-second soundbites.

–DE

PROLOGUE

TEL AVIV, ISRAEL
NOVEMBER 13, 2015

"I WOULD HAVE NEVER BELIEVED President Taylor would sell us out." Prime Minister David Feldman was angry—and desperate.

Yossi Winer, the National Security Adviser, lowered his head. "The Americans are an ocean away. President Taylor has no idea what it is like to be truly threatened, to live surrounded by enemies."

Also present in Feldman's office was his Intelligence Adviser, Benjamin Roshal. "Our agents report that the Iranians will renege on the agreement once international trade is normalized. The primary objective for the Iranians was to regain access to the billions of dollars in currency and assets frozen offshore, and the freedom to sell oil openly on international markets. Once their coffers are full again, their nuclear program will be resumed—almost certainly with the aid of Russia."

"Russia?" The question came from David.

"Yes. As you know, most of the enriched uranium that was

manufactured by Iranian scientists was shipped to Russia."

"Thousands of tons," Yossi added. "It is no secret that Russia and Iran have been forging a closer relationship."

David shifted his eyes to Benjamin. "How long?"

"Until they have an atomic bomb?" He shrugged, calculating the numerous variables. "Within five years if they have to rebuild their key reactors and resume processing fuel. However, if the Russians or Pakistanis help, it could be much sooner."

"With enough money, anything is for sale," Yossi added glumly. "Once the sanctions are lifted, the Iranians will have plenty of money."

"What are the most likely scenarios?" David asked from behind his desk, leaving his advisers standing.

"Benjamin and I have studied this risk in great detail. When the sanctions are lifted—"

"You think there is no hope that we can convince the West to stall?"

"No, sir," Benjamin answered. Months ago he had resigned himself to the new reality for Israel—the reality of a nuclear-armed Iran.

David raised a finger and swirled it in a circle aimed at Yossi, his signal to continue. "With a few hundred million dollars, Iran can buy a weapon from many sources. Most likely, from a disgruntled former Russian officer. Possibly from the Ukraine. Or, maybe from the Pakistanis."

Benjamin nodded, his expression dour. "Our agents believe that Hezbollah might be the eager recipient of such a weapon. Iran would be able to deny they had any role in the deal, and Hezbollah has hundreds of loyal soldiers who could smuggle a bomb into Israel."

"We need to increase the number of radiation scanners at the border crossings," David said to neither man in particular, but Yossi took it as an action item.

"You cannot guarantee the survival of Israel with radiation scanners," Benjamin said.

David cast a piercing gaze upon his trusted advisor. "And what would you have me do? Iran outnumbers our military four to one. They have a capable navy, as well as sophisticated missile systems. Our nuclear arsenal has been the only deterrent we enjoy. And, if your predictions are accurate, that will soon be nullified."

"If Iran attacks the homeland, the U.S. and NATO allies will rush to our side," Yossi observed. Israel had always been a very close ally of the U.S. and most European countries. Ironically, Germany had evolved to be one of Israel's strongest benefactors, second only to the United States. It seemed that modern German governments were still repenting for the horrors wrought by the Nazis.

"And what good will that be if Tel Aviv is a smoking ruin?"

"Perhaps," Benjamin offered, pressing a finger to his lips, sensing the time was right, "perhaps, we should think proactively rather than reactively."

David and Yossi both looked at the Intelligence Adviser. Benjamin allowed a moment to pass, ensuring he had their full attention. "The fathers of Israel would never have allowed such a threat to exist. They would have dispatched it before the threat was material."

The Prime Minister narrowed his eyes. "Are you suggesting a pre-emptive strike?"

"We've done it before," Yossi said. "Air strikes, sabotage. We've even destroyed key reactor parts and uranium fuel being readied to ship from ports in France."

"I'm quite familiar with the Begin Doctrine," David answered, referring to a fundamental tenet of Israeli foreign policy to use pre-emptive force in self-defense.

Yossi deferred to Benjamin. "David, one simply needs to read the newspaper to understand that Jews are constantly under threat. Persecution of our brothers and sisters is becoming more common. Last week a teenager was knifed to death in Lyon, France, by two immigrants simply because he was Jewish. In London, the Faithful have been advised not to appear in public wearing the *kippah* for fear of retribution by Muslims. Hezbollah continues to harass our northern border, and Fatah is constantly planning and launching raids across our southern border. And it has only been three weeks since the terrorist attack in Eilat. We know that attack was orchestrated by Hezbollah and financed by Iranian agents."

The Prime Minister's shoulders slumped under the great weight of it all. The deadly terrorist attack at the gorgeous Hilton Queen of Sheba hotel in the port city of Eilat was still a fresh wound in Israel. Known for the gorgeous snorkeling and scuba diving nearby in the Red Sea, the Queen of Sheba hotel was packed with tourists, mostly Israelis, on holiday. Six Hezbollah terrorists—three men and three women, posing as couples on vacation—went on a killing rampage. They wandered the halls and lobby of the hotel for over an hour, firing automatic weapons and tossing grenades into the terrified crowds using tactics copied from the Pakistani terrorists who had nearly destroyed the Taj Mahal Palace hotel in Mumbai in 2008.

Eventually, all six terrorists were shot dead by security troops, but not before 137 civilians—including children as young as two years old—were murdered. The nation was still mourning the loss.

"The Middle East has changed much since the 60s and 70s," David objected. "The Arab Coalition we faced in those days no longer exists. It has been replaced with new alliances—ones that are much stronger. You said yourself that Russia and Iran are developing ties. And what of China?" He shook his head.

"China does not have the energy resources she needs to fully modernize. Do you think China will miss an opportunity to ally with our oil-rich enemies?"

Yossi held his hands out at his sides, imploring the Prime Minister to keep an open mind. "David, please. Listen to Benjamin. Hear him out before you make a decision."

Feldman turned to Benjamin and dipped his chin in a curt nod. "You have a plan?"

"Indeed. We must strike Iran a deathblow before the hard liners acquire even one atomic bomb. We will take advantage of the animosity between the Sunni majority of Saudi Arabia and the Shia clerics who have ruled Iran since 1979."

For several silent minutes David Feldman considered what his advisers were saying. If Israel did strike first in accord with the Begin Doctrine, there was plenty of precedent for such action. Although the international community as a rule condemned first-strike military actions, the UN seemed to be willing to grant Israel more leeway in dealing with threats to her security.

"For the sake of argument, let's imagine Israel does attack Iran. What do you suggest is the objective? There are no operational nuclear facilities, are there?" He raised an eyebrow with this last question as he locked eyes with Yossi.

Benjamin cleared his throat. "No. For the moment at least, there are no nuclear programs of any significance underway in Iran. And we must ensure they are never able to develop or purchase such weapons."

"So you have said. What is it exactly that you suggest I do?"

Benjamin straightened his back and squared his shoulders. "For the sake of God, we must change the map of the Middle East forever. Our enemies must be defeated once and for all."

Slowly, David Feldman rose from his chair. In silent contemplation he rounded his desk and stood toe to toe with his National Security and Intelligence advisers. "We can do this?"

Yossi and Benjamin both nodded.

"You have a plan?" David asked.

"We do," Yossi answered. "I suggest we brief you fully, including the general staff."

"It would be a historic achievement for Israel." David rubbed his chin as he turned to pace across his office. "It would ensure our security for generations."

"You would be a national hero," Benjamin offered.

Feldman stopped, a disturbing thought suddenly coming to mind. "What if the plan fails? We cannot win a protracted battle with Iran. And what of Russia?"

For the first time since the meeting began, Benjamin Roshal offered a smile. "We have the backing of the American military. Russia will not intervene. And if the plan does not go as well as expected, the American war machine will prove to be an invincible ally as we defeat first Iran, then Syria and Iraq. Libya, Lebanon, and the Palestinian Territories will be ours for the taking."

David snorted a disingenuous laugh. "You can't possibly believe President Taylor will offer military support to Israel in this venture."

"No," replied Benjamin, a crafty smirk still plastered across his face, "but the next U.S. President will."

CHAPTER 1

ELI MOVED FORWARD in purposeful strides. Head down, he wore dark glasses, gloves, and a black beret. The collar of his black wool overcoat was turned up to ward off the frigid air. A stiff leather messenger pouch hung at his side, the contents given to him by Benny Goldsmith, the Israeli Ambassador to the United States.

An experienced agent of Mossad, Eli never questioned orders. Questions were a luxury for naïve idealists and dreamers. That was not Eli. He was a warrior fighting for the survival of his people, his homeland. It was not his job to make policy, to decide what course of action should be taken. Rather, he was an implement of action to ensure the desired results were achieved.

Sometimes, that meant exporting the violence, so that others would understand.

Everything Eli did this night, from the way he dressed, to the locations he scouted and ultimately selected, to the timing of his actions—everything—was coldly calculated to send a message.

It was 3:00 a.m., and the sidewalks were all but deserted. He turned the corner into an alley behind Langan's Pub, just off West 47th Street and a half block from Times Square. He passed a homeless man pressed tight against the brick wall, burrowed under a filthy blanket with the remains of a large cardboard box for cover. The rank odor of vomit, stale urine, and rotten food assaulted his senses.

Ahead, the mechanical rumble of heavy machinery announced the approach of a garbage truck a few seconds before its lights appeared at the opposite end of the alley. The truck was just turning off West 46th, right on schedule.

Eli jogged to a commercial refuse bin behind the pub. He only had a minute, maybe two, to complete his task without arousing suspicion from the truck driver. Plunging his hand into the messenger pouch, he retrieved a yellow-green object. It filled his hand as his fingers wrapped around the device, obscuring it from view of the security camera aimed from the far side of the alley toward the steel dumpster. With his free hand, he removed first a safety tie and then a metal ring attached to a pin. Then he carefully stuffed the grenade against a front wheel of the dumpster so that when the bin was pulled forward to be emptied, the lever would pop off and ignite the chemical fuze.

His task completed, Eli turned and swiftly exited on West 47th Street. As he crossed Times Square, the sharp report of the explosion was proof his mission had succeeded. He strode down another alley, placing three more grenades, before vanishing into the night.

The sanitation department driver was on autopilot. He'd been working this route for close to three years, long enough that the motions were more muscle memory than deliberate thought. With the diesel engine rumbling in idle, he hopped out of the cab and wrestled the dumpster forward about six feet. When the fragmentation grenade detonated, the driver was in the process of climbing back into the cab. The blast slammed the open cab door into his body, knocking him to the pavement. The dumpster cartwheeled into the air, landing with a clang 20 feet away. Dozens of steel fragments pierced the front of the garbage truck, including three that penetrated through the door and lodged in the driver's thigh and shoulder.

Almost immediately, passersby appeared from nowhere, drawn in the alley by the sound of the explosion. Soon, sirens blared and two police cruisers arrived on the scene, their flashing colored lights adding to the chaos. A civilian was applying pressure to the worst of the driver's leg wounds, stemming the flow of blood.

One of the officers was holding back the onlookers, whose ranks had grown to nearly a dozen, while the other was speaking over his radio to dispatch. "We have one victim, male, he's conscious with multiple wounds. Request emergency medical help; this guy is bleeding pretty bad."

"Dispatch. Roger request for med—"

The sharp crack of two nearly-simultaneous explosions drowned out the reply from dispatch. Reflexively, the two police officers ducked, but quickly it became apparent they were not in imminent danger. As the officer called in the report, one thought was foremost in his mind—*It's going to be a long night.*

With a 20-block area surrounding Times Square evacuated and sealed off, NYC police along with agents from BATF and the FBI, scoured the area for clues as well as additional explosive devices. The security tape from the video camera by the first bomb had been reviewed, and law enforcement knew their prime suspect was male, with short black hair—possibly Middle Eastern—but it was not possible to pull many facial details from the images.

By noon, they had found only one unexploded device, a military hand grenade also placed at the base of a commercial trash bin close to Times Square. Fortunately, there was a surveillance camera nearby, and it showed images of the same suspect as from the first bombing. Declaring the streets safe, the evacuation order was lifted.

Considering the nature of the recovered device, plus evidence that the three exploded devices were fragmentation bombs, possibly hand grenades, the investigative lead was turned over to the FBI. Before the day was over, an explosive ordinance expert from the U.S. Army confirmed the unexploded grenade was of Iranian manufacture.

"You guys are lucky no one was killed," the expert explained. He was video conferencing with FBI agent in charge, Special Agent Wilhelm. "That's a fragmentation grenade. Killing radius is eight meters."

"We don't often see military explosives in domestic bombings," Wilhelm said. "Usually it's homemade IEDs. You sure it's Iranian?"

"Absolutely. The markings are distinctive, as is the overall design. It's a rough copy of the older pineapple-style hand grenade popular during the mid-twentieth century."

Wilhelm was studying the photograph displayed over the video link. "This is the condition of the grenade when it was found?"

"That's right. Apparently, a patrol officer found it at the base of a dumpster about a block away from the second explosion. The pin was still in place. It was completely safe."

"That's odd. Why would the bomber place three grenades, pulling the pin and setting each to explode when the trash bins were moved, and yet fail to arm the fourth device?"

The Army expert shrugged. "Can't help you there. Anyway, that's all I have. Let me know if any other questions come up during your investigation."

"Yeah, sure. Thank you." And then a moment later, just before the expert hung up, "Oh, one more question."

"Sure, what is it?"

"Any idea how someone in New York would come into possession of Iranian hand grenades?"

"Well, the obvious answer is your suspect is connected to Iranian military, maybe the Revolutionary Guards."

Wilhelm had already thought of that possibility. "Yes, but how does he get the grenades—let's say there were four of them—into this country? It wouldn't be easy to get hand grenades through airport security; I don't care what country you're in."

"Like I said, beats me. Maybe he's a diplomat?"

"Iran and the U.S. don't have diplomatic relations."

"Sorry, I can't help you with that one. Give me a call if you have questions of a *military* nature."

Special Agent Wilhelm eased back in his chair, deep in thought. *How would I smuggle grenades from Iran into New York?* If the answer involved secure diplomatic pouches, it would have to be through a government friendly—or at least sympathetic—to the Islamic Republic of Iran. *I don't even know how to begin investigating that angle.*

He decided to see what forensics came up with. Maybe the facial images captured by the security cameras would return a positive ID after running through the many data bases maintained by U.S. and European agencies.

Wilhelm sighed. He was a realist, and he knew that short of a miracle, if the facial recognition software came up empty, this case would go cold within a week.

CHAPTER 2

THE CHIME FROM EMMA'S PHONE woke her from a fitful slumber. She glanced at the clock—5:30 a.m. Hopeful that it was the email she had been expecting, she rolled out of bed, grabbed her laptop, and quietly entered the kitchen so as not to wake Kate. While her PC was booting up she heated a mug of water in the microwave and began steeping a tea bag—black tea infused with orange and spices—and returned to her desk. There it was, an email message from Jon Q with a single large PDF attachment.

The file was titled "Traitors Within." She thought that odd, but then realized almost everything about this contact was odd. The communication was always email, always using aliases, anonymity being of paramount concern. Emma knew almost nothing of her contact—gender, age, race—all unknown. She didn't even know if he—she had a mental picture of her contact as a nerdish male, about twenty-fiveish—lived in the United States or abroad.

And then there was this whole dark web thing. Emma wasn't a computer geek, but she had heard of the dark web—mostly in news reports about arrests of hackers charged with stealing financial and personal data. Emma had surfed several online forums about hacking government sites until she made the connection with Jon Q. That was almost three weeks ago.

When Emma explained her request and how it had irreparably affected her family, Jon Q bragged that he could access the Department of Defense records and get the information she was seeking.

"But how can you be certain?" she wrote. "You don't even know where this information is. It could be anywhere after all these years—or nowhere. For all we know, it may have been deleted as part of the cover up."

"Relax Cupcake." That was Jon Q's pet name for Emma. She hated it.

"With the exception of 18 minutes of the Nixon tapes, Big Brother never deletes anything. The information is there—always is. Just waiting for me to find it and bring it into the light of day."

"Why do you do this?"

"It's my duty as a patriot to expose the corruption and waste that pervades every aspect of government."

"You're not a terrorist, are you?"

"Cupcake, you really need to chill. I'm not going to blow up anything. I'm not a terrorist."

"Then why are you doing this?" she wrote back. "You can't expect to change anything. People have tried before—you know, exposing government secrets, embarrassing secrets. And nothing changes, not really."

"I already told you. That and the money."

Emma sighed when she read that in the email. Of course she knew payment would be required. But it wasn't the first thing Jon Q demanded, so she allowed herself to believe that maybe he wasn't going to ask for much.

"Naturally," she wrote. "For love of country and money. Look, I'm a student. I don't have much."

"Already trying to negotiate my rate down, and I haven't even quoted you a price. Like I said, I'm on a mission—you might call it a crusade—to expose the lies and dirty secrets powerful people in Washington don't want Joe Citizen to know. Sounds like you might be onto something here, a really juicy secret. So, I'll cut you a deal. I'd normally get ten grand for this type of job. But for you, this job, I'll settle for five."

By the time the negotiation was concluded, Emma had worked the price down to $3,000—all of her savings—payable in bit coins. Harder to trace, Jon Q had explained.

That was two weeks ago.

She was beginning to believe that Jon Q was running a scam; that he had taken her savings and would never actually hack the records that had been buried for close to half a century: records of a violent battle that claimed her grandfather's life—a battle that should never have occurred.

Emma had not received any messages from Jon Q for close to two weeks, but now she had this email and file. She double clicked on the icon. Several seconds later the file opened and filled her screen.

The PDF document was actually a large collection of official reports and memos. At least they looked official, some with a Department of Navy header and seal, others from the State Department. There were even memos from the Department of Justice and the White House. The font was irregular, as would have been the case for typed documents from the period. They were all dated 1967, as early as June and then moving forward into July, August, and September.

Her hand gripped the teacup, squeezing until her fingertips

turned white as she read. And she continued reading, even as the tea cooled to lukewarm.

She never heard Kate approach, and when her roommate gently placed her hand on Emma's shoulder, she startled.

"You're up early. Is everything alright?" Kate asked.

"Oh, uh, yeah—just couldn't sleep." Emma minimized the PDF file, allowing Kate only a brief glimpse.

"What are you working on?"

"Oh this? Just some research for my history paper. Thought I'd get an early start on it."

Kate eyed her friend suspiciously. "You sure everything is okay?"

"Yeah, why wouldn't it be?" Emma knew she wasn't a convincing liar.

Pressed for time, Kate decided to let it go… for now. She chugged down a spinach-blackberry smoothie, a favorite concoction she had blended the previous night and stored in the refrigerator. "Hey, why don't you text me this afternoon if you want to meet after classes. Tim is tending bar tonight at Brother Jonathan's." Kate was smiling with her eyebrows raised as she mentioned this. For weeks she'd been trying to set up Emma with her friend, much to Emma's dismay.

"Yeah, okay," Emma said, her tone contradicting her words.

"I know that look. Let me know if you change your mind. Gotta go shower and dress; I'm already late."

Alone again, Emma returned to reading the Department of Navy memo. It was short, only three sentences, and addressed to the crew of the USS Liberty and their families. The order was simple, direct: *Do not talk to the press… to your friends… to anyone. The incident is classified, and violation of this order will result in legal prosecution to the fullest extent of the law.*

This information didn't help Emma. Her mother had already told her of the order to remain silent under threat of imprisonment at Leavenworth, the order still binding on descendants of the sailors who were engaged in the action. What Emma wanted—needed—were answers. She had tried in vain to get answers through official channels, filing four separate requests under the Freedom of Information Act. All were flatly denied.

She sighed and moved on to the next document, and the next—searching for answers as to why an obscure battle that took place so many decades ago was still highly classified.

Oblivious to the passage of time, Emma was completely absorbed by the documents, page after page. She stopped only long enough to grab a cup of strong coffee, hoping the caffeine would help to keep her mind sharp. As she read, she was taking notes, laying out the chronology of the attack on her grandfather's ship.

Her mother had told her some of the facts, such as the date of the attack—June 8, 1967. As well as the casualties—34 Americans killed and 171 wounded. Emma knew that the *Liberty* was heavily damaged and came close to sinking—probably would have had it not been for the heroic leadership of Captain William McGonagle and the desperate, tireless efforts of the crew.

Other information about the attack she had gleaned from several books and Internet sites. All of the public sources retold nearly the same story.

On the morning of June 8, four days into the Six-Day War, the *USS Liberty* was in international waters in the Mediterranean, off the coast of Egypt. Several Israeli aircraft flew over the *Liberty* that morning. However, the U.S. officially maintained a neutral position during the Israeli-Arab war, and Captain McGonagle had no reason to suspect his ship and crew were in danger.

The attack commenced suddenly, and without provocation or warning. Israeli jet fighters repeatedly strafed and rocketed the lightly-armed intelligence ship. The crew fought back as best they could, but with only .50-caliber machine guns, they could not mount an effective defense.

Another wave of jets came in and dropped napalm on the foredeck of the ship. Ablaze, the crew ducked bullets and rockets to fight the fire, eventually bringing it under control.

The stars-and-stripes flying above the ship was shot down, only to be replaced.

With ordinance expended, the Israeli aircraft broke off, making way for an even deadlier assault. Three torpedo boats motoring at high speed aimed directly for the *Liberty*. They launched five torpedoes. Miraculously, only one struck the crippled ship, blasting a hole nearly 40-feet across. In that split second, Emma's grandfather and 23 other servicemen lost their lives.

Emma felt her anger rising as she read the account again, this time directly from the official reports and memos. She closed her eyes and imagined the screams from the wounded. The blackened steel plates, blood-splattered decks and bulkheads, limbs and corpses strewn haphazardly by the rocket explosions and large-caliber machinegun fire.

She knew her grandfather was a radio operator and his desk was in a cabin below the waterline, exactly where the torpedo exploded with devastating effect. Like countless nights before, she envisaged the terror of water flooding into the ebony-black tomb. And like before, she prayed he had perished instantly from the explosion. To suffer through drowning, alone and in black isolation, was certainly hell on Earth.

A myriad of questions swirled in her mind, festering over the years without answers. Now she was on the verge of unravelling the mystery, or so she hoped. Yet despite her optimism, after reading more than half of the documents in the file, she still was no closer to knowing why. Why did Israel conduct a protracted air and sea attack on a U.S. Navy surveillance vessel? Why did the U.S. Naval command recall fighter aircraft that could have helped to defend the *Liberty*? And why did the Navy, the Congress, and the President cover up the whole affair?

She was beginning to think that this was a fool's errand, that she had drained her savings and received useless information—likely acquired illegally—in vain. But if Emma was anything, she was determined.

The next memo had been typed on White House letterhead. Across the top read CLASSIFIED TOP SECRET. It was a short memo and didn't take long to read.

"Oh my God." Emma mouthed the words, her voice not even a whisper. Her pulse was racing, her mind swirling in a tangle of thoughts.

She would have to go to the press, naturally. She'd start with the Bend Bulletin and convince them to write an exposé. But any journalist would demand proof that the documents she possessed were genuine.

That was a troubling question, since Emma had received the file from an anonymous hacker. Maybe the file wasn't genuine? Maybe Jon Q had compiled a fake?

No, she wouldn't let herself believe that. She would print several of the most damaging memos and use that to garner the reporter's interest. Maybe she would eventually share the emails and electronic file, too. Then it would be up to the reporter to authenticate the information. After all, that's what a good investigative reporter does, she reasoned.

The doorbell interrupted Emma's planning. Through the sidelight she saw a man at the door. He was dressed in a gray suit with tie and wearing dark sunglasses. His black hair was cropped short, military style.

"Hello," she said as she opened the door.

"Good morning, ma'am. I'm with the FBI, Portland office." He held out his ID next to a metal badge. Emma looked hard at the ID.

"Agent Barnes?" She read his name.

"May I come in? I need to discuss an ongoing investigation concerning cyber security."

With paranoia gnawing at her gut, she motioned him inside.

The rented house had a small living room. Emma directed Agent Barnes to an armless padded chair, and she sat at one end of the sofa. She hoped her mounting fear wasn't showing.

"What is this about? Why do you want to talk to me?" she asked, trying to keep her voice even. *How would someone normally act,* she thought. *Curious, I should be curious.*

Barnes made a show of looking at his pocket-sized notepad. "Miss Emma Jones, is that correct?" he asked, ignoring her question.

"Yes, that's right."

"I need to ask you some questions about your email. Is that alright?"

Emma's pulse quickened. *Stay calm,* she thought. *He can't possibly know about the messages from Jon Q And so what if he does; I haven't hacked into any restricted servers.*

Emma nodded.

"Do you receive a lot of junk mail or spam?"

"Sure, I suppose. What's a lot?"

Barnes seemed to be looking right through her, trying to interpret her body language. It was normal for people to be anxious and uncomfortable when questioned about a case. Often perspiring, sometimes stumbling over words to construct a coherent sentence. In fact, it was the criminals who were most likely to be casual, uncaring in their response, thinking that was the normal reaction.

"Over the last few days, have you received any suspicious or odd emails from anyone you don't personally know?"

"Well," Emma said, "you mean other than the spam?"

"Yes. Other than the usual junk messages and advertising."

Emma felt the weight of his stare as she thought how to answer his question. *Surely he knows. Maybe I should just tell him the truth.*

"Miss Jones. Please answer my question."

As Emma rubbed her hands, they felt clammy. "Well, let me think..."

Barnes held his pen, ready to scribe her answer in his notepad.

"No," she said, shaking her head. "No, I don't think so."

Agent Barnes leaned back in the chair and laid his pen down.

"Miss Jones." He spoke in an even tone, his words measured, carefully chosen. "I don't believe you are being completely honest with me. You are pretending to be ignorant. Now, why would you do that?"

She stared back, chewing her lip.

"I know that a file was emailed to you last night. It came from an individual who likes to call himself Jon Q. And I also know he sent several other email messages to you over the past three weeks. It seems that you and Mr. Jon Q had a rather extensive correspondence."

Emma felt her heart pounding, beads of perspiration threatened to slide down her forehead. She was squeezing her hands so tightly the knuckles were white.

Under the FBI agent's withering gaze, she slowly nodded.

Barnes sighed and then placed the notepad in the breast pocket of his suit jacket.

"I didn't do anything wrong," Emma said. "Honest! You can read the emails yourself."

Barnes had heard it all before. He sighed again, this time louder, and placed both hands on his knees. "Okay. I believe you. But you will have to cooperate with the investigation. You will have to truthfully answer all my questions."

"Okay," she nodded.

"Let's begin with the emails. Let's look at your computer."

"It's in the dining room, I was reading his last message when you rang the doorbell." She rose and walked toward the table next to the kitchen, Barnes following closely.

"Here," she pointed at the laptop, the screen still displaying the White House memo. "This file was attached to his last email. I really think this is important. It should be made available to the public. My grandfather was on the *Liberty*. He was one of the sailors who was killed."

Barnes leaned in and inserted a thumb drive into a USB slot. Then he took a step back.

"I'm sorry for your loss Miss Jones, but it was a necessary sacrifice. Now, please save that PDF file to the thumb drive."

She entered a few keystrokes to transfer the data, then ejected the portable drive.

"Thank you," he said, and pocketed the thumb drive. "I just have a couple more questions—" Barnes coughed. "Do you have some juice, or a soda?"

"Sure." Emma wanted to be helpful. She believed that if she fully cooperated, the FBI would treat her as a witness rather than someone who helped in the crime.

She turned her back to Agent Barnes and walked to the kitchen, opening the refrigerator.

"That's fine," he said.

Emma looked over her shoulder into the barrel of a gun. She still had one hand holding the refrigerator door, her eyes wide in fear.

"Who are you?" Emma asked.

Her question was met with a silent glare.

"Please, just let me go."

"I can't do that." He held the gun steady.

Tears welled up in Emma's eyes. "Please…"

That was the last sound she heard.

A small red circle formed instantly between her eyebrows, and Emma collapsed to the floor.

Barnes holstered the weapon, slipped on gloves, and then proceeded to ransack the house. He entered the bedrooms and dumped the drawers onto the floor. In the dining room there was a small desk, and he again tossed the contents on the floor, pocketing a ten-dollar bill he found in the pencil drawer.

Satisfied, he turned his attention to the laptop. Reinserting the thumb drive, he opened an executable file. Soon, he was prompted to type in and confirm a new password. His job nearly completed, he gathered the laptop.

As he closed the front door, Barnes glanced around the neighborhood. It was quiet, with older ranch-style homes set well back from the street on large lots. Every house had at least one mature pine tree in the front yard. It was mid-day, and no one was strolling the sidewalk; no cars or delivery trucks were moving on the street.

Agent Barnes walked to his car, placed the laptop on the passenger seat, and drove away.

CHAPTER 3

THE YELLOW CRIME-SCENE TAPE spoke volumes. Behind closed doors, the neighbors all asked the same question: What happened? By the time the ambulance arrived, a crowd of about two dozen had gathered on the far side of the street. Some were holding cups of coffee; a few were drinking from beer bottles. The atmosphere was one of morbid curiosity.

The local television station had their van parked nearby and was transmitting live updates. The cameraman was there to film the covered body wheeled out on a gurney late in the evening, footage guaranteed to be played on the 11:00 p.m. newscast.

The forensics team was still busy collecting evidence, room by room, and documenting the crime scene. It was going to be a late night.

Standing in the living room, Ruth Colson was looking toward the kitchen and dining room. Colson was a handful of years away from retirement, yet her energy and passion for solving crimes had not abated in her 34 years of police work.

Her gray hair was short, giving her a masculine appearance. She had been on her feet almost continuously for the past three hours; thankfully, she was wearing her trademark neon-green Oregon Duck sneakers.

With both hands braced on her narrow hips, she said, "No shell casing... we have a small-caliber entry wound, but no exit... and no stippling on the victim's face, consistent with a lack of observable GSR..."

Standing beside Ruth was her junior colleague, Niki Nakano. "The lab may still find gunshot residue on the victim's clothing."

Niki was relatively new to the Detective Unit and had been mentoring under Ruth for close to a year. A third generation Japanese-American, her parents had instilled in Niki a thirst for excellence and success that drove her from Patrol to Detective by age 32.

"True, but for now all we know is that GSR is apparently lacking, suggesting the shot was fired from a distance."

Detective Colson stepped toward the kitchen until she had a clear view of the refrigerator. She stretched her left hand out, miming a gun. "If the perp was standing here, the gun would be only five or six feet from the victim. At that distance there should have been extensive blood stippling on her face from the powder and bullet residue."

Niki walked around the dining room, which was separated from the kitchen by a wall of cabinets with a pass-through counter. Finding the spot where she had an unobstructed angle on the refrigerator, she repeated her mentor's exercise. "This is as far away as the shooter could have been; and it's still—what—maybe 12 feet?"

"Plus, the shot would have just missed the wall and cabinets," Ruth pointed to the wall on either side of the pass through. "Make sure they swab this area for GSR." She leaned in close, careful not to brush her face against the painted surface, her flashlight on, scrutinizing the white paint for particles that could have come from the discharge of a firearm. She shook her head. "I don't see anything."

"None of the neighbors reported hearing a gunshot. Maybe the shooter used a silencer?"

"No, it just isn't right. In order to account for the evidence, the theory is getting too complicated. We have what appears to be a simple home invasion burglary that went bad because Emma Jones wasn't supposed to be home. But why?"

"Sorry?"

"Why this house? It's a rental. Two students. They don't own much property of value. And to suggest that a silenced weapon was used… that's for the pros. It doesn't fit. This crime screams amateur."

Niki understood. "Except for the ballistics."

"Could be subsonic .22 ammunition."

"Maybe. We'll know more once the lab results are in."

"The roommate—Kate—what did she say when asked what was missing?"

Niki referred to her notes before answering. "She didn't take an inventory, she was pretty distraught. But she said they didn't have much—no money or jewelry, no guns or expensive electronics. She did mention that Emma's laptop was gone. She said it was on the table when she left in the morning, that Emma was working on something. We'll have her go through the house later, probably tomorrow if she can handle it. She was taken to the station for a complete statement."

"So only a laptop was taken. And we have a most unusual head wound on the victim."

"I don't know what to make of it," Niki said.

Ruth frowned. "Neither do I."

Sheltered from North Pacific storms by Vancouver Island, the quaint port city of Friday Harbor on San Juan Island is a recreational paradise. Accessed only by boat or plane, getting to and from this sleepy town takes just enough effort to keep the population at a little over 2,000.

When Mitch Kemmel dropped out of college to pursue his computer interests, Friday Harbor suited his needs well. With good civic infrastructure, including an undersea cable providing electricity and high-speed Internet, he had all the modern necessities his newfound profession demanded. Yet he was far enough away from Big Brother that the thought of government oversight was almost laughable. Many of the people calling San Juan Island home embraced bartering to avoid taxes and aligned themselves with the most liberal political positions. Mitch had two friends living on acreage outside the city limits who had gone completely off the net—hadn't filed tax returns in years and, for all intents and purposes, didn't exist in the eyes of the local or Federal Government.

Like most other days, Mitch was working at his office—a study in his modest house on Browne Street. The solitary window was covered with aluminum foil, ensuring no one could spy on his activities. He preferred a more powerful tower PC to a laptop for most of his coding. On the desk were three monitors side-by-side between two art-glass desk lamps.

Mitch lived on the dark web. He had complete confidence in his hacking skills to keep his actions untraceable. Now he was searching a popular bulletin board for the next opportunity.

The project he had just finished on the *USS Liberty* was sufficiently interesting to compensate for the poor payout. He'd added those files to his growing library, all stored on a server in the corner of his office. He was too paranoid to store information in the cloud—one never knew when the software and search-engine giants would be forced to grant back-door access to Big Brother.

Hell, maybe they already had for all he knew.

It was midafternoon, and he wasn't expecting any visitors, so when the doorbell rang he ignored it. Then it rang again. Annoyed, Mitch left his study, ready to tell whoever it was to go away.

Through the peep glass in the front door, he recognized a mail carrier's uniform, complete with a satchel hanging from her shoulder by a wide leather strap. The woman was holding a white box with red and blue markings indicating it was Priority Mail. The annoyance subsided, and he opened the door.

She said, "Mitch Kemmel?"

"Yes, that's me."

"Priority package," she said as she extended the box forward.

Mitch grasped it with both hands, surprised at how light it was—as if the box were empty. "Thank you," he said as he looked at the mail carrier.

Rather than a pleasant face, he was looking directly into the barrel of a gun. The carrier pulled the trigger and with a whisper of a metallic clang, Mitch Kemmel was dead.

The shooter glanced around quickly while pulling on latex gloves. Not seeing any passersby, she dragged Mitch inside and closed the door. Moving quickly from room to room, she tossed drawers in the bedroom and then found the study. She stashed a half-dozen memory sticks and about 20 CDs inside the satchel. Then she used a set of screwdrivers to expertly remove the solid-state hard drives from the tower as well as the server, placing everything into the satchel.

In less than 15 minutes, she picked up the empty Priority Mail box and was out the door, driving away in a white minivan with red and blue tape striping and a U.S. Postal Service magnetic placard on the door.

CHAPTER 4

DETECTIVE COLSON HAD DONE EVERYTHING she could; now it was time to wait and hope for a break. In the week following the murder of Emma Jones, the forensic evidence had been cataloged and secured, lab reports had been completed and reviewed, and witnesses interviewed. Kate Simpson, Emma's roommate, had been very cooperative over hours of questioning. She still insisted that nothing of value was missing, other than Emma's laptop.

Although the crime appeared to be a standard home invasion burglary turned violent, Ruth resisted that theory. Too much of the evidence didn't fit. Especially bothersome was the unique nature of the bullet that killed Emma Jones.

The autopsy revealed it to be magnetic, not made of copper or lead as are the overwhelming majority of bullets. The projectile also lacked the linear striations indicative of rifling. Ruth had never encountered anything like this type of projectile, and she was pinning new hope on this unique evidence.

She emailed photos of the bullet and other ballistic evidence to the Oregon State Crime Lab as well as those of neighboring Washington, California, and Idaho. She even sent the package to the FBI—hoping that another lab would have helpful information; anything to shed light on this puzzle.

"Bingo!" Ruth nearly jumped from her chair as she read an email from the Washington State Police.

Niki looked up expectantly, waiting for the explanation she knew was forthcoming.

"Just got a lengthy reply from the State Patrol Crime Lab in Seattle. That magnetic projectile the ME removed from our victim's head—well, they have one, too."

"Wow, that's a lucky break. What do they have to say about it? Anything on the type of gun that fires it?"

Niki walked around the desk so she could read the message over Ruth's shoulder. "No, nothing on the gun." Ruth sat down. "I don't believe it." She touched the monitor with her index finger. "Their case file was opened a week ago, just like ours."

Niki read further. "The victim—Mitch Kemmel—was shot at his home in Friday Harbor on the same day that Emma Jones was murdered. In both cases the time of death was early afternoon."

Ruth leaned back in her chair, staring at the screen. She had hoped for answers, additional clues. What she got was another conundrum.

"Friday Harbor is more than 400 miles north of here," Niki said, "so obviously we are dealing with two killers."

"Well, time for some old-fashioned detective work. I hope you're wearing comfortable shoes."

"What do you have in mind?" Niki raised an eyebrow.

"We have two murders at about the same time—400 miles apart. The lab reports say the ballistics are identical and unlike anything anyone in the department or crime lab has ever encountered. So, let's talk to the local experts. Maybe someone knows something."

On their fourth stop, at Lost Creek Armory, the detectives finally caught a lucky break. The owner of the gun shop, Tom Lewis—a fit man of about 40, clean-shaven and with short dark hair showing below a Boston Red Sox ball cap—provided their first tangible lead. Although Mr. Lewis claimed he had never seen a magnetic projectile, he suggested the detectives talk to Peter Savage. "He owns EJ Enterprises," Lewis had explained.

"And the connection is?" Niki prodded Lewis to be more specific.

"They design and manufacture magnetic impulse guns for the military. Thought you'd know that. His shop is in the Old Mill District—in the old Power House brick building."

"You seem to know a lot about EJ Enterprises. Why is that?" Ruth Colson asked.

"I've known Peter for more than 10 years. Used to be neighbors back when I was just getting my store going. He's been a good customer. Still see him at the range now and then."

It only took 15 minutes for Ruth and Niki to cross town. They pulled the white unmarked cruiser into a visitor slot in front of a large, three-story brick building with three enormous chimneys projecting through the roof. An American flag flew from the very top of the center stack. Adjacent to an upscale shopping and dining district, the old Power House building was overlooked by most locals and tourists since it did not house a restaurant, art gallery, or clothing boutique.

The detectives were dressed casually, looking very much like the passersby strolling past the shops, looking in the windows, some darting in to explore further and maybe make a purchase. There was little signage indicating the location of

EJ Enterprises, only black block lettering on a glass door. Ruth and Niki entered the lobby where they were greeted by the receptionist.

"I'm Detective Colson and this is Detective Nakano. We'd like to speak with Peter Savage."

"Just a minute. I'll see if he's in."

A minute later a man approached the lobby from a hallway that connected to other rooms farther back in the business. Ruth's trained eye sized him up quickly, a habit she had honed over a career working in law enforcement. He stood about six feet tall, medium build—maybe 170 pounds she thought—brown hair in a conservative cut. When he stopped to introduce himself, she noticed the eyes—steel gray, determined.

"Hello. I'm Peter Savage."

The detectives offered their badges. Peter looked at each carefully, not rushing the inspection. "If you don't mind, we have a few questions we'd like to ask," Ruth said.

"Certainly. We can use my office." It was at the end of the hallway, and Peter showed the detectives in, directing them to two chairs in front of his desk.

"How can I help you?" he asked pleasantly.

Ruth shared the photos of the two magnetic projectiles and the lab analysis proving they were made of metals used in rare earth magnets. She did not mention either homicide. "Tom Lewis suggested you might know something of these projectiles. They are very unusual."

Peter read the report. "Neodymium magnets. Twenty-five caliber." He raised his eyes to the detectives. "These would be fired from a Mk-9 magnetic impulse gun."

"I've never heard of a magnetic impulse gun," Niki said.

Peter smiled. "I'm not surprised. We manufacture the weapon for the military, primarily Special Forces. The technology is classified and sales are restricted—closely regulated by the Department of Defense."

"Then it's safe to say you don't sell these magnetic impulse guns to the public," Ruth said, angling for a clear yes-or-no answer.

"That's right. We sell only to the U.S. Department of Defense. As I said, the technology is restricted. I can't even sell to NATO allies, not even the Brits."

"Have any of your weapons been stolen?" Ruth asked. She knew that nothing had been reported to the Bend Police Department about a burglary at EJ Enterprises; she'd verified that on the short drive following their conversation with Tom Lewis.

"No," Peter said. "What is this about?"

"Am I to understand that you manufacture and sell these magnetic impulse guns only to the military, not anyone else? And your shop has not been burglarized?"

Peter nodded. "Yes, that's right."

Ruth shared a glance with Niki. "Then, would you mind telling me, Mr. Savage, how two of your weapons were used in crimes committed on the same day, 400 miles apart?"

"That's impossible. You must be mistaken."

"You read the forensics report. Those two projectiles— neodymium magnets—were removed from the skulls of a victim in Friday Harbor and a second victim here, in Bend."

Peter stared back blankly.

"I'm open to suggestions," Ruth said.

"I don't know."

"We'll need to audit your inventory and sales records. Everything—parts and completed weapons—going back a year. Maybe more. Oh, and the ammunition—do you make that, too?"

"Yes." Peter was still trying to understand exactly what was happening.

"Then we need to audit that as well. Maybe someone—one of your employees—has been stealing and selling this stuff on the black market."

"I don't believe that."

"We'll need to check your personnel files, too. I can be back with a warrant if necessary."

Peter raised his eyebrows and exhaled deeply. "Of course, I have no doubt. When do you want to start?"

"Now is good."

CHAPTER 5

CLIFF ELLISON STROLLED beside the Reflection Pool; his polished black wingtips, pressed gray slacks, light blue oxford shirt, and red tie clearly separated him from the multitude of tourists enjoying this scenic and historic stretch of the Mall in front of the Lincoln Memorial. He snacked on a bag of popcorn while the woman next to him spoke in a low voice. The conversation ceased whenever a stranger passed by.

"Spare me the suspense, Angela. Just get to the point," Ellison said. He seemed to wear a perpetual frown.

Angela Meyers was widely considered a political genius. Several times a year she was offered jobs by members of the Congressional Black Caucus who chided her for working for a middle-aged, white, male, career politician: Abe Schuman. And her decision had paid off, as Schuman was now Speaker of the House and only a few months away from winning the Republican National Convention. Angela was his principle campaign advisor and chief of staff.

"We ran into a minor issue, but everything is fine now."

"That's good news. I knew I could count on you."

Angela Meyers flashed a brief smile. She was tall, equaling Ellison in height. But her slim figure was in stark contrast to his muscular build. "Naturally, we will continue to monitor the situation. If anything develops, we'll deal with it."

"Hmm. Discretion is vital."

"No worries, Cliff." This time Angela held the smile as Ellison studied her demeanor. Her face conveyed confidence. And yet the issue was important enough to warrant an in-person, private meeting.

They walked on in silence, save for the crunching of popcorn. When Ellison finished, he crumpled the bag and tossed it in a green trash can.

"You know," Ellison said, breaking the silence, "I don't understand why we can't simply destroy the original records."

"Cliff, we've been over this. The records include physical papers as well as electronic copies and other files. They are scattered in too many places. And if we did delete electronic files, we'd likely be caught since the file size and time of last update is automatically compared to the backup copy every time the computer systems undergo maintenance. Trust me on this: it's best to leave this secret buried… deep and forgotten."

"Yes, but things have changed. The files were hacked, and we were forced to take drastic actions. It could happen again."

"No—" She cut off her reply as a tourist—a young man in plaid Bermuda shorts and a neon T-shirt—walked by at a brisk pace. "No, it won't happen again. As I told you, that problem has been fixed."

"What if you're wrong and some other hacker suddenly has interest in this obscure bit of naval history? Maybe a historian, or a poli sci student working on his master's thesis. Then what?"

"Cliff, come on. You already know the answer to that

question. All of the files are flagged. I'm notified the instant anyone accesses them. Their email address and their local server address are immediately sent to me. Relax. There's nothing to worry about. Trust me on this."

Ellison stopped and faced Meyers. He studied her eyes, searching for a sign of uncertainty, of weakness. "Okay... for now," he finally said.

She checked her smart phone. She had been away from the Speaker's Office for almost an hour. Checking the calendar, she said, "I need to get back. Schuman has an important meeting at 2:00."

"Busy schedule? How's Abe holding up?"

"He's been on the road almost constantly for the past six months, coming back to D.C. for key votes, but otherwise he's been on the campaign trail. I have to say, that man can charm just about anyone. He's been smashing his closest rivals. Cleaned up in nearly every primary so far, but most importantly Texas and Florida. And he's projected to win landslide victories in both New York and California."

"That's just the first step. The real question is, can he beat Taylor in November?"

With less than seven months until the Presidential election, and with Abe Schuman very close to being the presumed Republican candidate to challenge President Taylor, the talking heads had plenty of material to keep them going 24/7. Television ads were dominated by attacks on the other candidate, paid for by super PACS, of course. President Taylor and Speaker Schuman continued to elevate themselves above the muck, leaving the mudslinging to their supporters.

So far, Schuman was ahead in national polls by seven to 12 percentage points. With a huge war chest and a long list of prominent endorsements, the Speaker was well on his way to the Oval Office. He had managed to sell his agenda—domestic growth, stability in the Middle East, a hard line against terrorism, sensible immigration policies—to a broad range of voters.

"Are you kidding me? He's going to crush Taylor. Under Schuman's leadership, the House and Senate overwhelmingly passed a resolution condemning Iran for those bombings in New York two months ago. And with nearly the same margin, he ensured passage of a historic bill affirming our support for Israel in the event she is attacked—by Iran or any other country."

"So? President Taylor vetoed that bill."

"Exactly, and look what it cost him—the next day he slid another three percentage points in the polls. Just last week, during a speech at a VFW Convention in Minneapolis, Abe drew a standing ovation when he promised a vote to override Taylor's veto."

Ellison gripped her shoulder firmly. "You'd better be right about this. A lot of important people have invested a fortune in your boss. These people only get a return on their investment if Schuman is elected president. You *do* understand me?"

She pulled his hand away and looked him straight in the eyes. "Are you threatening me?" she asked.

He shook his head. "No, I like you Angela. Consider it a warning. You're mixing it up with the pros here. And in this league, failure is not acceptable."

Peter instructed his entire staff to stop what they were doing and assist the police officers. It turned out to be less disruptive than he had initially thought, as his accounting department was able to direct the detectives—Colson, Nakano, and two others—to all the records they requested. They went through manufacturing records, order and sales records, invoices, payments, and ammunition manufacturing and sales documents.

By early evening, the detectives had what they wanted, at least for now. But the tone of Detective Colson's order was clear. "You are not to destroy any records. No one is to delete emails. This is an active investigation into a homicide. Failure to follow this simple order will likely lead to arrest and criminal charges. Am I clear?"

Peter nodded, as did the accounting staff. "I'll make sure the rest of my employees understand," he assured Detective Colson.

After the detectives left, Peter returned to his office and accessed the electronic archives for the Bend Bulletin newspaper. He went to the edition from the day following the murder of Emma Jones. The account was dry and devoid of many facts about the crime. He learned that Emma attended the local community college, as did her roommate, Kate Simpson. The paper reported that the murder had occurred during a burglary in the middle of the day. Although the specific house address was not printed, the story did give the street and block number which, when combined with the published photo of the house, was enough for Peter to nail it down.

He decided a conversation with Kate Simpson was necessary. Based on the limited information shared by Detective Colson, it certainly appeared that a gun made by his company had ended up in the hands of a killer. And Peter needed to know how it happened.

He found the house easily and parked in front. After ringing the doorbell, he stepped back, trying to be as non-threatening as possible.

Kate opened the door, perhaps thinking this stranger was another police officer or detective. She had been allowed back into the house only two days earlier, when the yellow crime-scene tape was removed, and since then a seemingly endless parade of law enforcement officers had come by, always with a new list of questions—most of which she had already answered.

Don't they share what I'm telling them?

"Yes?" she said, not concealing her irritation.

"I'm sorry to bother you. Are you Kate Simpson?" Peter explained his reasons for being there.

"So, you're not with the police?" she said.

"No, ma'am."

With a shrug, Kate let Peter in. He noticed a glass of red wine on the coffee table.

"How are you holding up?" he asked. The dark shadows under her eyes couldn't be missed. Her face was drawn, but despite this, Peter was captivated, especially by her eyes. They were the same shade of chocolate brown as her shoulder length hair. Understandably, there was no hint of joy or welcome. Her entire demeanor conveyed surrender—a recognition that she must accept the circumstances, even though she hated it. And yet, despite all she had endured—and would endure—the hardship could not suppress her simple beauty.

Kate's mouth turned up in a mirthless smile. "As well as can be expected, whatever that means. Emma was my friend. She was like a sister. How should I feel?"

"I'm sorry. I know what it's like to lose a loved one."

"Yeah, I hear that a lot. Like it's supposed to help, or something."

"No. There's nothing I can say that will help. I'm sorry." Peter shrugged. "It sounds trite… because it is. I've been in your shoes—felt the pain, the loneliness…"

Kate looked into Peter's eyes. She saw a measure of sadness and sincerity that had been absent in every other face that had expressed condolences.

"So tell me, how long does it take?"

Peter shook his head. "I don't know. I still feel it." As the words came out, she saw his eyes glisten. "Eventually, the grief passes, but not the pain of loss. It's always there."

"Great." She sat down and took a gulp of wine. "Have a seat. Want a glass?" She extended the bottle.

"No. Thank you. I won't be long. I was hoping you could help me."

"I've already told the police everything."

"I know. Detectives Colson and Nakano interviewed me earlier today. Naturally, they shared only what they believed absolutely necessary," Peter said. "My company makes advanced weapons for the military. Our sales are tightly controlled, and our manufacturing volume is small. Yet the detectives believe that it was one of my guns that was used…"

"You mean, to kill Emma."

Peter nodded.

"I don't know how I can help you."

"The newspaper said this was a burglary. If I knew what they stole, maybe that would help me find a connection."

"They only took Emma's laptop. They killed her for an old, crummy laptop computer."

Peter cocked his head. "That's all that was taken?"

"Yeah, that's all. We don't have anything worth stealing." Kate motioned, indicating the few pieces of used furniture. The walls were decorated with some cheap prints and photographs. It looked very much like a rental occupied by college students.

"That doesn't make sense. Why would someone break into your house?"

Kate shrugged. "The police said there wasn't any evidence that the doors or windows were forced. They think Emma let the killer in."

"Really? That's different than the story in the newspaper. They made it sound like Emma surprised whoever had broken in. Would you mind if I look at the door locks?"

"Why not."

Kate followed Peter as he checked the front and back doors. He didn't see any scratches that would indicate someone tried to pick the locks. And the doorjambs and hinges were free of unusual marks. "Well, I don't see anything that looks out of the ordinary."

Returning to the living room, Kate refilled her glass and pushed the bottle toward Peter. He shook his head. "Can you tell me what happened that day?"

She cupped the glass in both hands, hesitating to speak. "I woke up late and was in a rush. I work part time at the Student Union. Emma was already up. She was sitting there at the table." She pointed toward the small dining nook adjacent to the kitchen. "She was working on her computer."

"She did that often?"

"No, that was the odd thing. Emma never got up early unless she had to be at class. I think I startled her."

"What was she working on?" Peter asked.

"She said it was research for a history paper, but I don't think so. She closed the file so I couldn't see whatever it was."

"And you don't think it was for a term paper."

"No. Emma was never a good liar. I could see she wasn't telling the truth. Anyway, I got ready and left for campus. When I came home at the end of the day…" Kate started to cry.

"It's okay," Peter said softly, gently, and he placed his hand on Kate's. She sniffled and regained enough composure to continue.

"She was in the kitchen, next to the refrigerator. It was open. The door couldn't close because…" she forced back tears. "Because Emma was blocking it."

"Emma was killed when she walked into the kitchen and opened the refrigerator." Peter was imagining the scene. "But if she let the killer in, and then opened the refrigerator, she must have been engaged in a conversation. Why would she open the refrigerator? Maybe to offer a drink to her visitor?"

Kate looked at Peter with puffy eyes. "I don't understand. Why is that important? Who cares why she opened the refrigerator." Her voice had an edge of irritation.

"Because I don't think this had anything to do with a burglary."

"Well, that's what I know—what I told the police."

Peter thought about the laptop, why anyone would be so interested in a student's computer that they'd kill for it. "Did Emma have any secrets?"

That triggered a short chuckle from Kate. "Like I said, she was a terrible liar."

"Did she receive any odd or threatening emails, or phone calls?"

"No. What are you thinking?"

"It sounds to me that this was planned. Which means someone had a reason for murdering your roommate. And that reason has something to do with her computer. My guess is the answer might be in her email."

Kate was calmer now, hopeful that Peter may be able to find the killer.

"Do you have the password to access Emma's email?"

She shook her head. "But maybe the police can help."

"Maybe. If not, I know another way."

"You'll let me know if you come up with anything?" Kate asked.

Peter nodded.

She wrote something on the napkin she'd been resting her glass on, then handed it to Peter. "Here's my number. I'm creeped out staying here, so I'm moving in with a friend tomorrow."

CHAPTER 6

"DETECTIVE COLSON," she said as she answered the phone.

"Detective, it's Peter Savage. Do you have a minute?"

"I'm surprised to hear from you. Look, if you're going to tell me you're lodging a complaint with the department, save your breath. Our review of your records was by the book, and I've already briefed the chief."

"No, actually, that's not why I'm calling. Have you considered the victim's email?"

"Look, Mr. Savage. I am not at liberty to discuss this investigation with you. You'll be hearing from either myself or Detective Nakano if we have any questions for you."

"Yeah, I get it." The friendliness was rapidly leaving his tone. "So I won't ask you any questions. But here's a suggestion. I was talking with Kate Simp—"

"Now you listen here," her voice was hard, threatening. "You'd better stop poking your nose into *my* investigation, or I'll book you into jail myself!"

"Calm down. I'm not interfering with your investigation. And there's no law against me talking to Kate."

"You're walking on a razor's edge, Mr. Savage."

"Look, all I want to *suggest* is that there may be something of importance in Emma's email. Think about it. This wasn't a random burglary, and you know it. This was planned. Why would the killer be after the laptop?"

"Stay out of this investigation before you muck it up!"

"I'm not in *your* investigation. Just tell me you're going to check into her email account."

Ruth Colson debated for a moment before replying, "We already have."

Peter was surprised. "Okay. And?"

"I shouldn't tell you this, but it's not important to the case anyway. Nothing, okay? We found nothing."

"What do you mean? She didn't have any emails?"

"No…" Ruth replied irritably. "What I am saying is that there was nothing—no messages sent or received—that in anyway were out of the ordinary."

Peter felt deflated. After his conversation with Kate he was certain he was on to a useful lead—something that would help explain how a magnetic impulse weapon had made it into the hands of a murderer.

"We've questioned Kate Simpson at length. We've gone at this from every angle. Trust me on this—we're not a bunch of dummies. I've been a detective for close to 15 years. I know what we're dealing with, and it's not a standard burglary. Now, if you have something useful, let me know. But I'm warning you for the last time: stay out of this."

Richard Nyden—alias Agent Barnes—was enjoying the crisp, clear morning. This was his first visit to Bend, and he felt it suited him well. Nestled on the eastern slope of the Cascade

Range, he had a panoramic view of snow-capped peaks from his hotel on the bluff overlooking the Old Mill District. He was well into a 10-mile run—working off the culinary indulgence from the previous evening—when his phone rang.

He stepped off the trail paralleling the Deschutes River to answer the call. "Did you read my report?" he said, already knowing the other party by the caller ID code name.

"Yes. That was smart, planting a bug in the house. I trust you hid it well?"

"Well enough," Nyden said. "Plus, there's no reason for anyone to suspect listening devices were planted, so no reason to search for them. Got three of 'em: in the living room, kitchen, and bedroom."

"Just the one meeting?" he heard the voice say.

"That's right. And the police don't seem to have any clue—no pun intended."

"What is the probability that this guy—Savage—will find something you missed?"

"Zero. I didn't miss anything. We accessed her email account and deleted the emails. Done. End of story. They've already gone through a backup cycle, so even if someone got overly suspicious, there's nothing on the backup server either. But, if you're losing sleep over this, I can take care of it."

The other party on the call knew exactly what Nyden meant. He was an accomplished killer. Trained by the Marine Corps, battle hardened, resourceful, and intelligent. Richard Nyden had planned to complete at least 20 years with the Corps, then retire and go into the private sector—corporate security, hired gun with few questions asked.

But that plan evaporated one day when he shot an entire Afghan family. Three generations, dead. All because Nyden snapped—that was the diagnosis from the base shrink. For three weeks the Marines had been taking heavy casualties from sniper fire and IEDs. One of Nyden's buddies was killed and two more severely wounded when a roadside bomb was remotely detonated as the patrol passed. Despite three to four patrols each day, the Marines were never able to catch the insurgents or get the villagers to identify them. So, following a tip, Nyden took care of the problem himself.

His fellow Leathernecks refused to testify against him. They had all said the Afghan elder had a rifle, but none was found during the investigation. With only circumstantial evidence, and it being a war zone, Nyden was acquitted of murder and manslaughter. The best the Court Marshal could do was convict Nyden of conduct unbefitting a Marine, and he was out. Seventeen years of honorable service wiped from the records.

Upon returning home, Nyden was unemployed for less than a month. He soon learned that there was an underserved market for a man with his particular skills. He was hired by a secretive organization known as the Guardians, although exactly what they were guarding was never clear. He usually worked alone, other times in a small team of two or three. Orders came from encrypted email and phone calls. Money was wired into one of several accounts in each of his aliases. He was almost always travelling and had no need for a permanent address.

The money was extremely good, especially since he didn't file a tax return—Nyden didn't believe in paper trails. He liked living off the net, using different aliases so there were no records of his existence. He was an apparition; at best, a distant memory in the minds of family and friends he had once known.

"No need to get heavy handed; not yet anyway. I've got a contact at the Cyber Crimes division of the FBI. He's at the Portland office."

"And what's he gonna do?" said a skeptical Nyden.

"Don't worry. He's not in your league. But for a few

thousand, he'll open an investigation into Peter Savage. Hacking government databases or something. He'll create a credible story to support the allegations; enough so, anyway, to get the local Bend police interested. Maybe even arrest Mr. Savage."

"What good will that do? We both know the charges won't stick—unless you're also planning to fabricate incriminating evidence."

The voice didn't answer right away. Nyden assumed the other party was contemplating doing just that. "No, too much time and possible links that could expose us. I think it will be sufficient to implicate Peter Savage on multiple federal offenses. He'll be so busy trying to clear his name that he won't have time to probe any deeper."

Nyden listened. So far this was interesting but irrelevant to him.

"I did some research on Mr. Savage," the voice said. "He owns a business that makes special weapons. Something you might be familiar with—they call it a magnetic impulse firearm. Sound familiar?"

Nyden smiled at the irony. The inventor who manufactured his preferred assassination weapon was about to be falsely implicated for hacking government databases. All to cover up a crime committed with one of his guns—the gun itself being illegally acquired by the Guardians. *Brilliant!*

"Orders from the Department of Defense will dry up as soon as word gets out—and I'll be certain the FBI issues a press release and internal memos right away accusing Peter Savage of identity theft, wire fraud, espionage… I'm sure my contact will produce a long list of allegations."

"So what do you want me to do?" Nyden asked.

"For now, stay glued to that bug you planted in the house. Let me know immediately if there are any more conversations between Peter Savage and Kate Simpson. If Ms. Simpson gets curious and starts sticking her nose in our business, you know what to do. Oh, and when the police take a renewed interest in Mr. Savage, I'll want your report without delay."

CHAPTER 7

"HEY GARY," PETER GREETED his childhood friend. "Say, I've got a bit of a problem here. Turns out to be more serious than I had thought, and I could use your help."

"Do I have to fry in the desert, get pummeled by genetic mutants, or shoot anyone?"

Peter chuckled briefly. It was good to hear that his friend could now joke about their expedition to rescue Ethan, Peter's son, from the Sudan—an expedition that nearly cost everyone their life. "None of the above."

"Okay, I'm in. What do you need?"

"Some computer forensics." Peter spent the next 30 minutes laying out the details, including his conversation with Kate and the many exchanges with the detectives.

Gary and his wife, Nancy, ran a cyber-security business from their home in the foothills just east of the California capital. He and Peter became fast friends in their teens, growing as close as any brothers could be. With his curly blond hair, easy

49

attitude, and quick wit, Gary Porter often left the impression that he was interested in little more than riding the next wave. But underneath that veneer was a sharp, analytical brain. Peter was absolutely confident that if there were any clues to be found in the email of Emma Jones, Gary would find them.

"Easy enough to peruse through the email account. Emma Jones, right?"

"Yeah, but I don't want you doing this from your office. Since I don't know where this is going, there shouldn't be any connection to you. If Detective Colson discovers what we're doing, I have no doubt she'll arrest me. And I'll need you out on the street to figure out what's going on, who's doing it, and why."

"Gee. And I thought you were going to say you didn't want me to get arrested, too."

"Well, yeah," Peter added quickly. "But that goes without saying. Look, if I do get arrested they won't hold me for more than a couple days, but I don't think it will happen. The detectives seem to be convinced there is nothing of interest in the victim's email account."

"Compared to my usual weekly challenges, this is child's play. I can do this from your office—"

"No," Peter cut him off. "From my home. I don't want any connection to EJ Enterprises either. The police have already taken copies of our manufacturing and sales records. Even the slightest suspicion and they'll be back confiscating our computers, and I'll be shut down for a long time."

"Either way—makes no difference to me. I'll book the first flight from Sacramento and text the schedule. You can pick me up at Redmond Airport."

After ending the call with Nyden, Angela Meyers called her contact at the Portland office of the FBI.

Andrew Shooks answered on the third ring. "Long time, no

hear," he said. "I was beginning to think you didn't appreciate my services or something."

"Relax. I can do without the snark," Meyers answered. "I've got a job. Should be pretty easy for someone in your position." She quickly explained what she wanted, and when.

"The usual arrangements?" Although Shooks was confident that the phones were not tapped, he could still be overheard by his colleagues.

"Ten grand. Small bills. Same drop as last time."

Ten thousand dollars of unreported income for a couple hours of computer work. Not bad, Shooks thought. He went to work setting up a false investigation report naming Peter Savage of Bend, Oregon, as the suspect. He entered it into the Cyber Crimes database, and forwarded a copy to the Bend police department, where he knew it would be forwarded on to Detectives Colson and Nakano.

Agent Andrew Shooks leaned back in his chair and folded his arms behind his head. Closing his eyes, he was already thinking about the new drift boat he would buy with the payoff.

Gary met Peter at the curb in front of the terminal shortly after 9:00 p.m. The regional airport at Redmond, Oregon, was not large, and only six other cars were there to pick up passengers. Gary tossed his duffle bag on the back seat and set his briefcase on the floor.

Leaving the airport behind, Peter headed south on Highway 97. Traffic was light, and the drive back to Peter's house on the floors above EJ Enterprises went fast. He used the time to answer a string of questions Gary had about the crime, the potential tie-in with the victim's email, conversations Peter had with the Bend Police Detectives, and other curiosities. By the time they arrived, Peter felt that Gary had a complete understanding of the background.

When Peter opened the door he was greeted by Diesel, his 70-pound red pit bull. Peter had rescued the dog as a six-month-old puppy from the Humane Society. The puppy had been taken from a dog-fighting ring, more dead than alive; the scars on its neck and muzzle, still fresh and festering, were ample evidence of the fate awaiting the bait dog.

Although the scars on the dog's face had faded with time, Peter still vividly recalled his first meeting with the pit bull pup. It was inside the kennel area—an indoor enclosure with concrete floor and block walls. There were no windows, no natural light. Chain fencing separated the dozen kennels. The air smelled of bleach and dog excrement despite the best efforts of volunteers to keep the area clean.

One of the staff members introduced Peter to the puppy amid the near constant barking. The ravaged dog approached with its head lowered, ears back, crouched, and tail tucked between its trembling legs. When the dog lifted its head, its eyes met Peter's. In those eyes he saw fear and innocence and instantly made his decision: he would nourish the dog back to health and give it companionship and love—a life in stark contrast to the terror and pain that had dominated the puppy's short existence.

Peter and Diesel immediately connected, and the bond between man and canine grew exceptionally strong. With Peter now an empty nester, Diesel was his constant companion.

The dog knew Gary from past visits, and waggled up to him, tail swinging from side to side. Gary reached down and rubbed Diesel's ears and neck. "Hey there, boy."

Peter returned from the spare bedroom after dropping off Gary's bag. "Hey, I know it's late, but if you're hungry I've got some pulled pork in the refrigerator. Can warm it up in a few minutes."

"Thanks, but I had a salad in Portland. Coffee would be

good though."

"Make yourself comfortable by the fireplace and I'll get it brewing."

Diesel followed Gary as he plopped into one of the overstuffed leather chairs facing the stone hearth. He settled at Gary's feet, then rolled onto his back and began snoring. Gary chuckled. "So much for the image of a fierce guard dog to protect you and your castle."

"He knows you. If he didn't, might be a different story," Peter replied from the kitchen.

Gary was staring at the glowing embers when Peter returned with two mugs of coffee. Peter poked the coals and then tossed in some more firewood. Shortly the flickering yellow light from the flames illuminated the room again.

The massive fireplace and rough-hewn timber mantle dominated the wall. The fire crackled and popped, and Gary sipped the coffee as he readied his laptop. He spent the next 15 minutes laying out his plan: he would hack into Emma Jones' email account using standard tools—programs written to either identify passwords or bypass them—and see what was currently on the server. Then he would use programs he'd written to find and recover deleted messages. That was the plan, but with deleted messages there was no guarantee they would still be intact. He estimated an hour or two and they'd have all the current emails plus whatever fragments remained of deleted messages going back three months.

"I'm in," Gary announced several minutes later.

"Was it easy?"

He shrugged. "The password she'd selected was not a word in my password dictionary—"

"What's that?" Peter interrupted.

"I maintain a dictionary of all known English words, many common foreign language words, and other passwords

I've come across over the years. My first step is always to run the dictionary past the password challenge. It takes about two minutes and you'd be surprised by how often it works."

Peter nodded. "Hence your insistence on strong passwords. I get it."

"Since that test failed, I used a special program that accesses the back door built into standard ISP email hosting software. It bypasses the password challenge and allows access so the account can be reset if the password is lost."

Peter was looking over Gary's shoulder, watching a list of email messages scroll by. "These are the messages in her inbox. Does anything grab your attention?"

"No. But I don't know what I'm looking for."

"It all looks pretty routine to me. Let's see what's in her sent box."

Again, they scrolled through the emails but didn't see any that looked unusual. Certainly nothing that would justify murder.

"Well, I really didn't expect to find any clues since the police have supposedly already checked her email," Peter said.

"Okay. Here's where I earn my pay. Let's see what deleted messages we can find."

While Gary was focused on his work, Peter returned from the kitchen with the coffee pot and refilled the two mugs. Then he threw another section of cordwood on the fire and gave it a couple pokes for good measure.

"Now we're talking!" Gary said, drawing Peter's attention.

"What do you have?" He moved close so he could see the screen.

"Several messages from someone named Jon Q." They both read the emails, although several were fragments rather than complete messages.

"Emma was definitely looking for classified information,"

Peter said. Then he pointed at a particular passage. "Look, the information she wants is related to a ship. The *USS Liberty*."

Gary moved his cursor to the next message and clicked on the attached PDF file. When the file opened, he let out a whistle. "We hit the jackpot. We're lucky the file still appears to be intact."

"You're not kidding." The PDF document contained about a hundred pages, and Gary was scrolling through, occasionally slowing, then moving fast again.

"This appears to be a collection of memos, reports, letters— all from various branches of the government," Gary said.

"Yeah, and they're all stamped top secret."

"I don't think Emma Jones was supposed to have this file. This information is radioactive; it could easily be why she was killed."

"It's all related to the *USS Liberty*…" Peter mumbled, deep in thought, while Gary continued scanning through the pages.

"Gary, where's this information going? Not the cloud, I hope."

"Honestly? It hurts that you would even think that. You know nothing is safe in the cloud."

"So, you're sending this to your server, right?"

Gary frowned. "Do I need to answer that? Of course."

"Good, I knew I could count on you." Peter entered his study and returned with a small memory stick in his hand. The solid-state device was as wide as the USB male connector and only half as long as his thumb. He gave the memory stick to Gary.

"Copy everything onto this drive and delete the files from your server."

"Why would you want me to do that?"

"This information is top secret and dangerous; you said so yourself. If someone from the government comes looking for it, and somehow they trace it to you, you'll go to prison for a long time."

Gary frowned. He couldn't argue with Peter on this one. "Alright," he reluctantly agreed.

"Promise me you'll do it."

"Yeah, I will. My number one rule in life is 'Stay out of prison.'"

Peter grinned. "That's a good rule to follow. Oh, and then send that PDF file to my printer. Looks like it's gonna be a late night."

It was well past midnight and several mugs of coffee later when Peter and Gary, with leaden eyes, finally finished with the hardcopies.

"It's no wonder these documents are still stamped top secret," Peter said. "I don't think the American public would be too pleased to learn what really happened to those poor sailors on the *Liberty*."

"You mean how they were sold out and abandoned by their government and then left to die in the Mediterranean?"

"Only they didn't all die."

"Hence the cover up. They couldn't afford to have anyone talking."

Peter set his stack of papers down and slumped back in his chair. "Whoever *they* is."

"Well, of course it had to be the President and his administration. Who else?"

"I suppose you're right. But why is this information so important now? Why haven't all these documents been released to the public? This incident happened in 1967. LBJ has been dead for decades."

Gary silently eyed his friend, his lips downturned.

"Who would commit murder over this, and why? That's the

question."

Gary had no answer.

"I need a Scotch," Peter said.

"Me too."

The wall opposite the enormous fireplace was covered floor to ceiling with a bookcase. In the center of the bookcase was an opening that connected the great room to the kitchen and dining area. Peter rose and removed a bottle of Oban single malt from a shelf between rows of books. He poured a generous portion into each of two narrow shot glasses.

Gary stood, careful not to spill his drink or step on Diesel, and turned his back to the fire, letting the heat radiating from the coals and masonry soak into his back. As he held the shot glass, the warmth from his grip enhanced the aroma from the West Highland whiskey. For a few minutes the room was silent save for an occasional crackle from the dwindling fire and the rhythmic breathing from Diesel. The muscular pitty was stretched out on the plush area rug, sound asleep, immune to the intrigue unfolding in his company.

"There's so much in these documents," Peter finally said. "It's going to take some time to piece it together. But it seems that President Johnson didn't want to alienate the Israeli lobby and possibly lose their political support. That's why he didn't come down hard on the Israeli government after they attacked our ship."

"But Johnson didn't run for re-election. Remember? He refused to accept the nomination from the Democratic Party."

"Yeah, but remember the time. This incident occurred in the summer and early fall of 1967. Johnson had not yet made his decision. He was still in play for re-election to the Presidency."

Gary nodded. "Makes sense. So he was thinking he'd like to do another four years. Many of his top advisers were Jewish."

Peter took another sip of Scotch. "Yeah, but it still doesn't make sense."

"Are you trying to confuse me? You just said this was about Johnson trying to maintain support from the Israeli lobby."

"That's right, after the fact. These White House memos clearly prove that Johnson was being advised to go easy on Israel on the matter of reparations and public statements, referring to the incident as an accident. But the evidence presented at the Naval Court of Inquiry, including eyewitness testimony by the officers and crew of the *Liberty*, indicates that the Israeli military clearly knew they were attacking an American ship. And this evidence was confirmed by communications with the Israeli Ambassador."

"You've lost me, buddy. Where are you going with this?"

"Simple. Once the attack was over, Washington did what it always does: it went into cover-up mode. But that ignores the bigger question."

"And that would be?" Gary said.

"For hours, in broad daylight, the crew fought off wave after wave of aircraft and torpedo boats. At first, their antenna was destroyed, but somehow they managed to get it repaired and a mayday was sent out. It was received by the *Saratoga*, the flag ship of the Sixth Fleet."

For a moment Peter paused. He tipped his shot glass, taking in the last of the Oban. His countenance was like stone; eyes forward, seemingly mesmerized by the flickering fire. "According to the Naval investigation, we had two carriers— the *America* and the *Saratoga*—steaming 400 miles west of the *Liberty*. When the distress call was received, Admiral Geis launched strike aircraft—not once, but twice—and both times they were recalled by none other than Defense Secretary McNamara. Those planes could have arrived in time to stop the torpedo boats and save 26 lives."

"Yeah, I got all that. But you haven't said what's nagging at you," Gary said.

"McNamara recalled those planes, presumably at the direction of the President. They abandoned our sailors; left them to die. So, the question is: was that treason, or murder?"

CHAPTER 8

IT HAD BEEN A LATE NIGHT. After Gary retired, Peter took the memory stick and approached the bookcase. He pulled a horizontal latch underneath a low shelf in one panel, unlocking a secret doorway. He swung the panel open and entered his safe room. Except for the vintage weapons displayed artfully on wall mounts, it could almost pass for a modest armory. His eyes skimmed over the replica flintlock and percussion rifles, muskets, and pistols hanging from brass hooks. In another era, these weapons were state-of-the-art and represented formidable firepower. But those days were gone.

His eyes settled on a Brown Bess musket. The smooth-bore weapon, so named for the corrosion-resistant brown patina on the long barrel, was the standard gun by which the British Army once controlled a far-reaching colonial empire. The large flintlock held a square flint the size of a postage stamp, and if Peter chose, he could load and fire a .75 caliber lead ball. With one hand he removed the long weapon from its mounts and held the memory stick in his other hand. Tonight, he had a different use in mind for the antique musket.

The last thing Peter did before retiring was to throw the paper copies he and Gary had been studying onto the glowing embers in the fireplace.

The black sheet-like ash was still visible in the morning, though none of the writing was discernable.

"Coffee?" Peter said by way of greeting Gary as he wandered into the kitchen. His eyes were a little puffy, no doubt a result of too much Scotch and not enough sleep.

"You need to ask?"

Peter smiled and then sipped from his mug. He enjoyed Gary's dry, sometimes sarcastic, way of communicating. They had met in high school and spent a good portion of their youth together camping, fishing, and hunting. For several years, before either settled down and married, they were inseparable and often confused as brothers.

"The cups are in the cabinet," Peter motioned with the mug in his hand.

After Gary filled his cup, Peter asked the obvious. "Any new thoughts about our discovery last night?"

Before Gary answered, there was a knock at the door. Mug in hand, Peter passed through the great room, Diesel at his side. Ten feet from the door, he commanded his pit bull to stay.

When Peter opened the front door he was surprised to be greeted by Detectives Colson and Nakano, plus two other police officers in uniform. Detective Colson thrust folded sheets of paper at Peter. "We have a warrant." She started to push in, and then abruptly stopped when she saw Diesel, muscles tensed and ready to spring, eyes locked on her.

"Is that dog safe?" she asked.

Peter turned and said, "Diesel. Fireplace. Stay." Obediently, the dog sauntered to his spot in front of the hearth and dropped to the floor like a sack of potatoes.

"What is this about?" Peter asked.

Colson, followed by Detective Nakano and the two patrol officers brushed past Peter and entered the great room. They turned around, taking their bearings. Detective Nakano directed the patrol officers to explore through the kitchen. She noticed the black ashes from burned paper in the fireplace and turned to Peter. "Looks like you burned some documents."

"So what?" he replied. "Old tax returns."

"Carefully collect what you can," Colson instructed her junior partner.

As Detective Nakano proceeded to collect evidence, Colson addressed Peter. "What's upstairs?" indicating the spiral staircase reaching upward from the great room.

"A game room, and the master bedroom."

"This warrant authorizes our search of your residence and car, plus your business—EJ Enterprises."

Gary had left the kitchen and was standing next to Peter. "Search for what?" he asked.

"What is your name and relationship to Mr. Savage?" Nakano asked.

"Gary Porter. I'm his friend. And who are you?"

"Let's see your ID."

"You first," Gary said waspishly. "We have rights, you know."

Detective Nakano rolled her eyes. She and Colson extended their shields for Gary to inspect, which he did in a most methodical fashion, serving only to further irritate the detectives.

"You still haven't said what this is about," Peter said, his voice even.

"Computers, data storage devices. We have a federal warrant for your arrest on charges of espionage and violation of the Computer Fraud and Abuse Act."

"What? I haven't done anything wrong."

"Save it—not my call," said Colson.

"You have the right to remain silent," Nakano was reciting Peter's Miranda Rights when the patrol officers emerged from the guest rooms with Gary's laptop and another laptop taken from Peter's office.

"Didn't find any portable memory devices—no server either," one of the officers reported.

"Okay," Colson said. "Search upstairs. When you're done here we'll move on to his business. It's on the ground floor below the residence."

"Hey, that's mine!" Gary said, referring to one of the laptops in a black nylon carry case. "You can't take that!"

"This warrant says we can. Now, Mr. Porter, stand aside or I'll arrest you for interfering with police business."

"Relax, Gary," Peter said. "I have no idea what this is really about, but we both know I didn't break any laws. Call Martin Hanson; he's my attorney. You'll find his card on my desk. Tell him about our conversation last night."

"What conversation?" Colson asked. "Is there something you want to tell me?"

"Dream on, Detective. Looks to me like playing nice is over."

It took all day, but Martin Hanson had bail posted shortly after 4:00 p.m. An hour later, Peter was released from detention with orders not to leave Bend.

"The charges are serious, Peter." Martin leaned back in his chair. His office was across the street from the jail. "I had to call in a huge favor from Judge Sullivan just to get you bailed out today. Fortunately for you, the jail is full and since you are a first-timer and non-violent, the judge agreed to expedite my request. The espionage charge is the most serious. The Government alleges you accessed secured data files and removed highly classified information. For the moment, they only filed charges for one count of espionage. But, in theory, they could charge you separately for each document that was illegally taken. If convicted, you could be sent to Federal Prison for the rest of your life."

Peter's shoulders slumped. "I don't know where to begin."

"This is usually where my clients tell me they didn't do it, and explain why."

"Of course I didn't access classified documents. I wouldn't even begin to know how to do that, even if I wanted to."

"That's well and good, but you did end up in possession of the documents. Gary Porter explained everything to me this morning after the police arrested you."

Peter shook his head. "That's the weirdest part of this. We didn't see those files until last night, about 11:00 p.m. or so. We were still reading them into the early morning hours."

"You didn't access those files from a government site? Gary Porter said he hacked into the email server and recovered deleted messages between Emma Jones and a Mr. Jon Q. Is that what happened?"

Peter told his story, confirming what he was certain Gary had already shared with Martin. "So, how come the police are knocking on my door with a warrant less than 12 hours after we gain access to these files from a deceased person's deleted email? How did they even know that we were reading them? I'm not the one who stole them from a government website. That was probably Jon Q—whoever that is."

"Is there a copy of those files on your computer?" Martin asked.

"No. And before you ask, Gary doesn't have a copy either. We printed out copies and read those, then burned them in the fireplace."

Martin folded his arms. "Well, if you didn't make any electronic copies, and the only paper copies have been destroyed, the DA won't be able to prove possession. And since you didn't hack into whatever site was breached, it doesn't sound like they'll have a case. In the morning, I'll file a motion to dismiss. The judge won't rule on the motion until the DA has enough time to review the evidence. That could take a few weeks."

Peter felt a pang of guilt for not telling Martin the whole truth. Sure, the files were not on his computer, but he did have a copy hidden away on a memory stick.

"In the meantime, stay out of trouble. And don't leave town. If something comes up—family emergency or something—talk to me first. Understand?"

"Sure. Thank you Martin; I appreciate your help."

Martin wrote a number on the back of one of his business cards. "This is my cell phone. If anything comes up—day or night—call me. That's my job."

"Thank you. Look, there's one more thing."

Martin raised an eyebrow.

"If anything should happen to me, contact Gary Porter. There's an item hidden away—think of it as an insurance policy—anyway, Gary will tell you where to find it."

"And what am I supposed to do with this *item*?"

"If it comes to that, you'll know."

Martin leaned forward, hands folded on his desk. "Peter, is there something you're not telling me?"

Peter looked at his attorney, but decided not to voice his thoughts. There were far too many pieces missing from the puzzle, and even he wasn't sure any of it made sense.

CHAPTER 9

IT HAD BEEN A LONG, stressful day, and Peter was emotionally exhausted. But he had one more thing to do. After he finished at Martin's office, he called Kate. Although she had not seen the emails or the classified files, Peter had a nagging fear that something deeper, something sinister, was in play.

"Have you had any recent contact with the police?" he asked.

"No, why? Is something wrong?"

"Yeah, you could say so. I was arrested for espionage. My attorney got me out on bail only a couple hours ago."

"What?" Peter could hear the concern in Kate's voice.

"I got a friend to help me, and we know what was in Emma's email." Peter paused to see if Kate was going to respond; she didn't.

"That's what got me in trouble. I need to talk to you... soon."

She hesitated. "Okay. I'm at the house, but only for another

66

hour. Just packing a few more things. I've been staying with a friend."

Peter drove directly to the rental where he had first met Kate. She must have seen him drive up, because she opened the door before he knocked.

Most of the furniture was gone. All that remained was the sofa in the living room and the dining table and chairs. Peter glanced into the kitchen and noticed many of the cabinet doors open. Cardboard boxes were on the floor and bubble wrap on the counter, ready to embrace the remaining glasses and dishes.

Kate looked exhausted. Her eyes appeared sunken with dark circles underneath, and she moved slowly, with effort. She looked at Peter, her arms folded across her chest.

"How are you doing, at your friend's place?" he asked.

"Fine. I'm almost completely moved. Sold some of the furniture—just the sofa and table left. Someone's coming tomorrow to look at them."

Peter nodded. He hated moving, and this was ten times worse for Kate. "Can I help you finish boxing up the kitchen?"

"That's not why you came here," she said.

"No, it's not. You said that Emma was working on something on her laptop early the morning she was killed, and that she tried to hide it from you."

"Yes. She said it was for a term paper, but I didn't believe her."

"I think I know what she was doing. We found a number of messages in her account. The messages had been deleted, but a friend of mine knows how to retrieve that sort of stuff."

"So your friend is a hacker." She said it as an accusation, not a question.

Peter tipped his head to the side, deciding how much information he would share. "Not exactly. More like computer forensics and cyber security."

Kate nodded.

"Anyway, this person Emma was corresponding with had emailed a large file late the previous night. I'd bet that's what she was reading when you spoke to her in the morning. The file details top secret memos and reports related to an incident that happened a long time ago—an attack on a U.S. Naval ship. A lot of sailors died."

Kate sat on the sofa and Peter followed her, taking the opposite end.

"I don't understand," she said.

"That information was not supposed to be released to the public. I think someone killed her because she had those files."

"This doesn't sound like Emma, not at all. She would never go looking for secrets, especially classified secrets. And you said the ship was attacked a long time ago, so why would anyone even care anymore?"

"That's what I want to talk to you about."

"What do you have?" Angela Meyers said, foregoing a greeting as a waste of time.

"It's that Simpson woman," Richard Nyden said. "She's talking to Peter Savage and somehow they've managed to recover deleted emails from that hacker in Friday Harbor."

"What do they know?"

"I'm listening to the conversation now. Savage claims they recovered the entire PDF file that was received by Emma Jones."

"Is he telling the truth?"

"You want me to ask him?"

"I want you to fix this problem for good!" Meyers nearly shouted into the phone.

"Yeah, I think Savage has read the file, or at least portions of it. He knows it's about the *Liberty* incident, and he referred to memos and investigative reports."

"Keep listening and find out if anyone else knows about this. And *deal* with those two!"

"I'm on my way there now," Nyden said and then ended the call. He was only a couple blocks away from Kate's house.

The street was deserted as before. "This is one quiet neighborhood," he mumbled as he parked the dark blue sedan across the street from Kate's rented house. He continued to listen to the conversation, adjusting the fit of the ear buds and turning the volume down a little. The bugs he planted—one in the living room inside a floor air register, one on top of a cabinet in the kitchen, and one in a floor register in the bedroom—continued to send a strong signal. The devices were very small and would remain powered by the internal battery for two weeks. To accommodate for the limited range of the transmissions, he placed a repeater in the hall closet on the top shelf behind a stack of bedsheets and towels. No one would find it unless they climbed onto a stool and searched all the way to the back of the shelf.

"Do you have any idea if Emma had a relative—maybe a father or uncle—who served in the Navy on the *USS Liberty*?" Peter said.

Kate was shaking her head. "No, her father works at a bank in Portland. He and Emma's mother visited here often, and always for the holidays—Thanksgiving and Christmas. They'd take us both to dinner, except for Christmas. But they helped Emma and me cook dinner, and they bought all the food. I never heard Mr. Jones talk about the military. I don't think he served."

Peter rubbed his chin. "I know someone who can check it out. There must be some connection, some reason—"

"Your hacker friend? I don't want him messing with their personal information. They're nice people."

"No, nothing to worry about. I'm thinking of someone else—he's in military intelligence and can check service records."

Kate nodded. "This is just so out of character for her. I don't understand."

"I'll continue to work on the why. But right now the bigger question is *who* is trying to keep this information secret?"

"It's the government, right? I mean, it's always the CIA or FBI." Kate looked like she was about to cry, but she held back the tears and chewed her lip.

"Sometimes it isn't that simple. Everyone is eager to believe conspiracy theories, but most of the time the truth is not so complicated."

"What happened to this ship, anyway?" she asked.

Peter smiled, appreciating the opportunity to move the conversation away from the grim reality. "It was the fifth of June, 1967, and the Six-Day War had just begun. Israel launched a pre-emptive attack on the Arab coalition—Egypt, Jordan, Syria, Iraq, Kuwait, and Algeria. In a brilliant move, Israeli warplanes destroyed most of the Egyptian air force on the ground, and then went on to decimate the air forces of Jordan, Syria, and Iraq.

"With air superiority, the Israeli Self-Defense Force launched a blitz against Egyptian ground forces in the Gaza Strip and the Sinai, quickly winning that territory all the way to the Suez Canal. Israel went on to defeat Jordan, capturing the West Bank and the Old City of Jerusalem, and they defeated Syria, taking control of the Golan Heights.

"It was on June 8, during the height of the conflict, that the *USS Liberty* was sailing in the eastern Mediterranean not far off the coast of Egypt. She was in international waters and flying the American flag."

"And the ship was attacked," Kate said, already knowing the

answer.

"That's right. She was attacked—by Israel."

Kate's eyes widened. "Why? Israel and the U.S. are allies. Right?"

"Yes," Peter said. "Israel claimed it was a mistake, but the attack lasted many hours and involved both fighter aircraft and torpedo boats."

Kate was speechless, her jaw slightly agape.

"Everything I just said is public record, a common narrative you'll find if you do a search on the ship's name. And yet, in that file emailed to your roommate, there are a hundred pages of documents that are still labeled classified—some from the White House, some from the Department of the Navy, some from the State Department—that reveal details that were never shared with the public."

"Like what?"

"There's a lot there. Some of the information corroborates what's in the public domain. To be honest, I've only read a small number of the documents."

"Did the Navy send other ships or planes to protect the *Liberty*?"

Peter shook his head. "The *Liberty* managed to send out a mayday radio signal that was received by the Sixth Fleet. They were also sailing in the Mediterranean. Attack aircraft were launched from both the *America* and the *Saratoga*, twice in fact, but those planes were recalled before they arrived on site."

"Surely that was a mistake," Kate said.

Peter shook his head. "No. Launching and recalling warplanes from the deck of an aircraft carrier is not done by mistake."

"Okay, so there must be a rational explanation. And I still don't see how any of this could motivate someone to murder Emma."

"I'm certain the answer can be found in those documents, but it's going to take a lot of time to read and digest that information, and then cross reference it with other sources."

There was a knock and Kate swung her head toward the front door.

"Are you expecting anyone?" Peter asked.

She shook her head.

Peter approached the door and looked through the narrow glass sidelight to the right of the entrance. He saw a middle-aged man with short, black hair. He was wearing a suit and tie. Beyond, on the other side of the street, Peter noticed a dark blue sedan—it had not been parked there when Peter pulled into the driveway.

He opened the door partway and leaned around the edge of the door.

"I'm Agent Barnes, FBI. Is Kate Simpson home?"

She was standing back from Peter, looking through the partially-opened door at the agent. "Yes, I'm Kate."

"I'd like to ask you a few questions. May I come in?"

"Just a minute," Peter said. "How about some ID first."

Agent Barnes reached inside his suit coat until he grasped a wallet from the jacket pocket. As the coat opened, Peter noticed the grip of his weapon, secured in a shoulder holster. With practiced fluency, Barnes flipped open the wallet and displayed the gold badge along with his ID card.

"If you're satisfied, may we move on?" Barnes said as he returned the wallet.

"You're from the Bend field office?"

"No, I drove from Portland. It's been a long day. Now, if you don't mind, I'd like to speak to Ms. Simpson."

"Why not fly? It's a lot faster."

Barnes placed his hands on his hips and addressed Peter. "Mister..."

"Savage, Peter Savage."

Exactly as Barnes thought. Now he had confirmation: both his marks were still at the house.

"Mr. Savage, you are very close to obstructing an official investigation. Now, my business is with Kate Simpson. So I'll ask once more. May I come in to discuss this matter, or would you prefer we continue in more official surroundings?"

"It's okay, Peter. Let Agent Barnes in."

Peter opened the door wider, but not by much. He kept his legs planted securely and his shoulder against the solid wood door.

As Barnes was passing through the opening, Peter suddenly slammed his weight into the door, driving it into the agent. Barnes was crushed against the door frame. His head bounced first off the door and then the frame. Already blood was seeping from a gash at the edge of his scalp.

Quickly, Peter opened the door and was straddling Barnes. He slammed his fist into the agent's face, bloodying his nose. Barnes was barely conscious, on the verge of passing out. Peter reached inside his jacket and ripped out the holstered weapon.

"This is a Mk-9 impulse gun. Where did you get this?" Peter said.

Barnes was lying on his back, his eyelids fluttering. He moved a hand to his head, and felt the wetness from the gash. When Peter's eyes moved from the agent to the gun, Barnes struck, lashing out with his fist, aiming at Peter's groin.

The blow connected and he went down, landing both knees on the agent's chest. The impact, backed by Peter's full weight, drove the air out of the FBI man's lungs and bruised multiple ribs.

The pain was excruciating, forcing Peter to further collapse over the body beneath him. As he did, he brought the grip of the pistol down hard on the bridge of Barnes' nose. There was a crack of cartilage, and Agent Barnes was out.

Peter rolled over, trying hard to catch his breath and counting the seconds until the agony waned. After what seemed like an eternity, but was less than a minute, Peter was able to rise to his knees. He checked for a pulse, relieved that the agent was alive.

After several more deep breaths, the worst of the pain and nausea had passed, and Peter became aware of Kate's voice. "Are you crazy?"

Peter finally stood, still gripping the magnetic impulse gun.

After two more deep breaths, he answered. "No, this guy is a fake." He was dragging Agent Barnes inside as he spoke. "This gun he was carrying—it was made by my company. They're only sold to the military, Special Operations. I recognized the two LED lights on the grip when he reached inside his jacket."

He shut the door. "And his car has Washington plates. If he was from the FBI's Portland office he'd be driving with Oregon license plates."

Kate sat down, her hand covering her mouth, frightened by the ever-growing vortex. Secret documents related to a decades old military incident… her friend murdered… and now a man impersonating an FBI agent assaulted in her home.

Peter sat next to her and placed his hand on her shoulder. "Kate, you need to listen to me, okay?"

She nodded.

"We have to go. I need to get you somewhere safe."

CHAPTER 10

WHEN RICHARD NYDEN FINALLY regained consciousness, his first sensation was intense throbbing in his face. He'd experienced that before and quickly surmised that his nose was broken. His chest ached too, and he felt a tightness of breath.

He began to stand, but stopped when his head pulsed in pain. He waited a minute and when the pounding ache subsided, he crawled to the sofa and eased into a sitting position. He punched a number on his phone.

"That was fast," Angela Meyers said. "You have good news, I assume." It was late in Washington, and Meyers was still at her office adjoining the Speaker's office. It was not at all unusual for Meyers to work late, or even all night, taking short naps on the sofa.

"Not good news. Savage got the jump on me. They got away, and he has my weapon."

"You idiot!" The screaming voice caused a flash of pain and Nyden pulled the phone further from his ear. The line was silent for a half minute.

Having quickly thought through the implications, Meyers issued new orders. "Stay there, but do not pursue Savage or the woman. Not yet. They are obviously on to you, and if you eliminate Savage the police may take the woman into protective custody. We can't risk that. I'll have my contact at the FBI issue a new arrest warrant—assault of a federal officer and kidnapping. That should get Peter Savage behind bars without bail."

"Should I look for Kate Simpson?"

"No, let the police find her. I'm going to call in another operator from Washington State. I believe you know her—Jana Cooke."

"That psycho? Yeah, I know her. Did a job together a couple years ago."

"Once Peter Savage is locked up, a woman's touch should be all that's needed to convince Kate Simpson to drop her guard. When that happens, terminate her. Oh, and make certain nothing—not a trace—is found."

Angela Meyers was fuming. It simply should not be this complicated. Her operators were all trained killers, physically fit, and with the best equipment and intelligence. How could it be that an ordinary man was causing so many problems?

Meyers placed the call to Jana Cooke. She was somewhere in the Seattle area, having completed the assignment in Friday Harbor. She was instructed to take the first available commercial flight to Redmond, Oregon. At the airport she would rent a car for two weeks, drive the short distance to Bend, and book a hotel room. While masquerading as a tourist, she would surveil Peter Savage from a safe distance. If there were any other persons involved, they needed to know and tie up the loose ends.

Now Meyers had to address a more delicate issue. She

debated waking Cliff Ellison or waiting until the morning. She decided to text him—if he was asleep, he'd get the message in the morning.

Surprisingly, a few minutes later her phone rang. "What's the problem?" he said. He sounded alert.

"I think we should talk… in person."

"It's after eleven. I assume this can't wait until morning?"

The pause was answer enough.

"Okay. Meet me at the Mayflower Hotel. Shouldn't take me more than an hour to get there. Look for me at the bar."

Angela Meyers slipped on some comfortable sneakers and then a light jacket. She pocketed her cell phone and left, locking her office door. A short distance from the Longworth House Office Building she boarded the metro, catching the last train of the evening. The trip was short and there were few other passengers at this late hour. She exited at Farragut North and walked the block and a half to the Mayflower.

She entered the lobby and then strolled into the Town and Country Bar. The lighting was dim, adding to the cozy atmosphere. Four men in dark suits were at the bar, talking loudly. Probably staffers. From the occasional slurred word, she suspected they had been drinking for a couple of hours. Meyers scanned the tables and booths tucked against the walls. Cliff Ellison hadn't arrived yet. She slid into a booth along the back wall. From her vantage point she would spot Ellison right away when he entered.

The cocktail waiter took her order: two whiskey sours. Meyers checked her watch and then her phone—no messages. The drinks arrived, and the waiter placed a bowl of mixed nuts on the table as well. The Mayflower was a favorite meeting place for celebrities, and the wait staff knew to be discrete. It was a favored meeting place for Ellison, too, a location he had frequented many times before as a lobbyist and sales executive for United Armaments.

When he strode into the bar, Meyers nodded and Ellison walked over to the booth. He was dressed casually in jeans, leather loafers, and a bulky knit sweater. Like many defense lobbyists, Cliff Ellison had served 20 years in the military— Army Rangers—before starting his second career, eventually advancing to Executive Vice President for United Armaments. He stood just under six feet tall and maintained a fit, muscular build through a religious regimen of physical exercise. His sandy blond hair was cut short, and his trim beard gave him a roguishly handsome look.

He casually looked around the room as he sat down—no one seemed to pay any attention, which suited Ellison just fine.

He took a sip of his drink, and then looked to Meyers for an explanation. "The problem has escalated," she said. "Peter Savage and Kate Simpson have been talking. It appears that they know more than I had thought possible."

Ellison remained silent, his teeth clenched.

"My operator placed several bugs in Simpson's rental house and has been monitoring for any useful information. It turns out that Mr. Savage managed to gain access to the electronic file from the email account of Emma Jones."

Ellison leaned forward, barely able to temper his mounting anger. "How is that possible? You know as well as I do what's at stake here. If that information is leaked to the press, they'll have a field day. The attention could easily turn public opinion against an override of Taylor's veto of the Israeli Security Act. It could give Taylor the boost he needs to win a second term!"

"Keep your voice down." Angela paused while Ellison regained his composure. She continued, "Besides, you think I don't know that?"

"You assured me those email files were deleted."

"They were deleted."

"But?"

"It seems that Peter Savage is a resourceful man." She leaned back in the booth. "I can't tell you how he did it, but somehow he managed to gain access to those deleted emails. Based on a conversation he had with Kate Simpson a few hours ago, I'm convinced he read some, or all, of the file."

"You have to stop him before he figures out what he found and goes public," Ellison said, his voice rising again.

Angela held her hand out, palm down. "You're going to attract attention," she said. Angela Meyers was adept at managing others. As an only child, her parents—both career military—had fawned over her, eventually sending her to Howard University. She majored in psychology and minored in political science, graduating top of her class.

She found that politics offered every challenge she ever wanted. It was an exceedingly competitive environment, and the intra-office politics were in a league of their own. Very quickly Angela learned that as an attractive female with a keen intellect, she had an edge on her male colleagues, and she was happy to exploit that advantage.

"If this information comes out," Ellison said, "we won't be able to contain it. The media will dig until they have enough truth or conjecture—it doesn't matter as long as they have a story to tell. It will be the scandal of the decade."

"I won't let that happen," Angela said in a soothing voice, a voice that conveyed confidence and control. "Have I ever let you down?"

He took a long sip from his glass, the whisky helping to take the edge off his anxiety. "We've come too far to fail. You have a plan, I assume?"

Angela glanced around the bar. The other patrons were paying them no attention. The four men at the bar were becoming more boisterous, a good distraction.

"Yes. I need you to contact David Feldman. Can you do that?"

"He'll take my call. We have history."

"Good. Set up a conference call and make sure it's a secure line. We need his help."

Ellison pushed his cuff back and read the time. "David is seven hours ahead of us. He'll be up now." He swallowed the last of his drink. "Why don't you pay the tab. I'll meet you outside and call him from a quiet spot along the street."

CHAPTER 11

Washington, D.C.
April 19

THEY EXITED THE MAYFLOWER and turned left, following Connecticut Avenue toward the White House. Ellison dialed the number and was connected on the fourth ring. "Good morning Mr. Prime Minister, this is Cliff Ellison," he said, his tone cheerful.

"It's not even 8:00 a.m. here, which means you're calling me in the middle of your night. Don't tell me there is a problem with approval of the arms sale—we need those F16s and missiles."

Ellison forced a short chuckle. *If only that was the problem.* "The House will vote to approve the sale tomorrow, and the President has promised to sign the bill."

"Excellent news. So, what is this about?"

"An issue has come up. One that could best be solved if we work together."

"I see. What do you have in mind?" the Prime Minister said.

"I'm on my way to my office now. Should be there in half an hour. Would you set up a secure conference line? Text the number to me, and I'll dial in."

The pair hailed a taxi and ten minutes later they were entering the office building where Cliff Ellison worked when he was in Washington. It was located next to the Longworth House Office Building and across the street from the Capitol. The lobby guard nodded. "Working late again, Mr. Ellison?"

He replied with a smile. "Good evening, Louie. Afraid so. Seems there is always some pressing matter to resolve."

With Angela Meyers standing at his side, he rode the elevator to the third floor and strode in silence to his office. The lights were still on—he never turned them off, a peculiar habit. Ellison felt the vibration from his phone: a text from David Feldman. It was a phone number, nothing else. He seated himself behind his desk and dialed the number. Meyers pulled a chair up to the opposite side of the desk.

"This line is secure," Feldman said. "I trust you have taken precautions at your end?"

Given his senior position within United Armaments— one of the largest defense contractors globally—Cliff Ellison utilized the latest encryption technology to ensure confidential communications.

"Naturally," he said. He had the phone on speaker so Angela Meyers would also hear the conversation in its entirety. "Thank you, Mr. Prime Minister, for making time in your busy schedule."

Cliff Ellison and David Feldman had known each other for years. In fact, Ellison had met many of the world's presidents and prime ministers, as well as genocidal dictators, through his business of selling weapons. One of the perks of the job, he thought, was to rub shoulders with the world's most revered and reviled leaders—sometimes both at the same social gathering.

A member of the right-wing Jewish Home Party, David Feldman could not have been more different from Ellison. In fact, if they did not share a common interest in arms, the two men would have little to bind their friendship.

David Feldman was ambitious, having risen to power after serving as the Minister of Defense under Benjamin Netanyahu. Past middle age but not yet old, Feldman believed he was destined to lead Israel to a greatness that would rival the achievements of King David, his namesake. The stress of office had not yet grayed his black hair or etched his face with deep wrinkles. He was single and often discussed in the tabloids as a womanizer, but nothing scandalous had ever been made to stick.

Prime Minister Feldman was immensely popular at home. He was a hardliner, appealing to a call for better security and a more nationalist government. His position was that you were either a supporter of Israel, or you were against Israel—in his mind there was no middle ground, no room for compromise. The Jewish Nation had to be strong to be secure. And that strength required a deeper level of military and political support from the United States.

"I'll get right to the point," Ellison said. "A situation has developed here that is most inconvenient. If it continues unchecked, the publicity will be detrimental to our mutual goals."

"Before you go on," Feldman said, "I should tell you that Yossi Winer is with me. We were discussing another matter, but since I value Yossi's opinion, I asked him to stay."

"Very good. I'm sure your National Security Adviser will have a strong interest in this... problem."

"Hello Mr. Ellison," Yossi greeted. "The Prime Minister speaks very highly of you. I look forward to meeting in person."

"As do I."

"Perhaps when the fighter aircraft are delivered?"

"Certainly. But now we must focus on another issue." He went on to explain the top-secret information that had been illegally accessed. He summarized the efforts to contain the leak but avoided mention of the two murders. Finally, Ellison concluded with the recent revelation that Peter Savage had somehow gained access to the files. Whether he had copies under his control or not remained unknown.

"The information, by itself, is of little value to anyone other than twentieth century historians," Yossi said.

"Historians don't hack into top-secret government files," Ellison retorted.

"I suppose you are right," Feldman interjected. "So, I assume you need help from Israeli Intelligence?"

"That's correct, sir," Ellison replied. "We need to know how the deleted emails were recovered from Emma Jones' account, and who did it. But more importantly, we must know the disposition of those files."

"I'm quite certain our cyber security unit can trace the activity related to the email account," Yossi explained. "But if files were downloaded it will be unlikely, perhaps impossible, to determine who has access to them now."

"Not impossible," Ellison said. "The files are coded with a unique lock that records both the computer IP address and the Internet service provider address—basically a tracking cookie. I will provide you with this log."

"Why not use resources in your country?" Feldman asked. "After all, you are saying the information was illegally acquired. I would think your FBI could solve this for you rather quickly."

"It's too risky, Mr. Prime Minister. If this information is somehow leaked, we will have a real mess. It would only take one whistleblower—someone like Edward Snowden—and our plans will be ruined. Can you imagine the public outcry if the truth were revealed?"

The line was silent and Ellison believed that David was doing just that, imagining what could happen if he refused to help. "Yes, I see your point. Yossi will have a team ready to track down the wayward path of this data file. Send the log and other relevant information to my email and I'll make certain Yossi gets it without delay."

"Thank you, sir," Ellison said. "Now, the second part of my request."

"There's more?"

"Yes, I'm afraid so. We need to be prepared to shut this down. In a little more than two weeks, the House and Senate will vote to override Taylor's veto. When Abraham Schuman secures that win in Congress, he will be unstoppable, sweeping the election in November. If the information leaks out after the election, it won't matter—it will be too late."

Yossi understood the implied message. "I presume you have operators there who can handle this situation. Why do you need assistance from the Israeli government?"

"Of course," Ellison said. "I am simply trying to mitigate risk. You see, my operators are all former military. If one or more were to be injured or worse… well, they will be easily identified through prints and dental records. That's a loose end we cannot afford."

"I see," Yossi replied.

The Prime Minister cleared his throat. "So, let's be candid, shall we? After all, this is a secure line. I have already taken on substantial risk by instructing one of our Mossad operators to plant those Iranian grenades in New York a couple months ago. That request came from Ms. Meyers, if I remember correctly."

Angela cleared her throat. "Yes, you are correct, Mr. Prime Minister. It was a useful measure to bolster opposition to Iran and strengthen popular support for Israel leading up to the vote on the Israeli Security Act. As you know, the Act was authored by Speaker Schuman."

"I see. And now you are asking if I will send a team to help you again. Agents who will not be easily identified by their fingerprints. Agents who are unknown to your law enforcement and government. Am I correct?"

Ellison exchanged a quick glance with Angela Meyers, and a small grin formed. "Yes. You are correct. It is merely an insurance policy, and I suspect your National Security Adviser would agree that this is a prudent measure."

Yossi didn't accept this simplistic explanation. "You would not require a covert team if there was no risk. We must consider this request with the understanding that these are loyal Israeli lives we are placing in jeopardy."

"True. However, Mossad operators accept risk every day. Israel has many enemies—your country is surrounded by hostile nations. The Prime Minister and I share a dream of a time, very soon, when Israel will be so powerful as to vanquish your enemies for good."

"Yossi and I will work out the details," Feldman said, ending the debate. "I'll provide Yossi's email contact. Please coordinate directly through him. Now, I presume that is all?"

"Thank you, Mr. Prime Minister. I'll work out the details with Mr. Winer. And I promise to see you in Tel Aviv when the aircraft are delivered."

CHAPTER 12

WASHINGTON, D.C.
APRIL 19

WHENEVER HE WAS IN TOWN, Abraham Schuman arrived at his office at 7:00 a.m. sharp. Today was no different. Dressed in a dark gray suit with white shirt and vivid blue necktie, he entered the outer office just as an antique American tall-case clock chimed the hour.

Although Schuman had several thousand square feet of rented office space nearby to manage his Presidential campaign, he seldom set foot there, preferring the familiarity and luxury of his Congressional office.

The outer office was understandably large—as Speaker of the House, Schuman was afforded an expansive piece of prime real estate. A hallway extended to the side where a half-dozen offices were located for his staffers. Two Chippendale sofas occupied the center of the room, facing each other with a cherry-wood coffee table separating them. The walls were paneled in oak that had taken a honey-colored patina over the years.

The office walls were adorned with original oil paintings of various historic battles from the War of 1812 up through the First Gulf War—gifts from the largest employer in Schuman's district.

Angela greeted her boss. She looked like she hadn't slept more than a few hours, which was pretty close to the truth. Her eyes were puffy and her clothes wrinkled from napping on the sofa in her office.

"Morning, Angela. Looks like you had a late night."

She faked a smile. "Good morning, Abe. Yes, very late. Some last minute complications with your energy bill," she lied.

"Everything okay?"

"Nothing to worry about. A last minute trade of favors with Representative Cartwright. He promises to deliver enough votes from the left to pass the bill. I think the Senate will go along without significant modifications."

"Good. So long as you didn't have to promise my firstborn."

It had been a slow but steady climb that landed Congressman Schuman second in line of Presidential succession. Abe had hired Angela Meyers to be his office manager when he was first elected to represent California's 17th District, encompassing a large portion of the south bay area just north of Silicon Valley. Abe's hair was beginning to gray when he first entered office; now that process was completed. The bulge around his waist was a direct result of too many meals at Capitol Hill eateries. He was especially fond of late nights at the Dubliner Grill, or enjoying a slice of aged beef and fine French Bordeaux at the Capitol Grille. Naturally, his constituent donors always paid.

Angela followed Abe into his office and prepared two lattes from the top-end Italian espresso machine built into the wet bar. While she was making the coffee drinks, Abe unloaded his brief case and fired up his computer.

He was just checking his schedule when she placed the cups

on his desk. "Senators Robinson and Putnam are meeting with me at 10:00 a.m.?"

"Yes, here in your office to discuss their rider on the appropriations bill. And you have lunch with Becky Winwood— she represents Winwood, Stuart and Kolb, a lobbyist for several of the major investment banking firms."

Abe rolled his eyes at the statement. He didn't like the way that the large Wall Street firms played the game and believed their reckless and greedy actions had directly cost his constituents—and Americans across the country—an incalculable amount of money.

"And what is she asking for? Or need I ask?"

"As you know, President Taylor has been pushing for banking reform. So far, it has just been speeches, but he has promised to introduce a bill by the end of summer if Congress doesn't take meaningful action first."

"Let me guess. Ms. Winwood wants me to block any bill from moving forward in the House."

"We've been over this, Abe. You need the support of Wall Street without appearing to be in their pocket. And the big firms are promising to make sizeable donations to your super PAC."

Schuman sipped from his cup and narrowed his eyes. "There was a time when I wouldn't have even considered such a request." He sighed and pushed his latte away.

Angela smiled softly. "There was a time when no one would have believed it possible that a Jewish American could be elected President. You are polling strong Abe—a double-digit lead over President Taylor. But the election is still many months away. Don't take anything for granted. You can never have too many backers."

He stared back at his Chief of Staff, his lips pursed and turned down.

"Besides," Meyers continued, "once you get elected, you can do whatever you want. No one remembers campaign promises."

The Presidential election was almost seven months away, and yet Abraham Schuman was the name people were talking about. President Taylor had served well during his first term, and if Schuman had not been so popular, Taylor would have been assured re-election.

Abraham Schuman seemed to be the right candidate at the right time. As Speaker, he remained enormously popular, working to reverse past bickering between his colleagues on both sides of the aisle. He had shepherded a new era of compromise and common sense governance, something the voters had been craving. Plus, it didn't hurt that Schuman had the backing of the American Israeli Lobby.

The son of Orthodox Jewish parents, Abe did not follow the strict religious practice, although he had visited the Holy Land as a young man. Schuman was the ultimate success story—his parents having emigrated from Europe in the late 40s. His grandparents on his mother's side, and many extended relatives, were murdered by the Nazis. He often told the story of his losses, his struggles, and finally of his achievements during fundraising events and on the campaign trail. It was a popular tale that never seemed to grow old.

"Fine, I'll play along. What do I get in return?"

"I threw out a number: five million. She agreed."

Schuman snorted. "Next time, ask for ten. Speaking of money, how are we doing?"

Meyers carried no notes with her, preferring to work from a near-photographic memory. "Very solid. Your super PAC is pulling in large donations from corporate America and wealthy individuals, and the grassroots fundraising seems to be resonating with blue-collar workers and young voters."

Abe nodded. "Good."

"Remember, this evening you are speaking at a dinner at the Hay-Adams Hotel. I'll make certain Regina has the final copy of your speech on your desk by noon."

"I still don't get why you picked the Hay-Adams. It's so small. You should have booked the Mandarin Oriental."

"Relax—and trust me. This is about image, and the Hay-Adams is as close to the White House as anyone will get short of being elected. Besides, we sold tickets to enough high-rollers to clear three million. Plus, with the auction of your memorabilia following dinner, we stand to pull in another two to three million."

Abe smiled. "What would I do without you, Angela?"

"That's right. Just remember that when you're elected President. A cabinet position will suit me fine."

"Secretary of State?"

Angela smiled.

CHAPTER 13

HE HAD ATTENDED TOO MANY fundraising dinners to remember. But what Abe Schuman did recall was that the food was always lackluster. The menu never showed any imagination or originality—chicken, fish, maybe a beef cut of some sort. The quality was subpar, even at five-star venues. If you were lucky, at least it was warm. His basic rule was to eat all the salad and add lots of salt and pepper to the main course.

Tonight, at least the wine was decent.

Abe started with a martini, and then a couple glasses of a full red, a merlot from the Napa Valley. Just enough to loosen him up a bit. Then his speech.

Like the menu, he delivered the usual fare—he could pretty much recite it from memory. But his staff liked to mix it up a bit, knowing the media was always watching and listening. If the message became stale, reporters would focus on that and not the substance.

He found his tempo quickly, and soon the showman part of

his personality took over. Abe knew when to pause for applause, when to slap his fist on the podium to underscore his hawkish views on the Middle East. All the while proclaiming he, and he alone, could restore America to its former glory.

He pledged to build up the military, reduce the budget for social programs, and create many new blue-collar jobs.

Abe Schuman cited his years of service in the House of Representatives and his current role as Speaker as ample evidence of his leadership abilities. And he proudly named several pieces of legislation that he shepherded through the House with support from both sides of the aisle. By the time he reminded the audience that it was he who authored the resolution condemning Iran for the senseless bombings in Manhattan, and it was he who spearheaded the appropriations bill for more military aid to Israel, his donors were responding with thunderous applause. And when he pledged to override President Taylor's veto of the Israeli Security Act, the audience signaled its approval with a standing ovation.

By the time Schuman finished his speech, everyone in the room—all the billionaires and captains of industry—knew that Abraham Schuman was their man to be the next President of the United States. Of course, they already knew that before the speech, which is why they had donated heavily to his campaign.

The only part of these fundraisers that Schuman really liked was the informal mixer after his speech. This was the time when alcohol flowed freely and he could speak one-on-one with various key supporters.

Which is why he was presently speaking with Claude Duss, CEO and principle shareholder of United Armaments.

"I trust you are finding my support... adequate?" Duss seemed to search for the correct word. He spoke with a mild French accent, something he had not been able to shed despite years of living in California. He was dressed in a classic black tuxedo with black tie. Abe knew him to be about 60 years old, and he was remarkably fit, both physically and mentally. He was thin, but not overly so, and had short black hair and a beak-like nose. His wife, a woman 20 years his junior, with blond hair and a tight evening gown, was hanging off his arm.

Abe smiled and raised his wine glass in a mock salute to Duss. "My super PAC appreciates your generous donations. My staff informs me we are well ahead of President Taylor in the total amount of funds raised to date. Thanks to substantial donations such as yours, the super PAC is flooding the networks with ads in the states holding upcoming primaries. Of course, this is only what I am told by my staff. Naturally, I have no direct dealings with the super PAC—that would be illegal."

Duss dipped his head. He would never verbally acknowledge gratitude. His peers—CEOs of blue chip American companies—universally saw Duss as ruthless. Unwilling to accept a good deal, he had to have the best deal, looking to get the last nickel on the table during a negotiation. Winning did not seem to be important to Claude Duss; destroying his opponent was everything.

The son of French parents, he had grown United Armaments from a small manufacturer of light weapons and guidance systems to the dominant defense contractor in the world through acquisitions and behind the scenes deals—payoffs and bribes that resulted in lucrative sales to many African and Asian countries. Along the way, he gained control of the Board of Directors and ensured that his stock holdings remained undiluted as new shares were sold.

By conservative estimates, he was worth about five hundred million on paper. Others pegged his net worth well north of two billion. Either way, what he was spending on Schuman's campaign was peanuts.

But money wasn't the only contribution from Duss and

United Armaments.

"I was actually referring to our other business concerns," Duss said.

Schuman glanced at a party of five nearby. They appeared to be engaged in conversation, but one could never be too cautious.

"Shall we take a short walk?"

Again Duss nodded, his wife following in obedient silence.

Once they were clear of potential eavesdroppers, Abe continued. "My chief of staff is in charge of the affair, as I'm sure you know. She and one of your executives—Mr. Ellison, I think—are in regular contact."

"Yes, I am aware of the measures you've taken to insulate yourself—"

Schuman interrupted. "As well as you."

Duss smiled. It reminded Abe of a snake. "Naturally. A wise move."

"If you are asking about my position vis-à-vis Israel, I've tried to be very clear. This has been a cornerstone of my campaign, and one that seems to resonate well with the voters. As you know, I led the Republican effort to nullify the nuclear treaty the present administration negotiated with Iran."

"As I recall, your leadership failed."

Abe sighed. "The math is quite simple. There were too many Democrats supporting the President's agenda. It was not possible to pass the legislation. However, public opinion has turned against the President. The street bombings in New York a couple months ago have been attributed to terrorists sponsored by Iran. Combined with Taylor's anemic support for Israel, we have a vastly different political climate than what existed when he returned billions of dollars in hard currency to Iran and negotiated away Israel's security."

"I'm not interested in excuses. I have made a significant

investment in you—and like all my investments, I expect a generous return. So far, your efforts to pass legislation favorable to my interests have been, at best, neutral—neither positive nor negative. You must do better."

Schuman glanced over his shoulder, ensuring no eavesdroppers were close by. "There are other ways to achieve our mutual goals—perhaps even better ways."

"Yes." Duss smiled again, and Abe fought back a shiver. "Mr. Schuman—Abraham—the United States and its allies appear to be locked in an intractable ongoing state of regional conflict in the Middle East. Recently, the Russians have decided to jump in as well. Many people see these events as awful, barbaric, filled with human suffering and loss, a failure of diplomacy and humanity. But in every failure there is opportunity. You understand, don't you?"

"Claude, my family has deep connections to the Jewish State. My grandparents suffered at the hands of the Nazis because of their faith. I have given my word to support Israel through what we all expect will be trying times ahead.

"Turmoil in the Middle East is as constant as the passage of time. Regime change has led to political vacuums. Governments are toppling at an alarming rate, and ideological leaders are replacing presidents and kings.

"The Middle East is, historically, a collection of tribes and religious subgroups of Islam. Sectarian movements overlay state borders, creating further unrest and mixed allegiances. If you ask me, the English and French really messed it up when they redrew national borders in that part of the world following the First World War."

At the mention of France, Duss returned an icy glare at Abe.

"There's only one way to fix that mess," Schuman concluded.

Duss nodded to his wife, and she slipped away in search of

a glass of Champaign.

"I imagine you are referring to the vote to override the Presidential veto. I understand this legislation is significant, more than just an appropriations bill."

Schuman nodded. "Indeed. It is the essential first step in my plan to bring stability to the region and ensure Israel, as a nation, can thrive."

"I see," replied Duss. "And President Taylor appears to be anti-Jewish by vetoing the bill, even though the language you drafted is untested."

"Not only anti-Jewish," Schuman explained, "but weak, pursuing foreign policy that is not supported at home."

"Some might view your bill as usurping Constitutional authority from the Executive Branch."

"Perhaps," Schuman answered with a sly grin. "But that's beside the point. The voting public is not educated in Constitutional law. No, this is politics—it's about persuading enough voters to support my position, and my candidacy. That wind of support is blowing strongly in my favor, and it will propel me to the White House this November. I promised you an override of Taylor's veto—and you'll get it."

"So then we understand each other." Duss leaned in close enough to smell the sour taint on Schuman's breath. "I will not be disappointed."

Abe felt his mouth go dry, and he gulped the remainder of his wine. "The votes are lining up. Soon, I will bring the matter before the House."

"Good, because I suspect you know what happens otherwise," Duss replied.

Silence hung heavy as Schuman tried to read Duss, an impossible task. "There's much at play here," Schuman said. "Has Ellison kept you informed?"

Duss remained impassive other than a raised eyebrow, his

eyes stygian black voids.

With a dramatic sigh, Schuman said, "Look, we have to be careful; discretion is of the utmost importance. That's why my Chief of Staff is liaising with Cliff Ellison, creating a buffer to insulate the two of us. You do understand the big picture?"

"I think you are getting to the point. Please. Continue."

Abe's eyes shifted right and left, ensuring they were well away from curious ears. "Prime Minister Feldman and I share a common interest."

"Pray tell."

Abe answered unapologetically. "The map of the Middle East must be permanently altered to ensure future peace and sustainability."

"Tell me," Duss said, "do you think the American public will support a full-scale war?"

"We've been in a near-constant state of war since Bush was in office. So what's new? Taylor's popularity has been slipping steadily since he pulled support for the Israeli Security Act. And did you hear the political pundits from both sides skewer him the day after his veto? Americans just don't agree with lifting the sanctions on Iran and essentially giving the Ayatollahs a green light to develop or acquire a bomb."

Impassively, Duss glared back at Schuman.

He nudged Duss toward a deserted corner. "Trust me. The pieces are falling into place. Once I'm elected, my first official action will be to correct decades of failed foreign policy."

This time, when Claude Duss smiled, it was genuine. "That will be good for business."

"So I trust I may count on your continued support?"

Duss extended his hand. "Of course. Cliff Ellison will keep me informed of his conversations with Ms. Meyers. Now, I should find my wife. One so beautiful should not be left alone for long."

After he'd crossed the room, Duss switched off the micro recorder in his jacket pocket.

CHAPTER 14

BEND, OREGON
APRIL 19

WHAT PETER NEEDED MOST was time. He'd taken Kate to his home above EJ Enterprises last night following the incident with the FBI agent. They made small talk while Peter prepared a light meal—microwaved soup-in-a-can, cheese, and carrot sticks. She picked at her meal, finally pushing it aside. "I'm scared. Maybe I should go to the police."

"They can't protect you, Kate. We don't even know who is behind this. There could be informants within the Police Department."

She stared back, exhaustion and fear etched on her face. Peter showed Kate to the guest suite down the hallway from the kitchen, and then excused himself, bidding her goodnight.

Making sure Kate's door was shut, Peter then opened the hidden door built into the floor-to-ceiling bookcase in the great room. He unlocked the gun safe and retrieved a Remington 12-gauge riot gun with one hand and a box loose-filled with 00 buckshot shells with the other. He was working his jaw as he stuffed shells into the tubular magazine. When it was full, he jacked one into the chamber and then pushed in a replacement. His anger was simmering, threatening to boil over. He needed to control his emotions.

Think. His home was on the second and third floors above EJ Enterprises, which meant that a forced entry was, for practical reasons, most likely limited to the front door or the door connecting to the staircase that led down to his business. Fortunately, both doorways joined to the great room. "Well Diesel, this is where we make our stand," he said to his ever-present companion.

Peter nudged one of the stuffed chairs in front of the fireplace, turning it so he could easily watch both doors. Then, resting the shotgun against the chair, he laid a fire in the hearth. There was enough seasoned wood stacked next to the fireplace to last all night. Next, he lit several survival candles and placed them at the corners of the room. The candles would burn for 10 to 12 hours and, combined with the firelight, would illuminate even the darkest recesses of the great room should the power be lost—or deliberately cut.

Peter had only met Kate Simpson on two occasions. Yet strangely he felt a connection to her, and the experience was foreign—forgotten. Was it only that they had both shared a tragic loss, or something more? *Focus. Don't go there—not now.*

"Well Diesel, looks like we have a job." Peter placed a couple of large logs on the growing fire and then relaxed into the soft chair. With the shotgun across his lap, he kept running the facts over and over in his mind. He felt himself moving over the edge, into a familiar space where everything was black and white, good and evil. He shuddered to recall some of the violent deeds he'd carried out when in this mental state—when forced to devolve from civilized behavior and the rule of law.

Diesel had already sensed his master's anxiety and edge. The powerful pit bull—normally extremely friendly and docile—sat at the base of the chair, muscles tense, his ears alert and eyes moving rhythmically from one door to the other—then back again.

Neither Peter nor Diesel would get any rest as darkness settled in. Kate couldn't have been better protected if a platoon of SEALs was camped out in the great room.

Throughout the night, Peter sat in that chair in front of the fireplace—occasionally stoking the fire, the pump-action 12-gauge never leaving his grip, and Diesel vigilant at his feet. If anyone tried to enter, they would be stopped—gravely wounded if not killed—before they cleared the threshold.

There was no doubt in Peter's mind that he could protect Kate—and himself—at his residence. But he also recognized that if the police came he'd lose that ability. It was only a matter of time before Detectives Colson and Nakano knocked on his door, no doubt with an arrest warrant alleging he had assaulted an FBI agent. He was convinced that someone within the agency was on the payroll of whoever was trying to keep the *Liberty* files secret.

He'd tried to reach Jim, but the call went to voicemail. If anyone could find answers and unravel this mystery, it was Commander James Nicolaou and his team of intelligence analysts at the Strategic Global Intervention Team, or SGIT.

Jim and Peter had become best friends in high school, before following disparate paths as adults. Fate intervened, reuniting the two friends a couple years ago. Since that time, Peter had provided assistance to SGIT—and vice versa—on several occasions.

The ring tone startled Peter. He'd been half asleep, still cradling the shotgun. "Yeah," he said.

"You awake?" It was Jim Nicolaou.

Peter quickly shook off the lethargy. "Good. You got my

message."

"Sorry I missed your call. What's going on?"

Peter filled in the details—Kate had spent the night at his place using the guest room, Gary had returned to his business in the gold country in the foothills east of Sacramento, and at any moment the police could arrest Peter again.

"This all began with secret files hacked from a government database?"

"That's right. I don't know why someone would commit murder over this information, or who is behind it all. But I'm running out of time and options."

"And you're certain that was not an FBI agent you assaulted last night?"

"He was packing a Mk-9 magnetic impulse gun and driving a sedan with Washington plates. Said he worked from the Portland office."

"Maybe he works for the Bureau and was also moonlighting for someone else?"

"Great. That would make him a crooked agent. Do you have anything encouraging to offer?"

"I'll get Lacey working on the secret files, see what she can dig up on the *Liberty* that isn't already public knowledge. Shouldn't be hard. In the meantime, what are your plans for Kate Simpson?"

"I need to get her to a safe location—hoping you'd help me with that."

"I can have the jet at the Bend airport in about two hours. She can stay here at SGIT in one of the dorm rooms we have for contractors." SGIT maintained a business jet and three pilots. The flight from McClellan Field in Sacramento, where SGIT was located, to Bend would take just about an hour, wheels up to wheels down.

"Thank you, buddy. It will be a huge relief knowing she's

there."

Peter filled Kate in during the short drive to the private airstrip on the east side of Bend. They'd left Peter's house shortly after his phone call with Jim. and were waiting at the airport when the SGIT business jet landed.

It taxied to a stop in front of the modest terminal, really a one room waiting area combined with administrative offices. The door opened and the steps were lowered. Immediately Peter recognized Jerry Balvanz—a.k.a Iceberg, for his mop of silver-blond hair—and Beth Ross, one of the intelligence officers. They'd met on previous missions.

"Good to see you again, Peter," Jerry said as he extended his hand.

"Thank you for making the trip. I feel better knowing Kate will be at The Office," he said, using the nickname for the SGIT headquarters.

Beth took Kate's small bag and turned, expecting Kate to follow her up the stairs into the waiting aircraft, engines still idling.

Kate offered her hand to Peter. "Thank you."

Peter's smile was warm, genuine. There was something about this woman…

"Don't mention it. I want to get to the bottom of this as much as you do. You'll be safe with my friends until it's over."

"And when it is over, I owe you dinner. I insist," her eyes gleamed, despite all she'd been through.

"It's a deal," Peter said, and released her hand. She climbed the stairs and disappeared inside the fuselage.

"The Commander says he'll have an update for you later today," Jerry said. He was taller than Peter by two inches, and his frame was solid muscle. "Lieutenant Lacey is already working the problem."

Peter nodded.

"What are your plans now, if you don't mind me asking?"

"I've got a phone call to make. Figured I should be the one to tell the Bend Detectives what happened last night before they hear about it through other channels."

"Understood. I'll fill in Commander Nicolaou. Well, time to go."

They shook hands again, and Peter turned to leave.

After returning to EJ Enterprises, Peter phoned Detective Colson. "I have an incident to report," he said. Peter explained everything in detail, including why he suspected Agent Barnes was a fake. She asked many questions, most two or three times. Peter imagined she was taking copious notes.

Finally she asked, "You said he had a Mk-9 impulse pistol."

"Yes, that's right. I took it from him. The serial number matches a lot we produced last year and sold to the Department of Defense along with 5,000 rounds of ammunition. The shipping records you have will confirm my statement."

"So it wasn't stolen."

"Like I said from the beginning: there hasn't been any theft of weapons or ammunition from my business. I suggest you check with the Pentagon. If you ask me, Agent Barnes should not have had that weapon. It is highly restricted. As far as I know, the Mk-9 is only available to Special Forces of the U.S. military."

"I'm going to need that weapon and a statement from you. I'll be right there. Don't go anywhere."

Peter sighed. He had known this was likely and preferred to get it over with. Still, he saw the endless questioning unnecessary and tiring, especially now that what he'd said from the beginning was being corroborated, at least regarding the disposition of the weapons his company manufactured.

"Fine," he said. "I'll be waiting for you in my office."

Detectives Colson and Nakano arrived less than 20 minutes later. As always, Colson had her notepad out—she was old school, preferring pen and paper—and was reading from it while Peter placed the Mk-9 pistol on his desk. Before either detective had a chance to ask, he demonstrated that it was not loaded while ensuring the muzzle always pointed safely to the side.

"You said you recognized it in the agent's shoulder holster," Colson said.

"That's right. See these two LEDs?" Peter pointed to a spot on the back of the action, just above the handgrip. "Pretty distinctive. Not found on any other handgun. The lights indicate the status of the magnetic impulse action."

"Just how does this weapon system function?" Detective Nakano asked. She sounded genuinely curious. Peter walked the detectives through the process, explaining the ten cylindrical electromagnetic coils spaced along the barrel; how they were sequentially energized as the magnetic projectile accelerated down the barrel.

Nakano was examining the gun. It was all black and looked much like an ordinary semi-auto pistol, except the barrel was a plastic tube. She pointed to a small black dial on the side of the action. "What is the function of this knob?"

"That's to turn the power up or down. You see, unlike conventional ammunition, in which the bullet velocity is largely determined by the powder charge in the cartridge, the Mk-9 is electrically operated. This means we can increase or decrease the strength of the magnetic field that accelerates the projectile, thereby changing the speed of the projectile."

"Why would you want to do that?" Colson asked, suddenly interested in the conversation.

"Special Ops. Sometimes they want a subsonic round for stealth, other times they want a high-velocity round for maximum effective range. Just depends on the specific circumstances. The soldier can make that determination on the spot, dial in the appropriate velocity, and let it go. No need to carry a range of special rounds, not to mention the time invested in changing loads."

"So, if this was dialed down in power, it would be totally silent?" Colson asked.

"Yeah. Except for a slight metallic click from the trigger mechanism. It's a single shot action, but it's not hard to learn how to load the next round without making noise."

She pressed further, developing a theory. "And if it was dialed down, say on minimum power or close to it, what kind of penetration would you get up close?"

"Not much. Depends on the medium—soft and fleshy or hard, like bone—and distance, of course. Even the lowest level of body armor would defeat the round. It might not even fully penetrate several layers of heavy clothing."

"What if clothing isn't an issue?"

"Like a head shot?" Peter asked.

Colson nodded.

"There wouldn't be an exit wound."

She locked eyes with her partner. "We'll run the ballistics. But I think we have our murder weapon."

CHAPTER 15

IT WAS LATE MORNING, and the Old Mill District was bustling. There was a steady flow of shoppers moving in and out and past the upscale stores. Cars moved by slowly, most seeking a coveted parking slot, others simply trying to exit and return to home or work.

From her seat at the coffee shop across the street from EJ Enterprises, Jana Cooke watched as the Bend Police Detectives got in their unmarked sedan and drove away. She didn't understand why police departments bothered with unmarked vehicles anyway—from the stock, basic model sedan, to the plain steel wheels, to the license plates indicating the vehicle was publically owned—you'd have to be blind to fail to recognize it as a police car.

She finished her latte—it was lukewarm—and considered ordering another when Peter Savage exited the building. He stood on the sidewalk, collecting his thoughts for a few seconds and breathing in the clean air, before turning and strolling toward the shops. She shadowed him from the opposite side of the street.

He passed several shops—an art gallery, a sandwich shop, two clothing stores—and came to a crosswalk. As Peter turned and crossed the street, Jana realized he was coming directly toward her. She pretended to answer her phone and pivoted to the right, entering a shoe store. From there she continued to watch Peter Savage for another half block before he was out of sight.

She quickly left the shoe store and almost jogged for a couple seconds until her mark was in sight. Abruptly, Peter stopped and turned.

For a moment their eyes met.

Peter instinctively sensed something was wrong. Sure, it wasn't uncommon for a gaggle of shoppers to slowly meander in the same direction, moving as if all were caught in some sort of invisible fluid, pushed along until—one by one—they peeled off into a boutique or eatery.

This was different. The woman had a determined glare, and she hesitated, just for an instant, when Peter turned. No, this wasn't a shopper or someone planning to meet a friend for lunch. This person was on business.

With nowhere to turn, and knowing Peter had made visual contact, Jana quickly decided that her only move was to keep walking forward, right past him as if he was of no more importance than any of the hundreds of other strangers on the sidewalk.

Peter stood there, hands by his side. "Hey, do I know you?" he said as she passed within two feet. He was looking over his shoulder and caught a second hesitation before she kept walking. Peter turned and followed.

Jana Cooke picked up her pace and turned right onto a walkway that connected to a side alley. She entered Pinnacle, a major outdoor equipment and apparel retailer. Peter followed only a handful of steps behind.

She moved deep into the store, passing racks of rain parkas and finding her way to the tents and sleeping bags. As she rounded a display shelf holding rolled-up sleeping pads, she glanced at Peter. His gaze never left her.

"May I help you find something?" a sales clerk asked Peter.

"Uh, no. No thank you." Jana made for the door while Peter was distracted by the clerk.

"Hey! Wait!"

He sprinted forward and reached out, grabbing Jana's arm.

"Sir!" the clerk said, her voice louder than it needed to be.

"Let go of me," Jana said, her voice menacing. Peter didn't loosen his grip.

"Is he bothering you? I can call security," the clerk said.

"Maybe you should," Peter replied, his head turned toward the sales clerk.

Jana Cooke was 50 pounds lighter than Peter, but an expert in hand-to-hand combat. Yet she was beginning to regret following him—what should have been a routine surveillance had now turned into a mess. And it would only get worse if the clerk followed through at Peter's goading and called security.

It was time to act. She could still salvage the mission, and the only consequence would be a tongue-lashing from her handler in Washington, who would assign another agent not recognized by Peter Savage.

Jana reacted, aiming to take Peter down. With blinding speed, she placed her leg behind him, pivoted, and grasped his shoulder with her free hand, yanking him backwards. Off balance, he tumbled, but maintained an iron grip on Jana's left arm. Peter managed to grab a handful of blond hair on his way down, just before he hit the carpeted floor. His attacker came, too.

Immediately, Peter twisted and pushed off Jana, blocking her attempt to regain her feet. When he reached his knees, Peter rammed a fist into her nose, immediately drawing blood. He pulled back, striking her again.

The sales clerk was panicking, yelling for him to stop. Three other patrons were screaming and running for the door.

Jana managed to land a blow to Peter's midsection, just missing his solar plexus. Forcing back the urge to double over, he slammed his fist into her face again, splitting her lip.

A middle-aged man with a beer belly and wearing a private security uniform grabbed Peter from behind and pulled him back from Jana. As Peter struggled, she rose to her feet and lashed out with a kick aimed for his groin. Peter twisted and the kick connected with the guard instead. He released his hold and bent forward in agony.

While Peter stumbled to the side, she uncoiled another kick, striking Peter's right leg. He felt a bolt of pain shoot up from his knee and he collapsed to the side.

The guard was rising from his knees, attempting to draw his Taser. Jana caught the movement a moment before the Taser would have cleared its holster. With blinding speed, she launched a vicious punch that struck the center of his face, bloodying his nose and rocketing his head backwards. As he fell, his skull hit the metal base of a clothing rack, splitting the scalp. Unconscious, his head rolled to the side, blood matting his hair.

"I think she killed him," a hushed voice said. Two young men had watched the brutal attack, and decided it was time to take action. One man stepped forward, his friend right behind him.

"You have to stop!" he commanded, his arm outstretched, pointing at Jana. She reached out, grabbed his arm, and yanked him toward her. At the same time, she struck with her right fist, crushing his windpipe. Stunned and unable to breath, he went down in agony, hands at his throat, trying desperately to suck in air, and failing as the tissue swelled, closing his esophagus.

His friend was next. She struck with a foot to his groin. He reflexively doubled over and she drove her knee into his face, breaking his nose and driving bone into his brain.

With the distractions eliminated, Jana stripped the Taser from the guard's belt holster.

Struggling to his feet, Peter saw the red laser-aiming dot on his chest. Jana fired.

As the dual darts shot forward, Peter pulled over a rack of flannel shirts. The barbs caught in the soft fabric and were pulled to the floor. While she was working to reload the Taser, Peter sprang at her, his right knee protesting as he pushed off.

He collided into her with all the momentum his 170 pounds could deliver. With outstretched arms, he latched around her legs and slammed her backwards. Together they tumbled into another display cabinet holding a dozen different hand-held GPS units arranged on a multi-tier shelf. Topographic maps were alphabetized in drawers within the base-cabinet below the shelving. She still had hold of the Taser, attempting to twist her right hand enough to point it at her adversary.

Using his left arm, Peter grabbed the weapon and struggled to wrench it from her grip. He landed another blow to her face, which was already turning purplish and smeared with blood and saliva.

Jana shifted on her back, pushing Peter to the side. She swung her fist, striking him in the ear. She swung again, hitting his temple. His grip slackened, and Jana sensed her opening. She brought her fist around again, this time more forcefully. The blow to Peter's temple nearly caused him to black out. He relaxed his hold and rolled away, trying to gain some distance, momentarily forgetting about the Taser.

He saw the black gun lining up on his body, and he ducked behind the cabinet. The darts shot forward, missing him by inches. Jana had risen to her knees, again reloading the weapon. From the far side of the display cabinet, Peter pushed the shelving holding the GPS units over. It tumbled onto Jana, striking her head.

Peter rounded the cabinet. Jana was dazed, but not out. She heaved the shelf aside, the Taser no longer within her grasp. She slowly righted herself, spit a gob of blood and saliva, and wiped away more blood mixed with mucous. She looked at Peter with unadulterated malevolence.

She charged him, head down, driving him backwards; somehow Peter managed to stay on his feet. They broke, separated three feet, and she kicked out again, aiming to cripple his right knee. Peter dodged the blow, and before he could regain his balance she launched her right arm forward in a stiff-arm punch that rocked Peter's head back.

He stumbled back several steps until he could retreat no further. Another short cabinet was blocking his withdrawal. He placed his hands behind him, not wanting to turn his eyes from Jana and yet needing to know what the obstacle was. His hand felt a familiar form on the cabinet, his fingers gripping the handle.

Just then, Jana launched herself at Peter. With nowhere for him to run, she was going to end the fight.

Peter swung his arm forward, outstretched, covering a wide arc. Within his grasp was a compact camp shovel. She didn't see it soon enough to halt her forward momentum. So she did the next best thing and bent her legs, trying to slide under the swinging implement.

It was a mistake.

The edge of the steel shovel sliced into her neck. Although not sharpened or designed as a cutting implement, the utilitarian tool still cut deep into Jana's tissues, severing arteries and veins, along with tendons and muscles. Her head fell limp to the side and massive amounts of blood gushed from the wound.

She dropped to her knees, one hand on the ugly wound, trying in vain to staunch the flow of blood, the other helping to hold her balance. With insufficient oxygen to her brain, she passed out, and a moment later was dead.

Peter dropped the shovel. He looked at the motionless body lying before him and couldn't recall what she looked like before he had bruised and bloodied her face. Later, the face would return—haunting his nights and terrorizing his sleep.

But now, he had to get away. He was in enough trouble already. But where? Where could he go where he wouldn't endanger others and yet he would not be captured by the police? It had to be someplace where he could defend himself, where he would have the upper hand. Then it came to him.

Returning to the cabinet that housed the topographic maps, Peter opened a drawer. He quickly worked his way until he found the quadrant he was seeking. It was a map of the Three Sisters Wilderness, just west of Bend. He ran to the checkout counter—everyone had fled the store by now—and used a pen to mark an X on the map.

Then, he placed the map on Jana's body. He only had a minute to get what he would require—an expedition hunting pack, a box of freeze-dried meals, a water filter and several plastic bottles, and a backpack cooking kit. He shoved everything inside the pack and grabbed the first sleeping bag he laid hands on—rolled tight and stuffed inside a nylon bag—as he made his way for the door. Before he left, he slipped on a down parka. He would need it where he was going.

From the fringe of the crowd a man with a flesh-colored butterfly bandage at the edge of his scalp and another bandage across his nose spoke into his phone. "Yeah, we have a problem here—a big problem."

CHAPTER 16

BEND, OREGON
APRIL 20

OUTSIDE THE PINNACLE STORE, a crowd was gathering. Sirens could be heard in the distance, the shrill sound growing in intensity—emergency vehicles no doubt summoned by many of the witnesses to the hand-to-hand combat.

"There are people inside who need help," Peter shouted to the onlookers, causing a dozen faces to inch closer to the windows, driven by morbid fascination. With the hunting pack slung over a shoulder and the sleeping bag clutched to his side, he pushed through the crowd, quickly putting the store behind him. He followed a zigzag path through the shopping complex and soon arrived at the stairs to his home on the floors above EJ Enterprises.

The sirens were much louder now, and then they silenced, indicating the emergency vehicles had arrived. There would be at least one ambulance and a couple police cruisers, Peter reasoned. More would be summoned once the first responders took stock of the carnage inside.

Taking the steps two at a time, his knee protesting every movement, he entered and was greeted by Diesel. He leaned over and rubbed his companion's head and ears. "We have to go," he said. Diesel looked at him and tilted his head, his amber-colored eyes suggesting understanding at a basic level.

Peter dropped the sleeping bag in the entry and went directly to the secret door in the bookcase and opened it. He bypassed the antique weapons for the gun safe. Where he was going would require substantial firepower if his worst fears were realized.

He spun the dial on the large safe—left, right, left, right— finally turning the lever handle. The heavy door swung open silently on greased hinges. Peter grabbed a worn pigskin bag from the floor of the safe and filled it with the ammunition he would need—shotgun shells, rifle and pistol cartridges. Next he retrieved a semiautomatic Colt .45 Government model. After placing the pistol inside the pack, he added the pigskin ammunition bag and a belt holster. Lastly, he included his Leica binoculars and spotting scope, and a set of third generation night-vision goggles. The optics alone would cost several thousand dollars to replace, which is why he kept them in this secret space.

After slinging the heavy pack on his shoulders, Peter finished his task by removing the Remington riot gun and one of his hunting rifles—a scoped Weatherby in .340 caliber. It was a powerful round with heavy bullets, favored for hunting bear and other dangerous game.

Peter hastily gathered up everything, closed the safe, then secured the secret bookcase panel before he called Diesel to his side. Lastly, he grabbed a bottle of ibuprofen from a kitchen cabinet on his way out. *No point locking the door. The police will be here soon anyway*, he thought. *Once they interview witnesses at the store and review the video from the security cameras, they'll come here for me.*

Ignoring the pain in his knee and general aches all over his body, he quickly climbed into his red Hummer H3 truck, having placed his possessions in the back. Diesel rode shotgun as was his preference. Trying to avoid drawing attention, Peter put the truck in gear and slowly backed out of his reserved parking spot in front of EJ Enterprises just as the receptionist came running out the door. She was shouting something incomprehensible. Peter made eye contact, shook his head, and drove away, leaving his receptionist wondering what was happening.

Within minutes, the red Hummer exited Bend, pointed west on the Cascade Lakes highway. Soon, Peter would be in spotty cell coverage, and he had one important call to make before he lost a signal.

"Jim, the situation here has deteriorated." Peter explained what had happened in short, almost cryptic, sentences, but it was enough for Commander Nicolaou to follow. He listened carefully, holding his questions until Peter was done.

"You understand that the police are going to perceive you as a violent criminal who has assaulted an FBI agent and is the prime suspect in the murder of one or more civilians. Whoever contacts you first—local police or FBI—will be predisposed to shoot first and sort it out later."

"That's why I'm not hanging around," Peter said. "I'll be in touch when and if it's safe to contact you. Don't try to reach me—you won't be able to."

"Where are you going? They'll find you—you can't hide."

"Don't worry. Where I'm heading law enforcement won't find me unless I want them to."

"Listen Peter. This isn't a good idea. Surely you recognize that the woman who attacked you today and Agent Barnes are almost certainly connected. Whoever these people are, they obviously have some heavyweight resources. And they won't hesitate to kill again."

"I know. I've thought this through."

Jim had heard the same raw determination in Peter's tone before, when the stakes were equally high. "They'll hunt you down... but you already know that."

"I'm counting on it. Only they'll be on my turf, under conditions of my choosing."

"You won't have any backup. You'll be alone."

Peter glanced to the side. Diesel was sitting at attention, watching the trees pass by.

"That's where you're wrong. I've got all the backup I need." Just then the line went dead as Peter's cell signal was lost. He was 20 minutes out of Bend and gaining elevation quickly.

The first responders were shaken by what they found inside Pinnacle. The paramedics quickly determined they had one survivor, a security guard, and rushed him to St. Charles hospital in serious condition with a suspected skull fracture. After the forensics team extensively photographed the crime scene and collected evidence from the bodies, the deceased—two men and one woman—were bagged and transported to the morgue for autopsy. Detectives were still combing through the scene well into the evening.

"Four homicides in less than two weeks. That isn't a coincidence," Detective Nakano commented to her partner. With a population of almost 90,000 and primarily known as a paradise for recreation, murder and manslaughter were rare—maybe one a year on average.

"Other than Peter Savage, what are the points of commonality between the Emma Jones murder and the three victims at Pinnacle?"

Niki Nakano shook her head. "Nothing."

"There's got to be more", Colson said. "We just haven't

found it."

"What do you make of the topo map on the deceased woman?"

"It's gotta be a message."

"Like in X marks the spot? But why? It doesn't make sense that he would flee and then point us exactly to where he's going."

"Yeah, I agree. But just in case, the Deschutes County Sheriff Department will check it out in the morning. Too dangerous to start the search at night."

Nakano understood. Besides, by morning they would know more. "Any word from the Feds yet on Agent Barnes?" she asked.

"No, not yet." Just then Colson's phone rang. She recognized the area code as Portland. "Speak of the Devil, maybe this is them now."

While Colson was on the phone, Detective Nakano returned to her pad of paper and the matrix she was constructing. A visual thinker, she preferred to use circles and arrows to indicate relationships between seemingly disconnected sets of facts. And there were a lot of discrepancies to sort through. Not the least of which, the eyewitnesses couldn't even agree on whether the deceased woman was an innocent victim or assailant. No one actually saw who killed the two men, although two witnesses did see Peter Savage strike the woman with the camp shovel. That would be easy enough to corroborate with fingerprints from the handle. She hoped they'd learn more when the security guard recovered enough to be questioned—assuming he did pull through.

She was chewing on her pen when Colson finished her call.

"Well, that was interesting. Agent Andrew Shooks—he's with the cyber-crimes division out of the FBI office in Portland—says Barnes works in his unit. He's requested access to everything—all the evidence related to this investigation and the Jones murder."

Nakano looked up from her diagram. "Why? The Feds don't have any jurisdiction here."

"Maybe yes, maybe no. There is the matter of unauthorized access to secret government files, allegedly by Mr. Savage. And even he admits he assaulted a federal agent."

"Not exactly. He claims that Barnes is a fake and not a federal agent."

"Regardless," Colson continued, "I doubt the Chief will want to get into a pissing match over this. But you want to know what's really weird?"

Her partner gave her the do-I-really-have-to-answer-that look. "Okay," Colson said. "It's Agent Barnes."

"What about him?"

"Well, Shooks sounded surprised when I asked how the agent was doing."

"Maybe Savage is right and Barnes is an imposter."

"You can't be serious. Anyway, he said we'll be getting an arrest warrant for Peter Savage within the hour."

Nakano raised her eyebrow. "Really? How come Saint Charles hospital has no record of anyone by the name of Barnes being treated in the last 24 hours? In fact, they haven't treated anyone identifying themselves as an FBI agent during the past six months."

Colson shrugged. "Agent Shooks says Barnes is doing well but will need several days to fully recover. That would be consistent with what Mr. Savage described for his injuries."

"Where is Barnes now? We should interview him."

"Good question," Colson answered with a frown. "Shooks wouldn't say and added that Barnes had been thoroughly questioned by the Bureau. Maybe the Chief can get a copy of his statement."

"Why wouldn't Barnes take himself to the emergency room

to get checked out? Without a proper medical examination soon after the alleged incident, there's no evidence an assault actually occurred."

"Except we have the statement from Peter Savage. And Agent Shooks has a written statement from Barnes that he was, indeed, assaulted last night, with injuries serious enough to keep him from work."

"This just gets stranger all the time," Nakano said.

"You got that right. I'll make sure the evidence techs get a copy of what we've got so far scanned and emailed up to Portland. In the meantime, we have local, state, and federal law enforcement searching for Peter Savage. I wouldn't be surprised if he's on the ten-most-wanted list by morning."

CHAPTER 17

PARALLELING THE PACIFIC OCEAN and forming the eastern boundary of the Willamette Valley are the Cascade Mountains. The volcanic mountain chain stretches from Northern California, through Oregon, Washington, and into British Columbia where it merges with the Rockies. With five peaks in Oregon higher than 10,000 feet, the Cascades provide an effective rain barrier resulting in the western third of the state being noteworthy for its precipitation, while the eastern portion is classified as high desert. The mountains are a sportsman's paradise with ample opportunity for hiking, backpacking, fishing, hunting—and hiding.

Diesel stretched, pushing his four legs against his master, waking him in the process. The morning air was cold, and frost covered the scattered bunch grass dispersed among the mix of pumice gravel and sand. Peter pushed up his brimmed hat exposing his eyes to a brilliant orange sunrise. He stretched, and Diesel groaned. "Me too," he said.

After leaving Bend, Peter drove the Hummer H3 pickup truck past Mount Bachelor to the turnoff for Todd Lake. Scattered patches of snow still frequented the forest floor—it would not be completely melted for another two months. But the road was open and Peter got about a mile off the highway before encountering the locked gate blocking the old gravel Forest Service road.

He knew this area well—knew that beyond the gate he could travel north, away from people. He was at ease in the wilderness, and he had the essentials needed to survive—*rather comfortably*, he thought. Water from melting snow was plentiful. He had food, and if needed he was perfectly capable of taking large or small game. But with the freeze-dried meals, that wouldn't be necessary unless he needed to stay in the high country for more than two or three weeks.

Here, on the eastern slope of Broken Top peak, at the edge of the Three Sisters Wilderness, he would hide out and let them come for him. Here, the terrain was his ally. He would set up hides well up the slope. The trees were thin, and with many open meadows, Peter would see his adversaries coming long before they knew where he was.

The backcountry was still considered closed to vehicles, and with only patchy snowfields, the cross-country skiers and snowshoers would be done for the season. It was unlikely any innocents would wander into the area.

Peter drove around the Forest Service gate and continued north, eventually pulling off the road and parking on a spur. He strapped the .45 caliber handgun to his waist and placed some last-minute items from the truck inside the pack—first aid kit, rope, knife, lighter, and a blanket. With Diesel by his side, he shouldered the pack and long guns before heading west on foot. After an hour of walking and with the last gray light from a faded sunset, he'd set up shelter beneath a dense fir tree. There, with Diesel resting his head on Peter's lap, he had fallen asleep.

With the beginning of a new day, Peter had work to do. He figured he had at least the morning to prepare, perhaps longer. The red Hummer H3, parked next to the road, would be found quickly. From there, trackers would follow his trail.

"Come on, Diesel." Peter was eying a rocky outcropping that rose about 30 feet above the meadow. "That point of land is our new home." It was angled to the northeast and had a reasonable covering of trees. From that vantage point, he could watch the entire length of the meadow, looking over their back trail.

Peter's knee felt better after popping several ibuprofens, but it was still sore and stiff. He estimated it was sprained and had wrapped an elastic bandage around it for added support. It helped, but only a little. His abdomen was also healing. The bruised muscles ached only when he took a deep breath.

After crossing the long meadow, they climbed the steep scree slope to the point, the only access avenue unless one was willing to climb the rock cliff face. Peter estimated that it would take a determined adversary at least two minutes to rush up the scree from the base, more than enough time to escape off the back of the point and retreat farther up the gentle slope.

The terrain was marked by a series of parallel drainages that funneled snow runoff to the east. At higher elevations from his current position, these gullies were separated by steep ridgelines. The drainages provided cover to disappear and relocate, while the ridges offered excellent hides to ambush any pursuers.

East, toward the road, the terrain was more densely wooded while the creeks, flowing slower at the lower elevation, meandered through innumerable grassy meadows, separated by pockets of fir trees.

Directly to the west was Broken Top, and extending north from the aptly-named extinct volcanic peak was a formidable natural barrier—the towering rock cliff known as Tam McArthur Rim. Peter had no intention of trying to drop over the Rim, but he could continue north and eventually work around the drop-off to access points deeper in the Three Sisters Wilderness. Within this vast tract of land, he could remain hidden for weeks, possibly months.

Although Peter would have preferred to be outfitted with his camo hunting clothing, the waterproof parka he'd pulled off the rack at Pinnacle was heavily insulated with down filling, and it came with a pair of medium-weight gloves tethered to the zipper—a package deal. Plus, he had luckily grabbed one in a slate-gray color, affording a decent degree of camouflage.

With the edge of his shoe, he scraped away loose rock and sticks from his vantage on the point. He planned to be here for a while—maybe all afternoon—so he might as well be comfortable. A rotting log lay between his scrape and the cliff, a perfect rest for the spotting scope. With the magnified aid of the scope, he would be able to identify faces at the far end of the meadow—more than a thousand yards away.

Peter and Diesel had already shared breakfast, and he wouldn't boil water and prepare food again until late afternoon—about an hour before sunset so the small cooking fire would be less likely to attract attention.

Stretching out on the ground and using the pack as a rest for his Weatherby, Peter got comfortable with the rifle. Next, he spotted several distinctive landmarks in the meadow—a boulder, a lone scrub pine, a bend in the stream flowing back toward the primitive road—and ranged the distance to each using the built in laser range finder of the Leica binoculars. He committed to memory the distance to each unique mark.

With his preparation completed, he took a drink of water from one of the plastic bottles and then poured some into one of the lightweight aluminum cooking pots. Diesel lapped until he had his fill.

Peter reached out and rubbed the pit bull's head. The dog sat and watched the meadow, just as Peter did. "Well Diesel, I guess all we can do now is wait."

Derek Hood was driving his Ford F150 pickup slowly north along the Forest Service Road. In the back was his Polaris Outlander ATV. He'd been working Search and Rescue as a Deschutes County Deputy for close to five years. He loved working outdoors, although he didn't care so much for the wintertime searches, especially during blizzard conditions.

He understood the unusual request for his present activity came through the Bend Police. Rather than searching for a lost hiker, he was looking for a vehicle thought to be associated with a wanted and dangerous man. Supposedly, the suspect had assaulted and killed three persons at the Pinnacle store in the Old Mill District. It didn't make any sense to him that a criminal would flee to these mountains—after all, they couldn't stay here forever.

The Ford managed the rough and rutted road with ease, and Derek knew he was on the fresh trail of a vehicle from the tire tracks traversing patches of snow covering the shaded sections of road. He rounded a bend and startled three does, the mule deer bounding off as the deputy's truck approached.

He was moving his head from side to side, plodding along, careful not to miss any sign of tire tracks heading away from the road. If he reached a snow patch without the tracks, he'd know he'd gone too far and would turn around and backtrack. Although technically vehicles were not allowed off the established road, he would use the Outlander if the trail led away into the wilderness.

At least the weather was nice, he thought. Sunny and mild temperatures made it comfortable to drive with the window down. He was wearing a long-sleeve uniform shirt and considered rolling up the sleeves. Thankfully, he didn't have his ballistic vest on—if he did he'd be roasting without the AC pumping out cold air.

So far he hadn't heard any engine sounds, other than his own truck. After rounding another bend and traversing up a shallow rise, he saw a glint of red. It was far ahead and could be just a trick of light on the earth. The lava that comprised these mountains exhibited a range of color, including rust and yellow. But he didn't think the color he saw was natural—it was too vivid.

The Ford slowed to a stop as Derek removed his foot from the accelerator. Leaving the truck in the road, he turned off the engine and exited the cab, leaving the door open so as not to make a sound. His pulse quickened. This was different than searching for a lost child or hiker; this time, the element of personal violence was very real.

His right hand fell to the Smith & Wesson .40 caliber pistol on his belt. Just to be certain, he brushed his left hand over the pair of chrome handcuffs. Derek took two calming breaths and then walked—in absolute silence—toward the patch of red behind a copse of young fir trees. After ten meters, he stopped to listen. The only sound was a soft whoosh from the gentle breeze moving through the evergreens.

Another dozen paces and he stopped again, this time along the edge of the road, using the vegetation to screen his approach. Still no sound.

With slow, deliberate movements he silently crept forward. Thirty more meters and he knew for certain this was a red pickup. Nine meters further and Derek was able to read the license plate on the rear of the truck. It was a Hummer H3, and the plate matched the information he'd been given.

His heartbeat ran up again, and he drew his sidearm.

Gripping the weapon with both hands, he cleared the fir trees and approached the truck. Only then did he recognize the passenger door was open. A head popped up—*must have been rummaging through the glove box or searching the cab.*

"Step out of the truck. Hands in the air," he ordered. Slowly, the man complied. His back was toward Derek, but his hands were up, fingers spread wide.

"Turn around and walk to me. I wanna see those hands!"

The man turned slowly, avoiding any sudden or provocative movements. Derek was sizing him up; well under six feet, slim and muscular, wavy raven hair and eyes like coal. His skin coloration was dark, but not African—Middle Eastern maybe, or Mediterranean. No, this person didn't match the description of Peter Savage.

"That's right. Come around the truck. Keep those hands up." Derek was moving backwards while the man advanced, taking a new position where nothing impeded his view of the suspect and he still had about seven meters of separation.

"Is that your truck?" Derek asked. He already knew the answer.

"No. It belongs to a friend. He took off that way." The man motioned with his head toward trees beyond the parked vehicle.

"And he just left you here? That's not very friendly."

The suspect stared back in silence.

"Does your friend have a name?"

He hesitated before answering. "Yeah. Peter Savage."

That was about the last answer that Derek Hood expected. He'd been a patrol Deputy for six years before moving into Search and Rescue, and during that time he'd caught all kinds of petty criminals in lies. And the lies were always lame, obviously untruthful, and often not even remotely believable. He'd expected exactly that now, from this man.

"You don't say. Well, he's just the man I'm looking for."

Derek cocked his head to the side and smiled. Maybe this was going to be his lucky day.

"He's a popular man, this Peter Savage fellow." The voice came from behind and startled Derek. Still, he had the presence of mind not to turn around. He held firm with his Smith & Wesson aimed at the suspect in front of him.

Derek heard the sound of boots on gravel as several pair of feet approached. Next he heard the distinctive sound of a shotgun action being pumped. Then the footsteps stopped.

"About time, where've you been?" asked the man in front of Derek. He still held his hands in the air and stood motionless.

"Relax Ben, we're here aren't we?"

Derek was sweating despite the cool temperature. "Ben is it?"

The suspect nodded.

"Well Ben, why don't you tell your friends to drop their guns and we'll have ourselves a nice, peaceful conversation."

Ben shook his head. "I have a better idea... Deputy Hood." Even from over 20 feet away Ben could read the nametag above the breast pocket on his uniform shirt. "If you want to live, put down your pistol."

Derek didn't answer. He knew that to surrender his weapon would leave him completely at the mercy of these people. And yet he still didn't know how many there were. Judging from the sound when they first approached, he was certain there was more than one gunman behind him. But where? How far away? He moved his eyes to the side trying desperately to see where they were, but he couldn't. And he wasn't about to let Ben out if his sights.

Ben motioned to the side with his head, still keeping his hand up. Again Derek heard the familiar sound of boots on the gravel road, and then two men appeared to his right and left. They were spread far apart, making it impossible for him to shoot both before one of them returned fire.

One man was brandishing a shotgun, the other a semiauto handgun. Like Ben, both had black wavy hair, dark brown eyes, and a tanned complexion.

Now that his colleagues were in view, Ben spoke again. "Last chance, Deputy. We can all walk away. It's up to you."

Derek held firm. He figured he could pivot to his right and take out the shotgun first. Then spin and blast away at the other guy. Ben wasn't armed, at least not that Derek could see. Now he regretted not wearing his ballistic vest. Against either the shotgun or handgun it would have given him the advantage, the ability to take a hit—multiple hits—and not be incapacitated.

"Well Ben, the way I figure it… the first bullet goes through your heart. I'll get one shot into your buddies before either knows it, and that gives me a better-than-even chance of coming out of this okay. But you won't. You'll bleed out before the gunfire is over."

Ben just smiled.

Click.

Derek heard the hammer cocking first, and then felt the cold barrel press against the back of his head. Before the thought fully registered in his mind, his life was ended.

Ben dropped his hands and strode forward. "Thank you, Nadya."

Nadya Wheeler holstered her pistol.

The Mossad team comprised five operators. All were fluent in English and had deeply established aliases, including expertly forged birth certificates used to acquire government-issued social security numbers, drivers' licenses, and U.S. passports. They had all lived in the United States since graduating from college and being recruited into the elite Israeli intelligence organization.

Nadya Wheeler—the team leader—and Joshua Nolan

were based in Los Angeles; Ben Jarmin, Seattle; and Marcus Black and Marie Vallejo were located in the San Francisco Bay Area. None of them had met or worked together prior to this assignment.

Mossad had many agents in the U.S.—the exact number was highly classified. The government of Prime Minister David Feldman believed it prudent to keep intelligence operatives in key positions in industry and foreign governments, always present to feed information back to his administration. Nothing was out of question when it came to preserving, and expanding, the Jewish homeland.

"What shall we do with the deputy?" Marcus Black asked, the shotgun slung over his shoulder.

Nadya sighed. "His vehicle can't be too far away. Go back down the road and find it, then drive it here."

Marcus left at a jog. Nadya was 10 years older than her colleagues and excelled at problem solving, especially under stressful situations. This certainly qualified as such.

"Joshua, Marie. Get our gear from the SUV. And try to push that red truck further off the road. Get a tarp and cover it—that color sticks out like a neon sign. Throw a tarp over the SUV, too. Make certain both vehicles are concealed well. Cut fresh boughs and maybe some small evergreen trees for camouflage. In a few hours, we have to assume there will be many law enforcement vehicles on this road searching for Deputy Hood.

"When Marcus returns, Ben, you and I will help him get the body into the passenger seat." She turned at the sound of the approaching Ford. It was white with green and brown stripes. When Marcus pulled to a stop and got out, Nadya recognized the Sheriff Department emblem on the door.

"He must have seen the red paint through the trees and stopped to investigate," Marcus said. "We should have hidden the truck right away."

"Don't worry," Nadya replied. "This plan is better. We'll give the authorities a diversion and send them looking in the wrong place. They'll waste days searching miles from our true location."

The three Mossad operators struggled but managed to get the body of Derek Hood into the passenger seat. Nadya buckled the seat belt across his torso to hold him in place when the truck crossed over rough sections of gravel road.

"Ben, dig a hole in the road bed and bury that blood," she said, pointing to the spot where Derek's head had fallen.

Nadya removed a topographic map of the area from a cargo pocket and opened it on the hood of the Ford. She got her bearings and then pointed to a spot several miles farther north of their current location. "Here," she said to Marcus. "Drive to this general location and find a spot to ditch the truck. Get it off the road, but not hard for the sheriffs to find."

He nodded agreement and leaned closer, examining the details of the terrain as shown on the map so he could identify the spot when driving.

"That looks to be eight miles in a straight line. Navigating back, it will be at least 10 to 12 miles. No problem." He was thinking he'd cover that distance in less than five hours. If he wasn't hunting Peter Savage, he was confident he could do it in three to four hours.

"Good. You'll rendezvous with us here." She stabbed her index finger at a location on the map about halfway between the road and Tam McArthur Rim. The many contour lines indicated the elevation gain he'd have to contend with, but his path would avoid steep slopes by following the meadows and drainages as much as possible. "We'll make camp there tonight."

"What if you encounter the target first?" Marcus asked.

"Then we kill him and radio you to meet here. With a little luck, we'll be out of here by tonight."

"And the police?"

Nadya smiled. "You worry too much, my friend. The police will be searching for Deputy Hood, being unable to reach him by radio. I suspect they'll know he was in this area, but not his exact location. Eventually, they'll find him and focus an intensive manhunt in that area. But it will take them time, and with nightfall only hours away, they won't be mobilized until midday tomorrow at the earliest."

"They'll have dogs," Marcus protested. "What's to prevent them from tracking me back to the rendezvous point?"

Nadya reached into her pocket, producing a plastic squeeze bottle. The top was sealed in shrink wrap. The liquid inside was yellowish.

"When you leave the pickup truck, head north for a quarter mile. Then squirt a small amount of this liquid on your shoes. It doesn't take much—10 drops or so. Every mile reapply five drops to each shoe."

She handed the bottle to Marcus. He held it up, shaking it slightly. "What is it?"

Nadya laughed. "Cougar piss."

CHAPTER 18

THE GUNSHOT WAS FAINT, but unmistakable. The sound roused Peter from a light sleep and he immediately grew alert. Diesel echoed his master's apprehension, his ears raised up and pointed in the direction the sound had come from. The problem was the ridge ahead and to the right. It towered 100 feet above the meadow and reflected sound that was originating from the direction of the road.

"That shot was a ways off, Diesel. It'll be easy enough for them to follow our trail across the meadows and snow patches." Peter had deliberately walked across the grasses as much as possible, knowing the flattened grass would leave an easy-to-follow trail for several days. He glanced at his watch. "I give them an hour."

The only problem was Peter didn't know who *they* were. Or how many, or what support they had. Suddenly, the confidence he had conveyed to Jim yesterday seemed hard to find. But it was too late to turn back.

Making use of the available time, he emptied and re-stowed everything in the pack. Then he checked all of his weapons again, making sure they were fully loaded. He expected he and Diesel would have to make a hasty retreat once first contact was made. The riot gun—only useful at close range—was strapped to the outside of the pack.

Pressure on his elbows and side was making it uncomfortable to lie still, so Peter stood and walked a short distance around the point, leaving Diesel on guard. He drew comfort from his knowledge of the terrain, and he knew exactly where they would go when they were pushed off the point.

In his mind it was only a question of how long they could hold back the enemy from this vantage. He knew it was indefensible given the ridgeline to the right towering above the point. Plus, there were multiple approaches, and if the enemy force was several men, they would surround him. He would retreat before that was allowed to happen.

After a final check that the spare ammunition was in outer pockets of the pack, separated by caliber, and that he had two loaded spare magazines for the Colt .45 in his cargo pockets, Peter settled in again. He looked at Diesel, studying the dog's face. The lines and folds of flesh seemed to echo the concern that was mounting within Peter.

Over and over he had considered his plan—anticipating every move they would make. He imagined them approaching up the meadow. Slowly, cautiously advancing. He expected a team of a half dozen men—a strike team like Jim led when SGIT was on a mission. And he knew that most of the force would be secluded within the tree line, keeping abreast of the trackers. Ready to lay down a heavy volume of fire once contact was made.

Peter looked through the spotting scope to the far end of the meadow, searching the shadows amongst the patch of old fir trees that separated this meadow from the next.

He was ready.

Nadya had Marie take point. She would follow the evidence of footfalls left across the meadow. The trail headed west, to higher elevation. The Mossad team had exchanged civilian camouflage clothing for their street clothes.

Still, there was no concealment for Marie in the middle of the meadow.

Nadya, Ben, and Joshua stayed within the tree line, at least 10 meters from the edge of the meadow. Through the breaks they could communicate using hand signals, and Marie kept the pace slow, frequently looking down, to the left and right, then forward again. She knew the grass had been flattened the previous day, since dewdrops uniformly covered the grass.

The team had two satellite phones—one was with Marcus and the other with Nadya. They were all armed with M4 rifles, and they each carried extra magazines, military-grade night vision goggles, spare batteries and food, and a sleeping bag. Each team member was trained in boreal forest and desert survival. They were also competent marksmen and skilled in hand-to-hand combat.

The chatter of a gray squirrel brought Nadya to a halt. She raised her clenched fist, signaling the others to freeze. After a minute and no further sign of disturbance, she resumed their advance. They reached the end of the meadow, and joined up with Marie, squatting in the dark shadows of old-growth timber.

"The tracks lead here," Marie said. "He probably crossed this wooded break. This entire slope is dotted with meadows."

Looking back, Nadya saw they had gained about 15 meters in elevation. She checked the time. It had been close to an hour since they left the road. *Marcus should be ditching the Ford pickup about now.*

"Okay," she said. "Let's go."

Peter was beginning to wonder if he'd miscalculated. More than two hours had passed since he'd heard the gunshot. *Maybe they're not following my trail?*

He looked again through the spotting scope. The shadows were growing long; the sun would set in a few hours. He was methodically scanning the tree line at the far end of the meadow—a skill he had honed over years of hunting—a few times from this very location.

The motion was fleeting, and Peter wasn't positive it was real, or what caused it. Could be a deer, or his imagination.

Or the enemy.

He left the scope fixed on the spot and watched, ever patient. Just as he was about to give up, he saw movement again. This time it persisted, and a person emerged from the shadows, following just to the side of Peter's track.

The terrain dipped where the creek exited the meadow, and for a full minute Peter lost the person. Then they climbed up the bank edging the creek and came fully into view. With magnification and a sharp image delivered by the Leica optics, he realized this was a woman. She was wearing camouflage, but not a military pattern. For a moment, he thought maybe this was just someone out for a hike. Maybe doing some early season scouting for deer. It wasn't unheard of, and Peter had done the same in other locations that were new to him.

As the woman approached closer, she stopped and leaned forward, like she was examining the tracks he and Diesel made. Or maybe she was just studying deer spoor.

He could tell she was carrying a rifle, but as the weapon was held close to her body, he was not able to positively identify whether it was a sporting rifle or military. She placed the rifle to the side, butt to the ground and stood. At that instant he had a clear view of the weapon: it was an assault rifle. If a legitimate civilian version, it would be labeled an AR15. If it was military, it was an M4—fully automatic and packing serious firepower.

"That's interesting, Diesel. A suppressor. Now I wonder why a hunter would have a suppressor on their deer rifle? I guess it's show time." Peter continued to divide his attention between the approaching woman and the trees to the left of the meadow. He discounted the ridge on the right—it was steep and would be difficult for individuals to traverse its slope. Occasionally a squirrel chattered, but otherwise the forest was quiet. He couldn't see any movement amongst the evergreens, but that was little assurance.

The woman continued her steady advance, staying just to the side of his trail. Exactly as would be expected if she was following it.

When she was about 400 yards out Peter snugged his rifle tight to his shoulder. With the variable-power scope turned all the way up to 20x, he acquired the woman's image. The crosshairs danced across her chest and face, then settled on a patch of bare dirt and gravel about 15 feet in front of her. Unless she abruptly changed course, she would walk right over the spot.

Peter started applying pressure to the trigger at the same time he was regulating his breathing. She was almost there, and he felt the flesh on his fingertip mashed against the trigger.

Boom!

Through the scope he saw the cloud of dust kicked up by the bullet cratering into the earth, not more than a foot away from her boot.

She froze as the echo faded away. Peter chambered another round, and held the scope on her.

He could see her eyes shifting, and then her head moved—

at first it was minimal, and then the movement became greater as she searched for the shooter.

"Stay right there!" Peter shouted. She was looking in the general direction of the point, but the movements of her head indicated she hadn't pinpointed Peter's exact location.

"Who are you?" he shouted.

"I'm just out for a hike."

"Nice try. I can make out every detail of your clothing, your face, and that assault rifle. You've been following the trail I left. Rather careless of you."

"What do you want, mister?"

"Where are your friends?" Peter was rapidly scanning along the edge of the meadow for movement but not finding any.

"I told you. I'm just hiking. There's no one with me."

"Is that so!" Peter shouted. "You act like someone who's used to being shot at. Most people, they would have dropped to the ground or run with a bullet that close. But not you. You're pretty cool under fire."

Peter had her in his scope again. He saw her eyes move toward the rifle she clutched. He read the face. There was no fear, just determination and… anger? He was still studying her expression, trying to predict her actions a second before she acted, when a string of bullets stitched a line up the edge of the cliff and across the log he was resting against.

At the same instant the woman raised her rifle, taking aim where her teammates were shooting. Peter fired.

The hunting bullet struck her torso—center of mass. It expanded quickly, dumping energy into her vital organs before exiting her back. She was dead before she hit the ground.

More gunfire, but it was muted and he couldn't determine the source. Peter suspected it was somewhere within the cover of the forest on the far side of the meadow, but he couldn't locate the shooters. He was moving the scope along the transition between grass and trees, desperately searching.

A volley of bullets ripped the air above his head. There! He just caught a glimpse of muzzle flashes.

Steady. Steady.

Although his pulse was racing, Peter controlled his breathing and steadied his rifle and scope. At 20x magnification, he had to be absolutely motionless or the image in the scope would be jittery, a blur.

Bullets impacted the log and then went high. They were zeroing in on the range. He and Diesel couldn't stay here much longer.

There! He made out a face, shoulder, and half of the chest. The shooter was male, and firing from a kneeling position next to a large fir tree. Peter rested the crosshairs on his chest.

Flashes of white light covered the image, and a second later he heard the bullets strike the rocky lip and log. Peter put it aside, concentrating on the crosshairs…

Steady… Squeeze…

Boom!

Through the scope he saw the man's arms fly outward, the rifle leaving his grasp.

Two down.

"Time to go, Diesel!"

Peter shoved the spotting scope into the pack and then inched backwards staying below the log so the assailants wouldn't see him pull back. The rocky ground sloped away from the lip of the point, and after covering sufficient distance, Peter rose to a crouch. Holding the straps of the pack in one hand, his rifle in the other, he scampered further away from the edge of the point.

There was more suppressed gunfire, and bullets were striking the log with regularity. Once he judged he was far enough from the edge that he wouldn't be seen, he straightened upright and slipped the pack on. With Diesel by his side, they jogged away from the point, following the slope downward to the creek. The last 30 yards was very steep, and Peter held his rifle high while sliding down on the seat of his pants. Diesel was waiting for him at the water's edge.

He turned upstream and continued at a jog, covering distance as fast as he could. Although the gully offered an escape route, he couldn't be caught in it. With the steep sides, he'd be trapped without cover.

Man and dog covered about 300 yards in five minutes. With adrenaline coursing through his veins Peter no longer noticed the protests from his knee. Directly ahead was a waterfall, and to the side a game trail was worn in the rock and dirt. Careful not to slip, Peter pushed up the side and emerged on the ridgeline. From his new location, he was about half a mile from the rocky point and at a considerably higher elevation.

By now the shooting had ceased. *Maybe they think they killed me*, Peter thought. Quickly he ducked into a group of trees that was stretched out along the ridge, running up the slope at least the length of a football field. Still, he crouched as he sought a good hide—a location where he could glass the approach from the rocky point and set up a solid rest for sniping.

Soon, they would discover he had escaped, and he knew they would pursue—exactly as he had expected. Peter knew he held the tactical advantage, even though he was clearly outnumbered.

He settled for an old fallen tree. The dried and weathered roots were an extension of the trunk, forming an immense radial pattern. Manzanita bushes and two small evergreens were growing around the dead tree. Peter and Diesel hopped into the depression left by the fallen tree. One of the roots was at an optimum height to support the rifle and still allow Peter the correct angle to sight down the slope toward the meadow.

As if they were following a script, two gunmen dashed across the meadow. As they approached the base of the rocky point, they split—one ascended the scree and the other approached from the western side of the point.

Peter continued to watch. The range was too far to see much detail even with the high magnification of the riflescope, but it looked like they were also armed with M4 assault weapons. He decided to conserve his ammunition and not give away his position—he'd watch for now.

And when they followed his trail, he'd take them out.

CHAPTER 19

"I'VE DUG UP EVERYTHING I can access," Lieutenant Ellen Lacey explained to her boss. "And I really didn't find anything that wasn't already in the public domain." Not only was Lacey brilliant in all areas of intelligence craft, but she was dedicated to the Strategic Global Intervention Team. Of Irish decent, her red hair, green eyes, and shapely figure attracted many of the opposite sex. But she had yet to find a companion who equaled her intellectually. In the end it had been a simple choice—the mental challenges of her chosen career proved far more interesting than the mindless small talk and gamesmanship of the dating scene.

"What surprises me," she continued, "is that even I can't access the top secret documents Peter referenced. In fact, I can't even confirm that they actually exist."

"You're not suggesting Peter imagined this," Jim said, his patience thin.

"Of course not. Just that I can't shed any light on this

mystery. Not yet."

It was a closed-door meeting in Commander Nicolaou's office. For reasons of security, Jim had instructed Lacey to keep this investigation within a small group that included the two of them plus Mona Stephens, one of SGIT's top intelligence analysts. She had proven her worth during the Belarusian affair. Presently, Lacey had Stephens researching relevant documents in the Library of Congress.

"I suggest we call Gary Porter," Ellen said. "Since Peter is not available, Gary is our best lead. Besides, he's something of a genius when it comes to hacking and cyber security."

Although Jim didn't care much for Gary's bohemian attitude and apparent lack of discipline, he had to agree with Lacey. He thumbed through his card file—preferring the old-fashioned address system to a computerized database precisely because of people like Gary—and dialed the number.

"Gary, it's Jim Nicolaou."

"Commander! I was wondering when you'd reach out to me. I've been waiting."

Jim bristled. "This isn't a social call."

"Of course not. I'd imagine you have questions about the files Peter and I read."

"That's right. In case you didn't know, Peter's in trouble."

"Of course I know. It's all over the national news. I can't reach Peter, and I suspect you can't either. That's why you're calling me."

Jim took two calming breaths. "Correct on both accounts. Those secret files… Lieutenant Lacey has been unable to access them. I understand that you and Peter read portions. What can you share with us?"

"Oh, there's a lot I can share—"

"Hold it there," Jim interrupted. "I have Lacey here in my office. I want to put you on the speaker."

"Yeah, sure," Gary answered. He paused until he heard the change in tone of the signal before continuing. "The documents were from many different government sources—the Navy, Congress, even the White House. They all were dated between summer and fall of 1967. But I didn't have a chance to read everything. In fact, we only scanned through maybe half of the memos and reports."

Gary spent the next 20 minutes relaying what he'd read and discussed with Peter. Jim and Ellen both took notes, occasionally interrupting to ask questions, seeking clarification before Gary continued. When he finished, they were dumbstruck.

The silence hung heavy. Jim was the first to speak. "If those documents are genuine, it's no wonder they were stamped with the highest level of secrecy and kept from the public."

"But why now?" Lacey asked. "I mean, the Six-Day War was a long time ago. Lyndon Johnson and Robert McNamara are both deceased. And why are these documents still classified?"

"And why did someone commit murder over them?" Jim added.

"If you ask me, maybe the *Liberty* really was spying on Israel and sharing information with Egypt. You know, covering our bets, just in case Israel lost the war."

Ellen Lacey rolled her eyes, earning a brief smile from Jim.

"Did you find any evidence to support that theory?" Jim asked.

"No, but you can't disprove it either."

"Be that as it may," Lacey said, "it wouldn't justify the on-going top-secret classification of the documents you read."

"Okay," Gary said defensively. "Maybe the government of Israel wants to keep the incident secret at all cost. Maybe they're afraid the U.S. will halt arms sales and other support. You know, we give Israel billions each year in foreign aid. If the public learned about the attack on the *Liberty* and the role Israel played, maybe they would force Congress to cut off support."

Lacey was shaking her head. "That makes no sense either. It's been public knowledge all along that Israeli forces attacked the *Liberty*. And the Israeli government paid reparations decades ago."

"Without time to carefully read or study all of those documents, I don't think we're going to figure out the *why*," Jim said. "So how about focusing on *who* and *how*?"

Gary was prepared for this opening. "I've been thinking about that, too. I can't say just yet who is behind the murders in Bend, but I may be able to tell you how they seem to know whenever the top-secret files end up in someone's electronic mailbox."

"That would be a good start," Jim said.

"A simple bot that phones home whenever the file or files are opened. That's how I'd do it if I were keeping tabs on information that no one was supposed to ever see."

"But you forwarded that file along with other emails to your server…" Lacey's voice conveyed confusion.

"And you're wondering why no one has shown up yet at my door to kill me?"

Lacey looked at Jim, who appeared equally confused.

"Elementary. I didn't open the file. Peter insisted I delete the PDF file and all emails I recovered."

"Let me get this straight," Jim said. "You don't have the files on your server?"

"Like I said, I deleted them. They were there for only a few minutes. I never even opened them. Actually, that's what clued me in. You see, if receiving the file triggered a flag, then I should have been stormed by now, too. But since that hasn't happened—and I haven't spotted anyone following me or otherwise being annoying, other than the cashier at the grocery store who wanted to chat way too much—I concluded that merely receiving the file was okay."

Jim raised his eyebrows. "It does make sense. Possessing the file is meaningless if the file isn't opened to read or print."

"Or copied. The flag would also have to be triggered if the file was copied. The IP address for whatever machine was opening or copying the file would be sent to the owner—"

Lacey interrupted, "Sorry. Owner?"

"Owner, file manager… whoever is responsible to keep the information under wraps."

"But you did open the file, and print it, at Peter's house," Jim said.

"Yes. Peter insisted I use his ISP address. He didn't want anything to be traced back to me."

"And you did?"

"Of course."

Jim and Lacey exchanged concerned looks. "So whoever is managing the file likely knows it was opened by Peter."

"Yeah, I'm afraid so," Gary answered, his tone conveying regret. "I could have spoofed a dozen ISP addresses from locations around the world. Had them following the trail for weeks. But Peter said that would tip them off and make it harder for us to figure out who they are."

"Well, what's done is done," Jim said. "Can you help us identify whoever is receiving notifications when the file is accessed?"

"Oh, this application of bots to notify a manager when a subject file is accessed is rudimentary, barely more advanced than child's play. Since this is my business, I figured it out pretty fast. But I'm certain you would have arrived at the same conclusion given enough time."

Lacey flushed at the put down, intended or not.

"We're working together, remember?" Jim said.

"Right. Sorry, I didn't intend to offend Lieutenant Lacey.

I'm sure she's good at that intelligence stuff."

"You just did it again. How about you stop trying to compliment my Senior Intelligence Analyst and tell us about this bot. How can we find out who it 'phones home to' as you phrased it?"

"I could hack into secret government servers, open the file, and see who knocks on my door?"

Lacey jumped in quickly, cutting off Jim as he was about to speak. "No! Under no circumstances are you to open or copy that file, or hack into any databases."

"Just kidding. You must think I'm crazy."

"Close," Jim said.

"Without opening or copying the file…" Gary repeated the conditions of the challenge. "Off the top of my head, I think I'd construct a bot to surf my server. Once it finds the file—that won't take long since I already know a lot about the file—it will access the data and search for a particular type of code."

"Slow down," Lacey said. "A minute ago you said you deleted the file and emails."

"I did. But that just means the file marker was removed. The information is still there. It shouldn't be hard to find. The code will be obvious."

"Code that would be used to send an IP address to a third party," Jim said.

"It's a little more complicated than that, but yes, you're basically correct."

"When can you start?" Jim asked.

"Am I going to get arrested for this?"

Lacey rolled her eyes again. "Mr. Porter. Your friend's life may be at stake."

"Still, I think that's a fair question. But relax. I've already started. Should have the bot constructed within a couple hours and the code debugged. Late today probably. Once I upload it to my server, it won't take more than a few minutes for it to find the relevant lines in the file."

"Thank you, Gary," Jim said. "Call me tonight, once you have that code."

"I will. And let me know when you hear from Peter."

CHAPTER 20

NADYA DIDN'T LIKE IT. Something felt wrong. She'd learned to trust her instincts years ago, on another mission, in Gaza. She had been ordered to infiltrate a cell loyal to Fatah. Mossad believed the cell was responsible for training and equipping two suicide bombers who had struck in Tel Aviv, detonating their vests on crowded city buses. More than 30 civilians had died, an equal number wounded. But it was the death of two toddlers—nine-month-old twin girls—that galvanized the government to take action.

After three months working undercover, pretending to be a radical wanting to join Fatah, she was invited to a meeting at a coffee house. There she was introduced to Farouq Salih, believed to be the leader of the cell. After nearly an hour of rambling conversation, she was asked if she was ready to be a martyr. Ever patient and cautious, this was the opening she'd been waiting for. The conversation was interrupted when Salih's phone rang, and he excused himself to speak privately.

Two minutes passed, then three. And Farouq Salih still did not return to the table. Some sixth sense told Nadya she'd been made, that she needed to leave right away. With the cell's leader nowhere in sight, she stood and went to the restroom. That's when she heard the explosion. Salih had placed a bomb in his backpack and left it on the sidewalk at the table.

From that day on, she never doubted her instinct. Now, she was tracking Peter Savage in the deep draw alongside the creek. A waterfall was just ahead. She saw the game trail coming down the steep slope beside the cascading water and easily surmised that he'd climbed out of the gully along that same trail.

There was another set of prints in the soft mud next to the creek—a dog. "Savage is not alone," she informed Joshua and pointed to the prints.

He stopped next to Nadya, speaking in a low whisper. "They left the point under cover of this drainage, that's why we never saw him leave."

"We must be extra cautious and quiet. The dog will hear us first." Nadya looked around at the steep edges of the draw. "We must go back."

Joshua looked confused and shook his head.

"Yes," she said. "He will be expecting us to crest the ridge there, following his trail."

Silently Nadya and Joshua backtracked a quarter of a mile. When she judged they were far from the spot Peter Savage would be watching, she climbed away from the creek, Joshua behind her. Before she reached the top of the ridgeline, she dropped flat and crawled until she could just see over to the next ridge.

There she lay. Motionless. Watching.

Perfectly still, she waited five minutes. Nothing. No movement, nothing that appeared out of place. Farther up the ridge she saw a copse of trees. From where she lay, the terrain was barren all the way to the evergreens. Just gravel, dirt, and an occasional boulder.

Pointing, Nadya leaned close to Joshua and whispered. "If he's on this ridge, that's where he'll be."

Ahead about 10 meters was a boulder, large enough for the two of them to hide behind while glassing the grove of trees. Nadya looked to Joshua and motioned with her hand, her fingers counting down... three, two, one. They rose and sprinted in a crouch for the boulder. Given the coarseness of the gravel, there was almost no dust as they slid in behind the igneous outcropping.

Nadya scanned the trees through her binoculars, resting against the rock for stability. She was methodical, searching the deep shadows for anything resembling a human form. The distance was significant; she estimated it be about 500 meters to the leading edge of the grove. She started glassing at the closest point, working back and forth, slowly, deliberately—searching.

Peter was beginning to wonder if he'd miscalculated. The two pursing him should have followed his trail along the creek and emerged over the lip of the ridge by now. *Something isn't right,* he thought.

He shifted his position and scanned with the binoculars further up slope. If they'd missed his tracks, they might be climbing to higher elevation. He followed the ridge—no sign of them. He checked the other ridgelines off to the right and left, systematically checking the boulders, fallen trees, and foliage for the gunmen.

After thoroughly glassing the terrain, he leaned against the root ball to think it through. What would he do? Diesel was sitting, muscles tensed, staring down slope. The canine was a frozen statue, reminiscent of a stone lion except many times smaller. Then his ears perked up.

A sound, and it had Diesel's full attention.

Peter was savvy enough to trust his dog. If Diesel was alert, Peter should be, too.

Then the realization came home. *They didn't go up hill— they went down to lower elevation.*

Peter leaned around the root ball, binoculars up.

⊕

Nadya saw the glint of light off the optics first. It was next to a horizontal log with root wood still attached, although most of the branches had long ago rotted away. She watched patiently, completely still.

"Gotcha," she mouthed, not risking being heard even at a whisper.

The image was of a man leaning into the dead tree. He was also holding binoculars, and looking in her general direction, but not directly at her.

She turned to Joshua. "Ahead, he's there. Against the fallen tree. He hasn't seen us yet."

Taking prone firing positions on either side of the boulder, the Mossad operators acquired Peter through their sights. Nadya held high, judging the amount of bullet drop. Her rifle was fitted with a two-power optical sighting system rather than a conventional scope, a reasonable compromise for close-quarter fighting as well as moderate distance. But right now, she would have preferred something with greater magnification.

She fired a single shot, and saw bark blasted off the log to the side of Peter. With her hold verified, and before Peter had time to comprehend what had happened, she let loose on full auto.

Joshua joined in, sending a barrage of bullets into the hide where Peter and Diesel had thought themselves safe. From their prone positions, the M4 rifles where held securely. With little movement of the muzzle from recoil, both operators emptied their magazines into the target.

Bullets impacted the log and the dirt that once anchored the root ball in place. Sixty rounds in total, in 10 seconds. Nadya and Joshua reloaded, and aimed, ready to shoot again if Peter presented himself.

All they saw was devastation—bullet-riddled wood and fresh gouges in the dirt from bullet impacts.

"Looks like we got him," Joshua said.

Nadya didn't reply. Instead, she started walking toward the patch of green, her weapon ready. Joshua was two steps behind.

CHAPTER 21

THE FIRST BULLET CRATERED into the tree only inches from Peter, bark and wood splinters erupting next to his shoulder. The cough of a suppressed rifle arrived a fraction of a second later, barely audible. But the crack of the supersonic bullet was unmistakable.

Before his next heartbeat, Peter was in motion, diving for the ground. He squirmed behind the tree roots as the volley arrived, thankful for the protection provided by the once-giant fir. The root structure stretched out several feet to each side, and he pulled Diesel in tight to his chest.

As soon as the gunfire ceased, Peter was on his feet. He slipped on the pack. "Let's go, Diesel!"

Peter had already thought through the next location—a crescent-shaped mound of igneous rock and boulders at the edge of a flat meadow. It would make a good defensive position. Plus, it offered shelter with nightfall not long off. The temperature would plummet once the sun settled behind the peaks, and with the dropping temperature there would be a heavy dew as the air shed its moisture. That dew would likely freeze to ice crystals in the early morning hours.

The pair worked through the trees and around rocks, staying within the cover as long as possible. Soon, they reached the end of the grove. Now, there was no choice. They had to dash across the open and drop down into the next creek drainage, hopefully without being seen.

Peter expected the gunmen to cautiously approach the grove, not certain if they'd killed him. He was counting on them being preoccupied with his last known position, not looking further up the slope.

He broke out into the open, running hard. Diesel stayed by his side, matching his pace. In a dozen strides he was at the edge, descending into the next gully.

The soft earth compressed under each step, sliding forward and threatening to upset Peter's balance. He slowed and shifted his trajectory, angling to the left, further away from the pursuers. It would not be long before they discovered he had escaped.

Breathing hard, Peter jumped across the rapidly flowing water and angled up the opposite side. His pace slowed markedly as he climbed, and his knee ached in protest. Diesel plunged ahead, his powerful hind legs propelling him forward.

This ridgeline extended only 50 or 60 yards to the west before expanding and merging with the next ridge. He was close to the spring that fed the creek. By now his pace had slowed to a jog, and his breathing was deep and labored. He felt the ache in his abdomen; the pain was stronger than it had been earlier in the morning. The strenuous activity combined with the altitude—close to 7,000 feet—were taking a toll on his body, threatening to undue the healing that had transpired over the previous 24 hours.

He pushed onward to a small cluster of stunted trees where he was marginally concealed by their branches. He needed to rest momentarily and catch his breath. Even Diesel was panting, his tongue hanging long as he gulped down air.

Peter looked around, checking his bearings. His destination was ahead and slightly to the right. He'd adjust course now that he was above the numerous springs fed by the melting snowfields.

He ventured to gaze back, around the small trees to observe the trail he and Diesel left. There was certainly no trouble seeing it. The soft gravelly dirt was disturbed by their forceful strides, the deeper coloration of the exposed soil leaving a track easily followed by his pursuers. But Peter had learned from the last encounter—they wouldn't come from that direction. They'd most likely split, flank the trail and approach from opposite sides.

It was a good plan.

Peter started running again. Not far to go, but he had to get there and settle in. Here he was exposed with little cover to fight from.

Onward he pushed, his faithful companion beside him.

He was holding a constant elevation now. Far below, to the east, the trees were thick. But at this altitude, the evergreens were small and sparse. He could see at least 100 yards in any direction.

There, just ahead, was the rocky outcrop. Without climbing gear it could be reached only from the left, the upslope side. Peter had discovered this location years ago when deer hunting in these woods.

Without slowing, he navigated around the fortress-like projection and entered a large grassy expanse. It was almost perfectly flat, and Peter surmised that dirt and gravel had washed down over eons, filling up behind a semicircular thrust of hard volcanic rock. Near the center of the arc was a slight cave. It didn't extend far, only eight feet or so, but enough to offer protection from rain or dew, and the surrounding rock would radiate meager warmth to chase away the chill at night. On previous visits, he'd had a campfire in front of the cave entrance. Not tonight.

"Diesel, stay." The red pit bull sat at the cave and waited obediently while Peter conducted a quick inspection. It was exactly as he'd remembered. Near the ends of the arc were large boulders, offering a protected view of the approach. Unless the gunmen went far upslope or down to lower elevation and then circled back, Peter would see them coming. And he didn't think they'd make such a long detour since there was no reason for them to suspect that he was making a stand at this location.

Peter leaned the Weatherby against a boulder and removed the pack. The exertion had raised his core temperature, and he needed to cool and allow the sweat to evaporate before sunset. Hypothermia was a real danger if his clothes were soaked from perspiration.

He removed a water bottle from the pack and consumed the contents. Taking out a second bottle, he called Diesel and poured some into a small pot. The dog lapped up the water eagerly. Peter poured out more, allowing his companion to drink his fill. Using the binoculars, he glassed the terrain. The enemy wasn't in sight.

There was no time to prepare a meal, and Peter wouldn't take a chance with a fire anyway. The next best thing was jerky and salty crackers. He shared some of both with the pit bull. The salt tasted good and would help to restore his electrolyte level to normal.

Between bites Peter was using the binoculars and searching for any sign of his pursuers. They had to be close now. He switched to his riflescope. Although the field of view was not as great as with the binoculars, the magnification was equivalent and he would be ready if—when—he spotted their approach.

The adrenaline was still pumping through his body, but at least his breathing had returned to normal. And he was cooling down, the sweat-soaked portions of his shirt feeling cold. Before long the moisture would evaporate completely.

The shadows were growing longer by the minute. In less than an hour, the sun would drop behind the Tam McArthur Rim. He hoped to put an end to the chase before then.

Nadya surveyed the numerous bullet holes gouged in the log and the old, dried roots of the fallen tree. Somehow, Peter Savage had escaped. There was no blood. Nothing was left behind.

"We will follow the trail, but stay to the side. And stay within sight of me at all times."

Joshua acknowledged the order, and they set out. The path was easy to follow. Rather than descend into the creek drainage, Nadya led Joshua around the spring since they were able to see the tracks emerging up the far slope.

There, above the spring, she picked up the trail again, with Joshua keeping pace to the right of the footprints. She was constantly looking ahead, using the binoculars to search for hiding spots and to follow the footprints. As long as she could see the path leading forward and not circling back, she was reasonably confident that Peter Savage was ahead, probably still running. But eventually, he would have to stop.

Nadya signaled for Joshua to join her at a cluster of manzanita bushes. The open terrain made her nervous even though she could clearly see the disturbed ground where feet landed heavily and pushed off.

She removed the satellite phone. It was time to coordinate with Marcus. After a short pause, he answered. Nadya quickly updated him on the loss of Marie and Ben, and she gave her location as coordinates displayed on the handheld military GPS unit. Marcus had heard the gunfire, but was still about two miles away.

"I can be there in about half an hour," he said, entering the coordinates Nadya had given him.

Nadya and Joshua separated again, paralleling the trail. Heads swiveling from side to side, searching for danger, they stalked forward. Ahead, Nadya saw that the footprints lead directly to a rocky outcrop, and then turned to the left. Made sense since it was very steep to the right.

They continued their approach.

At first, Peter didn't recognize the small shapes. They were gray-brown and blended well with the earth, passing easily for rocks. Plus they were moving slowly and directly toward Peter, such that he didn't recognize their motion until they were much closer. At about 250 yards out, he suddenly realized the shapes were getting larger.

Those aren't rocks. He looked through the riflescope. The gunmen were bent over, trying to maintain a low profile given the lack of cover. Peter recognized the figure to the right as a woman, and neither showed any indication they'd spotted him.

"Looks like our guests have arrived, Diesel." Peter shifted his gaze to the other figure, the man, and followed his approach. Then he swung the scope to the woman. They were now about 200 yards out, he estimated.

Abruptly, the woman looked directly at Peter. It was as if she suddenly knew he was scoping her. She dove and rolled to the same cluster of stunted trees that Peter had stopped at earlier.

He squeezed the trigger, but immediately knew he'd missed. The bullet kicked up a dust cloud where she had been only an instant earlier.

Peter spun to his left. Gunfire rippled through the thin air, but the bullets were high. He settled the crosshairs on the man who was struggling to cover the distance uphill to his partner. Peter tracked him. Smooth and steady.

Boom!

The man plowed forward in a somersault, coming to rest on his back. Motionless. Dead.

CHAPTER 22

THE BOT THAT GARY HAD CONSTRUCTED was nothing more than a collection of code. Lines of software following a logical series of instructions to achieve a desired goal. Despite the implications of the name and the way he spoke of bots as if they were mechanical or living beings, nothing could have been farther from the truth. In fact, there was nothing tangible about bots at all—they existing only in the digital world of zeroes and ones.

After completing a rigorous debugging exercise, the bot was uploaded to his server. Although it housed terabytes of information, the bot would be directed to the specific file of interest. There it would read every digital bit. Its function was simple: find and highlight sections of code that matched essential programming for the file flag to function.

Gary executed the program and unleashed the bot. He routinely used bots to search his massive digital depository, searching for the presence of malware and viruses. Although the commercial antivirus software was fine for the vast majority of PC users, Gary had rather special needs in his business of cyber security. Plus, he'd made a few enemies over the years fixing breaches for corporate clients, making his own computers something of a tantalizing target.

The first problem was that his security bots were not programmed to find the lines of code he presently sought. By reprogramming a security bot he'd addressed this first challenge. He was confident the secret files on the *USS Liberty* did contain a flag, a short executable file that would send the IP address of any computer that opened or copied the file to a third party. He needed to know who that third party was.

That led to the second problem—how to identify a specific person or persons associated with the file flag. He hoped he would be rewarded with an active IP address. If so, he'd plant a packet of code within the recipient's email account. That packet would spoof the account to reply to his server with a message that would provide direct connection to a real person.

Or so he hoped. There were many ways his plan could fail: the email account could be a cover—lacking identifiers of the account holder. Or the IP address could be fake, one of many that would have him chasing a digital ghost around the globe. If the roles were reversed and Gary was managing the secret file and file flag, he'd have implemented these shields in the event someone discovered the flag and attempted to trace it back. But then again, Gary was counting on the file manager being sloppy, or at least not as good at cyber security as he was.

Gary was leaning back in his chair when a brief message appeared on his monitor.

Program complete. Suspicious code identified and downloaded to desktop.

He worked his keyboard and opened the file. Next he copied the IP address from the code and placed it in the program of a spoofing bot. Using a generic Internet-access portal, he sent the bot to the IP address. In a few minutes he'd know whether or not his worries were founded.

Unlike many cyber security experts, Gary Porter had never used hacking maliciously. He'd never broken the law to illegally gain access to files and accounts that he had no legitimate reason to open. But his ability to think like a criminal was uncanny, and it had earned him a reputation as a genius at solving data breaches. Working mostly for Fortune 500 corporations, he'd earned an enviable income and purchased a large ranch in the gold country of California, east of Sacramento. He lived in a modern ranch house with his wife and business partner, Nancy, and three llamas, two dogs, a miniature horse, and seven goats. Due to the risk of wildfires in the foothills of the Sierra Nevada Range, the Porters designed their home to be constructed from concrete and cement block. An added advantage was that his servers were housed in a bunker-like room that offered a high degree of protection from just about any assault, including fire, water, and people.

A chime sounded, indicating an email message had arrived. Gary clicked on the message, and read the name and email address of the sender. He looked at the time—just after 6:00 p.m. He phoned Jim Nicolaou.

"That was fast. What did you find?"

"It was there, as I expected. Whoever programmed this flag was rather careless; they should have attempted to hide the code."

"Where you able to trace it to a person?"

"The name doesn't ring a bell. But the email address is the House of Representatives—the U.S. Congress." Gary smiled, imagining the surprise that would accompany this revelation.

Jim eased back in his chair, trying to understand what it meant.

"Hey, Jim, can you hear me? You still there?"

"Yeah, still here."

"Did you get that? The IP address is a computer at the Capital."

"What's the name on the email account?"

"Angela Meyers," Gary replied.

Jim rolled the name over in his mind. "No, I don't recognize it, but that doesn't mean anything. I'll have Lacey or Stephens look it up. My guess is it's the name of a staffer. Are you certain this is the person managing the secret file?"

"No. I already explained how the real manager might shield their name from this type of cyber discovery. But then again, this code doesn't show signs of being written by anyone trying to do something unique. If it were me, you'd never get a name that easily or quickly. So, no guarantees. It could be a diversion."

"Well, it's the only solid lead we have at the moment. And it makes sense that someone within the government would be trying to maintain government secrets."

"Did it ever occur to you that it might make too much sense?"

"You're paranoid, Gary," Jim said, refusing to allow his hopes to be dashed.

"Yes, I am. And it's because there are a lot of people out to get me. I'm something of a legend, you know. There's even a rumor that my servers have a bounty on them of fifty grand each if destroyed and one hundred grand each if delivered in operational condition."

"Your servers are wanted—dead or alive—is that what you're saying?" Jim chuckled, finding the analogy irresistible.

"You may think it's all fun and games, but this is serious business," Gary said defensively.

"No argument from me on that point. Look, is there anything more you can do to verify that information?"

Gary thought for a moment before answering. "Maybe. I can send a phony email message to Angela Meyers using a government email address, only her reply will be routed to my account. She'll only see the government address, and if the message is intriguing, she'll reply—basic human nature. That will tell me the account is real and active."

"You can do all that?" The skepticism came through in Jim's tone.

"Really? You still doubt me? After all I've done?"

Jim couldn't hold back the laughter.

"Ha ha," Gary said. "Now, if I'm done entertaining you, I have work to do."

"Thank you. Really, I mean it. Peter is fortunate to count you as a friend."

"Yeah. Just so you know, he's the brother I never had. Now, you need to do something for me."

"And what's that?" Jim asked.

"You watch after him. Do what you do best."

Lieutenant Ellen Lacey and Mona Stephens were sitting at Jim's desk. He'd called them in immediately after his call with Gary Porter.

"I know it's the end of the day," Jim said, "but we have a lead. And it can't wait until morning." He went on to share his conversation.

"I'll get on it right away," Lacey said. "It won't take long to find out if an Angela Meyers truly does work for the House of Representatives."

"Thank you," Jim said. Turning to Stephens he asked, "Was your search at the Library of Congress productive? Did you learn anything about the *Liberty* incident that might shed light on this mystery?"

She leaned forward in her chair. "Maybe. I read many

reports run in major newspapers and scores of statements given by members of the House and Senate. There was certainly a large population at the time who believed Israel committed an overt act of aggression against the United States, maybe even an act of war. The question was—and still remains—why? Why did Israeli forces attack the *USS Liberty* with a determination to sink her?

"*The New York Times* ran a series on the incident, concluding that the Israeli government had acted in self-defense, fearful that the *Liberty* had intercepted radio communications just prior to the Jewish attack on the Golan Heights."

Lacey added, "Recall that at the time—four days into the war—negotiations were underway to end the conflict and freeze all military forces where they were. Had that diplomacy been successful, Israel would not have captured the strategic Golan Heights creating a buffer with Syria."

"And the thinking was," Stephens continued, "that if the Johnson administration had known of the impending invasion, they would have pressured Levi Eshkol, the Prime Minister of Israel, to stand down."

Jim nodded. "So they aimed to sink the *Liberty*. Dead men tell no tales."

Stephens went on. "Only the *Liberty* didn't sink. The rest of the story we know."

Jim stood and paced behind his desk, arms folded across his chest. "There's more to the story—has to be. Why won't the government, to this day, declassify every document related to the incident? And why did the possession of some classified files result in murder?"

"I've been working on that," Lacey said. She opened a file folder she was holding, and read from the contents. "Both the *America* and the *Saratoga* launched aircraft multiple times to defend the *Liberty*. And every time, the planes were quickly recalled by Robert McNamara."

"The Secretary of Defense. Yes, I recall this. But why would he countermand such an order?"

"Exactly," Lacey said. "Answer that question, and you'll have solved the riddle."

"That was a question asked by several lawmakers from both sides of the aisle," Stephens explained, "but no answer is published in the Congressional Record. As strange as it seems, the White House did not put that query to rest. And what's even stranger is that no one—no journalist, no member of Congress, no one—insisted on an answer."

"What about the newspapers?" Jim asked.

"Not much more. Some editorials stopped just short of accusing Johnson and McNamara of treason. It was a politically-charged time: the Vietnam War was underway and the Arab Coalition was aiming to destroy the Jewish state."

Jim rubbed his thumb and index finger over his eyes. They could speculate all night and still not be any closer to solving the mystery. Maybe Lacey would be more successful in her search of Congressional staffers. Sooner or later, they had to get a break in the case.

CHAPTER 23

NADYA STARED AT THE LIFELESS BODY, the young man she knew as Joshua. Somewhere, probably in Israel, he had a family. Would they ever know where Joshua died? Probably not. The Mossad was renowned for secrecy—in life and death.

Her thoughts drifted to her own family. She had a younger sister living in the U.S., but both parents had died years ago. She recalled pleasant memories from her childhood, laughing with her sister on the farm her parents owned in the Golan Heights. She was born on the farm; her parents were settlers who benefited from cheap land—land she knew was captured from Syria. It was a standard practice in her homeland. Settle the captured territory, make it part of Israel, and it will be impossible for the international community to force a return to pre-war boundaries.

The Jewish state needed buffers all around. The nation was surrounded by hostile neighbors, countries that had recently fought to destroy her homeland. She was taught that her government was justified in settling these captured territories. It was a fair price to extract from the aggressors as compensation for the Jewish lives lost, the millions of dollars and resources simply wasted.

Nadya was glad she could not see Joshua's eyes.

She turned away from her fallen colleague and called out. "Don't shoot!" She held her rifle out in one hand, the other hand raised. Slowly, Nadya stood.

"Don't shoot!" she shouted again. She was scrutinizing the rock fortress.

"What do you want?" Peter shouted in return. "Why are you trying to kill me?" Nadya was looking directly at Peter's hide between two boulders, at the left end of the outcropping.

"You shoot well. Were you a sniper in the Army?"

"Never served," he answered. "Why are you trying to kill me?"

"Can we talk?"

Peter considered the request. It surprised him, but he did want answers. Plus he had her in the crosshairs and could drop her easily.

"Very well. You can walk toward me. I'll tell you when to stop. And if you don't stop when I tell you to, or if you make any threatening movement, I'll kill you where you stand."

Nadya stared across the open expanse. She was surprised at his determination. Most civilians would have crumbled under the fear and pressure.

"Do you understand me?" Peter asked.

"Yes, I understand." She started walking forward, hands still raised.

Peter tracked her step by step. She walked easily, not showing any sign of fatigue. She was composed, remarkably so, especially since he'd already shot dead three of her associates. When she was close enough that they could talk without shouting he said, "That's close enough."

Nadya stopped. She could see Peter's face now, at least the left side not hidden behind the hunting scope.

"Now. Carefully place your left hand on the rifle stock."

She did as instructed, aware that he could place a bullet in her heart at any moment if provoked.

"Place your right hand on the barrel, close to the muzzle, and heave that rifle toward me. One handed! I don't want to shoot you, but I will if you try anything."

Nadya slid her right hand to the muzzle and flung the rifle forward. It travelled maybe 20 meters before landing muzzle first in the dirt. Even if she could somehow get to the weapon without being shot, she wasn't confident it would cycle without first being field stripped and thoroughly cleaned. And if dirt was stuck in the barrel it might even blow up on her if she pulled the trigger.

"Okay lady, what's on your mind," Peter said.

"A trade. Let me go, and you walk away."

"I could kill you now and still walk away."

"No, you won't shoot an unarmed woman."

"Why are you trying to kill me? Who sent you?"

Nadya turned up the corners of her mouth. If the situation was not dire, the naiveté of the question would be humorous. "I suspect you know how this works."

"What do you mean?"

"Come now, Mr. Savage—"

"How do you know my name?"

"I was briefed." She paused. If Peter was surprised, he didn't let on.

She continued. "Your knowledge of tactics is commendable. And you seem to take killing in stride, like a man who has killed before and is good at it."

For a moment Peter wondered if her assessment was true.

Is this really what I've become? The thought was disgusting. She was right, of course. He had shot many men, but only when they were threatening him or his family. He wanted to believe that was the difference—the distinction between being a cold-blooded killer and someone who was only reluctantly forced into self-defense. But was that boundary really as clear as he wanted to believe? *In the end, people still died... by my hand.*

"No, that's not who I am."

"Do you really believe that? Your actions here today would argue otherwise."

Peter felt his finger brushing the rifle trigger. *Why not kill her, too? No.* She could taunt him, but he was not a killer. Not like she was. He was defending himself.

"Who sent you to kill me?"

"It's always the same answer, isn't it?" She sighed. "A government sent me, and my team."

"You're trying my patience. If you really think I'm a killer, remember which end of *my* rifle you're looking at."

"You know what, Mr. Savage? I don't think you are a killer." She took a step forward.

Peter squeezed the trigger—heard the report and felt the butt stock shoved violently into his shoulder.

Nadya saw the eruption of dirt an inch in front of her foot. Dirt and gravel sprayed against her boot and leg. She froze.

"Okay, point taken."

"Who sent your team to kill me?"

"I work at the pleasure of a government. An ally of the United States. Your only true ally in the Middle East."

"Israel," Peter said. But this answer just led to more questions. "Why would the Israeli government want to kill me?"

Nadya shrugged. Even if she had known, she would not have shared that information.

"They don't want the file on the *Liberty* incident released to the public," Peter said. "Is that it? But why would they care? That happened so long ago."

"I'm a soldier. And like every good soldier, I simply follow orders and don't ask questions."

"So goes the justification for murdering innocent civilians. I'll bet you sleep well at night."

She shrugged again. "I do okay."

"Did you murder Emma Jones and send that woman assassin to kill me?"

"I don't murder innocent civilians, Mr. Savage. My country is at war with terrorists who wish only to see the Jewish people wiped from the face of the Earth."

"Maybe you missed the news, but the U.S. is also at war with terrorism."

Nadya tugged the side of her mouth in a mock grin. "So I've heard. While Americans hear about terrorism in the news, my people live it every day. You have no idea what it is like to wonder if the city bus you are riding will be bombed. Or if the man or woman passing you on the street will attack you with a machete. That's true fear."

"The ends never justify the means."

Nadya laughed. "You are naïve, aren't you? The ends *always* justify the means. Your government, above all others, lives by that simple rule."

The silence hung on the air: Nadya waited for Peter to make the next move, while Peter was uncertain what that move should be. He wanted to feel righteous, and yet her words stung with the unmistakable pain of truth.

She broke the silence. "So, I have answered your questions. Now, I will go."

The Mossad operator turned and began the long descent. Peter watched her leave, conflicted. True, she and her team had brazenly tried to murder Peter. But equally true, she was now seemingly unarmed and walking away.

Peter slid down and rubbed Diesel's head. The amber eyes peered backed at him. "I don't know what to make of that either."

Only after she'd covered half a mile and was within the trees again, did she key the satellite phone. "Marcus. Change of plans."

She gave Marcus new coordinates. They would meet, rest, and regroup. This plan had fallen apart almost from the outset. She had made the capital mistake of severely underestimating her opponent.

That would not happen again.

CHAPTER 24

JIM WAS FINISHING THE DETAILS of his plan when his phone rang. It was Lieutenant Lacey. "I checked current records of all staffers working for the House, and there is an Angela Meyers. She's the Chief of Staff for Abraham Schuman."

"The Speaker of the House?" Jim said.

"That's correct, sir. And she's his principal campaign manager as well."

"Doesn't get more high-level than that. We'll have to proceed cautiously."

"How do you want me to handle it?" Lacey asked.

Jim thought through the possibilities. "We still need confirmation that the email address Gary found is active, but I'm guessing it is. I want you to call Schuman's office and get an appointment to talk with Angela Meyers."

"Given the time difference, I won't be able to reach anyone in Washington until tomorrow morning. But she may be out on the road anyway. The Presidential campaign has got to be a huge commitment with a grueling travel schedule."

"I understand. Call first thing in the morning. If you get the brush off, tell them it's a matter of national security—make up a story, whatever is necessary—but I want you on the phone with Meyers tomorrow."

"Yes, sir. And when I do speak to her, what should I say?"

"Tell her we are investigating a security breach. Ask her what she knows about top-secret files from 1967. But don't mention the USS Liberty."

"You want to spook her, she if she slips up and says something incriminating."

"That's the general idea. Maybe she'll give us enough to get a warrant for a phone tap."

"Sir, we both know that is very unlikely. As a branch of military intelligence, we have no jurisdiction. And the Justice Department doesn't like it when we try to help them do their job."

"I am well aware of the situation, Lieutenant. I took the same oath as you—to protect our country against all enemies, foreign and domestic. And right now it's looking more and more like we have a very serious threat developing. Do what you can."

"Yes, sir."

"I still want to keep this under wraps, at least a while longer. Is Stephens enough support for you?"

"We're good. If I feel we need additional assets, I'll let you know."

"One more thing. See if Stephens can get any new information from the Bend Police Department or Deschutes County Sheriff."

"We're on it. I'll let you know when we have something new to share."

⊕

Mona Stephens spent about 30 minutes on the phone, being transferred from one desk to another, before she was finally connected to Detective Colson's desk. It was late in the evening. Luckily, the detective had her calls automatically forwarded to her cell phone when she was out of the office. And lately that was often.

"Detective Colson," she answered.

"Detective, my name is Mona Stephens and I'm working on a case involving national security. Do you have a minute?"

It took closer to five minutes to offer sufficient explanation for Colson to agree to share an update on her investigation. She concluded with a name to call within the Sheriff Department, Deputy Tom Hastings. "He's your best source at the moment. Two hours ago they found the body of a deputy sent to track down a lead. He was executed, his body and vehicle pushed off the road. State Police and Sheriff Deputies are organizing a manhunt."

"What lead?" Stephens pressed for more specific information.

"A location in the mountains, west of here—possible location of Peter Savage after he fled the crime scene in Bend. Three civilians are dead; a security guard is in the hospital with a skull fracture, he may not make it. Mr. Savage is our prime suspect. And now it looks like he's graduated to cop killing."

Stephens thanked Colson for her help and promised to return the favor should she learn anything new. No mention was made of secret files.

Next, she phoned the contact in the Sheriff Department. The phone rang six times before going to voicemail. Frustrated, Stephens phoned the non-emergency number, explained her situation, and asked how she could reach Deputy Hastings.

"I'm sorry, ma'am. He's unavailable now. I suggest you leave a voice message for him."

Stephens sighed. "Already did that. Thank you."

It had taken an hour to gather only a few additional clues, and she was frustrated she couldn't get a detailed briefing from either department. She walked down the hall to Ellen Lacey's office. The door was open. Still, she knocked before entering.

"Come in," Lacey said.

Mona Stephens closed the door behind her and took a chair in front of the desk. "The local law enforcement doesn't like to share much."

Lacey frowned. Seems like they still couldn't catch a break.

Stephens continued, "But I do have one additional clue. A sheriff deputy was checking a possible location for Mr. Savage. Somewhere in the mountains—I couldn't get the specific location. But it didn't go well. The Deputy was shot, execution style. The crime scene is still being processed, and the State Police and Sheriff's Office are coordinating a massive manhunt. The local news will probably air the story tonight, might get more details then."

"Probably, but we'll lose several more hours in the meantime. Maybe the Commander will have a guess as to where Peter might be hiding out."

Two minutes later Jim had joined his two intelligence analysts.

"The detective… she said *west*?" Jim wanted to confirm he'd heard correctly.

"Yes, sir," Stephens replied after checking her notes. "Detective Colson is her name. She said Peter Savage was believed to be at a location in the mountains to the west of Bend. Is that significant?"

"It might be," he answered. And then, almost as an afterthought, "Follow me. I need a large display."

They followed their boss to the nearest conference room. Jim booted up the computer and soon had a satellite map of the

Cascade Mountain range displayed on the large wall-mounted monitor. He focused in on the area due west of Bend.

"Peter often spoke of this area." He pointed with his finger to identify certain features. "Here's Mount Bachelor and Broken Top." He moved his finger a little to the north. "And these three peaks are the Three Sisters—North, Middle, and South." The satellite image showed snow on all the mountain peaks, but the lower elevations were shades of green and gray indicating foliage and open ground.

"Todd Lake was special to him. It's here, next to this unimproved road." Jim jabbed an oval blue shape with his index finger. "He often told me how he likes to hunt in the back country north of the lake and on the eastern slope of Broken Top."

"You think he might have fled there?" Lacey asked.

Jim stared at the map in silence. On many occasions Peter had spoken so fondly of his time at Todd Lake with his children and his late wife, Maggie. Those memories harkened back to happier times for Peter, when his life was full of hope and love; a time when the future held limitless possibilities. In those memories Peter found sanctuary, a spiritual comfort that he turned to in time of need.

Lacey's question still hung on the air when Jim answered. "Yes. I know that's where he is."

"Excuse me, sir," Stephens said, "but how can you be so certain. Reference to 'the mountains west of Bend' covers a very large territory."

"Because that's his refuge. He knows the area extremely well. Just being there is comforting to him. Plus, he can play a defensive game in that country without the risk of civilians getting hurt."

"Once that manhunt gets underway," Lacey said, "they *will* find him. And they believe he executed a deputy. Law enforcement won't be inclined to bring him in alive."

Jim folded his arms across his chest, his jaw clenched. "That's why I have to get to him first."

CHAPTER 25

NADYA NEVER TURNED BACK, didn't even look over her shoulder. Instead, she hiked directly back to the meadow beneath the rocky point. There, she picked up Marie's rifle and the extra magazines from her cooling body. There was no time to be sentimental. Marie and Ben and Joshua were dead. Others would deal with the bodies, when they were finally discovered. For now, she still had a mission to complete.

Shouldering the rifle, she referenced her GPS and set off on a new bearing—one that would take her to the rendezvous location. This was one of several locations agreed to in advance and pre-loaded into the hand-held navigational unit of each team member. The destination was overlaid on either a topographical map or a satellite photo, depending on settings she selected. Currently she was using the topographical display and following a course that would avoid any difficult terrain. She had a mile to cover.

When she reached the coordinates, the sun was behind the

mountains and only twilight remained, soon to be followed by an ink-black night sky speckled with starlight. She'd familiarized herself with the lunar tables and knew the quarter-moon would rise after midnight.

Because of the detour Marcus had to take when the rendezvous location was altered at the last minute, Nadya arrived first. She unlimbered the rifle at the sound of a twig snapping. *Careless*, she thought. She had her body pressed tight against a large tree to breakup her outline. In the ever-dimming light it was impossible to discern details. Through her night vision glasses she watched the approaching figure and raised her rifle. She called out in a low voice, "Marcus?"

The figure froze. "Nadya? It's me."

Nadya exhaled in relief, lowered the rifle, and stepped into the open. "Over here," she said.

Marcus also was wearing his NVGs and joined up with her.

"Where are the others?" he asked.

"Dead."

Surprise was evident when Marcus spoke. "But how can that be? We were hunting only one man."

"One very dangerous man. The plan has changed. We were sent in poorly prepared. Now, we are going to change that."

She placed a call on the satellite phone.

The voice had a hard edge. "This better be important."

"It is," she said calmly. "If you want the mission completed, you need to send in a fire support team and heavier weapons."

"What? Lady, you've got to be kidding me. Your team was supposed to handle this easily and quietly."

"My team is no longer functional," she answered through gritted teeth. "There are only two of us left. The target has detailed knowledge of the terrain and is picking us off before we can get close enough to kill him. Now, as I said, if you want this mission to succeed, send in more firepower."

As a member of the Guardians, Richard Nyden was the coordinator for the Mossad team. He'd arranged to supply their weapons and gear and had provided the intelligence that led them to this location. But he was not supposed to have contact with the team again—too risky. Rather, they were to complete the mission, leaving the body to be discovered months or years later, probably by backpackers or hunters. They were to dispose of the weapons in the forest after wiping them clean of prints, pack up, and drive out.

A simple plan.

Nyden sighed, "Okay. I'll get the firepower. What are your coordinates?"

Nadya provided her location and agreed to check back in two hours. They would review the new plan at that time.

She turned toward Marcus. "Now we wait. Try to get some sleep. I'll take the first watch."

Richard Nyden was furious. He had never been on a mission with so many screw-ups. Who was this Peter Savage anyway? Every contact with him proved to be trouble.

He dialed Ellison's number. "We have another problem."

"You and problems seem to go hand in hand. I have to say, you are leaving an impression."

Nyden silently cursed Ellison. *I doubt that desk jockey has spent any time in the field*, he thought.

"The Mossad team has suffered heavy casualties and is no longer able to pursue the mission objectives." He went on to brief Ellison and make his request for a backup team.

After he finished, Ellison said, "Anything else that I should know about?"

"Just this: the Mossad team leader—Nadya Wheeler—had a brief conversation with Peter Savage."

"She what? How can that be? Why didn't she kill him as

ordered?"

"It seems he got the jump on her. Anyway, they had a short conversation. Wheeler says that Savage mentioned files on the *Liberty*. She wanted to know what that was about."

"What did you tell her?"

"Nothing, of course."

Ellison answered through gritted teeth. "Very well. You'll have your backup. Make sure this job gets *done*. Only now the parameters have changed. I want Peter Savage alive, if at all possible."

"That won't be easy."

"There's a bonus to whoever sees to it. I don't care how you hurt him, as long as he can answer questions. I need to know how deep his knowledge of the files goes, and if he's talked to anyone."

Much farther up the slope, Peter and Diesel were preparing for the night. Uncertain if the woman would come back during the cover of darkness, he decided they'd make their stand where they were. The shear rock cliff provided protection, the only likely approach being from the west.

Still foregoing a fire, Peter drained the remainder of the water, sharing it with his companion. "I guess tomorrow we need to fill up the bottles."

A chill had settled upon their encampment—or was it just the effects of coming off the Adrenalin rush? Peter wrapped his parka around his shoulders. "It's gonna get cold tonight." He caught the glint of starlight off Diesel's eyes. In the dim light, he could just make out the fat, droopy lips. It always reminded Peter of the late actor Edward G. Robinson.

Peter unrolled the sleeping bag and laid it on the ground at the base of the rock semicircle. He sat with his back to the rock, and Diesel settled in next to him. From his position he had an unobstructed view up the slope. The terrain was mostly open, so it would be difficult for someone to approach unnoticed, especially with a clear sky. The Milky Way already shone brilliantly, adding to the glow from countless stellar bodies.

Diesel was relaxed, a good sign. Peter trusted his dog's hearing to alert him to danger. Donning the civilian night vision goggles, he watched for any approaching danger. It was going to be a long night.

The minutes slowly became hours, and Peter found himself nodding off. He turned off the NVGs and tilted his head skyward just as a shooting star streaked by and then burned up in the atmosphere, providing a flash of light at the end. He saw several more streaks of light, all moving in the same direction. *A meteor shower.*

Without light pollution from the city, combined with the elevation, the heavens were unbelievably clear. It was one of the joys of the mountains, one that Peter had missed lately. He tried to remember when he last spent time in these woods. *Was it two or three seasons ago?*

He was still marveling at the multitude of stars when a bright pinpoint of light moved from south to north—it was moving too slowly for a meteor. The light faded and vanished. He knew this to be a satellite. There were so many objects in orbit—mostly space debris—that seeing the sunlight reflect off a passing object was common.

It was on nights like this that Peter had spent time with his children, Joanna and Ethan, in these same mountains. He remembered looking up at the clear night sky, teaching the youngsters how to distinguish passing aircraft from satellites and meteors.

Later, when Ethan was a teenager, Peter took him backpacking along the Tam McArthur Rim on the youth's first deer hunt. They spent a week in the woods, with Peter teaching

Ethan survival tradecraft.

Now, in the silence and solitude of his surroundings, he longed for those days. His mind shifted to Maggie and he closed his eyes, her smiling face vivid in his memory. How many years had passed since she died? She loved these mountains, too. As Peter recalled memories of love and life, tears traced a wavy track down his cheeks.

"I can't do this, not now," he said to Diesel. His companion was breathing deeply, and at the sound of Peter's voice, he opened his eyes, failing to understand.

The air was still, and cold was seeping into Peter's flesh with the lack of activity. It would only get worse as the night wore on. Diesel moved in closer, sharing body heat with his owner. Peter reached down and folded a portion of the sleeping bag over Diesel as well as his own legs. *It just might be a three-dog night,* Peter thought. He turned on the night-vision goggles and returned to watch.

A-couple-thousand feet lower in elevation and miles to the north, a bevy of law enforcement officers was busy setting up their base of operations. Their vehicles were parked in a rough circular arrangement off the gravel road not far from the location where Deputy Hood had been found. His body had been removed a couple hours ago. Although an autopsy would be performed, the cause of death was obvious to the officers on the scene. It was also clear that he had been murdered elsewhere and his body positioned in the truck.

A mobile communication center with state-of-the-art equipment was the nerve center. The heavy-duty truck frame housed a box-like shelter, patterned after military mobile command centers. From here, the State Police and the Deschutes County Sheriff's Office would coordinate a search using dogs, ATVs, and an army of law enforcement officers—

most of whom volunteered, eager to capture or shoot the cop killer. And everyone understood that the latter option was definitely preferred.

The search had started out promisingly when the dogs quickly found a scent trail leading away from the deputy's Ford truck. The trail headed north, and the handlers expected it would lead to a campground a few miles away. But unexpectedly the dogs either lost the scent trail or broke away from it. One handler suspected some cover scent had been laid down to mask the path—maybe cougar urine. Dogs were naturally fearful of the large feline predators, and unless they were specifically trained to hunt the cats, no dog would follow the trail.

Opting to wait the night out and resume at first light, the senior officers put their time to good use laying out search grids and assigning personnel to each quadrant. Beginning in the morning, they would search in shifts, working outward from the base camp, until a fresh scent trail was picked up.

CHAPTER 26

JIM WAS STILL STUDYING the satellite photos and topographic maps long after he dismissed his intelligence analysts, Lacey and Stephens. It was time to take action, even though he had no authorization to do so. He could contact Colonel Pierson, the Pentagon officer who oversaw SGIT, explain the situation, and request approval for the mission. But he also understood that the odds of permission being granted were very close to zero. *We'll just pass this off as a training exercise.*

He left the conference room on his way for the armory. Sergeant Jesper Mortensen had the shift rotation. A veteran of SGIT, Jesper had been recruited from the Navy SEALS. He was tall with nearly black hair, clean-shaven, and had cobalt blue eyes. He had the highest level of respect for his commander, having served under him during many missions. Normally, SGIT operations were organized around a team of six operators. So he immediately recognized the irregularity of his commander's request.

"Who's filling out the team, sir?" Jesper ventured the question.

"There is no team, Sergeant. This is a solo exercise. A training mission. I'll check out an M27 and ten extra mags." Jim preferred the M27 Infantry Automatic Rifle, based on the H&K 416 rifle and adopted by the U.S. Marine Corps, over other options, which included automatic shotguns and .50 caliber sniper rifles.

"That's double the normal load out of spare mags, sir."

Jim sensed where this was going. "Is there a problem, Sergeant? Because if there is, I advise you to follow standard procedure and state your concern in writing. You may register your written complaint in person in my office tomorrow morning. Are we clear?"

"Yes, sir." He glanced to the wall clock. "Sir, it's almost 2400."

Jim ignored the comment. What he was about to do went beyond irregular, and could lead to his court martial and the end of his career.

"I'll take a light excursion pack, range-finding scope, NVGs, spare batteries, MREs for three days, standard med kit, and satellite phone."

Jesper left the counter to gather the requested items. The armory—or more correctly, the storeroom—was to the SGIT soldiers what a high-end outdoor gear store is to the hunter and fisherman. With row upon row of steel shelving running the length of the room, everything that might be needed for a mission was neatly organized here. Weapons, ammunition, medical kits, optics, GPS, NVGs, special clothing and packs, meal rations, and on and on. All laid out in groupings of like supplies.

Sergeant Mortensen returned with everything his commander requested. "It's all in the pack, sir." Then he handed the rifle across the counter, bolt open and lacking a magazine.

Jim accepted the rifle and was inspecting it as Jesper left, only to return in short order with a light pack on his shoulder and a second M27 in his grip. "I'm going with you, sir."

Jim didn't even look up from his task. "The hell you are, Sergeant."

Jesper didn't give in. "Look, sir. There's a rumor going around that Peter Savage is in a tight spot. And I suspect you aim to help him out."

Without raising his head, Jim shifted his eyes to Jesper, noting his determined look, and then finished checking the bore and chamber. Spotless, as expected.

"You know he saved my life in the Sudan," Jesper said by way of explanation. "I won't turn my back on him."

"You *will* follow orders, Sergeant."

"I know the flight crew is preparing the bird." That was the nickname for their one-of-a-kind, specially modified HC-130J Combat King IIB aircraft. "You could use my help. Without backup, what are your odds?"

Jim inserted the bolt back into the rifle and drew in a deep breath. He knew Jesper was right. It was borderline suicide to embark on the mission alone.

"Alright, you win. But understand, this could end my career—yours, too."

Jesper nodded agreement.

"And you still want to volunteer?"

"You know the answer."

"Very well. Sign out a pair of comms. I'll brief you during the flight. It will be a short one, so don't count on any sleep time." If it had been only Jim on the mission, the squad communication equipment would have been unnecessary. But with Jesper joining him, the prospect of needing encrypted communication between the two was a very real possibility.

With a grin on his face Jesper Mortensen walked beside his commander to the waiting aircraft.

They climbed onboard, and Jim instructed the pilot to taxi and takeoff. The Office was located within the old airbase complex that had been McClellan Field. A former SAC installation, it still maintained a long runway.

Now that the two warriors were on a mission, they shifted to their call signs.

"The plan is simple, Homer," Jim began. He ran through the plan as best he had it worked out. The problem was that there were a lot of unknowns and variables. He also shared what he knew about the civilians killed in Bend and the Sheriff Deputy who was murdered not far from where they were going.

"Any questions?"

Homer shook his head. "It'll be a piece of cake, Boss Man. We parachute into the wilderness, aiming for a meadow to avoid snagging a tree. Then we find Peter. What's to go wrong?"

"Just remember, you volunteered."

For the first 30 minutes of the hour-long flight, the men had little to say. But Homer had been thinking mostly about Peter Savage. He easily recalled how Peter had stayed by his side in the Sudan, fighting off the enemy against overwhelming odds. "May I ask you a question, sir?" he said.

Boss Man shrugged as he looked at Homer, his expression inviting his sergeant to continue.

"Peter is… unusual. He's not like any other civilian I've met. But not really military either. I mean, he has a lack of respect for authority sometimes."

That last comment brought a smile to Jim. "Sounds to me like you pegged him pretty well." He paused, studying Homer's face. In it he saw genuine interest and concern. "What's on your mind, Sergeant? You may speak freely."

"I'm curious what makes him tick. He's so different from

anyone I've ever met."

"Where to begin..." Jim leaned back in the jump seat and stretched out his legs, crossing them at the ankle. "I met Peter in high school—we became the best of friends. After school, he went to college and I joined the Navy. Didn't stay in contact much. I missed his wedding to the love of his life—a woman named Maggie. We exchanged Christmas cards and occasional phone calls, but it wasn't until a few years ago that we reconnected."

"That's right," Homer recalled. "The mission to the Aleutian Islands."

Jim nodded. "You remember his father, too?"

"Yeah, a professor right? Ian Savage."

"I reconnected with Peter just prior to that mission. I was trying to persuade the good professor not to travel to Alaska. Thought Peter could help me. But if there's anyone more stubborn than Peter, it's his father."

Homer laughed. He had first-hand experience with Peter's dogged persistence. But then again, that character trait had saved Homer's life in North Africa.

"Anyway, at first Peter seemed like the same kid I knew in days past, except older and more mature. But when his back was pushed against the wall by the Ramirez brothers, he changed—it was like he snapped. I don't really know how to describe it, other than it was as if another side of his personality was unleashed. Make no mistake, Peter can be as hard and cold and cunning as you or me."

"Hey, you don't need to convince me of that. Remember, I've seen him in action."

"And there's a lot you haven't seen. Peter has worked with me on several missions. The Colonel considers him an honorary member of SGIT."

"So why this place?" Homer asked.

"You mean our drop coordinates?"

Homer nodded.

"That part of the Cascade Range is spiritual to Peter. He and his wife—"

"Maggie?"

"Yeah, Maggie. They loved camping and hiking in that area around Todd Lake, Broken Top, and South Sister. Peter told me that he and Maggie came up with the name of their first child at Todd Lake. They'd often go there for picnics—the children loved it, too. And Peter has hunted that piece of forest for years—taught his son how to hunt there."

"So Peter knows the terrain well. I get it."

"No, I don't think you do. You see, when Maggie died, Peter was heartbroken. A part of him died with her. On that forested land around Todd Lake and Broken Top, he feels a tangible connection to her—to some of the happiest moments of his life. He's there now—to be close to her, to draw strength from that spiritual connection. He's there because he feels he's been backed into a corner. You think you've seen Peter in action—something tells me we're about to be enlightened."

"Thank you, sir," Homer replied grimly.

"Check your gear again; we'll be at the drop zone soon."

Again Homer ensured his weapons were functional and with full ammunition magazines, but no round chambered to avoid accidental discharge. For the fourth time he confirmed the number of spare magazines he was carrying, his medical kit, rations, water, knife, and other essential items. He would be wearing the NVG set, and he confirmed he had plenty of spare batteries.

"So, once we're on the ground," Homer asked, "how do we locate Peter?"

Jim had worried about exactly this question. It was by far the biggest gap in his plan, and his plan was full of gaps and shortcomings. First, they would parachute—high altitude, high opening, or HAHO—and glide to coordinates that were supposed to be open terrain. Hard enough in daylight, but they would accomplish this feat in darkness. Even so, would they even be close to Peter? An unanswerable question since they had no intelligence as to his exact location.

"By sound," Boss Man answered.

Homer scrunched his mouth. "I don't get it."

Jim looked at Homer. His eyebrows pinched together, eyes reflecting cold reality. "By sound. We follow the gunfire."

Any illusion that Homer might have had that this would be an easy mission immediately vanished.

"Assuming I didn't guess wrong, and we land somewhere in the neighborhood where Peter is hiding out, then we wait and listen. If he's alive, and the bad guys are after him, there will be gunshots. We follow the sound, and we get him out. The sat phone is to contact Lacey. She can coordinate with the local badges once we have Peter in our custody."

"Law enforcement may not look kindly upon the military taking custody of their suspect."

Jim nodded. He'd already thought about that potential complication.

"Lacey will work out authorization through Colonel Pierson. You have to trust the Colonel. He'll do the right thing. Once we have Peter safe, and get his side of the story, it'll all make sense. Right now, we have too many questions and not enough answers. But I tell you this: Peter did not execute a Deputy. That's not him. It's against every moral fiber in his body."

"I know, sir."

They synchronized their wrist-mounted GPS units with the plane's navigational computer. Both men were wearing heavily-insulated jumpsuits to protect against the frigid outside temperature and 350-knot wind they would experience when they jumped out the back hatch.

With guns and packs hanging low and in front, they checked each other's straps. After final adjustments were made, it was simply a waiting game. But they didn't have long to wait before they'd be at the jump location—an imaginary point in three-dimensional space where the two soldiers would leap into the sky.

Homer had one more question nagging at his mind. "Sir. What if we don't hear any gunfire?"

"Then either I guessed the wrong location, or we arrived too late."

CHAPTER 27

PETER WAS FINDING IT HARD to keep his eyes open, not to mention actually focus on the expanse to the west. The night seemed to drag on, minutes passing with excruciating slowness. He looked at his watch again, only eight minutes since he last checked the time. Shaking his head and shifting his shoulders, he tried to stir from his lassitude.

Diesel heard it first, pushing up from his warm cocoon against Peter where he had burrowed under the sleeping bag. Ears forward, Diesel stared across the opening to the scattered and stunted trees. Peter felt the motion, and the tense muscles in his dog. He looked to Diesel, and then in the direction he was fixated.

Even with the electronics amplifying the ambient light, Peter could not see anything out of the ordinary. Yet he continued to search, trusting the dog.

With quickened pulse and a jolt of Adrenalin, Peter no longer felt sleepy. Diesel had heard something—but what? It could be a harmless rodent, or maybe a coyote on the hunt.

It could also be one of the enemy.

Diesel was sitting upright, staring ahead into the darkness, as still as a stone statue.

Peter's hand rubbed the soft fur and thick flesh at Diesel's neck, but even that didn't disturb the canine's concentration.

And then… movement.

Peter's pulse raced and his right hand moved to the trigger of his rifle, anticipating an order not yet sent by his brain.

He stole a quick glance at Diesel—the canine was still focused ahead. *What did you hear?*

Slowly, it appeared. Emerging from behind a cluster of dwarf fir trees, moving at a deliberate pace. At first it appeared as a shadow. But eventually the shadow took form, and a small doe ambled into sight.

Peter exhaled and relaxed. "It's okay, boy." He rubbed Diesel's head and thick neck, pushing his fingertips against the dense muscles that surrounded the oversized head and lent immense power to the stocky jaws and large teeth. He kneaded the loose skin on the canine's neck—a defensive feature bred into the dog for fighting.

Diesel relaxed his limbs and let out a breath he'd been holding. Sensing the doe was not a threat, he lowered his head.

The deep thundering bass of the rotors beating the air could be felt as much as heard. Against a black early-morning sky, Nadya and Marcus could barely see the helicopter hovering above the meadow with only instrument lights illuminated in the cockpit. If they had not worn light amplification goggles, the aircraft would have been completely invisible.

The Sikorsky S-70 Battlehawk was squat and wide, reflecting its evolution from helicopter troop-transports. It was a prototype, one of several in testing. The matte black fuselage bore no markings.

The pilot and passengers all wore NVGs. Still, what they were doing was a highly dangerous exercise.

From open doors on both sides of the airframe, thick black ropes were dropped. Then, while hovering 50 feet above the wind-whipped bunch grass, as close to motionless as possible, nine armed men fast-roped down the lines. All were dressed in digital camouflage in shades of black and gray.

At the same time the men were slipping away from the hovering Battlehawk, two creatures in slings were rapidly lowered. Through her night vision goggles, Nadya recognized them as some breed of dog.

The men spread out in a circular pattern and took up defensive positions while their team leader made contact. The helicopter didn't loiter—once the last man was down a crew member dropped the heavy lines and the helicopter departed, hugging the terrain as it did on the inbound flight, too low to be tracked on civilian air-traffic radar.

Nadya's satellite phone squawked. "We're on the ground. Do you have a visual?"

"Affirmative," she replied. "We are a party of two, just inside the tree line northeast of you, maybe 400 meters. Entering the clearing now."

Richard Nyden watched Nadya and Marcus approach. Wisely, they left their weapons shouldered and held their hands out to the side, clearly visible. After entering far enough into the meadow to be seen, they stopped. Nyden quickly moved his team to join the two Mossad agents rather than remaining in the open any longer.

Following personal introductions, Nyden distributed communication headsets to the foreign agents. The comm gear had limited range, but every member of the team could send and receive messages over the squad network.

DAVE EDLUND

It was an hour before sunrise.

"I doubt Peter Savage has moved during the night," Nadya explained. She had already briefed Nyden prior to their arrival, explaining the loss of most of her team.

Only hours ago, Nyden made the phone calls and assembled a squad of other Guardians, all hard men with military training and prior combat experience. Pilots and aircraft owned by United Armaments were used to ferry everyone to the staging area at a secluded UA test facility stretched across a remote patch of desert in Eastern Oregon.

The giant defense contractor also fully armed the team and provided the Battlehawk. The helicopter, an armored version of the venerable Black Hawk, was employed by UA as a test platform for a new laser-guided missile system it was developing.

"If we move quickly, we can be at his location in less than an hour," she added, her voice barely a whisper. Marcus stood to the side, silently sizing up Richard Nyden.

"You know his location, so why wouldn't he move on?"

"He thinks I am the only survivor, that he killed the rest of my team. Plus, he has a good field of view and a stone fortress for cover."

"And if he's not there?" Nyden said.

"Then we track him. He has his dog, so the trail will be unique, easy to follow."

She indicated the location on her GPS in topographical display mode, zooming in so the features of the crescent-shaped stone formation were evident. Then she switched to satellite display to reveal the scattering of trees amongst an otherwise open landscape.

"It's a good defensive position," Nyden said. "With good weapons and visibility, he can hold off a considerable attacking force."

"Now you understand," Nadya said, sarcasm evident in her voice. Nyden let it go. He wasn't sure yet what he thought of these Israeli agents, but he had a score to settle with Peter Savage. At least for the moment, that's where he would channel his aggression. Of course, it didn't hurt that he'd negotiated a bigger payday late last night in the process of organizing this assault team. It seems the escalation of events with law enforcement and the elimination of two-thirds of the Mossad team had motivated his employer to finish this assignment quickly.

"Do you know if Peter Savage has NVG equipment? Civilian or military?"

"It's possible, but I didn't see any," Nadya answered. "All of our encounters were in daylight."

"Although it would be very unusual for him to have night vision equipment," Nyden observed, "Mr. Savage has already demonstrated he is a very unusual man. Plus, my sources tell me he has contacts within the Defense Department. So, we will assume he has NVGs. Maybe not current generation, but we will proceed on the assumption he can see in the dark."

"We have to be smart, advance cautiously. He will wait for our approach, and then pick us off one by one, just as he did to my team."

"Not this time," Nyden remarked disdainfully. "The Guardians are all handpicked. They know combat."

Nadya cast her gaze around the assembled mercenaries. "Maybe you're right. We have enough men. We can get into position, surrounding him before sunrise."

Nyden considered his options as he surveyed the land. Everything shown clearly although the electronically amplified images were in shades of green and gray. Naturally he had reviewed recent satellite images of the mountainous terrain prior to helicoptering in, but there was no substitute for first hand observations. The rises and dips all looked steeper in person, the open expanses larger.

He opted for a different plan, one that would keep his numbers hidden from Peter Savage until contact was made.

"Ashcroft," Nyden called.

A man—several inches shy of six feet, and with three parallel scars across the side of his face—was standing in front of Nyden in four strides. Beside him were the two dogs that had been lowered in slings.

Marcus and Nadya stared at the beasts. They were not the largest dogs they had seen, probably a little over two feet at the shoulder, but they appeared massive—thick limbs, and bulky chest and head. Thick, long fur covered their bodies, even cascading over their eyes.

"What are those?" Marcus asked.

With pride, Ashcroft answered, "Black Russian Terriers. They were bred by the Soviet Army at the Red Star Kennel during the Cold War. Their goal was to achieve the perfect military and police dog."

"You can discuss canine genetics and breeding after the mission."

"Sorry, sir," Ashcroft replied.

Now that he had Ashcroft's attention, Nyden explained the plan. "We will split into two squads. You and the dogs are with me." He turned his attention to Nadya and pointed at her. "You'll lead the second squad. I want you to go north, circle around the target's coordinates. I'll take my squad south and approach from that direction.

"We are to take Peter Savage alive if possible. A bonus will be paid to the persons who apprehend him in one piece. My boss has some questions he'd like answers to."

"Well, I doubt he will just give up and walk out with us," Nadya said.

"Wound him, incapacitate him if you can. If not, kill him. But remember, the bonus is paid only if Savage is alive."

Silently, like a pack of wolves on the hunt, the nine Guardians and two Mossad operators moved out at a fast pace toward their objective.

"That didn't sound like a search and rescue helo," Jim said. "And I didn't see any running lights."

Boss Man and Homer had jumped out at 30,000 feet and glided in the still night air to a perfect landing. With no idea where Peter might be, they moved slowly and stealthily within the trees, aiming to be positioned on the slope of Broken Top by daylight.

At the sound of the approaching helicopter, they dropped and squeezed up against the closet tree or boulder. If the helicopter was hostile and equipped with thermal imaging, they'd almost certainly be spotted.

But the thump of the rotors soon gave way to the whine of receding twin turbine engines as the aircraft passed over. Seconds later, the sound became consistent in pitch and intensity, indicating the helicopter was in a hover, and not far away. Moments later, the sound faded.

"Could be a Black Hawk," Homer whispered.

"If it is, they just inserted up to eleven combat troops, all gunning for Peter."

"It would seem you guessed correctly and Peter is in these woods."

They stalked in the direction they estimated the helicopter had hovered prior to departing the area. It was impossible to be certain how far away that was, but based on the attenuation of the sound, Boss Man and Homer both agreed it had to be at least half a mile, maybe farther.

Had it not been for their NVGs, it would have been

impossible to move through the forest and maintain any progress. With a clear sky, there was abundant starlight to amplify, enabling easy visibility even within the tree line. The biggest obstacle was the never-ending collection of dry branches on the forest floor. A heavy boot snapping a dry limb would be a sure signal of their presence.

The frigid night air was now a blessing, for Boss Man and Homer could move swiftly without overheating. Balancing pace with stealth, they advanced along the vector where the supposed Black Hawk was heard. If it was a Black Hawk, then it would have unloaded military men—mercenaries who fought for money, not ideals. Trained men, deadly men, who had no qualms about killing anyone for any reason as long as there was a payday at the completion of the job.

Ahead, the trees thinned. Cautiously, Boss Man and Homer crouched and approached, stopping at the edge of the wooded patch. The meadow opened up before them, and continued to the west, following the slope upward.

Boss Man turned on his GPS system. "This would be a good spot to rappel men."

"The distance we traveled is about right," Homer added in agreement.

Boss Man was still studying the GPS unit when Homer asked, "Where to now?"

"If it were me, I'd be ahead of the enemy, up at high elevation. Make them fight up hill."

"Any of these groves of timber could make reasonable defensive positions, especially for an ambush."

But Boss Man had his eye on another location on the GPS display. "We'll stay in the trees and keep moving up to high ground."

CHAPTER 28

PETER AWOKE TO A DEEP bass-like reverberation. He stretched his limbs, and his knee immediately protested. Probing his other injuries, he drew in a deep breath, expanding his chest slowly. At least the bruised ribs were barely noticeable.

He immediately recognized the sound for what it was—a helicopter—and he silently cursed for having fallen asleep. *How long was I out?* He checked his watch—he'd been asleep for almost an hour.

The rhythmic sound of beating air was growing louder, although Peter estimated the helicopter was still a considerable distance away. He was searching the night sky to the east, where the sound was coming from, but could not make out any aircraft running lights. After half a minute, the sound began to recede.

A minute later and silence returned to his wilderness.

It was the lack of aircraft lights that had Peter worried. He looked to Diesel—his companion was watchful, staring into the darkness beyond.

Peter's anxiety only increased as he thought through the possibilities—none of which were good. Only a search and rescue helicopter would be out here in the dark, and they would be flying with their exterior lights on. By logical deduction, he concluded that a new enemy had arrived, a black ops team. How many men, he had no idea.

Peter thumbed his GPS and the screen illuminated, showing a detailed map of his present location. He considered his options. He could stay, but the woman knew his location. Although defensible, if there were enough enemy, he could be surrounded and forced to fight off an attack from the front and rear. Not a good proposition, even at his current fortified location.

"We have to go, Diesel." He selected a set of coordinates and saved them to the GPS memory and then downed another couple ibuprofen tablets. Although he was reluctant to leave his defensive position, at least he could still use the element of surprise to his benefit.

About a mile to the east of Peter's presumed location, Nyden split his team and sent six, including the two Mossad operators, to the north, while Nyden's squad broke to the south. Each squad would follow a course on their GPS that would take them another mile from the crescent rock formation and loop them around to the west. From a higher elevation, the two squads would fan out and assault the stronghold from the west. With eleven guns engaging Peter along a long front, Nyden and Nadya were confident in success.

Each squad continued to move along their routes at a brisk pace, almost a jog. As much as possible they stayed just within the tree line, but at this high altitude the trees were less frequent, giving way to large open expanses of powdered pumice and gravel.

Nadya and Marcus stayed close to one another; they weren't sure yet how deep their trust of the Guardians went. They each held their rifles with both hands, ready to snap the weapon to a firing position.

Even with six pair of boots pounding the ground, the sound was barely audible. The green-tinted image projected by the NVGs made the path as clear as if it were a sunny day.

Both the north squad and the south squad kept up their pace despite the thin air and steep slope; there was no time for even a short break. To the east, the horizon was beginning to take on a light glow: sunrise would arrive soon.

Both squads reached their GPS coordinates at almost the same time. They were about 300 meters to the west of the geologic anomaly. Nadya spoke into the communication headset. "We're in position."

A moment later came the reply from Nyden. "Copy. South Squad is also in position. I can see clearly into the crescent formation, but no one's there."

Nadya was studying the curve of fractured lava rock as she listened.

"Are you sure this is where you encountered Savage?"

"Yes, I'm certain," she replied irritably.

"Well, unless there is a cave or something down there, our target's gone."

Eleven pair of eyes were scrutinizing every inch of the rock and boulders. Nothing.

"I suggest we move closer," Nadya advised.

Nyden considered his options. He glanced at Ashcroft. The Black Russian Terriers were sitting obediently at his side—motionless, quiet. Failing to think of a better course of action, he agreed. "Everyone spread out in a line. Use whatever cover you can, but move forward in unison. Halt when I give the order."

They still had the advantage of darkness, although not for long. Of course, if Peter Savage had night vision equipment, he would have already spotted them.

Without a sound, the 11 assailants formed a line 100 meters in length and descended toward the flat meadow filling the west side of the rock crescent. When Nyden estimated they had closed to within 200 meters, he ordered the team to stop. They took what cover they could find, some lying prone and motionless on the gravel.

"If he had NVGs, he'd have seen us by now," Nyden said.

Nadya replied right away. "Or he's asleep. I still don't see any sign of him, but the dirt looks disturbed at the right end of the ledge. Do you see it?"

Several seconds of silence passed while Nyden—and every other team member—scrutinized the ground where Nadya had directed their attention.

"Yeah, I see it," Nyden answered. "I don't like it. If he's there, why haven't we spotted him yet?"

It was a good question, and Nadya did not have an answer.

"Here's what we're gonna do," Nyden said. "Nadya and Marcus, you split, flanking right and left. Search the formation and we'll cover you from here."

She looked to Marcus, who was by her side. He nodded, signaling he was ready. As one, they rose and darted down the slope, separating as they advanced. Soon they each arrived at opposite ends of the lava protrusion. Then, with rifles pointed forward, they advanced methodically—always aiming wherever their eyes looked.

Nadya came across the disturbed ground where Peter and Diesel had settled in for the night. No objects had been left behind. She continued her search and soon found the shallow cave; again marked by footprints and paw prints, leaving no doubt they had camped here.

Continuing to work her way forward, searching along the junction between meadow and rock, she found more footprints. But there was no other cave, no hiding spot to conceal his presence.

There was only one conclusion—Peter Savage was gone.

Peter and Diesel had climbed quickly and were now close to the Tam McArthur Rim. With the sheer cliff to his back—to the west—he could focus his attention on the lower approaches from the east. *That is the direction the enemy will have to come from.*

The terrain was close to level at the edge of the Rim, and Peter selected a spot at the cusp, where the land just began to slope downward. The trees remained stunted and scattered, but the volcanic origins provided plenty of dense igneous rock formations for shelter.

He selected one particularly promising thrust of rock about three feet thick, with a sloped side facing downhill and a perpendicular face on the opposite side. It was plenty wide and cleft in the middle, the crack wide enough to peer through. He settled in behind the shield, testing his field of view. *Good enough,* he thought.

The sky to the east was grey, and soon the sun would rise above the horizon. *Not ideal at all. I won't be able to get a clear image in the scope when the sun is low in the morning sky.*

Peter shouldered his rifle and scanned the terrain before him. Nothing. No sign of anyone—just wilderness.

With the approach of dawn, the forest was slowly waking up. First it was the gray tree squirrels descending from their homes in an endless search for food. Then the ground squirrels emerged from burrows on a similar quest. As the sky continued to lighten, the feathered inhabitants—nuthatches and chickadees—began to stir. All this activity created a commotion that was in stark contrast with the stillness and silence of night.

Every disturbance of air or rustling of foliage became a new focus of interest for Diesel. His head was in a constant state of motion as he swiveled to each new sound.

Against this curtain of life, a deadly threat approached undetected.

CHAPTER 29

STILL ON HER FIRST CUP OF COFFEE, Lacey was reviewing the latest intelligence updates that had come in overnight when she was joined by Stephens. They each had their laptops open and a scattering of papers covered a major portion of the conference table.

"I phoned Angela Meyers already and left a voice message. Nothing useful from the local law enforcement."

Lacey was tapping the table with her pen, only partly aware of the brief report from Stephens. Suddenly she rose and started to pace the length of the conference room.

"What is it?" Stephens asked.

Lacey held up her index finger. "What if this has everything to do with the *Liberty* incident, and yet nothing at all?"

"I don't understand, ma'am," Stephens replied as her mind immediately went into overdrive, trying to catch up with whatever line of reasoning her boss was following. "How can it be both?"

"That's an excellent question." Lacey regained her chair and selected a paper from the dozens on the table. She slid it across to Stephens.

A minute later her eyes widened. "Wow! Are you suggesting what I think you are?"

Lacey nodded and sipped her coffee, her gaze locked on her associate. Stephens finished reading the document, and then typed in a search phrase on her laptop. A couple seconds later the reply flashed on her screen. "Speaker Schuman has the endorsement of the American Israeli Foundation."

"Correct. And he's the son of Jewish parents. In fact, his family history is quite interesting. He has plenty of material for a riveting autobiography—a surefire best-seller."

"Let me get this straight," Stephens said, her voiced edged with excitement. "You're suggesting that Abraham Schuman is in collusion with the Israeli government to keep the details surrounding the *Liberty* attack secret?"

"No, not exactly. I am theorizing that Schuman has formed an alliance with the office of Prime Minister David Feldman, and that together they want to maintain secrecy surrounding the extent of U.S.-Israeli involvement in the *Liberty* incident."

"Okay," Stephens said, her eyes narrowed. "There is certainly a religious and cultural connection between Schuman and Israel, but the same is probably true for a dozen or more members of Congress. Why is this case special?"

"Well, Schuman is going to be the Republican Presidential candidate, for one. But bear with me." Lacey retrieved another paper and shared it with Stephens. It was a list of attendees at a private fund-raising dinner three nights ago at the Hay-Adams Hotel in support of Schuman's Presidential campaign.

Stephens read the list and looked back at her boss with a blank expression.

"Think about it," Lacey said.

"I am," she protested, her arms open. "We have a Jewish-American, highly-respected member of Congress—the Speaker of the House for God's sake—running for President. He has the usual corporate donors—many, no surprise, from his own district. And he has the endorsement of the American Jewish Foundation." She shrugged her shoulders. "Put it all together, and I just don't see any illegal conspiracy. It sounds pretty much like politics in America."

"What if I said that David Feldman is a member of the Jewish Home Party?"

"Not surprising. The party has been riding a wave of popular support for a few years. With a struggling economy and a continued threat of terrorism from Islamic fundamentalists, the Israeli people are eating up the right-wing, nationalist agenda."

"Exactly," Lacey said, her green eyes sparkling. "An ultra-nationalist Jewish government supporting the leading challenger to President Taylor's re-election bid. What if Schuman is elected President? There's no doubt he'll extend U.S. support to Israel."

"But every U.S. administration supports Israel. I don't see anything nefarious in that."

"And if it draws us into another war? Schuman is the lead author of the Israeli Security Act, and he's been very vocal that he has the votes to override President Taylor's veto."

Mona Stephens looked again at the list of donors to the Schuman campaign. "A lot of these corporations are in defense."

"That's right." Lacey leaned back in her chair, allowing time for Stephens to make the connections.

With only the ticking sound from the clock on the wall, Lacey waited.

Stephens raised her eyebrows. "Let's assume Schuman is elected and pledges strong support to Feldman's government.

That could be all the encouragement the Prime Minister needs to pre-emptively attack Iran or Syria."

"Israel has made no secret of their dislike for the nuclear treaty President Taylor signed with Iran. And their warplanes did bomb the Osirak nuclear reactor near Baghdad years ago to slow Iraq's progress toward nuclear arms."

"Right." Stephens said, still pulling the threads together. "So, hypothetically speaking, Israel launches a pre-emptive military strike against Iran or another of its belligerent neighbors, confident that the U.S. will provide military and intelligence support."

"Plus airpower and troops if it goes badly."

Stephens nodded. "Yes. They could draw us into a regional conflict again."

"With Russia backing Syria and possibly Iran, it could outgrow a regional conflict," Lacey said with a grim look.

"But Schuman and Feldman are betting that they can contain the conflict. After all, it's worked in all previous Arab-Israeli wars. So, Israel attacks her neighbors first—my guess is an air strike against military facilities in Iran followed by an invasion of Gaza. Later they'll turn on Syria."

A thin smile appeared on Lacey's face. "Did you notice who the number one donor is to Schuman's campaign?"

Stephens looked at the list again. There it was, the first name—United Armaments.

She looked across the table at her boss. "So the defense industry makes billions supplying weapons to support the Israeli conflict. Even better if the U.S. is drawn in."

Lacey smiled. "It's only a theory, but it does make more sense when you hear someone else say it."

Stephens smiled. She understood, of course, the element of self-doubt that could stifle deductive reasoning unless one had the benefit of bouncing theories and speculation off another person. She had these same feelings many times before. It was one of the aspects of working for Lieutenant Lacey at SGIT that she especially valued—she could freely hypothesize and refine theories through intelligent dialog with the other analysts. No one ever thought less of her for sharing half-baked ideas, and the resulting informal group discussions had always been beneficial.

"There's just one thing I'm still missing," she ventured. "You said you thought this puzzle—the murders—has everything to do with the *Liberty* incident, and yet nothing at all to do with it. I'm still not making the connection."

"The answer is as elementary as it is fiendish. The events surrounding the attack on the *USS Liberty*…"

"Yes?"

"I think that was the blueprint."

Mona Stephens pushed her laptop aside and leaned over the table. "Whoa. Let me get this straight. Schuman and Feldman are following a plan that was first put into play by the U.S. and Israeli governments during the Six-Day War?"

"I do. Given the information Gary Porter shared about the contents of those classified files, that has to be the connection.

"In 1967, Israel felt threatened and desperately wanted to expand its geographical boundaries to put a significant buffer zone between the homeland and her Arab neighbors. In particular, the Golan Heights were a strategic priority to deny Syria the high ground. That fear lead to an Israeli first strike in June, the beginning of the Six-Day War.

"Many of Lyndon Johnson's cabinet members and closest advisers—including Arthur Goldberg, the U.S. Ambassador to the United Nations—were Jewish and staunch supporters of the hardliners in Tel Aviv. Defense Secretary McNamara had positioned the Sixth Fleet in the Mediterranean, not far from Egypt and Israel. Most noteworthy is that both of the fleet's two aircraft carriers—the *Saratoga* and the *America*—were on station as part of a large naval task force in the Eastern Mediterranean.

"There is only one reason for that amount of U.S. naval power in proximity to Egypt, the Sinai Peninsula, and Israel. Johnson had us poised to intervene on a moment's notice if the tide of battle turned in favor of the Arab League."

"I'd love to read those top-secret documents," Stephens said, shifting in her chair. "It just doesn't make sense to me that Israel would attack a U.S. ship. I mean, how could they benefit from doing that?"

Lacey raised her eyebrows. "That's a question that historians, someday, will spend thousands of hours investigating. And those secret documents that Peter Savage and Gary Porter came across will likely shed some daylight on this mystery. At this time, all I can say is that based on public documents, it was a mistake on the part of a local commander. That was the official position from the White House and State Department as well."

"Mistake? I don't believe that."

"Neither do I, but it's easy to imagine such mistakes could happen during the heat of battle. It was a blitzkrieg—lightning war. Israel was fighting on multiple fronts against a coalition of nations. June 8, the day the *Liberty* was nearly sunk, was the eve of the invasion of the Golan Heights. Two days later the war was over. A ceasefire was negotiated by the UN, and although there are those who will argue that Israel wanted to press her military advantage and take more territory, the weight of international pressure prevailed and the hostilities ended with a negotiated settlement.

"The *Liberty* began its life as a Victory Ship, hauling cargo. But she was reconfigured and modernized by the Navy to become an Auxiliary Technical Research Ship. In other words, a floating surveillance post. On the eve of the invasion, Israeli command would have been very sensitive to their radio communications being intercepted. They would have never agreed to sharing sensitive information such as troop movements and timetables with anyone for fear of the information being compromised. That fear would be sufficient grounds for an attack. But that decision could have been made at a low level—say a base commander.

"So, the *Liberty* is under attack—by accident or on purpose, it really makes no difference—and Admiral Geis does the right thing and launches aircraft from each of his carriers. Not once, but twice, to defend the intelligence ship—"

Stephens interrupted, "And those aircraft are quickly recalled by none other than the Secretary of Defense himself: Robert McNamara."

"That's right," Lacey added. "Once the attack on the *Liberty* began, Johnson, or maybe one of his advisers, recognized the opportunity. If the *Liberty* had sunk, the American public would have screamed for an immediate and decisive retaliation against the assumed aggressor—the Arab Coalition."

"The crew of the *Liberty* were nothing more than sacrificial pawns."

For a moment the two analysts looked each other in the eye, feeling the full weight of their assessment, and its implications to both historical perspective and current events.

Lacey exhaled, feeling some of the weight released with her breath. "Really, when you think about it, the plan was close to perfect. Israel, with the tacit approval of the United States—perhaps even a handshake deal between Lyndon Johnson and Prime Minister Levi Eshkol behind closed doors—launches a first-strike, a highly-successful military campaign against her Arab neighbors. In the process, the Jewish State captures vast territories that have never been returned."

"And if it weren't for the tragic events surrounding the

Liberty, no one would ever know the truth." Finally, the missing pieces fell into place and Mona Stephens understood. "If your theory is right, President Lyndon Johnson and Defense Secretary McNamara collaborated with a nation that was attacking a U.S. Naval vessel, deliberately sacrificing those poor seamen."

"If I'm right," Lacey said, "Speaker Schuman and Prime Minister David Feldman want to repeat those events. They want Israel to pre-emptively launch a military campaign to change the face of the Middle East. And drag the U.S. into war."

Stephens leaned forward again, her hands gesticulating her concerns before the words escaped her mouth. "Somehow we have to get word to Commander Nicolaou. He could be walking into a very dangerous situation!"

"Not yet. He was very clear to me. We have to get more evidence—concrete evidence. Then I'll get Colonel Pierson involved."

"But ma'am," she protested as Ellen Lacey held her palm out.

"I share your concerns. The murders in Oregon could have been committed by elements of Mossad or private security forces funded by U.S. defense companies. The Commander knew what he was getting into; he knows how the game is played. Without hard evidence, all we have is a story. Now, if you want to do something helpful, get me something tangible. Preferably on Schuman or Meyers."

CHAPTER 30

WITH A PLAUSIBLE THEORY to guide their investigation, useful information finally began trickling in. Lieutenant Lacey was reading the latest update from MOTHER, the SGIT super computer, when Mona Stephens knocked on the door.

"Come in."

Stephens marched directly to Lacey's desk and planted herself in one of two chairs. "Good news from the Bend Police," she said excitedly. "They asked for our assistance in providing any information on an FBI agent out of the Portland office named Barnes. The detective seems to think he may be an imposter."

"That's interesting," Lacey replied. "Anything else?"

"Yes. The deceased woman at the outdoor equipment store has no priors with local law enforcement, and her prints are not in the usual databases."

"Not even the FBI?" Lacey asked.

"No, ma'am."

"And this is supposed to be good news?"

"It is. Detective Colson—she's the lead investigator for the Bend PD—is pretty sharp. She sent the fingerprints off to the Defense Office of Personnel Records and requested a cross-check against service records."

Ellen Lacey straightened at this news. "Any word yet?"

She shook her head. "No, not yet. It could take days. The case is relatively low priority since it is not related to national security or terrorism. But…"

"You want me to make a phone call or two and bump up the priority," Lacey said, her mouth turning up in a subtle grin.

Stephens nodded in agreement.

After a moment's thought, Lacey said, "We can do better than that. MOTHER can access the records request and execute the crosscheck. We'll expand the search to all accessible military and other databases. We should have the result within an hour. And this Agent Barnes, do you have a copy of his prints?"

"I do. Colson already sent them to my email."

"Good, we'll run his, too."

"Excellent," Stephens replied. "That's all I have for the moment. Any word from Commander Nicolaou?"

"No. I don't expect to hear from him until the mission is completed. Probably later today. You need to stay focused. The Commander is the best there is; he knows how to handle these situations."

"Even with the lack of intelligence? An SGIT strike team is normally well briefed when they enter a hostile zone. Commander Nicolaou has nothing—no intelligence about the force he is facing."

"You mean potentially facing. We don't know that anyone is in the Oregon mountains other than the local law enforcement search team. We don't even know that Peter Savage is there. That map trick may have been nothing more than a diversion to draw attention away while he fled east into Idaho or Wyoming, or north to Canada."

"With all due respect, ma'am, I don't think you believe that. And, for the record, I don't either."

"What I believe doesn't matter. Right now we need evidence—tangible evidence that I can share with Colonel Pierson."

"I understand," Stephens said, her face devoid of expression. "May I make a suggestion?"

"Of course."

"Angela Meyers is not taking my call. And she won't return my voice messages. So we need to push this along, elicit a response."

"Go on." Lacey tilted her head to the side, intrigued with the possibilities that her top analyst might offer.

"Have Mr. Porter email that file to MOTHER."

The Lieutenant didn't like the idea at all. Death followed that file.

"No. It's too risky."

"But we can protect him. Send SGIT operators to his home prior to emailing the file. When the bad guys show up, we apprehend them."

"I said no. Commander Nicolaou would never agree to placing a civilian intentionally in grave danger."

Mona Stephens sighed; it was worth a shot. "Yes, ma'am."

"I need you to get MOTHER working on those prints. Let's see who Jane Doe and Agent Barnes really are."

"I'm on it." Stephens rose to leave.

"One more thing," Lacey said. "Take a look at this." She pushed a sheet of paper across her desk. It was only one page, and Stephens lifted it and quickly read the contents.

As she neared the end, she raised her eyebrows and her mouth fell agape. Before she could speak, Lacey answered the

DAVE EDLUND

most obvious question.

"That came from a search MOTHER has been doing. It's an obituary for Chief Petty Officer Tony Hart, printed in a small-town newspaper, somewhere in northern Georgia, I think. That's why it took so long to find it. MOTHER was programmed to search records following a hierarchy that placed higher priority on more significant publications and news broadcasts. This newspaper must have been pretty far down on the list.

"In 1967, Mr. Hart was stationed at a U.S. Navy relay station in Morocco that handled radio traffic between Washington and the 6th Fleet."

"According to this report," Stephens said, "Mr. Hart overheard the communications between Rear Admiral Geis and McNamara. He says Geis refused the order to recall aircraft from his carriers, aircraft that were launched to protect the *Liberty*."

"The Admiral insisted he would only do so if President Johnson gave the order directly. So Johnson gets on the phone and does just that, saying he didn't care if the men on the *Liberty* were killed and the ship sunk."

Stephens handed the paper back to her boss.

Lacey placed it back in the ever-growing stack of documents. "Since Geis is dead, as are McNamara and Johnson, no one can corroborate this recounting of events. But there must be something in those files."

"My God, you were right all along," Stephens said. "No wonder they buried this deep and still won't disclose what really happened. Johnson and McNamara are guilty of treason."

CHAPTER 31

OREGON STATE POLICE CAPTAIN Oscar Sheffield assembled his team early, an hour before sunrise. They would eat and be briefed, ready to renew the search for Peter Savage even before the first rays of sunlight. The night had been clear, cold, and still. *Good*, he thought. *The scent will still be reasonably fresh, and tracks will be undisturbed.*

Using a mug of coffee as a hand warmer, the fuzzy collar of his issued jacket flipped up to keep the chill off his neck, Sheffield addressed the assembled men and women. The dogs would pick up the scent trail again and, if thrown off, circle in ever-widening arcs until they picked it up once more.

"McGregor. I want you and Vashal on the ATVs. Start here," he pointed to a location on the large topographical map and traced an arc with his finger. "That will put you far out in front of the dogs. Maybe you can pick up a trail or something. Work your way west from the road, a couple miles. Some of the terrain will be difficult—even with the ATVs—but do what you

223

can."

The two Sheriff Deputies nodded understanding.

"Any questions?" the Captain asked.

"Yeah," came a voice from the back of the group. "When we find him, what then?"

Sheffield understood what was on everyone's mind. Peter Savage had murdered—executed—a fellow lawman.

"You will apprehend him and bring him to justice. Until he is proven guilty—"

A groan of protest rippled through the crowd.

"I'll repeat. The suspect is innocent until proven guilty." The captain looked across the faces. They were devoid of emotion.

"Does everyone understand me?"

A reluctant chorus of yes slowly rose above them.

"Good. Thank you for that question. I'm glad we cleared the air. Anything else?"

"Yeah." It was the same office who had asked the previous question. "What if he resists arrest? You know, doesn't want to cooperate."

The captain's eyes narrowed as he looked across the faces, making eye contact with as many as possible. "In that case, you have a weapon. The DA won't have any problem if you act in self-defense."

A smile spread across the face of the man who posed the question.

"Alright, anything else?"

No one spoke up, and the captain ended the briefing. The dog handlers were still the priority. If they could stay on the scent, they would have Peter Savage in hours, tomorrow at the latest. The dogs were excellent trackers and would keep going well into the night. The hard part would be for their human handlers to keep up. If necessary, they would use the ATVs to keep pace.

McGregor and Vashal fired up their machines and let the engines warm for two minutes while they gathered helmets, lunch bags, and filled insulated bottles with black coffee.

"Ready?" McGregor said.

"After you," came the reply from Vashal.

They departed base camp, single file, following the gravel road south, back toward Todd Lake. They rode for about 10 minutes and then turned west, into a meadow that promised to stretch farther upslope into the wilderness. Once off the gravel road, they had to greatly reduce their speed due to the numerous bumps and rocks littering the meadow.

McGregor held the lead, and Vashal tried as much as possible to follow his tracks. They reached the end of the meadow, a couple hundred yards off the road. The terrain became steeper, and they knew from the maps that the next meadow was just beyond a row of trees. At this point, the two deputies split. Vashal would explore farther to the north, but still making his way to higher elevation. McGregor would keep pushing west. His plan was to go as far as Tam McArthur Rim before turning back. Once he rejoined the road, he would radio Vashal, compare notes, and agree on the next area to scout.

McGregor advanced the throttle. The engine revved a little and the ATV rolled up the slope. As he entered the copse of trees, he had to steer around patches of snow, fallen logs, and tree trunks. Progress was slow, and he kept the ATV in lowest gear. But eventually he emerged on the other side of the trees, facing another long meadow. Gunning the engine, the deputy picked his way along the side of the creek that meandered through the grassy expanse.

He made better time, and soon was facing another rise and patch of thick forest. McGregor picked his way through the evergreens and around deadfalls. When he emerged from the dark timber, he had another slope to cross, and then the meadow was mostly flat and level. From the seat of the ATV he could see the blown out side of Broken Top. The layers of rock were shades of red and yellow and gray. And with the sunlight just falling on the highest portions of the ancient peak, the color was stunning.

Running the engine at higher speed, the small olive-green machine bounced along on knobby tires that vaguely resembled balloons. It was still at least two miles to the Tam McArthur Rim, but with most of the forested sections behind him, McGregor figured he would make good time.

He drove around a rocky point that looked back over the valley, missing the body that Nadya had pulled back into the trees. As he left the meadow the slope grew steeper, and the Deputy found it necessary to stand on the footpegs and lean forward to maintain balance. If he didn't shift the center of gravity forward, the vehicle could flip over backwards, potentially causing grave injuries.

The machine topped the rise with a spray of gravel from the tires, and McGregor brought the ATV to a stop. He was on a small plateau. Before him were another half dozen short ridgelines and an ever-increasing rise to the Rim.

To his left, the gravelly land fell off into yet another drainage. He would stay to the right, skirting around the scattered groves of evergreens that dotted the high mountains.

"Hear that?" Nyden said to the Guardian nearest him.

"Yeah, and it's coming our way."

"Stay here." Nyden split off and ran toward the sound of the machine. He didn't worry much about making noise since the rider would never hear him anyway.

He ran through the trees, using the deep, dark shadows to conceal his advance, homing in on the engine noise.

It was getting louder, and Nyden picked up the pace.

Inside the forest, the soil was firmer, not sandy and loose. He jumped over a log, and ducked low-hanging branches, his ribs protesting as he drew in volumes of air.

He was racing forward. The engine was revving up and down, and it was close. Then, Nyden saw movement ahead, through the trees. He stopped so as not to attract attention, and moved his head from side to side, trying to get a better view of the machine and who was riding it.

From his vantage within the timber, he saw the ATV and rider crossing the relatively smooth gravel along the top of a finger ridge. He was approaching quickly.

Nyden dropped to a knee so he could see more clearly under the needle-covered branches. He squinted, and recognized the green polyester jacket with the shield emblem on the shoulder. *Sheriff Deputy.*

The rider continued his approach, completely oblivious to the assassin just yards ahead in the trees. Nyden set his rifle down, and removed a silenced Glock from his side. He aimed, tracking the approaching rider.

But too many branches were in the way, so Nyden crept to the edge of the timber, and waited. The deputy was concentrating on the path of his ATV, mindful of rocks as well as holes left by industrious ground squirrels.

As the driver reached his closest point to Nyden, the assassin opened up. He fired four shots; three struck the deputy. His body armor may have saved his life if all the shots had hit his chest. But the one round that entered his temple did the job.

Nyden chased after the ATV, which, without a pilot, veered off and stopped against a small tree. He turned off the engine, and then returned to the deputy, firing an insurance shot into the man's forehead.

With his pistol holstered, he returned to the seclusion of the timber and scrambled to rejoin his team.

CHAPTER 32

WITH A TRAIL LEADING UPSLOPE from the crescent rock formation, it was clear what direction Peter Savage had taken. "Okay, listen up," Nyden announced over the squad communication net. "That engine sound was a Sheriff Deputy on an ATV. We're running out of time."

"They should be searching miles north of here." Nadya made no attempt to disguise her surprise. "Marcus disposed of the truck and body just off the road, near the rim before it drops down to Three Creeks Lake."

"Tell that to the dead deputy," Nyden replied. He looked to Ashcroft, who returned his gaze with a slight nod.

"Time to speed things up. Ashcroft, take the dogs and follow the trail. With the rising sun behind your back, it'll be impossible for Savage to get a bead on you. But move fast—once the sun rises he'll have a clear view through his rifle scope."

"What about the rest of the team?" Ashcroft asked.

"We need the dogs to find him. If we're all running around,

Savage is likely to locate us first. Once you engage him, we'll move in and complete the mission."

Ashcroft made a clicking sound, and the Black Russian Terriers stood alert at his side. In the twilight of dawn, the dogs looked like black holes, blacker than anything else. Even the charred stumps from long-ago fires were not as black as the thick, shaggy canine coats.

All of the field signals between Ashcroft and his dogs were made with a series of clicks and soft whistles. Ashcroft touched his nose and then the ground where footsteps had disturbed the earth, presumably Peter Savage. The black hounds lowered their heads in excitement and eagerly drew in the scents. After a half minute of scenting, he issued a low whistle followed by a click. His purpose-bred military dogs took off in a run following the trail. They would only venture 50 to 100 meters ahead of their handler, allowing him time to stay within communication range.

Everyone watched the black beasts charge up the slope, followed by Ashcroft. Nyden was using his binoculars to follow their progress. He had no idea how long it would take to track down Savage, but sooner was preferred. With at least one deputy out in the area, more law enforcement may be nearby.

He was confident his team could dispatch any officers that stumbled upon them, but his mission parameters were simple and clear. Avoid contact with the police and bring back Peter Savage, alive if possible. Otherwise, proof of death would suffice.

Unlike hounds running down a feral pig or cougar, Ashcroft had trained his animals to remain silent. When they struck, it was always from close distance and without warning.

The black terriers reached the crest of the slope, Ashcroft laboring to keep up. Nyden watched as the canines hesitated while their handler closed the gap. Then the group disappeared from sight.

The seconds ticked by into minutes. Nyden was not watching the time, instead staying focused along the ridgeline, glassing with his binoculars. He knew that beyond the ridge was the Tam McArthur Rim, a formidable natural barrier. Unless Savage had serious rock climbing gear—harness, rope, pitons, carabineers—he couldn't depart in that direction.

He was moving the binoculars slowly, systematically taking in every detail, when he saw it. A glint of light, a mere flash of sun, from beside a large boulder not too far up the slope. He ordered his team to stop while he glassed the area with his binoculars. There it was again. A brief flash of light, although nowhere near as bright this time.

"There you are," Nyden muttered to himself. He continued to study his adversary through the high-power optics. He saw enough of Peter's face to recognize him as the man he'd met at Kate Simpson's home—the same man who had split his skull and knocked him out. He felt his face flush with anger and his temperature rise.

Peter never heard the footsteps, never saw them coming. With the sun's rays low on the eastern horizon, his scope was useless looking in that direction. So he focused his attention farther to the north, carefully searching for approaching enemy.

He was balanced on one knee to hold his rifle steady, Diesel by his side as usual. He was doing his best to ignore the rumbling of his stomach, not to mention his growing thirst. They had departed the crescent formation too quickly to eat or fill their bottles with water. Now he regretted not getting water during the cover of darkness. They could do without food, but water was a different matter.

Fortunately, the air temperature was still very cool. Peter considered working his way to lower elevation and finding one of the dozen or more springs and small streams filled with the remnants of the winter's snowmelt. Just the thought of the cold, fresh water a half-mile or so away seemed to amplify his thirst.

He was still scanning the distance through his riflescope when Diesel emitted a low, guttural growl.

An alarm.

A warning.

He reached down and laid a comforting hand on his companion, but to no avail. With lips drawn back causing the flesh on Diesel's nose to wrinkle like a prune, four ivory fangs were prominently displayed. The claws on all four feet were clenched into the earth—leg muscles tensed like giant, powerful springs.

In the blink of an eye, Diesel launched at some unseen threat behind Peter. He spun around, trying to bring the rifle to bear, but it was too late. A massive black creature was in the air flying at him like a missile.

Knowing he couldn't avoid the impact, Peter extended the rifle and the black terrier clamped its jaws down on the barrel and stock. He heard the sound of splintering fiberglass, the synthetic stock yielding to the bite pressure exerted by the powerful jaws.

For the moment, it was a standoff. The dog held fiercely to the rifle, as did Peter. At the same time, he heard the terrifying sounds of a pitched battle, deep growls mixed with high-pitched yelps and cries.

Peter hazarded a glance to the side and saw Diesel locked in mortal combat with another black beast. The red pit bull was half the size of his adversary, and Peter feared for his dog. But a glance was all he could steal. His attention brought back to his own struggle. The black creature tried to twist its head and dislodge the rifle from Peter's grip. But he maintained the advantage of leverage as he shifted his hands to the opposite ends of the weapon.

The pit bull and Russian Terrier were fighting viciously. Red and black tumbling, separating, and pouncing. White teeth flashing like daggers. Blood-tinted saliva streaming from open jaws. The rapid attacks and parries became a blur as the animals clashed, driven by the most basic of natural instincts: kill… or be killed.

Black and red fur rolled, becoming one and then separating, only to repeat as the melee continued. Each advance an attempt to clamp down on the other's throat or soft belly. Once a firm bite was achieved, the animal would wrench its head violently, ripping and tearing muscle and skin in the process.

Peter saw Diesel flip the Russian Terrier and slip between its legs, then bite down, only to be thrown away with a powerful kick. In a flash, the larger hound pounced on Diesel. The black jaws bit deeply into the red neck as a huge paw and leg pushed down on Diesel's shoulders. The terrier was aiming to pin the pit bull to the ground and crush his spine or rip open his throat. Either way it would claim victory.

Diesel yelped over and over. In a madness bred of pain and desperation, he twisted and slipped the jaws, but the creature was still over him, viciously snapping blood-covered teeth, seeking any hold it could get.

The blocky red head turned and mashed down on a black front leg. Like a steel trap, the jaws squeezed and locked into place. Then the head shook brutally, separating muscle and bone. Punctures opened to gashes, spilling blood.

With lighting speed, the black head came down, jaws open, teeth bared. It grabbed the first thing it contacted and ripped off half of Diesel's ear.

Diesel released and yowled in agony, the high-pitched cry penetrating the din of noise. The black terrier, perhaps confused that it's bite had so easily given way, pulled its head back and spat out the piece of fleshy cartilage. In that opening, the pit bull lashed out and closed on the exposed throat of its larger opponent, crushing the windpipe in a fraction of a second. Then Diesel planted his hind legs against the belly of the black dog and pushed, flipping it onto its side. He was still locked down on its throat, slowly depriving it of air.

But the fight was far from over. Both dogs were pumped full of adrenaline, obscuring pain and driving them berserk with the single-minded purpose of killing the other.

The hound attempted to twist free, but with one mauled front leg and the pit bull on its throat, it had no leverage. Diesel pressed his advantage, and rocked his head. At first the motion was limited, but as blood crossed his tongue, the thrashing escalated. It became more and more violent as the Russian Terrier slowly succumbed.

Finally, Diesel released his prey.

Peter did not witness the outcome of the battle. He was pitched in a deadly fight of his own.

With teeth clinched down on the rifle, Peter twisted the gun to the side. The beast went with it, coming to rest on its back.

Without a pause, Peter dropped his body, aiming his knee at the dog's chest. Upon impact, the canine released and exhaled a grunt, then kicked with all four legs.

Peter felt the claws rake against his arms and legs, renting his jacket and pants. Blood soon filled the coarse gashes, now aflame in burning pain. Still over the dog, he slammed the rifled down. But the black terrier grabbed the barrel and stock again and shook its mighty head. It was all Peter could do to maintain his grip. Then the dog kicked again. This time one of the muscular hind legs connected with Peter's groin. It felt like he'd been hit with a tree limb.

The air left his lungs and his grip weakened. The creature wrenched again and yanked the rifle from his hands. Peter leaned to the side, trying to avoid another powerful kick.

Dropping the lifeless rifle, the beast lunged for him, aiming for the throat. It launched, mouth agape and fangs glinting in the sunlight. Peter raised his left arm, intending to sacrifice it to the jaws.

A flash of red slammed into the side of the black beast. The pit bull's legs where open, encircling the larger canine as it bit down on the back of the ebony neck. Insane with fury, Diesel stayed on the beast as they slammed into the ground. The terrier attempted to roll free, its four legs thrashing wildly. Driven by crazed fear, the pit bull refused to release, instead squeezing its jaws tighter.

Peter was scrambling to regain his composure. He saw a bloodied Diesel struggling with the black monster, and reached for the .45 pistol holstered at his side. His hand found the grip when the black creature stopped moving. Diesel had crushed its neck.

CHAPTER 33

THE SAVAGE ENCOUNTER had lasted less than 90 seconds—not enough time for Ashcroft to engage. He was still running forward when the second Black Russian Terrier was killed by Diesel. He screamed in rage and raised his rifle.

Gunshots filled the air.

Unsteady from breathing heavily, his shots missed. The bullets cratered in the dirt and rock near Peter.

Despite his wounds, Diesel launched on the new enemy, closing rapidly. Ashcroft adjusted his aim, trying to shoot the pit bull, but was too slow to connect with the rushing red dog.

Peter twisted his upper body and aligned the sights on Ashcroft. He fired and a .45 caliber bullet slammed into his chest. He stumbled backwards but didn't go down.

Body armor.

It was enough to cause Ashcroft to lose his aim. Peter lowered his sights and fired again. The bullet crushed through his pelvis just before Diesel plowed into his chest—70 pounds of berserk muscle and teeth in an adrenaline-fueled frenzy.

Ashcroft threw his arms up and latched onto Diesel. But it was too late. The teeth had already penetrated deep into his throat. A bath of hot red blood ensued as Diesel pulled up, ripping his throat open.

Peter hobbled forward and called Diesel off. The animal hesitated, and Peter called again. This time, it let go and limped back to its master.

With considerable effort, Peter hoisted Diesel into his arms and retreated to the rock shield.

After several deep breaths, the pain in Peter's groin and abdomen subsided. The torn flesh on his arms and legs burned, but clotting had already stemmed the bleeding. He began to inspect Diesel's wounds. His fur was mated with blood. It was impossible to determine how much was Diesel's and how much was from the Russian Terriers and Ashcroft. One ear was half-gone and bleeding. There were deep gouges along his chest and belly. Several were bleeding, and would likely require stitches. His neck was both punctured and lacerated. Fortunately, the copious loose skin there probably saved Diesel's life—the terrier grabbing nothing more vital than a fold of flesh.

As he held Diesel, the canine lowered his head and began trembling. Spasms surged through his limbs in waves and he licked his lips, his eyes closed. *Shock is setting in.*

"Hang in there, buddy. I'll get you out of this; get you patched up."

Peter had no idea the second wave was close.

Nadya's team—the north squad—was the nearest to Peter's position. She had ordered her squad to split into two-man teams and to spread out. Although she didn't know the exact location of the target, that became apparent when Ashcroft opened fire.

"Keep north of his position," Nadya ordered her team. "We

have to get to the side of the boulder."

Her communication set crackled to life, and through the earbud Nadya heard Nyden's voice. "South squad is moving up."

She glassed the target location with her binoculars one last time and then, in a crouch, scampered to a group of bushes not far away. She was being extra cautious, recalling Peter's skilled performance picking off her team from a distance.

"Use the cover as much as you can," she said to Marcus. But that was proving difficult as the vegetation was sparse and stunted.

Suddenly the air was split by the report of a rifle shot. The sound was distinct and different from the small-caliber military rifles deployed by her team. Nadya looked over her men and saw one of the Guardians in the pair to her left laying prone and motionless. His rifle was a few feet to his side.

More gunfire erupted, this time much farther to the left, the morning calm now a distant memory. It was Nyden's south squad opening up on the sniper. Nadya shifted her gaze uphill and saw the bullet strikes against rock and dirt, kicking up small dust clouds.

"Keep moving," she urged her team. "Stay to the right. We need to flank his position."

Peter had just caught a glimpse of motion several hundred yards down slope and a bit to the north. He swung his scope and was rewarded with a clear image, free of the glare from the rising sun. The figure was wearing camouflage fatigues and carrying an assault rifle.

He lined up the scope reticle and adjusted the hold high, slightly above the figure's head, to account for bullet drop over the long distance. He was laying prone for a steady rest. He moderated his breathing, and gently squeezed the trigger.

Boom!

He saw the enemy figure fall, his rifle thrown to the side.

Peter was thankful the stock damage inflicted by the Russian Terrier was only minor and didn't seem to influence the rifle's performance. After working the bolt to chamber another round, he was searching for more assailants. *Where was the woman he had conversed with the previous day? Did she call in reinforcements, or were they already here? How many are there?*

Just then a barrage of bullets struck his rock shield and the dirt before him. Reflexively Peter pulled back behind the stone barrier. Diesel was curled in a ball, shaking almost constantly from the pain of his wounds. Blood clotting in his fur had seemed to stem the loss to minor seepage.

As quickly as it started, the gunfire stopped. Peter knew that meant the men were moving toward him. They would stop only to fire. Otherwise, they would advance and attempt to encircle his position.

He scoped to the right and left. At first, he didn't see any enemy. But he kept searching knowing they were there. Then he spotted a figure moving quickly, almost running, across an opening, aiming for a decaying log. His progress was slowed by the soft soil that was more like sand than dirt. The enemy slid to the ground and rested his rifle on the log.

From his elevated location, Peter was looking down on the man. He had his weapon resting on the log and was aiming at Peter. And then he fired, but Peter ignored the bullets as they cracked over his head.

He placed the cross hairs on the target, centering on his back. Peter fired, felt the rifle stock shove forcefully into his shoulder, and chambered another round. The man was still shooting. In less than a second, the scope was centered on the enemy target again.

Peter fired once more, the heavy bullet cratering into the man's back, shattering his spine and smashing his vital organs.

South squad was down to four men, and Nyden ordered them to stop advancing and seek cover. To the north, Nadya was facing a similar dilemma.

She urged her team forward. They had to advance fast and flank Peter. "Can you engage him from your location?" Nadya had radioed Nyden, explaining her plan.

He ordered his men to fire single shots, not full automatic. They had to conserve their ammunition and prolong the covering fire.

North squad advanced.

They had covered another 30 meters when Peter spotted them darting across the barren slope. It was clear that they were working their way around him. But they were still within rifle range.

Peter moved behind the igneous stone fortification, and repositioned himself on the opposite side. From this location, he had a better view of the approaching squad and was protected from bullets fired by the south squad.

He lined up the Weatherby rifle, taking careful aim. The figures were moving at the pace of a jog. He counted four of them, and he could almost see the strenuous exertion of their charge up the sandy slope. He led the first enemy, holding a little high, and fired. The bullet struck the man's abdomen and he tumbled forward.

The other three assailants kept running, spurred forward by the loss of their comrade. Peter picked out the next target, lined up the sights, and fired. The shot missed, and the man kept moving. He adjusted his aim and fired again, this time connecting. The man fell, his femur shattered.

Now Peter's rifle was empty, and he had to reload.

But Nadya wasn't taking any more chances. She held her ground.

"He's shooting a sporting rifle!" Nyden said over the communication network. "The magazine only holds three or four rounds. Then he has to reload. Count the shots, and advance when he's reloading."

Peter pushed the last round into the magazine and was searching for targets again. He focused to the north, fearing that they were closest to flanking him.

CHAPTER 34

THANKS TO THEIR NVGS, Boss Man and Homer had covered a lot of ground in the darkness. At one point, just as the sun was rising, they heard an engine, but it was distant, and the sound stopped abruptly. Although Jim worried that it might be the search party, he had more pressing concerns to focus on.

They had climbed a considerable distance, avoiding open terrain as much as possible. That decision forced them to follow a circuitous path. But then again, they had no clear idea where Peter might be—until the gunfire erupted.

"Let's go!" Jim said to Homer. They picked up their pace, running in the general direction of the sound. The reports seemed to be coming from two different locations—one farther away and the other closer and to the left.

"The nearer location, that's automatic fire," Jim said. "That'll be the bad guys."

Opting to stay within the timber, they continued their approach. Then the gunshots changed to seemingly random, single shots—and much louder. Occasionally a deep report from farther away was heard.

Jim peered forward through a break in the trees. He couldn't see any persons.

"It's clear," he said, and they moved forward in a crouch. Ever alert, both Boss Man and Homer had their rifles shouldered, heads moving from side to side.

Suddenly Jim held his hand up and dropped to a knee. He pointed ahead. Homer edged up to his side. He squinted, trying to make out the target. Then he saw them: four men. Dressed in camouflage.

The distant reports resumed. One shot… two shots… three shots.

"That's gotta be Peter," Jim said.

The rifle fire was answered by a volley from the four men Boss Man and Homer had spotted. But there was a new sound, gunfire from the right.

"Sounds like they've flanked his position," Homer said.

As the words came out, they saw the four assailants rise and move in a straight line toward higher elevation. They were quickly greeted by another shot from Peter, then silence.

"Let's go! Follow me," Jim ordered.

He rose and took off in a dead run across the naked pumice gravel. The next copse of trees was a dozen strides away, and Jim counted on the enemy being distracted as they worked to gain a superior position on Peter's fortification.

They ducked into the trees and found a man-sized chunk of volcanic rock among the dwarf evergreens.

Peter's rifle fire resumed and was immediately answered by the two groups, quickly approaching him from opposite sides. "If they circle him, he won't have any cover," Homer said.

"We've got to slow them down. Give them something else to worry about." Jim raised his rifle and fired at the group of four.

They were still a long way off, 400 meters or more, but the bullet impacts from the SGIT soldiers were close enough to cause the Guardians to break off the attack on Peter.

Nyden ordered his team to return fire and seek cover. Then he radioed Nadya. "We're taking fire from a new team. Unknown number. East of my position. Have not located them yet."

North Squad had been reduced to only Nadya and Marcus, and they still had not been able to gain an angle to fire into Peter's location. She confirmed the transmission and reported the status of her team.

Homer and Boss Man continued to fire into South Squad, buying relief for Peter. He raised his head at the new sound of gunfire, farther off, but could not see where it was coming from. *Is this a new threat? No, if they were shooting at me, I'd know.*

Richard Nyden had no choice but to direct his weapons down at the new force, whoever it was. This was more than he had bargained for, and it fell outside his mission parameters. *Could it be the local police had discovered our operation?* His mind was searching for answers. It didn't make sense that military would be involved; this was a domestic police matter and there were laws against military action in such cases.

How could law enforcement converge on their position so quickly? The manhunt was miles to the north, and other than the lone deputy on the ATV, his team had not encountered any police or sheriff deputies. It didn't make sense. But what he did know was that his team had taken heavy losses already, and now he had a new threat to contend with. He grabbed the satellite phone and placed the call.

"You heard me right!" The report of gunfire served to reinforce his request.

"Yes, now!" He read the coordinates and the other party

repeated them back in acknowledgement.

"Yes. We'll pop smoke and mark our positions."

More words were exchanged, and Nyden felt his blood pressure rising. "Look, just get the bird armed and in the air. When you call back with the ETA, I'll tell you how we'll mark our locations and direct your fire to the assault team that has my squad pinned down. Once that threat is neutralized, you will take out the primary target."

The call ended just as rounds zipped past Nyden, clipping off several small evergreen twigs near his head. "Hold them here," he ordered his team. "Help is on the way."

"What about Savage?" Nadya asked for the remainder of the team to hear.

"Keep him pinned down! As long as you're blocking his retreat, he has nowhere to go."

Nadya and Marcus had found a depression next to a split boulder. A fir tree was firmly rooted in the crack, suggesting the fissure went deep. It provided adequate cover from which to ensure Peter Savage did not escape. If he rose, they would have him dead in their sights.

From the United Armaments test range in Eastern Oregon, the Battlehawk was already fueled and loaded with a dozen experimental surface-to-ground missiles. The aircraft was supposed to begin a test of the new laser-guided munition, but that was suddenly pre-empted. A new crew, comprising pilot and co-pilot, rushed to the helicopter and completed the preflight check.

The pilot started the engines. It didn't take long for the twin General Electric turbines to warm up.

The aircraft flew low to stay under radar. There was insufficient time to file a flight plan, and even if they did it was likely to be rejected on the grounds of the manhunt underway in the mountains between Todd Lake and Three Creeks Lake.

Eighteen minutes after Nyden made the call, the Battlehawk approached the target coordinates.

"Nyden," he said, answering the call on the sat phone.

"Approaching your coordinates," the pilot said. "I need a visual."

Nyden had one of his men pull the pin on a white smoke grenade. Marcus was doing the same from his location with Nadya.

"Affirmative; we have visual. Will make one pass, then come in hot."

"Roger that," came the reply from Nyden.

The helicopter came in low, just clearing the trees. It was a menacing sight: squat and wide, with stubby appendages to both sides from which weapon pilings hung, bristling with missiles. Beneath the nose of the black machine was a targeting pod for the 20mm gun system. The gun was slaved to a holographic reticle on the pilot's helmet. Wherever the pilot looked, the gun would point automatically.

Nyden's eyes narrowed and his mouth drew into a tight grin. *Now that's what I'm talking about.*

CHAPTER 35

VASHAL WAS RIDING HIS POLARIS ATV about a mile north of where McGregor was investigating. He was advancing his machine at a comfortable pace, slightly faster than a brisk walk. At this speed he could comfortably scan side to side, and still pay enough attention to the path in front to avoid major obstacles.

The distant sound of gunfire alerted him. Initially single shots, it was soon followed by rapid fire. *Either multiple weapons discharging or automatic fire.*

"What the hell?" He stopped the ATV and radioed McGregor. "McGregor, this is Vashal, over… McGregor, you copy? McGregor, this is Vashal, come in…"

The lack of response from his partner added to his mounting concern. He called the base camp, and dispatch immediately picked up.

"Copy you, Vashal," came the reply, loud and clear.

"I'm roughly two miles west of the gravel road, maybe four

miles south of base camp. Picking up a large volume of gunfire. And McGregor is not responding to my radio calls. What's going on?"

"Hold on, Vashal. Let me get Captain Sheffield." After a brief pause, a new voice came over the radio speaker.

"Dispatch is trying to reach McGregor," the captain said. "You're hearing gunfire?"

"That's right, Cap. Sounds like it's coming from close by Broken Top. But don't hold me to that. Sounds can echo off the ridges and get distorted."

"It's not our men. The hounds are still going at it, but the handlers think cougar urine was sprinkled on the scent trail to spook the dogs. We don't have anything yet."

"If you ask me, our suspect planned this pretty well."

"Take it easy, Vashal. We don't have all the evidence yet."

"Come on, Captain. You have to admit that this took some planning. I mean, who wanders around with a bottle of cougar urine?"

"I understand, Vashal. But what I think at the moment is irrelevant. We all have jobs to do. We apprehend the *suspect*, collect evidence, and let a jury settle the matter."

The silence felt heavy, stifling. Finally Vashal replied, "Has dispatch contacted McGregor yet?"

"No, they're still trying. Probably something wrong with his radio. Look, why don't you investigate the source of the gunfire. Maybe McGregor's there already. I'll radio in a preliminary report."

"Roger, sir. Out."

Vashal holstered his radio. He started the engine and accelerated in the direction the shots seemed to have originated. The ATV bounced over the uneven terrain, pulling the front wheels right and then left. With the engine revving a high-pitched, throaty whine, other sounds were masked, and at first he didn't hear when the gunfire renewed.

He advanced his machine, seeking the best path to maintain a respectable speed. The engine noise was constantly increasing and decreasing in both pitch and intensity as he shifted gears and throttled up and down. On the flat stretches he was able to open up the engine, and then when he had to traverse a steep climb or negotiate a fallen tree or other obstacle, he would ease back.

Vashal had just reduced his speed to a crawl to navigate around some large rocks, when he heard a sonic crack and recognized he was very close to whoever was shooting. He turned off the ignition and stood on the foot pegs, looking for the shooter. He couldn't see anyone.

More gunfire, both near and far. No doubt there were multiple shooters. He dismounted and removed the Glock from his hip holster. Holding his service weapon in both hands, he stalked forward.

The crunch from his boots on the pumice gravel seemed loud, and he tried to soften his footfalls. He was crouched, maintaining a low profile and meandering around the stunted vegetation.

The gunfire wasn't constant, and Vashal didn't know if that meant anything or not. He still hadn't seen or been able to contact McGregor, and the reports he was hearing sounded like rifle shots, not from a pistol.

Ahead was a small island of green, and he moved quickly for it. He jumped as the gunfire renewed, and dropped to a kneeling position among a group of manzanita bushes and fir trees. Glancing through the greenery, he could see ahead, across a clearing, and into another patch of trees.

There, he saw movement and recognized men dressed in military uniforms. With their camouflage, they blended in well, explaining why he hadn't seen them sooner.

He observed the two men for a long minute. Their attention was focused farther up the slope. As Vashal watched, points of light erupted—like a dozen flashbulbs going off—and punctuated the sparse foliage. The sonic crack immediately followed and he realized there were other men shooting at the two figures before him.

He advanced quickly, sprinting across the open land. Bullets struck the dirt in front and to his side so he zigged and zagged. He dove behind the closest cover, a modest chunk of igneous rock. Pushing his shoulder against it, trying to meld with the stone, he called out.

"Sheriff! Cease fire!"

Boss Man and Homer turned. The voice was close, but they didn't see the man.

He called again. "Cease fire! Put your weapons down!"

Vashal rose and placed his handgun on the boulder, sighting in the direction the shots had come from, although he still didn't have a specific target in his sights. He squeezed off two shots.

"There," Boss Man pointed. "Deputy! You have two U.S. military 20 meters in front of you. We are friendlies. Do not shoot!"

Boss Man and Homer were concealed from the Guardians except when they rose to fire. Right now, they were hunkered down, looking toward the Sheriff Deputy.

Jim faced Homer. "We're gonna give him some cover fire, get him up to our position. Ready?"

They turned and popped up, firing at the Guardians, enough volume to cause the assailants to keep their heads down. The deputy jumped up and dashed forward, tumbling into Jim.

They stopped shooting and slid down behind their cover.

"Who are you?" Vashal asked.

"U.S. military." Jim pointed to the American flag patch on his shoulder. It was in olive green and black so as not to pop out in bright color and spoil the camouflage.

Vashal noticed there was no nametag above the breast pocket of either man's uniform. "Yeah? And what are Uncle Sam's finest doing here in a firefight?"

"That's a very long story," Jim answered. "And I promise to tell you. But right now we have a problem."

Jim made a snap decision not to tell the deputy that Peter Savage was pinned down on the ridge. It would take far too long to calm the deputy down and convince him that Peter was not a cop killer. Instead, he stuck with the training exercise cover story.

"And how do those bad guys fit into your training?"

"They don't. Just our bad luck, I guess," Jim said.

Vashal looked at Boss Man and then Homer. He looked right into their eyes, studied their faces, the way they held his stare. He didn't know what to think, other than he was glad to have their rifles on his side.

"Tell me something? When did you guys start training with live ammo on public National Forest land?"

Before Jim could venture a reply, the air reverberated with a deep *whump, whump*: rotor blades. A helicopter.

And it was approaching fast.

CHAPTER 36

LACEY WAS BEGINNING TO FEEL like a conspirator in a low-budget Hollywood film. She was spending so much time in private conference with Stephens that she was certain rumors were spreading amongst her colleagues. As much as she wanted to, she was not to engage any SGIT personnel other than Stephens—Commander Nicolaou had made his orders unambiguous. The mission was classified "Need to Know," and that applied to her colleagues as well as outsiders.

"That's one down. We have positive ID on Jana Cooke," Lacey said as she and Stephens reviewed the personnel records displayed on the monitor. The two had taken over one of the secure conference rooms. With no windows and a high measure of soundproofing, they were free to carry on their discussion without being overheard.

She continued reading key portions of the file. "Former Army. One of the first women to qualify for combat positions. Discharged after seven years, eight months."

"Why?" Stephens asked. It seemed that Jana Cooke had everything going for her. She was at the leading edge of a major new transition in the U.S. military—allowing women into combat roles was a huge advancement in the bureaucratic thinking.

She scrolled further down, and then stopped. "Looks like Jana Cooke became a trouble maker when the Army failed to actually post her into combat positions."

"Can you blame her?" Stephens said. "Another example of sexism leading to discrimination. The Pentagon says what the politicians and public want to hear, but nothing really changes."

"Regardless, she left the military quietly, but not on favorable terms."

"What else did MOTHER find? Where did Cooke go after her discharge?"

"Let's see…" Lacey opened other files with reports from other government agencies—the Veterans Administration, Internal Revenue Service, U.S. Postal Service listings of address changes and postal boxes, Social Security, FBI—MOTHER even searched the databases used for background checks of a purchaser of firearms.

There were many false hits—the name matched but other essential facts such as age, race, and physical description did not. After removing those, the number of matches in the databases was very small.

"Looks like the last tax return she filed was the same year she was discharged. She listed a Seattle address." Lacey shook her head. "Nothing else. She dropped off the network."

"Well," Stephens said, "at least we know who she was."

"Yeah, a trained killing machine. There is a strong market for individuals with that skill set."

"Okay, what about this supposed FBI man—Agent Barnes?"

"From the fingerprints lifted from the Mk-9 gun he carried,

MOTHER found his Department of Defense personnel file. Like Cooke, he's ex-military."

"Interesting." Stephens said. She cocked her head to the side in thought.

"It gets better. Look at this…" Lacey pointed to the name at the top of the personnel file.

Stephens read it aloud. "Richard Nyden."

"So we know that Peter was right. Agent Barnes is not who he appears to be."

Stephens read down the file. "He was discharged from the Marine Corps after 17 years. Why?"

Lacey scrolled down. "Wow. That's quite the file. Accused of murdering Afghan civilians. Not enough evidence to convict on those charges, but the Corps ran him out anyway."

"Well, if he's not an FBI man, then who does he work for?"

"Let's see what his tax return says." Lacey opened the search results. "Huh. Just like Cooke, no return filed after the year he was discharged."

"We have two individuals with a lot in common tied to this case. Both ex-military. Both left the service under less than honorable circumstances. Both fall off the network following their discharge. What are the odds of that?"

Lacey considered the implications for a long moment before answering. "Neither Nyden nor Cooke received government support. Neither has filed a tax return in years. Neither has had any interaction with the VA. No post office box, no dealings with Social Security, no police records. For all practical purposes, neither person exists."

"Except they do. Jana Cooke's body is at the morgue in Bend, and Richard Nyden is still out there, somewhere." Mona Stephens knitted her brow. "What about medical records?"

"MOTHER only has limited access due to privacy concerns."

Stephens raised her eyebrows. "You mean it's okay for us to access IRS databases but not medical records?"

Lacey shrugged. "Hey, I don't make the rules."

"Maybe Mr. Porter can search for medical billing histories? It might yield an address."

"Maybe. But understand we never had this conversation. And if you talk to Mr. Porter, don't share it with me."

Stephens smiled. "Plausible deniability."

"Two of the most powerful words in the intelligence community."

"Got it. Never happened."

"Back to Cooke and Nyden, and the lack of records. Other than the two not being gainfully employed, what do you make of it?"

Stephens folded her arms, her mouth scrunched in a frown. "Well, like you said. There are a lot of private security firms out there. But if it was a legit company, they'd have a presence. Tax returns at the very least. So, maybe they were both hired by an illegitimate security firm. Maybe they were, you know, mercenaries."

"There's no work domestically for mercs. But the first part of what you said, that rings true."

"So what now?" Stephens asked.

"Now we have something to share with Detective Colson. Maybe the information will help break open their investigation. We're not getting anywhere with it."

"Yes ma'am. I'll phone her and get a copy of the DoD personnel files and IRS returns to the detective. I think she'll be surprised to learn that Barnes really is an alias."

Unexpectedly, Detective Colson picked up on the second ring. "Colson," she said.

"Detective, it's Mona Stephens with SGIT. I have some news

for you."

This wasn't Colson's first rodeo, and she immediately suspected a setup. "Yeah? And what do you want from me?"

Stephens was taken aback by the response. She'd imagined the detective would be ecstatic that this obscure defense intelligence agency was offering to share information. "I'm not asking for anything. Simply delivering on a promise I made to you."

"Okay, I'll play along. What do you have?"

"IDs and some background information. The deceased female from the Pinnacle store murder, her name is Jana Cooke. She's former Army. And Agent Barnes *is* an imposter."

Colson nearly shot out of her chair. "What?"

"That's right. His real name is Richard Nyden. He was run out of the Marine Corps after 17 years. Accused of murdering Afghan civilians, but they couldn't prove it."

"Unbelievable. I didn't see that coming. And you *will* email the personnel files to me?"

"Of course. Oh, you may also be interested to know that neither Cooke nor Nyden filed a tax return since they were busted out of the military."

"Really. And what do you suppose that means?"

"Pretty simple, we think. They are both trained to kill—experienced and accomplished at their craft. After leaving the military, Jana Cooke and Richard Nyden were recruited and hired for off-the-books operations."

"Hired killers…" Colson's voice trailed off as if she was formulating an important idea.

"Yeah."

"Thank you. This is helpful. Please email those records right away. Also the latest tax returns."

"I'm on it." Stephens was about to hang up when Colson stopped her.

"You aren't going to ask about the manhunt for Peter Savage?"

"Should I? Is there a new development to report?"

Detective Colson sighed. "No, nothing yet. Maybe later today. But this information about Barnes is important. I'll make sure the word gets out to the search party. Also, I need to have an urgent conversation with the FBI. They've got a serious problem at their Portland office. I'll let you know when I have something to share."

"Thank you, Detective."

"Oh, one more thing," Colson added, almost as an afterthought. "We found some charred papers in the fireplace. Apparently Mr. Savage attempted to destroy a large stack of documents. Except they didn't all burn to ashes."

This news certainly had Stephen's attention. She listened for the detective to get to the point.

"The top portion of several sheets was only partially burned. Although the full documents were too far gone to get the subject matter, Detective Nakano and I can make out government seals."

"Seals?"

"Yeah, you know. Emblems."

"Yes, I understand. What are they? What departments or agencies?"

"Oh, you'll love this. The White House and the Department of the Navy."

Stephens was still thinking about her conversation with the detective when her phone buzzed. It was Lieutenant Lacey.

CHAPTER 37

HOMER WAS LOOKING SKYWARD, searching for the bird. As the sound grew louder, it became more difficult to pinpoint a direction due to the growing echo.

"Does that radio work?" Jim asked, his voice anxious.

"Sure," Vashal said.

"Call your commander and tell him we have a terrorist action underway. Ground troops and aircraft. Automatic weapons. Give him these coordinates."

"Wait a minute, you said this was a training exercise."

"Just do it!"

Vashal keyed the radio and reported in.

At the same time, Jim was on the sat phone to Lieutenant Lacey. He had just established communication when the Battlehawk passed overhead. The missiles and 20mm gun slung underneath the cockpit left no doubt about its intended use.

"Lieutenant!" Jim shouted to be heard above the din of the turbine engines and rotors. "The situation has deteriorated. We

257

have located Peter, but we can't reach him. Presently engaged with approximately four, possibly more, hostiles."

"Copy that," Lacey replied. "What's that noise?"

"Attack helicopter, presumed hostile unless you're going to tell me it's ours."

"No sir. Colonel Pierson does not know of your action. Per your orders he has not been briefed."

The Battlehawk circled low while the pilot and copilot got their bearings, located the two groups of "friendlies" by the smoke, and identified the large rock feature where the primary target was located. As the bird came over Boss Man and Homer a second time, Homer opened up, stitching a line of bullets across the armored belly of the craft.

The pilot did what he was trained to do and twisted the collective control at the same time he ran up the engine throttle. The helicopter swiftly rose and accelerated away. He addressed his copilot and quickly ran his eyes across his instruments. All gauges and indicator lights were good, no damage was sustained. "Did you get the shooters?"

"Negative. I think they are to the east of the south squad, but I did not get a visual."

The pilot swung the Battlehawk around: it had traveled far beyond the Tam McArthur Rim. As he turned, he maintained a low elevation. To an inexperienced aviator, it looked like he might fly into the sheer cliff, but he cleared it by 20 feet. As they crossed the Rim, the land fell off and within a second Homer and Boss Man were shooting again at the attack helicopter.

This time the pilot and copilot saw the muzzle flashes. The pilot had just enough time to squeeze off a short burst from the 20mm gun.

The bullets impacted to the side of Jim's position. Any doubt Vashal had about the seriousness of the situation had just evaporated.

Lacey had a complete auditory record since Jim had not disconnected the call. He picked up the phone as the bird passed overhead. "We need air support now!" he shouted.

"I'm on it. Keep the line open; I'll be right back."

Jim set the phone by his side to grip his rifle with both hands. The change in pitch of the sound from the engine and rotor blades indicated the helicopter was turning to make another run. When he estimated it was within range he began shooting. Homer joined him, and a second later Deputy Vashal was discharging his Glock at the aircraft.

The Battlehawk was designed for combat, and as such, it's armored underside and front of the cockpit could take repeated hits from small-caliber arms. If they had a .50 caliber Barrett, or shoulder-fired missiles, they could bring the aircraft down. But they had neither.

Before Lacey dialed Colonel Pierson, she buzzed Stephens' office. "Stephens. I need you here now." Lacey didn't wait for a reply as she redialed.

On the second ring Colonel Pierson answered. How he managed to always be near a phone was a mystery to Lacey, but she was grateful nonetheless. After the perfunctory greetings, she got right to the point.

"Sir, Boss Man and Homer are on a mission in Oregon, mountains to the west of Bend—"

"Mission? I didn't authorize any mission to Oregon or elsewhere. And need I remind you of the delicacy surrounding military actions on domestic soil?"

"No, sir. I understand, sir. This is an urgent matter—life and death—and I don't have time to explain now. The Commander needs air support ASAP!"

Stephens crossed through the doorway and quietly closed the door. Hearing Lacey's strained voice, she took a chair at the desk.

"You know I can't authorize that," Pierson replied. "Even if I could, it would take hours for armed aircraft to get there by the time the request went up the chain of command and back down again."

"Sir, there has to be something—"

Pierson cut her off. "Lieutenant. There's nothing I can do to get Jim out of this pickle, whatever it is." And then he added, almost as an afterthought, "I wish I could."

Lacey was not surprised by the response or the brevity of the call. It was an unsanctioned mission. The rules about military undertaking action on U.S. soil were very clear—and sacrosanct. In time of emergency, the state governor could call up the National Guard. But unless the Guard was federalized, they remained under state authority.

"That's it," she murmured. Lacey pointed at Stephens. "Get on the phone to the governor of Oregon. Tell her it's urgent—terrorism or whatever. Just get the governor. We need her to authorize the Air National Guard to send an F15 to intercept an attack helicopter shooting up our men. You have the coordinates."

"Armed?" Stephens asked.

"Wouldn't be much use otherwise. Now go!"

She reported back to Jim. "Sorry sir, Pierson wouldn't authorize a sortie. His hands are tied since the mission is off the books."

"Understood Lieutenant—"

The rapid staccato of the 20mm gun swamped out Jim's words.

"Sir," Lacey added. "We're working on a solution. We might be able to get the governor to authorize the Guard to intercept."

"Get on it. We don't have anything to take down that helicopter."

She left the connection open and searched for a contact number for the base commander of the Oregon Air National Guard. She knew the 142nd Fighter Wing flew out of Portland, knew they had a pair of F15 Eagles on alert standby 24/7. She dialed, and after three transfers was connected to the base commander.

"Colonel, this is a priority request. It is a matter of national security. An unknown terrorist group is attacking personnel in the Cascade Mountains near Broken Top and South Sister." She gave the coordinates. "There is a State Police and Sheriff search underway near that location. We have reports that automatic weapons are in use, backed up by an attack helicopter."

"What?" the Colonel replied. He had never heard of military aircraft being used in terrorist actions. "Who did you say you were with?"

Lacey rolled her eyes, she didn't have time for this. "The Strategic Global Intervention Team. We are associated with the DIA."

"Uh huh."

"Look, sir. With all due respect, I have eyes on the ground. Trained and experienced combat soldiers. If they say an attack helicopter is shooting at them, that's what it is!"

"Look, Lieutenant. My pilots and aircraft serve under the authority of the Oregon governor. If she says to launch a pair of Eagles, my pilots are ready. Until then, I don't see how I can help you."

Lacey wasn't ready to give up, not yet. "I understand the chain of authority, sir. I also understand our duty to our brothers and sisters in uniform. Right now you have a couple dozen men and women on the ground in that section of wilderness with nothing more than small arms against a fully armed, military gunship! Sir."

For several long seconds there was no reply. When the

Colonel spoke his voice was even. "I'll phone the governor and relay this information, requesting we send a pair of Eagles to investigate. But mark my words, Lieutenant. If this is a hoax, I'll see you are busted all the way down to private."

"Thank you, sir. This is not a hoax. My people—they need help now. There must be something you can do. Are there any aircraft already in the air?"

Again the line was silent while the base commander considered the request. "I have two Eagles on a training exercise, logging hours. They are over water, near the coastline. I'll have them do a flyby. In the meantime, I'll call the governor."

"Thank you, sir!" She hung up and returned to the satellite phone.

"Commander, are you there?"

Her ear was filled with rapid gunshots and a very deep boom that she knew was an explosion.

Boss Man heard the tinny voice and picked up the sat phone. "I hope you have good news."

"Maybe. The Guard is vectoring a pair of Eagles over your position for a flyby."

"We need more than a flyby!"

"Understood, sir. Working on getting approval from the governor for an armed sortie. Don't know how long that will take."

What Lacey heard was an explosion so loud she thought it was in her office.

The satellite connection went dead.

CHAPTER 38

THE SECOND MISSILE DETONATED very close, showering Boss Man, Homer, and Vashal in rocks and dirt. Jim had dropped the satellite phone as he ducked and shielded his head. It landed hard, breaking the internal electronics.

"Let's go!" he ordered. The pilot had pinpointed their location. They couldn't hang around with high explosive missiles raining in.

The three men dashed for another stand of trees as the Battlehawk flew overhead. Jim wanted to be far away by the time it turned and came back.

They ran hard and fast and made it to the protective cover before being spotted. The Battlehawk fired another missile obliterating their former position.

"Those missiles are pretty accurate," Homer observed.

"Must be guided. Nothing that I know of—maybe experimental."

Jim turned to Vashal. "I lost the satellite phone. Do you still have your radio?"

The Deputy produced it as proof.

"Good. Brief your commander. They will have heard the 20mm gun and explosions. Tell him to call the governor. We need air support, and it can only come from the Air Guard under the governor's authority. Do it now!"

While Vashal was on the radio, Homer and Boss Man fired again at the helicopter as it passed, trying to further distract the pilot from opening up on Peter's hide.

It worked, and the pilot looped around, showing less fear of the damage the small arms might inflict on his aircraft. He came in slower, and stopped to a hover at the far range of the rifles.

Boss Man and Homer fired anyway, the muzzle flashes gave away their location. The pilot aimed the 20mm gun at them and fired. Jim dove to the side and Vashal and Homer ducked, trying to become one with the earth. A line of dirt geysers raced between them.

The SGIT soldiers came up shooting from behind two thick trees. Bullets pinged off the nose and chipped at the reinforced polycarbonate windshield but didn't penetrate. A flash of white light and a smoke stream marked the launching of another guided missile.

"Incoming!" Homer shouted.

The explosion was deafening as the missile detonated 10 feet up on one of the trees, cutting it in two. The top portion toppled over. Wood fragments—some large enough to impale a man—rained outward and down.

"Are you okay Vashal?" Jim shouted, his hearing just about gone, replaced by constant ringing. The deputy was sitting with his back to the tree, arms folded over his head.

"Vashal! You okay?" This time he turned his head and nodded. His lips moved, but Jim didn't understand what he said.

The Battlehawk stayed on station, hovering, watching for signs of activity—of life—but saw none and concluded the targets had been destroyed. Slowly, the helicopter turned, pointed to the large stone outcrop where Peter had been last seen.

A deep double boom arrived a fraction of a second before the pair of F15 Eagles. Jim and Homer both looked up just in time to see the sleek, gray aircraft sweep overhead. The leader and his wingman had been redirected from a maritime interdiction exercise just off the Oregon coast near Florence, being briefed on the new mission inflight. With afterburners on, traveling at Mach 1.2, they reduced throttle and dropped altitude as they came even with South Sister Peak just west of the Tam McArthur Rim. For the pilots, it sounded like another phase to their training. A dry run at an air intercept.

As the Eagles passed the coordinates at 200 feet above ground level, the roar from the engines was incredibly loud.

"Looks like the cavalry has arrived!" Homer shouted as he raised a victorious fist in the air.

The Battlehawk shook violently from the turbulent air in the wake of the high-speed fighters.

"What was that?" the copilot asked.

"An empty threat. Stay on task," the pilot replied.

The F15s banked into a tight turn, gaining altitude and bleeding off speed for a second pass. The leader radioed his flight command. "Blue leader. We are turning for a low-speed pass."

"Roger, Blue Leader."

Peter still cradled his rifle, pressing has back against the hard stone. He didn't know how he could defend himself against the helicopter and missiles. At least the enemy was also staying put.

He wedged most of his body into the cleft in the stone, shielding Diesel as best he could. Peter's spirits lifted when the two jet fighters raced by, but then sank again as they passed, the roar of their engines replaced by the high-pitched whine of the Battlehawk's twin turbines. He cautiously peered around the side of his stone shield and saw the helicopter hovering, pointed at him. He saw the flash as two missiles were fired, and he ducked back, pulling Diesel in tight.

The explosions were deafening. Peter couldn't hear anything for several seconds. Not the whine of the engines, not the thumping of the rotors, not the gunfire. Nothing. Then the silence was replaced by ringing.

He seemed to be engulfed in a cloud of dust. Gravel and fine dirt rained down, but the rock barrier held.

The two laser-guided missiles had impacted the soft earth a couple of feet in front of the stone outcrop, dampening the explosive force of the warheads. Seeing the cover still intact, the pilot started to fly the Battlehawk around to the far side.

Boss Man and Homer opened up again, but the pilot was no longer dissuaded by the impotent threat.

The black, menacing machine slowly came into view to the side the boulder. Peter had sensed its approach. As his hearing gradually returned, he noticed the changing pitch and tone of the rotor thump and engines. And he was ready.

The pilot came in close, wishing to end the mission. The arrival of military aircraft was a bad sign. It would not be long before reinforcements arrived, and he still had to escape.

As the cockpit came into view, Peter raised his .340 Weatherby. Aiming for the crew, he fired. He cycled the bolt, and fired again.

Unlike the assault rifles used by the Guardians and the SGIT soldiers, Peter was shooting a large caliber, heavy bullet.

Intended to dispatch the largest, most dangerous animals on the planet with a single shot, at close range the bullets smashed through the thick Plexiglas canopy—both rounds striking the copilot.

The pilot veered away. Cursing his lack of caution, he would use distance to his advantage, and terminate the target.

Blue Flight completed their turn and was approaching when the missiles exploded.

"Blue Leader. We have live ordinance here: missiles, small arms fire. Unidentified attack helicopter is firing on ground elements. Personnel only, negative on vehicles or heavy equipment. Request instructions."

Flight command came back immediately. "Say again. What are the markings on the attack aircraft?"

"Repeat, no markings. Looks like a Black Hawk but is heavily armed. Aircraft is unidentified."

"Affirmative. You are instructed to harass that bird. Try to drive it off."

"Roger. Be advised that Blue Flight is unarmed. Will try to shake off unidentified aircraft, but suggest command launches the alert aircraft ASAP."

"Affirmative, Blue Leader. Inbound alert flight on its way. ETA five minutes."

Blue Leader and his wingman completed their flyby, attempting to raise the Battlehawk pilot on standard military frequencies. They got no response, and he showed no indication of breaking off his attack. The helicopter had circled to the opposite side of the stone monolith and suddenly retreated.

"Making another pass," Blue Leader announced to his wingman. "I'll get a radar lock, see if he'll bug out."

The Eagles came in again, low and affording ample time to get a lock on the nearly stationary aircraft. If they'd been armed with missiles, either heat seekers or radar guided, it would have been an easy kill shot.

Inside the cockpit of the Battlehawk, the pilot's senses were inundated with a shrill warning of missile lock. His training took over, and he advanced the throttles to the stops, ejecting flares and chaff as he maneuvered his aircraft away. The closest route of escape was over the edge of the Tam McArthur Rim.

Peter watched with relief as the black helicopter fell out of sight.

"Vashal! Get on the radio. Tell your captain we need backup. Have him get everyone here!"

He nodded, and spoke frantically, relaying what was happening. At the command base, they could hear the sounds of the battle but had no ability to see the confrontation. Captain Sheffield had already recalled the hounds and other search teams upon receiving the first message from Deputy Vashal about the attack helicopter. His men were already assembled.

They had rifles and plenty of ammunition. His briefing was direct. Everyone would be armed with a rifle as primary weapon. They would be facing a paramilitary force. No, not Peter Savage—apprehending him was no longer the priority. At this moment their job was to save Deputy Vashal and the two soldiers he was with.

Dispatch relayed the message to the field teams. They would catch up as soon as they could.

A parade of vehicles departed their base camp and headed south, single file on the gravel road. They traveled fast and covered the few miles quickly. Sheffield was in the lead, and he abruptly pulled off into a meadow. This is where they would continue on foot.

Now the sounds of battle were much louder: explosions. Gunfire. And then the roar of jet engines as two aircraft flew over at low altitude.

Sheffield swore he could even see the pilots.

CHAPTER 39

LIKE A PHOENIX RISING from the ashes of death, the black machine climbed above the edge of the cliff. It kept rising vertically, the dual weapon platforms aimed at Peter.

The F15s circled back when they saw the helicopter had been spooked but didn't flee. "He's probably figured out we're not armed," Blue Leader said to his wingman.

The Battlehawk was lining up on Peter, working to gain enough elevation to ensure a clear flight for the missiles.

Blue Flight started their pass. "Let's see if this guy wants to play chicken," Blue Leader said.

"I'm on your six," replied his wingman.

The first Eagle came screaming in from behind the Battlehawk. Blue Leader had to get his approach right. Too close and a mid-air collision was the likely outcome—too far away and the turbulent jet wash would have negligible effect on the helicopter. Blue Leader got his line and held the stick expertly, pulling up and applying throttle as he passed over the

Battlehawk. His wingman was right behind, also pulling up.

The helicopter shook violently and was shoved up and down, side to side. At the moment the first Eagle streaked passed, the pilot pressed the fire switch. But the guidance lock had been broken during the severe turbulence. The missiles detonated short.

If the helicopter pilot had not been extremely skilled, he may not have regained control of his aircraft. As it was, he struggled with the cyclic and collective until the air stilled again. He maneuvered back into position, knowing it would take time for the fighters to circle back. And when they did, they would likely approach head on.

"Blue Lead to Blue Two. What's your fuel status?"

"Maybe another five minutes."

"Okay Blue Two, let's buzz this guy again. I'll try to shave it even closer."

The two Eagles lined up and came in again, one behind the other as before.

The pilot of the Battlehawk doubled-checked his weapon systems. Still plenty of 20mm rounds, and the targeting reticle was functioning. He held his ground in a stationary hover, allowing the jets a clear shot at the flyby.

He was ready.

He wanted it.

The lead Eagle came in—straight, level flight. The Battlehawk pilot lined up the sight, suppressing the urge to fire. He was calculating the distance, the speed of approach… waiting for the pilot to be fully committed… Now! He depressed the button and a stream of 20mm shells lanced out like a tongue of fire. The rounds punched holes through the middle and rear of the lead F15, destroying fuel and hydraulic lines, shattering turbines blades. The two massive engines ground to a halt, black smoke streaming behind the aircraft.

Blue Two saw all this, knew what had happened, and cursed. He pulled up and to the right, evasively escaping the same fate.

"Blue Leader is hit! I see a chute. Aircraft is lost. Aborting mission. Confirm, over."

The reply came back over the radio. "Aborting mission. Confirmed. Clear the area, return to base. Will dispatch a recue bird. Tracking beacon is reading strong."

As Blue Two gained altitude and turned north, he tipped his wing to improve the view below and to the west. A billowing cloud of smoke and yellow-orange fire marked the location where his flight leader's aircraft had slammed into the ground near the base of South Sister. He just glimpsed a parachute fluttering into the forest canopy before he lost sight of the crash scene.

Blue Two returned his attention to the pale blue sky, wondering what in hell was going on, just as a pair of Eagles rocketed passed his aircraft. And these F15s had Sidewinder missiles hanging under their wings.

Peter's hope had drained with the loss of the Eagle and the sudden departure of the second jet. He pushed his body up, felt the burning pain from the lacerations clawed into his limbs, the ache in his abdomen and chest.

"Come on, Diesel!" His companion looked up, but the eyes lacked the will to move. "Diesel, let's go! Come on boy!" He whistled as best he could through dry lips. "We have to go!" Slowly the dog rose and stepped forward on unsteady and trembling legs. Peter forced his feet to move. They felt like limp weights, and every step seemed to require an inordinate amount of energy.

He moved forward, down slope, Diesel by his side.

They made it only 10 feet when Nadya and Marcus

opened up. Bullets flew high, but he heard the rifles and knew the shooters where in front of him. He couldn't flee in that direction, he'd be walking right into them. He dove to the side, in front of the rock barrier, his rifle and scope slamming hard into the ground. He squirmed his way to a slight depression. Diesel followed him and collapsed at his side.

At the same instant an explosion blasted away the earth where he and Diesel had just been. The Battlehawk was back.

Peter closed his eyes. *How many more missiles do they have?*

With the F15s gone and the Battlehawk blasting out Peter's hide, Richard Nyden ordered his squad to engage Boss Man and Homer. The Guardians spread out in an attempt to flank their enemy.

Boss Man and Homer fired at every target of opportunity, but the enemy was skilled and moved in short dashes from one cover to the next.

"Running low on ammo," Homer exclaimed.

Boss Man squeezed off a couple shots to his left. "Fall back!" he ordered.

With Deputy Vashal between them, the two SGIT warriors retreated, firing to slow their pursuers. They worked back 50 meters and found themselves at a group of boulders large enough to offer limited, but welcome, protection.

"Vashal, time to check in. Where's our backup?" Boss Man said.

The deputy keyed the radio. To his surprise, he connected directly with Captain Sheffield rather than the dispatcher.

"Vashal! What's your location? I've been trying to reach you."

"Sorry, Cap. I didn't hear the radio squawk with everything going on here. We're retreating toward you. Hold on…"

The deputy conferred with Jim who checked his GPS and

gave the coordinates to Vashal.

"Copy that," Sheffield replied. He was holding a GPS unit and entered the coordinates. "We're close, maybe a mile away."

"Roger that. Hold on Cap, someone here wants to talk to you." Vashal handed the radio to Boss Man.

"Captain Sheffield, my name is Commander James Nicolaou." Jim finished the introduction and exchanged a few more words with Sheffield. He concluded with "Thank you, sir," and gave the radio back to the deputy.

"Vashal, your Captain has a lot of men not far away. That's good for you. We," Jim cocked his head toward Homer, "have a friend we need to rescue. He's up on that ridge, where the helicopter was attacking."

Vashal put it all together. "You came for Peter Savage, didn't you."

Jim nodded.

"He's a cop killer. He murdered another deputy, a friend of mine."

"I don't think he did; he wouldn't do that. I suspect these people who are trying to kill you and me—and also Peter—are the ones who murdered your fellow officer. But right now that's not the point. We can sort all that out later."

Vashal stared back at Jim, his face firm.

Jim continued, "Homer and I are going to provide covering fire. You run like hell back that direction. You'll find Captain Sheffield at the next meadow down the slope—it's not far. Have him split his men into two squads, one on either side of the meadow. If any of the enemy follows you—well, your Captain will know what to do."

"Where are you going?" Vashal asked, although he thought he knew the answer.

"To bring home a friend."

"Green Leader, I have visual confirmation. The bogie is engaging ground targets. Request permission to engage."

A moment later confirmation was received.

"Roger, this is Green Leader. Going in."

The two F15s circled around the battle site, preparing to line up for the kill. As they passed the Battlehawk, the pilot turned his head, following the lead aircraft and fired the 20mm gun.

"Bogie is firing at us Green Leader," came the warning from his wingman. From his position, the arc of the tracers falling underneath the first F15 was clearly visible.

"Roger Green Two. Pull up and break right. Let's get a lock on this guy."

Green Leader advanced the throttles, turned, and climbed. The gun slung underneath the helicopter could not shoot upwards at a steep angle.

The maneuver away from the bogie had taken the fighters out of missile range and firing position, and the Battlehawk pilot knew that. He circled his aircraft around the target, maintaining a greater distance. He suspected the missile had fallen short. Peter had been on the run when he fired.

The Weatherby roared, the bullet chipping the front windscreen in front of the pilot. But the impact was off, and even if the bullet had penetrated it would have missed the pilot. Peter had no time to correct his aim before Nadya and Marcus returned fire. Bullets raked across the dirt at the edge of his depression.

"Green Two. Come up on my nine so your seeker won't lock on my tail."

They were closing fast.

The Battlehawk was steady and had locked the missile laser-guidance system.

Green Leader fired a Sidewinder heat-seeking missile, and

a heartbeat later Green Two also fired.

The twin missiles streaked at supersonic speed, making minute course changes to fly unerringly at the blazing hot helicopter exhaust.

The Battlehawk pilot had his finger on the switch, ready to depress—

Twin explosions thrust the cockpit into a forward roll. The pilot struggled with the controls as he felt his aircraft tumbling through space. And then it crashed in a ball of fire and secondary explosions, incendiary debris raining over the Tam McArthur Rim.

CHAPTER 40

EASTERN DRAINAGE OF BROKEN TOP
APRIL 22

AS THE PAIR OF F15 EAGLES circled overhead, smoking cinders of metal, fabric, and polymer dotted the land around Peter. A piece of burning rubber the size of a marble landed on his arm, melting the synthetic fabric on a path to flesh. He slapped it with his hand to extinguish the fire.

The sound of the twin explosions was replaced by the grinding and rending of metal as the helicopter shattered on impact, the rapidly spinning rotors disintegrating on contact with earth, scattering more debris across the crash site. As the seconds ticked by, that, too, subsided.

The reports from multiple guns reached Peter's ears. It was coming from hundreds of yards down slope. He didn't know who was fighting—maybe law enforcement was engaging whoever was out to kill him?

Peter raised his head to search for the assailants he knew to be to his front. A handful of bullets scraped across the gravel only feet away. Still there.

"We move forward, one at a time," Nadya ordered Marcus. She went first. Jumping to her feet and sprinting forward in a crouch while Marcus continued to fire selectively, just enough to force Peter to stay down.

And then Marcus ran forward while Nadya provided covering fire. Peter slid back into the depression, focusing down the slope, seeking a way out. There wasn't one.

He squirmed back to the lip of the depression and aimed his rifle. The crosshairs settled across Nadya's chest as she ran toward Peter. He squeezed the trigger, felt the recoil, and then immediately settled the scope again where she should be laying. Only she was still running. He pulled the bolt back and then forward, ramming home the last cartridge, and fired again.

This time Nadya went down, but not because she suffered a bullet wound. His rifle was no longer shooting true.

She had taken cover behind a cluster of fir trees. With a wave of her arm, she motioned Marcus forward.

Rather than taking time to reload the rifle, Peter cast it aside and shouldered the shotgun. The two assailants were just outside the scattergun's range, but not for long if they continued to advance.

Nadya noted the lack of rifle fire and thought maybe Peter Savage was out of ammunition. Marcus passed her position, aiming for a group of bushes, when the riot gun roared.

Peter fired once, twice—a volley of buckshot spread in a deadly circle as it flew at Marcus. The pattern opened up too much and by the time the shot careened off the ground it had lost nearly all its effect.

Nadya fired and rose to her feet, advancing quickly, sensing the end was near. She had angled up the slope about 20 meters and now she had a vantage looking down at Peter. She fired twice more, and ordered Marcus to advance.

Peter fired rapidly, pumped the next round into the

chamber, and fired again. There was no time to aim—point, shoot, repeat.

He fired the last shot shell when Marcus was only 50 yards out. Still a considerable distance for buck shot, though a pellet managed to strike Marcus in the thigh. He stumbled, but stayed on his feet.

Marcus aimed and fired, the bullet striking the ground in front of Peter and ricocheting high. Peter edged back into the depression, grabbing for the pistol holstered on his hip.

"Enough!" Nadya shouted. Peter froze, and looked up at the woman, immediately recognizing her. She was close now, within a stone's throw. She could easily shoot him if he made a threatening move.

Slowly, Peter removed his hand from the Colt .45 pistol, and raised them in surrender.

Marcus hobbled in closer and Nadya joined him.

"Are you alright?" she asked. Marcus looked at the wet stain on his pant leg. It was dark, venous blood. The shot hadn't exited the back of his leg.

"A field dressing will take care of it. I can walk."

Together they approached Peter. "Hands up! On your knees!" Marcus shouted.

Peter complied, wincing as he kneeled. Diesel was by his side, but unwilling to stand. Still, he issued a deep, guttural growl that caused Marcus to hesitate.

"Get your dog under control before I shoot it!" he yelled.

"Diesel, quiet."

Nadya looked at Marcus, his face a mask of fear as he lost sight of Peter, focused instead on the dog.

"Marcus! We still have a job to do."

The pair drew nearer, rifles pointed at their mark. "What do you want?" Peter said.

"Yesterday, it was to kill you," Nadya answered.

"And today?" If they had wanted to kill him, they would have done so by now he reasoned.

"Someone wants to talk to you. They have questions, I suppose."

"What if I don't want to talk?"

Nadya shrugged. She and Marcus were very close now. "That's not my concern."

"And my dog? He needs care, medical attention."

Marcus shouldered his rifled and aimed at Diesel. "The dog can't answer questions—"

"Stop!" Nadya shouted.

"We should kill them both. I don't care about the bonus. Let's get on with it before the police find us."

Peter still held his hands high. "Why is the Israeli government so afraid of the *Liberty* file being made public? What is in that file that is so important today?"

Gunshots reverberated from below, reminding Nadya that they could not continue to talk indefinitely. "I'm not the person who can answer your questions."

Peter saw something in her face, a hint of concern, maybe, or was she questioning her mission directives? "You know don't you?" Peter said.

"Know what?"

"The *USS Liberty* was attacked in 1967. A lot of innocent seamen died in that attack. We were allies!"

"Yes, I know how history records that tragic event," Nadya answered, her eyes conveying a measure of sorrow. As a Mossad operator, she had known loss, as many Israelis had.

"Is that all it is to you? A tragedy to be forgotten?" Peter's voice raised in genuine anger.

"No, not to be forgotten," she answered to Peter's surprise. Then she turned again to Marcus. "Lower your weapon."

Marcus was anxious, refusing to lower his rifle. His body

appeared tensed, his jaw line tight and hard. "Nadya! We have to shoot them and get out of here!"

"Put the gun down, Marcus," she said in a soothing voice. It was a request, not an order.

"What are you talking about?"

"Marcus, I said—"

Peter sensed an opening. "I'll go with you. But first promise you'll stop at a vet clinic and drop off Diesel so he can be cared for."

"You're in no position to bargain." Marcus spat out the words.

"If you kill me, that file will be released to all the major media outlets."

"You're bluffing," Marcus said.

Peter grimaced as he shifted his weight, his knees objecting strenuously. "My attorney has a copy."

"Then we'll kill him, too. Isn't that right, Nadya?"

She appeared to be studying Marcus. He was not the calm, calculating Mossad agent that she was. She had assumed all agents passed the same training and exhibited the same cunning and deadly skills that she possessed. But Marcus was an amateur. He was crumbling under the pressure.

"Lower your weapon, Marcus."

"Not until he's dead."

Nadya saw his grip tighten on the rifle, his eye squinting. "No!" she yelled.

Boom!

Marcus dropped the rifle, his mouth hung open as he looked upon Nadya in disbelief. She pulled the trigger a second time, the bullet blasting through his chest. His eyes slid closed as he collapsed, unmoving.

Peter was stunned, still holding his hands up. Nadya swung the barrel toward him.

"Do what you will with that file. I will not be responsible for any more killing over it."

"Then I may go?"

"Go! Before I change my mind."

Peter lowered his hands and rose to his feet. Then he cradled Diesel in his arms. When he looked up, Nadya was almost out of sight.

She was running for the Tam McArthur Rim.

CHAPTER 41

THE SPORADIC GUNFIRE HAD CEASED at the same time Nadya released Peter. He completed a couple dozen strides, stumbling more than running, when he heard a familiar voice call out. "Peter! It's Jim!"

The initial confusion soon gave way to a feeling of relief. With Homer by his side, Commander Jim Nicolaou stepped into the open where Peter could see him.

"I can't begin to tell you how glad I am to see you," Peter said, barely restraining his emotions. "Diesel's been mauled pretty bad. We have to get him to a vet."

Jim nodded. "We will. First, where are your weapons?"

Peter nudged his chin indicating up slope. "Near that large boulder."

Homer took off in a jog. "It's safe now. We captured three of the gunmen. They're being held by the State Police and Sheriff Deputies. They had a large manhunt searching for you."

"Figured they would."

As Jim filled Peter in on the details, the murdered deputy, and the theory Lacey was building that there was a conspiracy involving Speaker Schuman, plus the urgent call to the Oregon Air National Guard, Homer arrived back with Peter's rifle and riot gun.

Against the backdrop of high-performance jet engines from Green Flight, Jim re-established communication with Lacey. It was awkward, having to use Vashal's radio and being patched through from the State Police dispatcher. His first request was to maintain the air cover as long as possible just in case another attack helicopter arrived on scene.

"Given the circumstances with the loss of Blue Leader, I don't think there will be any reticence to provide an air cap all day," Lacey replied. "The search and rescue helicopter is on the way to recover the pilot. The Air Guard is reporting a clean ejection. Sounds like the pilot will be fine."

"Request the Guard dispatches a crash investigation team here ASAP. There may be some useful evidence in the wreckage of the attack helicopter."

"Yes, sir. Were you able to identify the type of aircraft?"

Jim thought for a moment, picturing the helo hovering and firing rockets and the 20mm gun. "It was a prototype Battlehawk, armed with missile pods on both sides of the aircraft and a gun slung underneath the cockpit."

"I'll let the base commander know. If nothing else, they should be able to recover serial numbers from major portions of the airframe and, hopefully, the engines. That information will point to the owner. I can't image there are many of these aircraft outside the direct control of the Army and Marine Corps."

Jim signed off and then turned his attention to Peter. He was sitting, with Diesel lying motionless at his feet. Homer had shed his pack and was completing a preliminary medical examination.

He finished applying a hemostatic gel to Peter's arm and legs to encourage blood clotting then turned his eyes up to his commander. "Nothing major, no bullet wounds. Bruising and lacerations. Several will need stitches."

"Blood loss?" Jim asked.

Homer shook his head. "Should be okay."

"We need to get Diesel off the mountain and into care," Peter said.

Jim squatted and carefully examined Diesel, gently raising first one leg, then another. The dog's chest and face were plastered with drying blood. He grimaced at what he saw. He looked to Homer, and nodded his head almost imperceptibly, but Homer didn't miss the unspoken message.

Jim stood and offered a hand to help his friend to his feet. Peter was unsteady, his eyes unfocused.

When Homer stood, he had Diesel snuggled in his arms, cradling the dog's body so that the legs and head would not flop as he marched down the slope.

Anticipating Peter's next question, Jim offered a preemptive explanation. "The fastest way out is to hike back to the road and evac using the emergency vehicles. I'll ask the State Police to radio for a civilian air ambulance."

Exhaustion and dehydration were beginning to set in as the adrenaline rush wore off, and Peter suddenly felt extremely fatigued. He nodded, choosing not to waste the energy to form words.

The trio covered a couple hundred yards in silence. Even Diesel was still, the tremors having ceased as his body was slowly succumbing to shock and blood loss.

They met the law enforcement contingent, about equal numbers of Oregon State Police and Deschutes County Sheriff Deputies, who had a dozen guns trained on the three surviving assailants, hands on their heads. Their camouflage uniforms made them look like American soldiers, but Peter knew differently. He approached in silent apprehension, flanked by Jim on his left and Homer on his right.

As they closed the distance, a lone State Trooper stepped forward. He stopped right in front of Peter.

With hands on his hips, the Trooper spoke. "You must be Peter Savage."

Three nodding heads was his reply. Peter made note of the nametag above the Troopers breast pocket. "Officer Sheffield..."

For an uncomfortable moment, neither man spoke. Peter expected to be handcuffed and taken into custody; he hoped Jim could persuade them to get Diesel into medical care first. Then, Peter would gladly cooperate with the authorities.

Captain Sheffield spoke, breaking the silence. And his words were the last thing Peter expected to hear.

"Let's get you out of here. It's been a helluva day."

In another place, another time, Peter would have smiled.

Sheffield shouted over his shoulder. "Vashal! Give Mr. Savage a hand. Looks like he's taken quite the beating. He could use some help."

Deputy Vashal presented himself, standing to the side of Captain Sheffield. He extended his hand in greeting. Peter accepted it, still not fully understanding the situation.

"I thought you'd arrest me," he said.

"Maybe later, we'll have to see," Sheffield replied. He narrowed his eyes as if he was looking into Peter's soul. "Yesterday, any of these men would have shot you on sight. But Deputy Vashal reported the battle that transpired here. Seems you're not the criminal mastermind we thought you to be."

"We need a medevac," Jim said, his voice communicating a sense of urgency.

Hearing the words, both Vashal and Sheffield scanned Peter from head to toe again, this time noticing the degree of injuries.

Then Sheffield took in Diesel for the first time.

"That your dog?" Sheffield asked.

"He's my friend."

The Captain's features softened as he examined Diesel. "I'm rather partial to dogs myself. Have two, a pit bull and a Shar Pei."

He turned to Vashal. "Get ahold of dispatch. Tell them we need an air ambulance ASAP. We'll meet them at Mount Bachelor, the main parking lot."

Then he addressed Jim. "Commander, I suggest we go. We have vehicles at the road."

Vashal finished on the radio and then wrapped an arm around Peter. Jim was on the opposite side. Together, they moved as fast as possible down the slope, aiming for the gravel road to the west.

Homer was jogging, leading by only a few steps. Holding Diesel as still as possible, he sensed time was of the essence. He had no way of knowing how much of the blood covering the dog was its own. Diesel had become disconcertingly quiet and still, his breathing shallow. Hopefully, they still had time.

For his part, Peter accepted the pain that seemed to be everywhere at once—his groin, his abdomen and chest, both arms and legs. But all he thought about was Diesel. The dog had stood by him, ever loyal, guarding his front and back.

Without slowing, Peter said what was weighing on his mind. "You've got to get him to the helicopter."

Jim understood who Peter was referring to. "We will. The road is just ahead. Ten minutes to the highway, and another three minutes to the parking lot. The air ambulance will be waiting there."

The trio pressed onward rather awkwardly, trying to synchronize their steps. Peter stumbled, pulling Vashal and Jim down with him. The air expelled from his lungs with a grunt as he hit the ground. Two pair of hands grabbed hold of Peter's clothing, attempting to pull him to his feet.

Homer heard the commotion, and stopped, turning back to his commander. He stood there, waiting for the trio to get their feet under them and moving again.

Peter glimpsed Homer and Diesel as he struggled for balance. "Go!" he shouted.

Homer shot a questioning glance to Jim. "Go ahead! Get the dog on the medevac!"

Vashal questioned Jim. "Sir, that helo is for Mister Savage."

Before Jim could offer a rebuttal, Peter reached out and latched a hand on Deputy Vashal's shirt. "Diesel saved my life. Get him on that ambulance. Please!"

Vashal's jaw dropped at the visceral response. He stood there speechless. Jim wasn't surprised at all. He tipped his chin to Homer. "Move it soldier! That dog is your priority. Get him on the helo pronto!"

"Yes, sir!" Homer turned, pulling the 70-pound canine to his chest, and sprinted for the road.

CHAPTER 42

HOMER WAS OUT OF BREATH as he ran up to the lead truck on the gravel road. A deputy was holding the passenger door open. "Captain Sheffield said I'm to get you to the air ambulance ASAP."

Homer gently laid Diesel on the seat, and conducted a swift examination. Fresh blood was oozing from several lacerations on the dog's neck and chest. Homer tore open another packet of hemostatic gel and spread it over the wounds. He scooped up Diesel, then sat and cradled the battered animal on his lap.

"Hand me those compresses," he instructed the deputy. Homer applied pressure to stop the bleeding, but the lacerations were too numerous and lengthy to cover all of them.

The deputy stomped down on the accelerator, sending a plume of dust and gravel into the next vehicle in line. He kept his focus on the rutted and bumpy road, both hands gripping the steering wheel tightly. Twice, the pickup fishtailed as it came into tight turns too fast. Somehow, the deputy managed to stay on the road and avoid sliding sideways into trees or boulders.

The bumps and jostling—some severe enough that Homer hit his head on the roof liner—seemed to have no effect on Diesel. The canine appeared to be unconscious and unresponsive. Homer placed a hand on the dog's chest, and thought he felt a heartbeat, but he couldn't be certain. "How much farther?"

The deputy stole a quick glance sideways before returning his attention to the road. "Not far now. Maybe another five minutes."

Homer had enough advanced first aid training to recognize that severe hypovolemic shock due to excessive blood loss had set in. Diesel's battered body was losing the battle. His kidneys and gastrointestinal tract were likely being starved for oxygen as the limited remaining blood was shunted to his lungs and brain. Homer had rendered aid to critically injured men before. Based on his assessment of Diesel's condition, he wasn't sure they had five minutes. "Go as fast as you dare. We're running out of time."

The deputy coaxed more speed out of the truck and still managed to stay on the road. He flipped a switch and the red and blue lights came on along with the siren. They were speeding toward the Cascade Lakes Highway, just ahead. The deputy slowed enough to make the tight left turn then floored it again. Cars on both sides of the highway pulled over, allowing the emergency vehicle to pass. Homer glanced at the dashboard: the speedometer registered 100 miles per hour.

Homer was pitched forward and the tires squealed when the deputy braked for the turnoff to Mount Bachelor then raced again toward the empty parking lot. The air ambulance was already there, the rotor blades turning and the whine of the turbine engine overpowering the roar of the truck engine. Locking up the brakes and spinning the wheel, the deputy drifted the truck sideways and came to a stop near the helicopter.

Homer pushed the door open and rushed to the air ambulance, his arms folded around the pit bull. The EMT accepted the dog without a word—if there was any surprise, he didn't show it. Captain Sheffield must have radioed ahead and made it clear that this was not going to be a routine transport. Homer climbed in and held Diesel on a gurney while the EMT secured the door. The helicopter rose, and as soon as the pilot had sufficient altitude to clear the trees, the aircraft was streaking forward toward Bend.

The EMT placed a stethoscope against Diesels chest. "Pulse is faint and rapid." He reached into a compartment and removed an IV bag. It took some searching to find a vein that he could use, but soon saline fluid was dripping into Diesel's body. It would help to raise his blood pressure and buy some time, even if only a few minutes.

With the movement that had occurred, Diesel's wounds started bleeding again, the compresses were bright red and some looked to be nearly saturated. While the EMT was monitoring heart rate, Homer ripped open a packet of sterile bandages and laid several over the chest wounds. Then he gently lifted Diesel while the EMT wrapped a roll of wide gauze around the canine's chest to secure the bandages.

Suddenly the helicopter started to slow and then hover. Looking out the side window, Homer saw they were setting down in another parking lot. *Glad the parking lot isn't packed with cars*, he thought. As the air ambulance touched down with a bump, Homer noticed the sign above a wall of windows— Animal Emergency Center.

The EMT thrust open the door and Homer slid out. He once again cradled the red pit bull, laying the IV bag on top of the dog. Ducking his head until clear of the rotors, he dashed for the door, already held open by a woman wearing dark blue scrubs. "This way!" someone shouted, and Homer ran toward the voice. Three women were already in the surgical suite, waiting for him. They all wore white surgical masks and latex gloves.

One woman stepped forward. "I'm Doctor Kumar. This is Alicia and Courtney. They'll be assisting."

Homer nodded. "Jesper Mortensen."

"Your captain called and told us to expect you—this dog was in a fight?"

"Yes, it was bad." He didn't see any reason to go into details.

"Just lay him on the table," Doctor Kumar instructed. As Homer did so, Alicia lifted the IV bag and hooked it on a stand. Doctor Kumar proceeded to check the heart beat while Courtney replaced the IV with a fresh bag. Homer stood back, out of the way.

Suddenly, Kumar shouted, "Cardiac arrest!"

Both techs jumped into action. One prepared a defibrillator while the other began CPR. Doctor Kumar grabbed Diesel's snout, gave three quick puffs, and then reached for the defibrillator pads, placing them on either side of Diesel's chest. "Clear!"

A brief convulsion marked the electric shock. Doctor Kumar placed her stethoscope against the dog's chest. She listened intently, moving the diaphragm as she concentrated. "Pulse is faint and rapid. Breathing is shallow. I'm not picking up any fluid in his lungs. Administer Vasopressin and insert a breathing tube; I want him on oxygen. Get his blood typed and a transfusion started. We have to get some blood back into this guy before he goes into cardiac arrest again."

Courtney gently grasped Homer's arm. "You should wait in the lobby, sir."

He nodded, looked at Diesel once more, then turned and left.

⊕

About six miles away, Peter was wheeled on a gurney into the emergency center at St. Charles Hospital. En route down from the mountains, the Sheriff's SUV was met by an ambulance dispatched from Bend. Sheffield, Vashal, and Commander Nicolaou escorted the gurney down the hallway to an examination room.

When the ER doctor entered, his attention was immediately drawn to the armed escort. "Would someone mind telling me what's going on? Is this patient a threat to my staff?"

"No sir," answered Sheffield, his voice calm and even.

Doctor Prescott exhaled deeply, his brow knitted. "All three of you may wait in the lobby."

Jim remained rooted in placed, his hands relaxed by his side. Sheffield and Vashal followed his cue.

"I said—"

"We heard you, Doctor Prescott," Jim answered, pre-empting the objection about to be issued. "Mr. Savage is under our protection. We will wait at his side while you treat his injuries."

Not easily intimidated, Prescott eyed Jim, taking in his uniform and shoulder insignias. He also noticed the rifle slung over Jim's shoulder, muzzle pointed down, magazine removed from the receiver, as well as the large pistol in a tactical holster at his thigh.

Jim stood straight and tall, never blinking.

"Nurse!" Prescott called, and then moved past Jim to begin his examination of Peter. First, he conducted a superficial examination of the arm and leg wounds. Satisfied that blood loss was not a life-threatening issue at the moment, he placed his stethoscope against Peter's chest while the nurse measured his blood pressure. Prescott looked up at Jim. "Lungs are clear. Heartbeat is strong."

The nurse interrupted. "Blood pressure is 80 over 55."

The ER doctor placed his hand on Peter's forehead. The skin felt cool and dry. His coloration was slightly pale, but not sufficient to suggest excessive blood loss.

"Start a fresh bag, normal saline. I think he's probably dehydrated. Draw a blood sample and have the lab run a complete analysis."

Doctor Prescott returned his attention to the lacerations, manipulating the deeper cuts between his thumb and forefinger, drawing fresh drops of blood. Peter winced in response. "Sorry about that. Can you tell me where you hurt?"

"Every—" Peter's mouth felt dry, and it took some effort to moisten his tongue so he could enunciate clearly. "Everywhere."

"Can you tell me your name?" Prescott asked.

"Peter. Peter Savage."

The doctor continued his examination, making small talk as he palpated various areas of Peter's chest and abdomen. "Looks like you rolled around with a wild animal," he said. He pushed against the lower ribs. "Does that hurt?"

Peter winced and nodded his head.

Doctor Prescott stood and approached Jim. "The good news is that I don't think he suffered any internal injuries. His ribs are pretty tender, maybe only bruised, but I'll want a chest x-ray to be sure. Also, I recommend a CT scan. There's some bruising on his forehead. Looks like he took a pretty good blow to the head."

Jim nodded. "Whatever you need to do."

"It may help to know what happened to this man."

"It's classified."

CHAPTER 43

THREE DAYS HAD PASSED since Peter and Diesel were rushed out of the mountains. True to his word, Captain Sheffield declined to press charges, although he did confiscate Peter's weapons for ballistic testing. He also cautioned Peter to stay in Bend and remain available should the need arise for further questioning.

After being held at the Animal Emergency Center overnight and well into the next day for observation, Diesel was released to Peter with an upbeat prognosis. Doctor Kumar pronounced the dog lucky to have no broken bones or internal bleeding. Plus, there was no evidence of brain damage—a concern given the extensive loss of blood he suffered—and no internal injuries other than massive bruising. Detectives Colson and Nakano wasted no time in questioning Peter, and he had spent the past day and a half answering their questions. In great detail, Peter had explained how he first encountered the woman—he now knew her name to be Jana Cooke—at the Pinnacle store. He explained the ensuing fight, how Cooke injured the security cop and murdered two bystanders. Fearing others would come for him, Peter explained his plan to flee to the mountains. On his turf, he stood a chance, and without innocent civilians at risk, he would see the fight to the end.

Peter patiently explained that he knew nothing of the murdered deputy. He'd stashed his red Hummer truck alongside the road knowing that if he was being followed, his pursuers would find it quickly. The map he left on Cooke's body was a sufficient clue, he reasoned.

He marked the locations on a topographical map where the bodies of the assailants who had accompanied Nadya could be found. It didn't take long for the Bend Detectives to receive confirmation from the Sheriff that the bodies were exactly where Peter had said they would be. The fact that all were armed except one corroborated Peter's story, which seemed almost unbelievable at times. The State Police crime lab was already running ballistics on the recovered weapons. But without a bullet from the slain deputy, a ballistic match would never happen.

Near the end of the second day of questioning at the Bend Police headquarters, Peter had already recounted his version of events three times. He was tired and feeling the pain from his injuries. The fact that he refused to take the Vicodin, prescribed by Doctor Prescott, added to his misery.

"That's quite the yarn, Mr. Savage," Detective Colson challenged. She decided this was the time to see if his statements would hold together. "You'd have us believe," she motioned with her hand to Detective Nakano, sitting beside her at the table, "that you single handedly took on these trained and armed assassins?"

Peter looked back at her with drooping eyelids and a blank expression. "You know what, Detective? I really don't care anymore. I'm tired, and I feel like I was run over by a truck."

"Seems there's a trail of bodies following you everywhere you go."

"Yeah, I've noticed."

Colson sighed and glanced at her partner. Detective Nakano shrugged. Colson decided to try a different approach. "What I don't get is how you could know that these terrorists—"

"Assassins," Peter interrupted.

"Assassins. How did you know they would follow you into the mountains?"

Colson leaned back and folded her arms across her chest. So far, everything Peter had said held together. They even had the testimony of the Deputies and State Police about the gun battle that had transpired up close to Tam McArthur Rim. Plus the weapons and bodies. And then there was the wreckage of the attack helicopter.

What really bothered Detective Colson, though, was why?

"It's like I told you already. I didn't *know* they would follow me. Look, you have three murders in Bend that I think are related. It wasn't safe for me to stay here. And anyone near me was also in danger."

As Colson thought about the answer, Nikki Nakano picked up the questioning. "Why didn't you come to us with your concerns? Why didn't you turn yourself in and report the murders at the outdoor store?"

"I told you already. You wouldn't have believed me. You'd have locked me up."

"You should have reported—"

Peter cut off Detective Nakano. "Don't give me that!" The frustration and fatigue was clear in his tone. "I did what I did. End of story. Now, I've answered your questions. Check it out. Talk to the law enforcement officers who were there. Talk to Commander James Nicolaou. For Chrissake! A military attack helicopter was shot down there after it tried to blow me up with missiles!"

The two detectives had left the interrogation room, made some phone calls, talked to their captain, and finally returned. Detective Colson placed her hands on the table and leaned in toward Peter. "Okay, Mr. Savage. You can go—for now. Just don't leave—"

"Yeah, I know the drill. Don't leave town. Look, detectives, no disrespect intended—but I've told you everything. I didn't murder anyone. Cooke and the people I shot, that was self-defense."

"Just stay in town, okay?" Colson shot Peter a stern look. She was serious with either three or four murders to resolve, not certain whether she believed Peter that killing Jana Cooke was self-defense. The last thing she needed was to add to that workload with the prime suspect on the run.

"I'm going home," Peter said. "I'm going to have a Scotch— very likely two. Then I'm going to bed."

He did just that, and rested soundly. He woke in the morning feeling better, but still stiff and in pain. He downed a couple ibuprofen tablets with his first coffee. Had it really been only three days since his ordeal and near death?

Peter then checked on Diesel. His companion wagged his tail by way of greeting. Peter rubbed his head, careful not to disturb the ear that had been ripped off and then surgically removed so that only about a quarter of the appendage was still there. While in recovery, Diesel was enjoying a larger than normal portion of cheese and meat as supplements to his kibble.

"Hey boy. Stay here. I'm just going out for the paper." Peter patted Diesel on the head and then closed the door on his way out. He descended the steps to the street level. On a post beneath the mailbox was a holder for the *Bend Bulletin*. With his attention focused on the daily headline, Peter didn't notice the person silently step in behind him.

"I think we should talk," the person said.

Peter froze in his steps. He recognized the voice, but didn't think it possible she could be here. Slowly, he turned and faced her.

"I thought you were gone."

She shrugged. She was dressed in blue jeans and a bulky sweater. Peter couldn't tell if she had a gun in a belt holster underneath the sweater; at least her hands were empty and in plain sight. "Let's go inside."

Peter forced a short, insincere chuckle. "And why should I invite you into my home?"

"Because I have the answers you seek."

CHAPTER 44

PETER LAID THE NEWSPAPER on the counter and then poured a cup of coffee for his unexpected visitor; he slid the mug across the granite countertop to her. She grasped the handle but did not sip. For the first time, Peter noticed her appearance. She was younger than he was, late thirties, with tanned skin, a high forehead, a long and thin face, and dark brown eyes. Her light brown hair was gathered up in a ponytail that went below her shoulders a bit. She was a few inches shorter than Peter, and her physique was lean and muscular, the appearance of someone who worked out regularly.

From the great room Diesel rumbled a guttural growl. It was impossible to mistake the intention behind that primal warning. "It's okay, boy," Peter said, his voice light and soothing.

"How is your dog?' she asked.

"He was badly mauled. But you knew that." His clipped words replacing the civil tone from a moment ago.

The woman nodded, knowing there was nothing she could

say to change what had happened nor assuage Peter's concern for his companion. She decided to move on to business.

"My American name is Nadya Wheeler. I work for the Israeli government—Mossad."

Peter paused, absorbing what he had just heard. Another piece of the puzzle. He tried to downplay his surprise. "I thought as much." Although she had admitted to working for Israel, he had not known in what capacity. "Why didn't you kill me up there? Those were your orders."

She tilted her head to the side. "Yes, they were." She paused, deciding how much to say. "My Hebrew name is Danya. It means judgment of God. I'm not a killer—not like you think."

"Really. And just what do I think?"

Nadya kept her eyes locked on Peter's. "I've killed many people, that is true. But it was always for the greater good. The people I killed deserved to die. They were evil. Terrorists, for the most part. Sometimes those who financed terrorism or gave the orders."

"And that's supposed to make you a saint?"

"Mr. Savage. I do not seek your approval. I accept responsibility for who I am and what I've done. The day will come, no doubt, when I will answer for my deeds. But that is not why I'm here."

"Okay then. Let's get down to business."

"Business," she echoed and lifted the mug to drink. "My superiors believe you have knowledge of a secret file that contains everything related to the 1967 attack on the American ship. The USS *Liberty*."

Peter raised his eyebrows. "And what if I do?" He had his arms crossed, but was already thinking of the weapons within his reach. Kitchen knives, a sealed bottle of wine. Both choices primitive, but still possessing lethality.

"As long as Mossad believes you have those files, they

will hunt you down. Mossad agents are very accomplished assassins."

"I've done pretty well so far."

Nadya pursed her lips. True, Peter had proven to be a capable opponent, but she knew the ways of her agency, knew they would eventually kill him. Realizing intimidation would not work, she decided to tell the truth. "You should understand those were dangerous and unstable times. The nation of Israel was young, and we were surrounded by enemies who sought our total and complete destruction."

"I know something of the history of that era. The Six-Day War. The number of dead and wounded seamen from the *Liberty*." Peter felt his blood pressure rising at the thought of the suffering—men burned from napalm, shot, limbs severed by shrapnel, others drowned as seawater flooded in through the gaping maw created when the Israeli torpedo detonated on the hull plates. "That ship was defenseless. The torpedo boats even machine-gunned the life rafts!"

Nadya looked into his steel-gray eyes. "It wasn't us."

"What do you mean—of course it was. The Israeli air force and navy attacked the *Liberty* for hours. How she remained afloat is nothing short of a miracle."

"I mean, the order did not come from Israeli command. The United States was our ally. Why would our military attack a U.S. ship?"

Peter stared back in silence. He had pondered this very question. The answers remained elusive. Perhaps, once he read the complete file, he would finally know.

"The answer is, we wouldn't. Israel would never attack America."

"But you did."

"Yes! We did. Because—" she hesitated.

"Go on."

"Because we were told to do so… by your President."

Peter's jaw dropped as he stared back at Nadya.

"Think about it," she went on. "Your Admiral ordered planes from your aircraft carriers to intercept, but they were recalled by Defense Secretary McNamara."

Peter's mind clicked into overdrive despite the pain and fatigue he was feeling. "And McNamara was working under orders from President Johnson."

"Yes," Nadya replied.

Peter was searching Nadya for a hint that she was deceiving him, but she remained calm, her eyes looking directly at him, unblinking.

"But why would President Johnson order an attack on one of his own ships?" he asked.

She was nodding her head. "Now you are beginning to think like an agent."

Peter didn't respond, uncertain if it was a compliment or not.

"When I learned that you had knowledge of the *Liberty* file," Nadya said, "I asked myself, why? Why should my team be ordered to kill you because of something that happened in 1967? So, I did some research; made some phone calls. The tragic attack on the *Liberty* is public knowledge. So, I thought, the reason had to be something else. But what?"

"And?" Peter encouraged her to get to the point.

"It seems my government had a secret agreement with the United States. You see, the Six-Day War was planned in advance by our joint militaries. The war was executed with the approval of the United States. Your UN Ambassador—Arthur Goldberg—argued in favor of Resolution 242, which provided Israel international support in seizing the lands captured during the war. Your intelligence agencies provided vital intelligence in the days leading up to the initial pre-emptive air attacks that destroyed the Egyptian air force. American military aid was shipped to Israel in violation of an embargo. And American Special Forces fought on the ground beside Israeli Commandos."

"And your contacts within Mossad told you all this?" Peter said.

"I understand you are skeptical. I would be, too. But I have been a loyal agent for 15 years. I have contacts, friends—yes. They looked into Israeli archives and shared this with me."

Peter shook his head. "I still don't get it. Why would we do this?"

"It seems that President Johnson saw the coalition of Arab countries as an unequivocal threat to the survival of Israel. He believed that together Israel and the United States would have to defeat our neighbors. Remember, your war in Vietnam was escalating then. The American President did not want to fight two wars at the same time.

"He thought that a decisive defeat of the Arab countries was necessary in order to avoid a protracted siege, a state in which Israel was under frequent assault."

"So Johnson colluded with the Israeli government to strike a decisive blow against your enemies, and seize strategic lands in the process."

Nadya shrugged. "It was necessary for the security of Israel."

"But none of this explains why the *Liberty* was willingly sacrificed."

"President Johnson required an incident so brazen that the American public would demand swift and total destruction of the Arab coalition."

"So he orchestrated the attack on the *Liberty*," Peter concluded. "He wanted the ship sunk so he could blame Egypt and enter the war."

She nodded.

Now it made sense to Peter.

"My government depended on American support. Even if our leaders wanted to, they could not defy Johnson's directive." Nadya sipped from her coffee mug again.

Peter was shaking his head, and he raised a hand waving off an imaginary object. "No, that still doesn't work. So what if all that happened? So what? Why would historical events from over a half-century ago be cause for murder today? Why would you be ordered to kill me simply because I might know the truth about U.S.-Israeli relations during the Six-Day War?"

Nadya raised her eyebrows. "Have you not heard the expression? History repeats itself."

Peter stiffened. He had been searching for an explanation in the events surrounding the *Liberty*—it had never crossed his mind that history had only a tangential relationship to the true motivation. "Are you saying that there is a new secret military alliance between the United States and Israel?"

"That is the only logical explanation. A military and political alliance that is modeled on the events of 1967."

"If that's true, then the goal is to start another war, one that will engulf all of the Middle East."

Nadya stared back in silence.

Peter pushed his mug aside and leaned forward on the polished granite surface. He held that position for a long minute of silence, absorbed in thought. A dozen questions were swirling in his mind—all equally unanswerable.

"Do you have evidence of this conspiracy?" he finally asked.

She shook her head. "No. Nothing definitive. David Feldman, our Prime Minister, is a right wing nationalist. He is paranoid that Iran will acquire a nuclear weapon and destroy Israel."

"If Israel attacks Iran, war is assured. But President Taylor may not be eager to commit American soldiers to such a conflict unless Iran is the first aggressor. Taylor supported the nuclear deal with Iran, and the lifting of sanctions."

"The Presidential election is only a few months away. Maybe President Taylor will not win."

The thought sent a jolt of fear through Peter. He knew that Abraham Schuman was very popular. "You think that if Schuman is the next President, he will support a pre-emptive attack from Israel on Iran?"

She crossed her arms. "It's guaranteed, whether Schuman wins or not."

"Why do you say that?" he said, his eyebrows pinched together.

"You know of the Israeli Security Act? A bill passed by your Congress but vetoed by President Taylor?

Peter nodded. "Congressman Schuman claims he has enough votes to override the veto."

"Yes. And what if he does?"

He shrugged indifference. "The bill increases the level of military aid to Israel; I don't see the connection here."

"That bill has a provision requiring that Congress views any act of military aggression against Israel as an act against America. Don't you see? Congress will be required to declare war."

Peter's jaw went slack. "So whether Schuman wins or not, war is virtually assured."

"Once that bill is passed into law, there is nothing to prevent a pre-emptive strike against Iran, which will trigger a retaliatory attack on Israel."

Peter's eyes were wide as realization set in. "We have to expose this plot."

"And who will believe us? All we have is conjecture."

"I have the *Liberty* files."

Nadya shook her head. "If those are historical files, as

you've suggested, there won't be anything there to connect to Schuman and Feldman."

"Then we need proof. We need to go to the media with evidence that uncovers this conspiracy. But how?"

"Trust me," Nadya said with a smile.

Peter cocked an eyebrow. "Really? You want me to trust you—the woman who tried to kill me a few days ago?"

"But I didn't."

Peter recalled her turning her weapon on her comrade and shooting him, just before he would have pulled the trigger.

"What's your plan?"

"Simple," she answered. "I still have my contact. He doesn't know that I'm here, talking to you. All I have to do is place a phone call and say that I have won over your confidence, and I set you up to be captured. They want to question you, find out what you know. I think that will allow us to get close to someone very high up in the organization. Maybe the leader."

"Who's your contact?"

"His name is Richard Nyden. He was leading the squad that attacked you from the other side."

Peter's eyes widened and he shook his head slightly, almost imperceptibly. "The other team was either killed or captured. Only three made it out alive, and I saw them taken into custody. Your contact—Nyden? He's either dead or in jail."

Nadya pulled her mouth back tight. She paced in a circle, thinking. "Okay. Then I reach out to the backup. They'll know Nyden is no longer actively engaged in this mission. My call won't be suspicious."

"You're sure this will work?"

"Yes," she replied.

"So I'm the bait?"

"Of course. There is no other way. But don't worry; I'll be there with you." Her smile didn't relieve Peter's growing fear.

CHAPTER 45

TOGETHER, NADYA AND PETER had spent the previous 24 hours planning and preparing. She would place a call to her alternate contact—a person she was to speak with only if Nyden had been eliminated. She had no name for the alternate, only a number. She wasn't even certain the number would still be active. Certainly, by now the leaders of the organization would have received news that the mission had failed.

Nadya had been well insulated from the organizers—she didn't even know what organization had orchestrated the attacks. Information had been compartmentalized and shared strictly on a need-to-know basis.

"Ready?" Nadya asked. It was early afternoon.

Peter nodded. "Make the call."

She dialed the alternate contact number from memory. After two rings, a person picked up. The voice was masculine. "Pizza and Pipes. May I take your order?"

"I'll have a medium California special, no garlic."

The line went silent for several moments as the other party identified the caller from the code phrase. The voice came back. "You have a status report?"

"Yes," she replied, matter-of-factly. "I have established contact with the package. Are you still paying a bonus for delivery alive?"

Silence again. Nadya imagined the contact was considering the risks of proceeding. "The terms of the contract still apply. How am I to trust you? Everyone was either killed or captured—but not you."

"I'm better than the others. Maybe you should make me an offer?"

"Maybe. But first, you claim you can deliver the package alive. What do you propose?"

Nadya relayed her cover story—how she had followed Peter for a day then intentionally bumped into him on the sidewalk outside his business, striking up a casual conversation. She charmed him, and they met the next day for a coffee. That led to Peter asking her to meet him tonight for drinks.

"I'll have assets there and a cargo van. We'll grab him outside his residence. Make sure you keep him distracted."

Nadya agreed and shared the address and time she was to meet Peter. Then she ended the call. Her eyes caught Peter's. She was confident, in stark contrast to his concern and apprehension. "Relax," she said. "Nothing to do now but wait."

A few minutes after 7:00 p.m. Peter greeted Nadya at his door. He smiled warmly and invited her inside. She was dressed for the cool evening temperature, wearing a light leather jacket with fur collar. The short jacket flared in at her waist, emphasizing her shapely figure.

With the door closed, she silently handed a small note to Peter. *Am being followed. They will snatch you on the sidewalk.*

Don't resist.

Peter nodded and threw the paper into the garbage disposal without making any noise. He expected she was wearing a bug, and her actions so far confirmed that suspicion.

"Let me grab a jacket," he said. Retrieving a tobacco-brown leather bomber-style jacket from the hallway, he added, "Shall we go?"

"Sure. I hope the walk isn't too far. It's chilly."

Peter held the door open for Nadya. "No, not far at all. There's a popular bar just a block away."

They walked side-by-side down the short flight of steps onto the sidewalk. They turned right and completed another half dozen steps when a cloth bag was thrust forcefully over Peter's head. At the same moment, a gun was pushed hard into his back. He felt the steel barrel digging into the soft muscle alongside his spine. A strong hand was clamped over his mouth. It pulled backwards. Peter tried to correct his balance but was tripped. Without sight and with the gun wedged into his back, down he went, landing hard on the concrete. Hands grasped his arms and legs, lifting him up and then heaving him into a van. Or at least he assumed that's what it was from the sound of the side door sliding closed.

He reached for the hood and had his hands slapped away. A cold gun barrel was pressed against his temple. "Leave the hood on," a gruff voice said. Then hands reached inside Peter's jacket and frisked him, checking for a concealed weapon. They removed his phone. "Nothing, boss."

"Who are you and what do you want?" Peter asked.

"Shut up!"

"Where's Nadya?"

He was answered with a perverse chuckle. "Don't worry about your girlfriend. She set all this up. Didn't you, Nadya?"

"Just do what they say, Peter. They have some questions for

you. Cooperate, and you might live to see another sunrise."

The van drove into the night, heading east on Highway 20 toward Burns. The passengers rode in silence. Peter estimated they had traveled for about an hour when the van slowed and turned off the paved highway onto a well-kept gravel road. Potholes and ruts were absent, and the sound of gravel striking the undercarriage was unmistakable.

A few minutes later, the squeal of brakes announced their arrival. Exactly where, Peter had no idea.

The side door slid open, and Peter was yanked out. He stood with his arms firmly clasped by two strong men; a third yanked the hood off and then wanded him with a small metal detector. "Clean, boss," he announced.

"Well, well. Look who we have here." Peter didn't recognize the man standing before him. "Peter Savage. Welcome! My boss has been looking forward to meeting you."

"And who would that be?" Peter asked.

The man smiled. "I'll let him handle the introductions."

"What is this about?"

"Enough chatting." He aimed his eyes at the two men holding Peter and motioned with his head. Then he pivoted and strode to the entrance to a large building.

Peter swung his head from side to side. The night sky was clear, and without any light pollution, the Milky Way was visible. Other than their footsteps crunching upon gravel, there were no other sounds. He estimated they were maybe 50 or more miles outside of Bend—most likely somewhere in the desert of Eastern Oregon as the terrain appeared relatively flat and he could not see any mountain peaks blotting out starlight.

A sign on the door read PRIVATE PROPERTY. NO TRESPASSING. The walls were constructed of concrete blocks and no windows were visible on the forward-facing exposure.

They entered, Nadya and two guards taking up the rear,

and proceeded along a short hallway. Darkened rooms to either side suggested offices or meeting rooms. Near the end of the corridor, the hallway turned a corner to the right and continued a short distance to a double steel door. The doors were pushed open and they entered a dark, cavernous space. Someone flipped on switches and dozens of overhead high-intensity lights clicked on, dim at first, then growing to a brilliant intensity as they warmed up.

Several square steel posts in the central portion of the space supported roof trusses 20 feet up. Roll-up metal doors were located along opposite walls for access by large vehicles.

Peter stood there taking it in. Two M113 armored personnel carriers were parked near the large doors, the rear of each facing the entry he had just passed through. The carriers looked like steel boxes on tracks, painted in tan camouflage. Machine gun mounts were on the top of each, but the guns had been removed.

Yellow tape marked sections of the concrete floor where toolboxes and shelving stacked with parts were located. A forklift was parked off to one side, next to rows of pallets loaded with crates and stretch-wrapped in plastic. Grouped in another area were tools—a lathe, drill press, a horizontal band saw, shear and press brake, and two computer-controlled milling machines.

"Restrain Mr. Savage to one of the posts."

"Yes sir, Mr. Ellison," one of the guards replied. Peter was shoved forward and spun around, his back slammed against the post. With a pistol pointed at his chest, a second guard pulled Peter's hands behind his back and around the post and slipped a FlexiCuff around his wrists, pulling the restraint tight.

"What is this place?" Nadya asked.

"Maintenance shop," Ellison said. "United Armaments owns 10,000 acres of land out here. It's surrounded on three sides by BLM land. Ain't nothin' but sagebrush and jackrabbits for 50 miles in any direction."

"When will I get paid?" she asked. "I'll want proof of the wire transfer to my account."

"Right to business. Okay. When my boss gets here, and is satisfied that you delivered the package, you'll get your money."

"When will that be?"

"You ask a lot of questions. Well, maybe you can answer some questions too."

"Like what? You have Savage. I delivered on my end of the bargain." Nadya was getting a feeling that something wasn't quite right. She'd learned to trust the feeling—like a sixth sense—it had helped her to stay alive through too many close calls in Gaza, Syria, and Iran. She casually walked to the side, away from the center of the group of men.

Ellison tracked her movement. "We'll come back to the package later. Right now, perhaps you can explain to me how my entire team was either killed or captured in the forest. Richard Nyden was very experienced and a capable operator. He's been in my employ for many years and has never failed."

Nadya continued edging to the side. "I lost my team, too: four Mossad agents."

"That's right, you did. And how is that?"

"You sent us in ill prepared," Nadya said. She surreptitiously shifted a hand behind her back. "We should have been better prepared."

Ellison snorted a mocking laugh. "Five Mossad agents plus nine of my Guardians—against one man." His eyes narrowed as he looked at Nadya. "A civilian!"

He paused and regained his composure. "How is it that you—and you alone—managed to slip away?"

"Like I told you before—I'm good at what I do." She felt the grip of her Glock. With her thumb, she flicked off the leather strap holding the weapon securely in its holster.

Ellison snapped his fingers and six guns were suddenly pointing at Nadya. "You're not that good. Raise your hands, slowly."

Reluctantly, she did as ordered, her eyes darting to Peter and then back to Ellison. "What are you doing?" she demanded, continuing to play her role. "We had a deal!"

One of the guards approached and felt behind her back. He roughly snatched the Glock and then ran a hand over her pockets until he found her cell phone, taking that, too.

"Did you really think me so stupid that I'd believe your silly story about how you tricked Peter Savage into asking you out?" He started to laugh. "To be truthful, I've never heard such a corny story. Seriously? You bump into a stranger and a day later he asks you on a date?"

Nadya stared back, hers eyes burning with defiance.

Ellison continued, "I think we know how you escaped from the mountain. You and Mr. Savage, you made a deal, didn't you?"

The ruse was up, and Nadya saw nothing to gain by debating. She remained silent, focusing instead on how to escape.

"Mr. Savage?" Ellison called.

"Yeah, I'm still here."

"My men tell me that you offered almost no resistance when they grabbed you outside your home. Perhaps you were expecting to be captured?"

"Oh, sure. You'd be surprised how often someone stuffs a bag over my head and throws me in a van. The novelty has kinda worn off."

Ellison motioned with his chin and a guard slammed a first into Peter's abdomen. He slid down the pole, doubled over as far as the restraints would allow. He coughed and gagged, trying to suck in air.

With a wave of his hand, Ellison said, "Tie her to the post with her boyfriend."

At the point of a gun Nadya was ushered to the post, and her hands were tied behind her back with a FlexiCuff. The super tough nylon was virtually indestructible, and struggling against the bond was only going to shred her wrists.

"We had a deal!" she shouted as Ellison and his men ambled to the door.

"Kennor, you stay here at the door. No one enters. Understood?"

The man named Kennor nodded and stepped through the doorframe, standing to the side. The rest of the men filed through, with Ellison taking up the rear. He stopped and turned back to his captives. "In 90 minutes Mr. Duss will arrive. Then we will all have a nice chat."

The door closed, followed by a click as the lock was engaged.

CHAPTER 46

ELLISON WAS CONFIDENT—too confident. With Peter and Nadya restrained to the steel post, all they had to do was wait for Claude Duss to arrive on the corporate jet, a Gulfstream G650. The flight from San Jose—a hub for corporate jets for the biggest Silicon Valley corporations—to the test range in Eastern Oregon would be a little more than an hour.

As soon as Ellison received the phone call that Peter had been bagged, he placed the call to his boss. While Peter was being ferried in the van to the desert test range, Duss was riding in the back seat of a limousine, headed for the airport. UA maintained a staff of pilots 24/7, and the G650 was always fueled and ready for flight.

Now, with an hour and a half to kill, Ellison and his mercenaries settled in the rec room, engaged in small talk and big plans of what they would each do with the bonus they expected from Mr. Duss. Not only were they delivering Peter Savage—alive, no less—but also the suspected traitor Nadya

Wheeler.

Several minutes passed in silence after Ellison and his men left the maintenance bay. Finally, Peter was satisfied that no one was returning immediately. Having caught his breath and standing again, he addressed Nadya. "Well, that didn't go as planned."

Nadya sighed. She preferred to save her breath for something important to say.

"I have a plan," Peter said. "Do you have a knife?"

Nadya rolled her eyes, but since they were back to back, Peter couldn't see her expression. "No! I don't have a knife. And they took my gun and my phone. Any more ideas?"

"Okay. Plan B. Slide down the pole and reach into the top of my right boot. There's a Boker folding blade there."

"But how... They ran a metal detector over you. How did they miss it?"

"Ceramic blade and synthetic grip. Almost no metal in the knife." Nadya was slowly lowering herself, back straight against the pole. Working only by feel, she lifted the pant leg and felt inside the top of the leather biker boots. There, her fingers touched one end of the folding knife. Deftly, taking care not to drop it, she lifted the blade from the small sheath.

"Okay, I have it." She pressed up with her legs and slid back up the pole. Peter heard the familiar click as the blade was unfolded and locked into place.

"I'll hold my hands as far apart as I can. Please be careful not to slash my wrists when you cut the nylon cuff."

"I'll do my best." Peter felt her fingers running over his skin as he strained against the plastic tie. And then, with a snap, the tie was severed and his wrists free. Wasting no time, he took the knife from Nadya and cut through the FlexiCuff binding her to the post.

Peter folded the blade and returned the knife to the sheath

inside his boot as Nadya was rubbing the chaffed skin.

"What about the guard outside the door?" she asked.

Peter nodded and hustled over to a large tool chest. He opened one draw after another until he found a suitable bludgeon. In this case, a large combination wrench for one inch bolts. *Crude, but effective*, he thought.

"I wish we had some firearms," Nadya said, keeping her voice low.

Peter hefted the wrench, and then looked toward the two M113 tracked vehicles. "Those have machine gun mounts up top. What do you think they have inside?"

She raised an eyebrow. "Only one way to find out."

The two vehicles looked identical. Peter walked to the back of the nearest one. The wide door was secured with a latch. He raised the handle slowly and opened the door, cautiously at first. Fortunately, the hinges were greased and the door opened silently, assisted by hydraulic springs.

Inside, there were bench seats at each side. Up front was access to the turret and the swivel gun mount. The driver's seat was also up front. Otherwise, it looked like an empty box. Small metal compartments were mounted to the armored walls, but there were no weapons.

Peter was about to exit, when he had an idea. He moved forward, close to the instrument cluster at the front. "Nadya, come here please."

She crouched to avoid hitting her head and joined Peter. "I think this is the radio." He was pointing to a black panel with switches and rotary knobs, and what appeared to be a digital display. "Do you know how to operate it?"

She leaned in closer, running her hand over the controls, as if she was gleaning information by touch as well as sight. "Yes, you are right."

She flipped a toggle switch and the panel lit up. The digital display showed a number that Peter assumed was a radio frequency. Nadya turned a knob to the left, the volume control.

"I'll raise the antenna," Peter said and he scurried outside. The whip antenna was folded down, and it was a simple matter to remove the metal whip from a hook and allow it to go vertical to its full height. He scrambled back inside.

"Is the radio working?"

"Yes, it checks out fine."

"Set it to 156.8 Mhz. That's the international distress channel."

"Yes, that's right. But how do you know that?" Nadya adjusted a dial until the digital display showed the requested frequency.

"I hang out with an interesting crowd," he answered.

She handed the microphone to Peter. "Just press this button to speak."

"Mayday. Mayday. Mayday." Peter released the button and waited for a response. Nothing. He tried again. "Mayday. Mayday. We are in urgent need of help. This is an emergency, over."

A tinny voice answered. "This is the Crook County Sheriff Department. State the nature of your emergency. Over."

Peter handed the microphone to Nadya knowing that a female voice would garner a greater sense of urgency than a male voice. "Tell them where we are and that a fugitive is threatening to blow up the building. Give them my name. Tell them I am wanted by the Bend Police Department. Tell them to speak with Detective Colson."

Nadya looked confused, and hesitated. "Just do it. It's the fastest way to get help here."

Nadya's brow wrinkled as she gathered her thoughts. Before she could speak, the tinny voice came back. "If this is a legitimate emergency, state the nature and your location. If this is a hoax, you are committing a federal crime and will be prosecuted."

"I need help. This is not a joke. There's a man—he says his name is Peter Savage and he is wanted by the Bend Police. He says Detective Colson knows who he is. He's threatening to blow up the building. Please, send help. I am at the United Armaments facility."

"Copy that. State again your location."

"I said *United Armaments*. They operate a facility in Eastern Oregon. I don't know exactly where it is. I was taken here against my will. I'm in a large maintenance facility. There are tracked military vehicles here. I'm using a radio from an armored personnel carrier."

"Copy."

"Stay by the radio," Peter said. "I'm going to try to get a weapon." He exited the tracked vehicle and silently approached the door. He needed to lure the guard inside without raising so much suspicion that the guard called for backup.

He grabbed a handful of smaller wrenches from the toolbox and slid beside the door, his shoulder against the concrete-block wall. Satisfied he was ready, he dropped a wrench from waist high. It hit the floor with a metallic clang.

Peter waited several seconds, but nothing. The double steel doors were sealed well around the edges, no doubt to reduce the sound of mechanics working on vehicles so as not to disturb the people in the front of the building.

He dropped another wrench. This one bounced off the floor and into the base of the steel door.

Three seconds later the latch turned and the door opened. The first thing Peter saw was a hand holding a Beretta semiauto pistol clearing the edge of the door. That was his cue. He rammed his body into the door with all the force he could muster. There was an audible thud as the steel slammed into a body or head just before the door closed on the arm. The crack of bone sounded clearly.

Crushed between the edge of the door and the frame, the guard dropped the firearm. "Ahhh!" he moaned.

Peter scooped up the Beretta and yanked the door open on the stunned guard. "Inside."

With the gun pointing at his face, the guard complied, cradling the broken arm against his chest. Peter grabbed him by the collar and spun him around, then closed the door.

"On the floor. Face down."

The guard complied, offering no resistance as Peter frisked him one handed. He removed his phone and two spare magazines.

"On your feet."

"You broke my arm! I can't get up."

"On your feet. Or I'll break your legs, too." Peter kept the gun trained exactly at the man's chest while maintaining a distance of several feet.

Slowly, he rose to his feet. His face grimaced in obvious pain. "Over there," Peter said, motioning toward the second armored personnel carrier, or APC.

At the rear of the APC were two massive steel tow loops—essentially round steel eyes used for the purpose of fastening chain to tow another vehicle.

"Sit down," Peter ordered. The guard settled to the floor, still holding his broken arm at chest level.

"Nadya, I need your help." Two seconds later she was at the hatch and hopped to the concrete deck. "Over there, in that tool chest, is a roll of wire. Grab it. And find some wire cutters and duct tape."

She nodded and jogged to the chest. Peter heard drawers open and close, but never removed his focus from his prisoner. A minute later Nadya returned, displaying her spoils.

"Good. Now, bind his ankles with wire. Make sure it's tight. And I don't care if it hurts."

With efficient movements, she bound the ankles and knees of the guard, wrapping three layers of wire for good measure.

"Okay. Take his good arm and wire his wrist to the tow loop."

Nadya grabbed the good arm, but the guard resisted her efforts. "Raise your arm," she said, her voice venom. "Or I'll break it and you can have a matching pair."

Slowly he relaxed and allowed Nadya to secure his arm to the tow loop and place a length of tape across his mouth. His eyes were narrowed and dark; his jaw set hard. But his focus never left the barrel of the 9mm.

CHAPTER 47

NADYA RETURNED TO THE RADIO, making certain the Crook County Sheriff Department was mobilizing. Finally, dispatch told her they found the location of the test range, but given the time needed to organize a hostage rescue team and the distance they would have to travel, it would take almost two hours for help to arrive.

She lowered her head. "Yeah, well, guess I'll just have to keep everyone entertained until you get here." She signed off, and stood at the open hatch. Peter was examining a pallet stacked with medium-sized wood boxes. She looked to their prisoner. He appeared to still be securely fastened to the steel tow loop.

With a sigh, she approached Peter, keeping her voice low once she was next to him. "Law enforcement says ETA is two hours."

Peter didn't break his concentration on the crates stacked before him. They were banded with steel straps. Each a little under a foot tall by a foot wide by 18 inches deep.

"You heard me?" Nadya prodded him. "Two hours." She checked her watch. "Ellison and his men will be back in 60 or 70 minutes, maybe sooner."

"Yep. And we'll be ready for them." He hefted one of the wood crates and set it on the concrete floor. Then he turned to a tool chest and removed a pair of metal shears, quickly snipping off the metal band securing the lid in place. He slipped the shears into a rear pocket.

The top lifted off. Peter was surprised it wasn't screwed in place, but then again the steel bands seemed to do a fine job.

Inside were two metal boxes, each standard GI-issue-olive-drab in color. Peter thought they were ammo cans for .50 caliber ammunition. But Nadya knew otherwise.

"Fuzes," she said. "But what good are fuzes? We don't have any explosives."

Peter smiled, popped open the metal lid, and removed one of the conical devices. It was unpainted. The bare, rust-free metal suggested aluminum or stainless steel. Peter placed the fuze in his pocket.

Nadya raised an eyebrow. "Did you find explosives while I was on the radio?"

"Sort of." He pointed at another stack of pallets, but all she saw were more crates.

"Okay. Where?"

Peter led her to the stacked goods, and then around to the far side. There, sitting on a lone pallet, were four 155mm artillery shells. They were the same dull green as the metal cans containing the fuzes. On each shell, stenciled in white paint, was the designation:

155mm
xxxAPERS
COMPOSITION-B

The four shells stood on their bases, and across the top was a cardboard placard that read: DO NOT STACK. The tip was missing from each shell.

"Without a fuze threaded into the nose," Nadya said, "these shells are inert. They can't be exploded."

"I agree, and that's not my plan. I'm gonna take the explosive out of a shell."

"Do you have any idea how long it will take to cut through the metal casing and remove even part of the explosive?" Nadya asked.

"We have power tools." Peter was not dissuaded in the least.

"That casing is at least half an inch thick, and hardened steel."

Peter shook his head. "No, not these. See that designation? XXX indicates these are experimental rounds. APERS means they are antipersonnel. I've heard about this."

"From your circle of friends?" Nadya said, not trying to hide her skepticism.

Peter nodded. "Actually, yes. I believe these are beehive rounds. They use an aluminum shell casing so it's easier to split open."

He strode to the tool chest and retrieved a magnetic tray about the size of a saucer—it was used for holding small nuts, screws, and bolts. Returning to the pallet, he attempted to stick the magnetic base against one of the shells. "See, it's not magnetic."

Nadya's eyes widened. "Tell me what I can do to help."

Peter refined his idea, thinking of the items he would need, and then rattled off the list. "We're gonna need some steel wool. Maybe there's some in the tool chest. If not, look around. Might be with sanding pads. Also, two extension cords, one long and one short. Plug the longer cord into the closest electrical outlet to the back of that APC." Peter pointed to the APC that their prisoner was not cuffed to.

"Got it." She set out on her scavenger hunt.

Peter snipped the metal band secured around all four projectiles and then hefted one; the injuries to his arms burned in a flare of pain. It was heavy, but manageable by holding the shell close to his waist. Without a moment to lose, he made directly for the horizontal band saw and gently laid the green shell on the cutting table. He shoved it back and forth, adjusting the cutting position, until the saw blade was about half an inch from the base. Then he reefed down on the locking block to hold the shell firmly in place.

Just hope this band saw is not too noisy. Peter flipped the switch and energized the drive motor. As the blade came down, the bi-alloy steel teeth cut through the aluminum casing with ease, hardly making a sound. A minor but important victory, and he let out the breath he'd been holding.

He glanced over his shoulder and saw Nadya had a coiled extension cord draped from her shoulder. She was searching through drawers at the bottom of the tool chest and abruptly stood, holding a plastic bag half full of steel wool.

When Peter looked back at his work, the blade was almost three-quarters through the projectile. *Good, didn't hit any of the steel flechettes.* He'd suspected the steel darts would be bundled and located farther up the shell where they would be propelled forward by the explosive charge in the base.

Another half minute passed and then the saw completed the cut. Peter turned off the power, unlocked the latch, and removed the severed base. A material the color of beeswax was exposed inside the aluminum casing. "Bingo," he mumbled too softly for Nadya to hear.

Peter met Nadya at the tool chest where he pocketed a putty knife. "Got it."

"The explosive?"

He nodded, seeming to hesitate.

"What else do you need?" Nadya asked.

He was studying one of the metal drawers in the tool chest, fidgeting with the glides along the side of the drawer. "Ah, there it is." Nadya heard the click and then the drawer slid free. Peter dropped to a knee and dumped the tools onto the floor, avoiding loud clanging noises.

"See if you can find some large nuts, like half inch or so. Maybe over there in those parts bins." Peter pointed to some shelves not far away.

"Nuts?" She wrinkled her brow.

"Yeah, projectiles. I'll pack explosive in the bottom of this drawer. Then we'll fill the top—covering the explosive—with nuts or bolts or whatever you can find. We'll wrap it in cardboard and duct tape to hold it all together and then stand it on edge, aiming at the door."

A sly smile creased Nadya's lips. "An anti-personnel mine."

"The detonator will be tricky, but I have an idea. See what you can find. We don't have time to waste."

Using the putty knife, Peter scraped around the edge of the Composition-B explosive, separating the waxy material from the aluminum case. He sliced the squat, cylindrical chuck of high explosive into three circular slabs, each about an inch thick. As he was layering the slabs into the bottom of the metal drawer, Nadya arrived with two bins filled with heavy steel nuts. She dumped the contents over the layered explosive.

Peter left a small section of explosive exposed at one end. Nadya cut a sheet of cardboard from an empty box and produced the duct tape she had used to gag the guard. She formed the cardboard over the top of the drawer to prevent the nuts from falling out while Peter fastened the cardboard in place with the tape.

"Time to see if it will stay together." Peter lifted the drawer so it was resting on the flat back end. Nothing shifted. Still, he decided to wrap more tape just to be sure.

"We should position our mine in front of the door," he said.

"How about at the back of the APC? It's about 40 feet from the door and the projectiles should spread to an effective pattern at that distance."

"Exactly. Set it on top of two of the fuze crates; we don't want it right on the floor. I'll get to work opening a fuze and removing the detonator."

"You know how to do that?"

Peter couldn't explain that, as a designer of magnetic-impulse small arms, he'd been asked to consult on development of the Navy's railgun, a ship-mounted cannon that used an enormous magnetic impulse to fire shells. Consequently, he was familiar with both conventional artillery shells as well as the specialized projectiles that would be required for this futuristic weapon system. But even if he could tell Nadya, he didn't have the time.

"Stories for another day—assuming we live to see another day." He filled his fists with several adjustable wrenches and screwdrivers, not knowing exactly what tools would be needed, and moved to a heavy-duty workbench. Mounted to the steel surface was a large vise.

The fuze was a couple inches in diameter at the widest part. At the base of the pointed tip was a smaller-diameter protrusion with threads around the perimeter. Peter knew from his work on the railgun that this threaded portion contained the detonator and a small booster charge. It fit into the recess at the front of the shell.

Carefully locking the conical section into the bench vise, Peter used a pipe wrench to gently remove the detonator and booster cup. Fortunately, the detonator was likely new and the two portions separated easily on lightly lubricated threads.

Peter held the booster cup before his eyes, examining its construction. To the side was the detonator. It looked like a large percussion cap. If struck forcibly by the firing pin, the detonator would explode and cause the booster charge to also explode. But without a means for striking the detonator with a firing-pin-like object, Peter had to come up with an alternative. He had been thinking through this problem and was convinced there was another way.

Holding the booster cup, Peter returned to the tool chest. In the top tray was a portable propane torch. He grabbed it and continued on to Nadya. She was busy placing the mine on top of two crates at the back of the APC.

Peter pressed the booster cup into the section of exposed Composition-B explosive at the top of the charge. It was immediately clear that it wouldn't stay there on its own. The explosive was barely moldable, and although he was able to press the booster cup into the slab of yellow-tan explosive, he was going to have to secure it in position.

"Nadya, I need a section of wire to hold this detonator in place."

She nodded, retrieved the spool of wire she used to bind their prisoner and the wire cutters, and handed them to Peter. Two wraps and a twist, and the detonator was secured.

Peter stood the portable propane torch on the crate next to the mine, and aimed the tip such that the flame would impinge the detonator. He estimated that within a few seconds of ignition, the intense heat from the torch flame would cause the detonator to ignite, setting off a chain of explosive events.

"I need the steel wool," Peter said.

Nadya handed a large bunch to him, and he pulled it a little to loosen the fibers; then he wedged it in the wire wrap near the torch tip.

Nadya looked at her watch. "We have to hurry. We're

running out of time."

Next Peter used the wire cutters to lop off one end of the short extension cord. He used his knife to cut back the insulation and expose the copper conductor of the two wires. He stuffed the bare copper wire into the steel wool, and then laid out the cord so the other end was resting on top of the tracks at the rear corner of the APC. Then he stood back, examining his work.

He moved his eyes from the makeshift mine to the door. *Yes, that should do it. Just hope the detonator works.*

"Is it ready?" Nadya asked.

Peter nodded. "Almost." He positioned the end of the long extension cord at the tracks of the APC. "Now, for a little camouflage." He rolled the large tool chest in front of the mine. When Ellison came through the door with his mercenaries, they'd have no idea what they were facing.

CHAPTER 48

STANDING BESIDE THE HUMVEE, Ellison looked to the clear night sky. In the distance, he saw a speck of light. It was moving, gaining size as it approached. Finally, he was able to make out the red and green wing lights. When the landing lights came on, he had to avert his gaze.

The Gulfstream landed and rushed past his position. After breaking, and turning around, the G650 came to a rest not far from the parked Humvee, the turbine engines whining like banshees. Ellison had cupped his hands over his ears.

Two minutes later, after cooling the engines, the pilot powered down the aircraft and the cabin door opened outward, allowing a stairway to fold down to the tarmac. Claude Duss stood in the opening, backlit by the dim cabin lighting.

Ellison had not been waiting long. He was standing on the tarmac flanked by two mercenaries wearing black BDUs, each armed with an MP5SD submachine gun. Presently, their weapons were pointed down, and held with a relaxed grip. No threat was anticipated.

Ellison stepped forward. "Welcome, sir. How was the flight?"

"I didn't come here for idle chit chat," Duss said. "You have Savage and the woman, Nadya Wheeler?"

"Yes, sir. In the maintenance depot."

Duss folded himself into the passenger seat of the Humvee while Ellison and his two men climbed into the back seat. It was tight, shoulder-to-shoulder, but the ride would be short.

With a squeal of brakes, the Humvee stopped at the depot. One of the bodyguards held the door open for Duss to enter, Ellison one step behind his boss. Once inside, Duss stood to the side, allowing Ellison to take the lead.

He strode to the end of the hallway, followed closely by his three guards and Duss. As Ellison rounded the corner, he froze. The closest guard almost walked into him, stopping only inches away.

"What is it, boss?" one of the guards asked.

"Where is Kennor?" Ellison said.

The guards looked at each other, as confused as Ellison was.

"Get the rest of the men." Ellison motioned in the direction of the rec room, and one of the guards dashed off. The other two mercenaries tightened the hold on their weapons and locked eyes on Ellison, awaiting orders.

"Mr. Duss. I suggest you wait here."

"What's going on?"

"I left Kennor here at the door."

Duss glared back at Ellison, his eyes narrowed and jaw set.

The sound of boots on tile echoed off the hard walls and soon all of Ellison's bodyguards—10 in total—were gathered outside the double steel doors. All were former military, now professional guns for hire. They no longer pledged their allegiance to country or ideals; their loyalty now was to a paycheck.

"Has anyone seen Kennor?" Ellison asked the assembly.

Ten faces stared back in silence.

"You led me to believe," Duss said, his voice menacing, "that the situation was under control."

"Jackson and Nye, you stay with Mr. Duss. The rest of you will enter the maintenance bay with me. Weapons ready. I don't know how Savage and Wheeler could have escaped, but we aren't taking any chances."

Ellison produced a Beretta 9mm pistol and pulled the slide back to chamber a round. He had a man grab the handle on each door, ready to throw it open.

"On three. Ready?" Ellison said. "One… Two… Three…"

The double doors flew wide and the guards poured in, fanning out as they entered the brightly lit service facility. Some dropped to a knee and shouldered their MP5SD submachine guns, the silencers making the barrels look fat, almost like a short-barreled shotgun. Others stood, brandishing submachine guns or pistols.

Peter was standing by the improvised mine when the doors burst open. With his back to Ellison's men, he opened the gas valve on the propane torch. Then he cast a glance to Nadya. She was stationed at the side of the APC, her hands were on the extensions cords, ready to plug them together upon Peter's order. The Beretta pistol rested on the tracks next to the electrical cords.

Ellison stepped forward and lowered his gun. He had half expected Peter and Nadya to be gone—to have somehow escaped and fled. The fact that they were still here was good. In a moment, his men would take them into custody again. This time there would be no delays prior to questioning. And when Claude Duss had his answers, when he had learned all he sought to learn, then Ellison would bury both Peter Savage and

Nadya Wheeler in the desert.

"The two of you make a very resourceful pair," Ellison said. Kennor struggled at his bonds and grunted, but no intelligent communication could escape through his taped mouth. "Perhaps later you'll tell me how you overpowered my guard. But first, my boss wants to have a discussion with you."

"Right. And exactly where is your boss?" Peter asked. He was standing between the mine and the tool chest.

Before Ellison could answer, Duss stepped forward. His arms were folded across his chest. "I must say, Peter Savage, you have caused me a great deal of trouble."

"Well, it's the least I could do," Peter replied. He looked at the black hair, thin face and stern features of Duss and wondered what the face would look like if he smiled. In his mind, he couldn't imagine anything resembling humor in those dark, threatening eyes.

"Step forward, both of you. Hands up!" Ellison ordered. Duss was standing by his side.

Nadya glanced to Peter, taking her cue from his actions.

Peter stood his ground. "Before we do, aren't you just a little curious what we've been up to?"

Ellison raised an eyebrow and cocked his head slightly. "Look at all these guns trained on the two of you. Do you really think you can bluff your way to freedom?"

Peter drew in a deep breath and exhaled. He pinched his lips together and drew back the corners of his mouth, but his gaze never left Ellison and Duss.

"If you shoot us," Peter said, addressing Ellison, "your boss won't be very happy."

"Correction. You mean, if I kill you. My men are excellent marksmen, and at this range wounding you will be easy. So, as the saying goes, we can do this the easy way or the hard way."

"I see." Peter paused, his eyes taking in the deployment

of men before him. It was impossible to predict what the spread would be for the steel nuts in the mine. But given their irregular shape, Peter assumed they would spread considerably. Naturally, the highest density would be directly in front of the mine. That's where Ellison and Duss stood.

Of course, it was also entirely possible that the mine would be a dud. If that happened, he and Nadya were doomed.

He quickly thought through the sequence of events again, picturing each step.

"Mr. Savage. This is my last warning. Raise your hands and—"

"Now!" Peter yelled. At the same instant he shoved his shoulder into the tool chest and heaved to the side. The chest glided on roller-bearing castors to the side and Peter pivoted, diving for the concrete floor. His body slid to the side of the APC.

As soon has Nadya heard Peter's signal, she plugged the electrical cords together, setting off an irreversible chain of events. Electrical current surged to the steel wool, instantly sparking it ablaze. The propane gas issuing from the torch ignited. The high-intensity blue flame impinged upon the detonator.

One full second after Nadya initiated the chain reaction, the mine detonated.

CHAPTER 49

AS SOON AS PETER SHOVED ASIDE the tool chest, Ellison was in motion, thrusting his body in front of Duss. When the mine detonated, Nadya and Peter were shielded from the blast wave by the body of the APC. Still, even with hands cupped over their ears, the sound was almost deafening, and painful. The blast wave punched their bodies, squeezing air from their lungs.

After taking a moment to suck in air, Peter rose to his knees and took in the carnage. Bodies lay scattered in unnatural positions, nearly all with blood pooling around them. Peter didn't see Duss, although he thought he recognized Ellison's body, lying face down on top of another. Only three men were standing, and they were dazed, unfocused.

Nadya recovered first and held the Beretta in both hands, squeezing off controlled shots at the highest threat targets.

Boom! Boom!
Boom! Boom!

Boom! Boom!

The mercenaries fell, each receiving two slugs in the chest.

Peter rose to his feet and scooped up a silenced submachine gun from the closest body. His head felt like it was tightly wrapped in a sound-proof blanket; the ringing in his ears was nearly unbearable. He saw Nadya slowly advancing, pistol pointing wherever her eyes looked.

Suddenly, two guards rushed through the doorway, firing and running. Nadya dove to the side, seeking cover behind the tool chest. A volley of bullets punched into the chest, only to be stopped by the steel tools within.

The guards turned toward Peter as he was raising the MP5. Bullets screamed past. He pulled the trigger and cut down first one guard, then the second.

For a long minute, neither Peter nor Nadya moved. Their eyes staring at the doorway, expecting another charge. It never materialized.

Although Peter's ears were still ringing, he was beginning to regain his hearing. Through his peripheral vision, he noticed Nadya rise from the protection of the tool chest and move from body to body. She was kicking weapons out of reach, nudging bodies with her foot, and checking for a pulse. All the while keeping the Beretta ready.

Peter fixed his gaze on Ellison; his back was riddled with blood. As he approached, he recognized the clothing on the body under Ellison. It was clothing Claude Duss was wearing, but the face was concealed under Ellison's torso.

Cautiously, Peter closed the distance. He heard the sound of a muffled groan, quickly silenced by Nadya's Beretta.

"Nadya." He moved his chin toward the two bodies. She understood.

Holding the pistol in her right hand, she extended her left hand and tugged on Ellison's collar. His deadweight was heavy and unyielding at first. She repositioned her feet, and pulled again, this time leaning back to free the tangle of bodies.

Ellison's corpse came free, and she nearly stumbled as her balance was thrown off by the shifting weight.

"Drop your weapons, both of you," Duss commanded. He was gripping Ellison's pistol and had it pointed at Nadya, only three feet away.

She hesitated, calculating her moves and the required time. Her pistol was in her strong hand, but it was pointed uselessly at the floor. She'd never bring it to bear on Duss before he shot her dead.

Peter also hesitated, shifting his hands on the MP5SD and lowering his head so his sight line was perfect. Very subtly, he pulled the gun into his shoulder and began applying pressure to the trigger.

"I said drop it! You too, Mr. Savage."

Reluctantly Nadya complied and the gun clanged on the concrete. Her training as a Mossad agent was to never give up your weapon in a hostage situation. But that instruction seemed senseless when she was literally staring into the barrel of Duss' gun.

"You can't get away with it," Peter said with a calm, controlled voice.

As if to underscore Peter's statement, sirens wailed faintly. They were still far off, but getting closer.

"Put your weapon down, Mr. Savage. This is your last warning."

"Don't listen to him, Peter."

"Mr. Savage. I never bluff."

"No, I don't suppose you do." Then Peter pulled the trigger.

At the sound, Nadya fell to the side, anticipating to be shot over and over. But she never felt the pain of slugs slamming into her chest.

Duss cried out, clutching his hand. The pistol was beyond reach even if he could have grasped it.

"You shot me!" Duss screamed. His eyes bulged, and spittle appeared at the corners of his mouth. He leaned forward, pulling the wounded hand in close to his chest, his blood mingling with that from Ellison.

"I'll kill you! You hear me? You're dead. Dead! I'll never rest until my men hunt you down."

"Yeah, well you've already tried, remember? And that didn't go the way you planned."

Duss tried to rise only to be shoved back down by Nadya. She was aiming her Beretta once again at him. For his part, he didn't acknowledge Nadya at all but glared at Peter with pure hatred.

The sirens were very loud now, and Peter estimated the first responders would be there in minutes. "So let me give you a reality check, okay? First, your men are either dead, or wounded and incapacitated. You are also wounded and incapacitated. There are two guns pointed at you, and either of us would gladly kill you if that becomes necessary."

The malevolence still burned fiercely in Duss' eyes. "So why don't you shoot me now? You want to."

Peter allowed his lips to twist into a cocky grin. "Actually, I don't. We were going to have a conversation, remember? Only now, I'll ask the questions."

"I'm bleeding. I need medical treatment."

"Don't worry," Nadya replied. "I'm sure there are EMTs among the first responders. They'll be here soon."

Peter walked over to the first aid kit mounted on the wall near the doorway. He opened it and soon found some gauze packs and a triangular bandage. "Here," he said, dropping the supplies in Duss' lap. "That'll keep the bleeding in check. So how about some Q and A while we wait for law enforcement to arrive?"

Duss ignored the question while he busied himself bandaging his right hand, the forearm streaked with blood to his elbow.

"Why were you trying to kill me?"

Duss finished snugging a knot by gripping a corner of the cloth in his teeth. His hand was wrapped in layer upon layer of gauze and white cotton, but blood was already beginning to seep through.

He remained defiant. "I don't have anything to say to you."

"It's the files, right? What's your connection anyway?" Peter prodded.

Nadya keep the Beretta pointed at Duss. She was becoming increasingly impatient.

"Well," Peter continued, "it doesn't really matter. I'll release the files to the media. Combined with the helicopter gunship attack in the mountains and this… event… here, I'm sure all the major newspapers and TV stations will pick up the story. It'll make national headlines for weeks."

Duss coughed out a mocking laugh. "You really don't get it. Even now, you still don't understand."

Peter's brow wrinkled. "Get what? Once I release the files, there won't be any secrets to protect anymore."

Duss laughed. "Are you really that stupid? Do you really think this is about an obscure event that happened in 1967?"

"No. I know it's more than that. You stand to gain handsomely if the U.S. goes to war. And war is coming if Schuman is elected President, isn't it?"

The mirth left Duss' face, his jaw taking a hard edge once again. "I run a legitimate business—essential to national security. I've done nothing wrong."

Peter met Nadya's gaze. The sirens were loud, and then one by one they went silent. Help had finally arrived.

Outside, law enforcement officers surrounded the building. Portable floodlights were set up and soon the sound of generators softly humming could be heard inside.

"Release the files; it doesn't matter any longer," Duss said. "And get used to looking over your shoulder. If you're lucky, you'll spend years in prison for murdering my men here. If you ever get out, you'll have a very large price on your head."

"This was self-defense." Peter felt his face flushing, heard his voice rising. "You're the one who will spend the rest of his life behind bars."

"That's not the story my attorneys will sell to the jury. Besides, I have a get-out-of-jail-free card." He shifted his eyes to Nadya again. "I understand the Mossad are very good at terminating their marks, and they never forgive, isn't that true?"

She lowered her gun a little and faced Peter. "He's right. If they mark you, they will never stop until you are dead."

A loud bang sounded at the front door. It wasn't a gunshot or explosion, rather metal smashing into the steel door.

"They're breaching the door," Peter said. He ejected the magazine from the submachine gun and threw it across the room. Then he cycled the action, ejecting the round from the chamber. Nadya followed his lead and tossed the unloaded Beretta well out of reach. Peter draped the black nylon-web sling over Duss's head and laid the MP5SB in his lap.

Another bang echoed through the hallway, followed by the slam of the door into the wall as it burst open under repeated blows from the battering ram.

Nadya and Peter sat, hands raised, to either side of Claude Duss, who was still holding his injured hand against his chest. He was attempting to slip the black sling off his shoulder when the first Sheriff Deputy edged around the corner of the hallway. He was leading with an M4 assault rifle.

"Don't move! Raise your hands!"

"I need medical help," Duss said. "They tried to kill me."

"Raise your hands!"

Slowly, Duss complied.

More deputies appeared and rushed into the large room. The smell of blood and urine and guts was almost as strong as the visual image of total carnage. It was the worst massacre any had seen. Bodies were bent at unnatural angles, flesh ripped from limbs. Other than the shuffling of their boots, it was eerily silent.

"Keep your hands up!" someone shouted, and a deputy roughly removed the weapon slung over Duss' head. Others walked among the corpses, occasionally checking for a pulse. A deputy rushed to the APC where Kennor was wired to the tow loop. He ripped off the tape and confirmed the man was alive.

One of them spoke into a microphone attached to his shoulder epaulet. "Secured. Send in the EMTs. We have four survivors. Looks like a gunshot wound to the hand of one of 'em."

"My name is Nadya Wheeler. I radioed for help."

She was met with a blank stare from the deputies. All rifles still aimed at the three of them.

"Is Detective Colson from the Bend PD with you?" she asked.

One of the deputies left and returned on the heels of the EMTs, Detective Colson at his side.

"I'm not injured," Nadya said to a pair of EMTs while others attended to Duss.

Colson approached Peter. He shrugged off the paramedics. "Well, well. Mr. Savage." She met his eyes with a stern countenance. "You do have a habit of being in the wrong place at the wrong time." Colson cast her gaze around the room. "Your doing?"

"My friend here," he nodded to Duss, "arranged to have me

plucked off the street a few hours ago by his goons. Right in front of my home. His men tied us up in this room."

"You and the young lady—Nadya Wheeler?"

Peter nodded.

"I did no such thing. He's lying."

One of the paramedics got in Duss' face. "You need to calm down, sir. We're going to put you on an IV and get some fluids in you. You've lost a lot of blood."

"They tried to kill me!"

"Sir," the EMT commanded, "you need to calm down."

Nadya addressed Colson. "Ellison, that man there," she pointed to the body, "worked for Duss. He was orchestrating the murders in Bend and the attack in the mountains."

"You seem to know a lot about this, so why don't you enlighten me?"

Nadya glanced at Peter, and then focused on Colson. "I work for Israeli intelligence."

"Don't listen to her!" Duss shouted as he was being strapped onto a gurney.

Colson rolled her eyes. "So much for wrapping this up quickly."

"I'll give you a full statement and answer all your questions at your headquarters."

"Yes, you will. You too, Mr. Savage."

CHAPTER 50

AFTER A LONG NIGHT of seemingly endless questioning by the detectives, Peter and Nadya were released with stern orders not to leave town. "I mean it, Mr. Savage," Detective Colson admonished.

After conferring with two Crook County Sheriff Investigators, who participated in the questioning, they decided there was insufficient evidence to implicate Peter or Nadya for any crime. For once, Colson had to admit that it appeared Peter was a victim.

It was still dark outside when the detective drove the two to Peter's home. "Remember what I said. Don't leave town."

Peter nodded as he stepped out of the unmarked car. He climbed the steps, unlocked the door, and held it open for Nadya. Diesel greeted him as usual, and this time the canine didn't growl at Nadya.

As tired as he was, Peter really needed to talk to Jim. He offered Nadya the guest room, but she wanted to participate in

344

the call. They sat at the counter in the kitchen, and Peter dialed the number.

"Jim, it's Peter. I have you on speaker. Nadya Wheeler is with me."

Nadya identified herself and gave the name of her superior in Tel Aviv.

"I'll have one of my analysts verify your identity. But until we do, this conversation will not be candid."

"Understood," Peter said. "I need to bring you up to speed. Last night, some hired guns working for United Armaments snatched me in front of my home. Nadya was taken also. They intended to question us at a test range in Crook County, Eastern Oregon."

Peter and Nadya shared the highlights with Jim. He waited to comment and ask questions until they were done. "We were able to connect that gunship to UA. The wreckage was badly burned, but we got a serial number from the frame. The assault team was mostly composed of mercenaries—ex-U.S. military. Although four bodies remain unidentified."

"That's probably my team. They won't show up in your databases."

"You sound pretty certain, Ms. Wheeler," Jim said.

"I am."

"Foreign agents acting on U.S. soil, attempting to murder an American. That will not go over well at the State Department."

Nadya understood the diplomatic fallout that was about to beset her government. She also recognized that Mossad might disavow her, or worse.

"We have a theory," Peter said, "that the Israeli Prime Minister and Congressman Schuman are plotting a pre-emptive attack on Iran."

"The Speaker would have to win the election first," Jim said, sounding almost philosophical.

"That's obviously his plan, but we think he's engineered a fail-safe. If Schuman succeeds in spearheading an override vote, and the Israeli Security Act becomes law, Congress will be forced to declare war on Iran when they retaliate. The *Liberty* case was, essentially, the blueprint. That's why they were willing to commit murder to keep it secret."

"Lieutenant Lacey and Mona Stephens have put forward a similar theory, although they have yet to find any supporting evidence. What did Duss have to say?"

"Nothing of value, really. And when I told him I was going to release the files to the public, he didn't seem alarmed. If our theory is right, they'll want to bury those files at least until the election is over."

"You have the files?" Jim asked.

With all that had happened over the past days—from the near-death experience in the mountains to the kidnapping by Ellison's men—Peter had not shared with Jim the thumb drive he'd hidden.

"I'll need that memory stick. Lacey and her team have been working to uncover who's calling the shots." Jim explained that Agent Barnes was an alias. Richard Nyden never was an FBI Agent. Furthermore, the mercenaries working for UA were known as the Guardians, and phone records from Nyden's cell connected him to both Ellison and Angela Meyers.

"That's incredible," Peter said. "You have a probable connection between Claude Duss and the Guardian's terrorist actions."

"Yes, and that's the problem. Nothing solid to connect Duss to any of this. Or to Schuman."

"Duss was there, at the test facility," Nadya added. "Flew in just to question us is what Ellison said. That makes him an accessory to kidnapping."

"No, Ellison is dead—and Duss will deny he knew anything

about the kidnapping." Peter stood and began to pace, but not straying too far from the phone.

"He's got an army of top-notch attorneys on his payroll. We have to have overwhelming evidence to get a conviction."

Peter leaned over the counter, suddenly energized. "Or, you need to turn him."

"Go on," Jim said.

"Can you have the FBI file federal charges? Terrorism? Firing missiles in a National Forest? Whatever. Anything and everything you can think of."

"I'm sure we can get the Justice Department to cooperate. What's the end game?"

As Nadya listened, Peter explained his plan.

"Well, it may be our best shot. I'll make sure Lacey and Stephens are prepped, and I'll phone Detective Colson and get the ball rolling. We'll need to move fast. In the meantime, you two should get some rest. Expect to hear from Colson later today."

"One more thing," Peter said before Jim ended the call. "How is Kate?"

"Good. She's safe here. Bored, but safe. She told me to remind you of your promise."

Peter smiled, his mind flashing back to their farewell as she boarded the SGIT jet. That seemed so long ago.

"Tell her I remember, and I always keep a promise." His smile faded.

After the call ended, Nadya looked at Peter like she was seeing him for the first time. "Who is Kate?"

"Someone who reminded me of something I'd forgotten."

"What would that be?"

He raised his eyes to Nadya, his mind suddenly turning melancholy. "Life shouldn't be wasted."

Peter dropped himself into one of the leather, overstuffed chairs in front of the fireplace and Nadya retreated to the guest room. They both needed rest; a full ten hours of sleep would be great. But there was too much going on for that to happen. The best they could expect would be a few hours of shuteye—fitful, but better than nothing.

Peter pulled the leather ottoman closer and placed his legs on it. The supple leather and plush padding felt luxurious in comparison to the night he'd spent on concrete, van floors, and hard chairs.

Very quickly his eyelids closed as his entire body relaxed. But deep sleep did not come. His semiconscious mind began wandering. How would Claude Duss react when confronted by the federal charges? What if the detonator had failed and the improvised mine had not detonated? Would he ever be safe? And what of his family, Ethan and Joanna?

He shifted his body, scrunching deeper into the stuffed chair, trying to clear his mind. He craved sleep, but he had to shut down his mind first. There were so many what-ifs. He thought back to the beginning, when he met Kate Simpson. That Agent Barnes would have surely murdered her had he not been there. What will happen to Kate?

He recalled her brown eyes, soft and gentle; when she smiled her whole face radiated joy. Peter pictured that smile, her chocolate brown hair shimmering as she moved her head, her infectious laughter. Then he pictured a different Kate, one who was terrified after discovering the body of her roommate. Peter had lived this before—when fear infected like a hideous disease, a disease that left the body gaunt and pale after attacking the soul.

Kate would be easy prey for assassins if he couldn't end this nightmare. Peter pictured her opening the door to a delivery person, or a police officer, only to learn too late that they were imposters.

No, he had to be certain the leaders were stopped—arrested and put in prison, or killed. It was the only way.

His mind shifted to Nadya and the moment she was prepared to kill him on the mountain. She had said Peter was a killer, no different from her or her team. He was angry at first; he wanted to believe he was different. But now, he questioned himself and his motives. Was he really any different?

He opened his eyes and checked the time. It was morning, and he had to concede he wasn't going to get much sleep. Maybe some fresh air would help. He patted Diesel on the head, but the canine showed no interest in giving up his warm spot on the rug.

Pocketing his cell phone and keys, Peter opened the secret panel in the bookcase and retrieved the memory stick he'd hidden there inside the barrel of the Brown Bess musket. He quietly left and locked the door, no reason to disturb Nadya. Clutching the memory stick he climbed into his H3 Hummer truck and started the engine.

His first destination was an office supply store to purchase another memory stick. Next stop was the library to use one of the public computers.

Time to double down on my insurance policy.

CHAPTER 51

PETER GLANCED AT THE TIME on his phone before answering the call. It was almost 1:30 p.m. The number was blocked on caller ID. *That was fast, thought it would be later.*

"Mr. Savage, it's Detective Colson. I was told you'd be expecting my call. I want you and Ms. Wheeler to participate in a meeting at Bend PD in a little over an hour from now. Say 3:00 p.m."

"We'll be there." Peter had already had lunch: a pulled pork sandwich and glass of IPA from one of his favorite brewpubs. He patted his pocket for the third time, making certain both memory sticks were still there.

On the short drive home, Peter was thinking over the anticipated meeting with Detective Colson. She did not want to say who would be attending, which suggested to Peter that Jim had succeeded in convincing the Department of Justice and FBI to play along.

Diesel greeted Peter at the door, tail wagging. It seemed that despite the sutured wounds and extensive bruising, the worst of the pain had passed. "Hey boy. Is Nadya still sleeping?"

Diesel returned his master's gaze, cocking his head to the side.

Peter walked to the guest room and knocked on the door. "Nadya, we have our meeting soon."

He expected to hear a groggy acknowledgement, or maybe stirring as she rose and moved about the room. Instead, he was greeted by silence.

He rapped his knuckles against the door, this time harder. "Nadya?"

Silence.

Peter turned the doorknob and pushed the door open, peaking around the edge, hoping she was just exhausted and sleeping soundly. The sheet and blanket were pulled back, and the pillow was pushed in, suggesting she had slept in the bed, but the room was empty. Nadya was gone.

"Where's Ms. Wheeler?" Detective Colson asked.

"I don't know. She left without a word. Not even a note."

"Great. Why is it that nothing's easy when you're involved?"

Peter shrugged.

"Never mind. Sign in so we can issue you a visitor's badge."

Peter filled out the log sheet and a uniformed officer gave him a clip-on badge. An audible buzz accompanied the click of a lock, and Colson held the door open for Peter to enter.

"You should have this. You'll find the contents interesting, to say the least." Peter held out a memory stick.

She raised her eyebrows as she pocketed the memory device. "Follow me," she said.

It wasn't far to the conference room, and Colson waved him inside. Jim and Mona Stephens were already seated at the table.

"Lieutenant Lacey couldn't break away from another

assignment," Jim said. "But Ms. Stephens has been on this case from the beginning. In fact, she's been our point of contact with Detective Colson."

An unfamiliar face approached Peter. "I'm Special Agent Markley," he said as he offered his FBI badge and ID for Peter to examine. "We've discussed this case in detail," he said as he motioned for Peter to take a seat. "I was under the impression that Ms. Wheeler would also be participating. We have some questions we thought she could help with."

"I don't know where Nadya is. She was staying in my guest room after the detective dropped us off early this morning. I went out to have lunch, and when I returned, she was gone."

"Did you ask her to join you for lunch?" Detective Colson asked.

Peter shook his head. "I assumed she was sleeping; I didn't want to wake her."

"We're checking her story," Stephens added. "It might take a few days to get a definitive answer if we have to involve the State Department."

"That's unfortunate," Markley said. "Under the circumstances, the Bureau has no choice but to place her on a watch list as a suspected terrorist. At the very least, we want to bring her in for questioning."

Jim cleared his throat. "We will provide you a full report once we have anything definitive from the Israeli government. However, under the circumstances, perhaps it would be more productive to focus on the bigger fish."

Markley frowned. "I'm coming to that Commander. Your participation in an advisory capacity is appreciated, but we do have a process to follow."

"Gentlemen." Colson interrupted sensing a turf battle about to erupt. "No one is suggesting we forget about Ms. Wheeler. But that's not why we are here. The question of national security must be taken seriously. If the allegations that Commander Nicolaou has shared are true, we have an extremely serious problem."

Markley held his hands out in a placating gesture. "Agent Elizondo is questioning Mr. Duss just down the hall. As you suggested, if he agrees to testify against Angela Meyers and Abraham Schuman, we are prepared to offer full immunity on all federal charges, including terrorism. I have to say, I never thought the AG would agree to these terms."

"Do you think he'll take the offer?" Peter asked. He had formulated this plan after thinking about the comment Duss made about being above the law, having a get-out-of-jail-free card, as he put it.

"I do," Markley replied. "It may not be enough to get a conviction against Schuman, but it should ruin his chances of getting elected in November. My guess is, Schuman will turn on Meyers, make her the scapegoat. For her part, Meyers has already given us the name of her contact at the Portland office— Andrew Shooks. He's had a lot to say about Meyers, but so far we're only getting hearsay on Schuman's role."

Peter nodded. "What about David Feldman?"

"That will be up to President Taylor's administration, assuming he wins re-election."

"Which is very likely if Schuman is disgraced," Stephens observed. "We've scrutinized both campaigns, and although Schuman is favored over Taylor, his popularity is driven by a large fraction of pro-nationalist, anti-establishment voters. But there is also a large block of swing voters. And once Schuman is discredited, facing criminal charges and a possible conviction, those swing voters will shift to supporting President Taylor."

"Israel has always been a very close ally," Jim said. "Even so, President Taylor does not take kindly to being played. I suspect the atmosphere between Washington and Tel Aviv will be pretty frosty for a while."

Peter folded his arms across his chest. "So, this all sounds good. But for the plan to work, it requires Duss to take the deal. Then, my friend Detective Colson," Peter motioned with his hand to the detective, "plays her cards."

"Already briefed the Chief," she said.

There was a knock at the door, and Peter swiveled in his chair to see who it was.

Markley addressed their visitor. "Agent Elizondo, this is Peter Savage." Peter stood and shook the agent's hand. Markley was standing now, too.

"Well?"

"After exchanging a few words with his attorney, he took the deal. That bastard is unbelievably arrogant. He didn't spend more than a minute thinking it over. He said the USS *Liberty* files were simply the blueprint, confirming your theory." Elizondo held his hand out toward Peter and Stephens.

The agent continued, "He said Schuman was worried that if there was renewed publicity about the role President Johnson played in that incident—the fact he committed the U.S. military to supporting a pre-emptive attack on the Arab Coalition, including willingly sacrificing the *Liberty* and blaming the attack on Egypt to drum up popular support—then the press would be sensitive to Schuman's collusion with Prime Minister Feldman to repeat that plan. Only this time, it would have been joint Israeli and American forces bombing and invading Iran, Syria, and Iraq."

"That's quite the story," Colson said.

"Yes," Elizondo replied. "As war spread—possibly even involving Russia—United Armaments, under the leadership of Claude Duss, would make billions from the sale of weapons. He claims to possess secretly recorded conversations with Schuman stashed in a safe deposit box. Based on what he shared, even if he suddenly decides not to cooperate, we have enough to get a search warrant. He must have anticipated that this could all blow up in his face."

"Naturally, the AG will downplay this deal," Markley added. "As Special Agent in Charge, I'll draft a press release pointing out the close cooperation between our departments. Of course, I'll need a quote from you, Detective Colson, and from your chief."

Colson stared at the two FBI agents. She was amazed they seemed more interested in the optics than in actually catching the bad guy and stopping a plot that would have drawn the U.S. into a full-scale war encompassing all of the Middle East.

"I assume you have what you want from Mr. Duss?" Colson said.

"Yep," Elizondo replied. "Signed, sealed, and delivered."

"Very well. Would you please escort Mr. Duss and his attorney in here? I don't expect he'll take what I have to say very well—better to have several witnesses. Besides, I owe Mr. Savage the satisfaction of being present when this comes to an end."

Elizondo nodded and, followed by Markley, left the room.

"I suspect that memory stick you gave me contains the *Liberty* files?"

"Yes. It's evidence. Thought you would need it." Peter expected a thank you, but Colson remained noncommittal.

"There may be complications with that evidence," Stephens said.

"Such as?"

"The government doesn't want it released. Our request to declassify all of the documents have so far been refused. No one will even admit that the files exist."

"I could simply release them to the press," Peter said.

Colson worked her lower jaw, not pleased about this new

revelation. "So, what you're saying, is that even if I wanted to return this data to Mr. Savage, I can't."

Stephens nodded.

"Well," Peter said, "someone should leak this information. Then the government would have to acknowledge its existence and explain why, after all these decades, they still don't want to make it public. I can't—"

Peter was interrupted by the opening of the door. Wearing an orange jumpsuit and with his hands cuffed to a chain around his waist, Claude Duss entered, followed by his attorney and the two FBI agents.

Colson rose and motioned to an empty chair. "Have a seat, Mr. Duss."

"What is this about?" his attorney objected. "We made a deal. Complete immunity from prosecution in exchange for my client's full cooperation."

"Yes, that is my understanding as well. Agents Markley and Elizondo have explained that Mr. Duss is very happy to be a cooperative witness, including sharing secretly taped phone conversations with Abraham Schuman."

The attorney was nodding vigorously. "And my client is afforded immunity from prosecution for all charges associated with the alleged crimes. I am confident the tapes and testimony Mr. Duss will provide will be very damaging to Schulman's defense."

Colson held up a finger. "Agent Elizondo, may I read the agreement signed by Mr. Duss?"

Elizondo held it out, and Colson read through quickly. "Ah, here it is. It says that Mr. Duss is granted immunity by the Attorney General of the United States from prosecution for all *federal* charges."

The attorney's eyes widened as realization dawned on him. "But the agents only mentioned federal charges—"

"That is correct," Markley said. "You do understand that the FBI has limited jurisdiction that does not extend to local policing."

"Which brings me to the point," Detective Colson said. "Claude Duss, you are under arrest—"

"You can't arrest me!" he shouted and lunged forward. Both FBI agents grabbed his shoulders and roughly shoved him back into his chair.

"You are charged with accessory to commit murder after the fact." Duss' eyes were wide and his teeth clenched.

Colson turned to the attorney. "You should expect more charges against your client as the investigation progresses."

Duss faced Peter, veins on his temples bulging, his face flushed. "I'll kill you!"

Peter stood. He'd seen enough. Duss was slippery, but with a pile of serious charges coming, it would take a miracle for him to walk. Peter paused at the doorway and turned his head toward Duss. "Like I said before: you tried that already, and it didn't go so well for you."

CHAPTER 52

BEND, OREGON
APRIL 27

PETER LEFT THE OFFICES of the *Bend Bulletin* about 30 minutes after his arrival. The meeting was necessarily brief. He had nothing to say "on the record" and insisted his identity be kept secret. Upon meeting the reporter, he retrieved the second memory stick from the knife sheath inside his boot, having left the folding blade in his truck prior to entering the police station. The reporter accepted the data storage device with an inquisitive expression. He estimated she was in her mid-thirties, and based on what he found online she had a decent resume. Probably the most seasoned reporter he would find in Central Oregon.

She listened carefully, taking notes and asking a few questions. Peter retold the events that transpired in the mountains west of Bend, culminating in the Air National Guard shooting down the United Armaments attack helicopter. He knew she would quickly confirm the events and glean other critical facts from an interview of the base Public Affairs Officer.

Then he walked her through the kidnapping and confrontation with Claude Duss at the test range in Eastern Oregon.

"Crook County Sheriff?" she had asked, just to be sure.

Finally, Peter handed over the memory stick. "The secret files—it's all there. You need to draw your own conclusions, but this is Pulitzer material."

Without looking up from her notepad, she asked, "How do I tie Speaker Schuman to this conspiracy?"

"Call Special Agents Markley and Elizondo, FBI, Portland office. I believe they are preparing a press release on the plea bargain struck between the Department of Justice and Claude Duss. I'm confident they'll be happy to talk to you—on the record."

"You know," she said, "Schuman has scheduled a vote in 10 days to override the President's veto of the Israeli Security Act."

"Sounds to me like you've got a tight deadline." Peter stood. "You'll want to go to press at least several days before that vote."

"How can I reach you if I have follow-up questions?"

"You can't." He walked away, but stopped and turned to face the reporter. "One more thing. You might want to talk to Detectives Colson and Nakano."

The reporter tilted her head. "Bend Police?"

"Yep," he said as he walked out the door.

He was running late and hoped that Kate wouldn't be disappointed. Peter parked at his home and walked the short distance to Anthony's restaurant. He entered the lobby and spotted her immediately. She was standing with her arms folded, scrolling through her phone.

"I didn't message you, and I'm sorry I'm late."

She looked up, her face radiant. She was wearing a yellow summer dress with a knitted shawl draped over her shoulders.

"You look beautiful."

"Thank you." She smiled and Peter felt like a young man

again, a feeling that had been absent for so long, it was hard to recognize at first.

The hostess led them to a quiet table near the large windows looking out toward the Cascade Mountains. The Deschutes River flowed lazily only 50 yards away.

"I phoned you several times over the past week. Where have you been?"

Peter sighed. "It's a long story."

Kate looked back into his eyes. "And you think I don't deserve to know the truth?"

Peter let the question hang until the cocktail waiter arrived. He ordered a bottle of Pinot Gris from Erath vineyard in Northwestern Oregon.

Kate raised her eyebrows. "Well?"

"I was up there." He pointed out the window at the mountains. "And then I was kidnapped, but I escaped."

She twisted her mouth into a crooked grin. "I see. So you don't want to tell me what's going on."

The wine arrived, and Peter had the waiter pour two glasses. "It began when your roommate was murdered and ended up being a case of national security. What I said was true. Mercenaries tried to kill me, and I fled to the mountains so no one here would get hurt."

"Like what almost happened to me?"

Peter nodded. "And what did happen to those people at Pinnacle."

"I was worried. The stories on the news said you were wanted for murder."

"It's cleared up now."

"Is that why you asked me to have dinner? So you could set the record straight?"

Peter met her gaze and felt his pulse quickening. "No." He reached across the table and found her hand. It was soft and warm. "No, I asked you to dinner because I wanted to see you again. I wanted to tell you that the danger is over. And, if you'd like, maybe we could have dinner again."

Kate rubbed her thumb across the back of Peter's hand. For reasons she couldn't explain, even though she hardly knew the man, she felt comfortable and safe in his presence.

She looked at the face across from her. When she'd seen it before, it was usually hard, the eyes cold. But not now, not tonight. The steel grey eyes flashed a hint of blue and glowed with warmth.

Kate smiled. "I'd like that."

AUTHOR'S POST SCRIPT

THE *USS LIBERTY* INCIDENT is, to most Americans, a little-known historical event. I became aware of this tragic affair by a documentary aired by Al Jazeera in 2014 titled "The Day Israel Attacked America." Here is the link where you can download the video: http://bit.ly/USliberty.

In addition, there are many books retelling of the incident, along with this website that purports to be the official memorial site for the *Liberty*: http://www.ussliberty.org/index2.html.

As you know by now, the *Liberty* was a U.S. Navy surveillance vessel stationed in the Mediterranean Sea off the coast of Egypt in June of 1967. The attack in broad daylight, deliberate and ruthless, should have been a low point in U.S.-Israeli relations. Except that's not how it played out. The facts of the attack, as retold in *Hunting Savage*, are true—I did not embellish them. Based on recently declassified documents and voice recordings of Israeli pilots engaged in the action, it is crystal clear that the military forces of Israel knew from the beginning they were attacking a U.S. Naval vessel. Exactly why, remains a mystery to this day.

It is equally disturbing that American aircraft were within range of the *Liberty*, capable of lending assistance and likely saving the lives of many seamen. Those aircraft were launched multiple times from the carriers *America* and *Saratoga*, only to be quickly recalled by the Secretary of Defense, Robert McNamara. Historians generally agree that the order to recall those planes originated with President Lyndon Johnson. The only explanation put forward for Johnson's decision is that he did not want to embarrass an ally of the United States.

That explanation insults the memory of the seamen serving aboard the *Liberty*, as well as all veterans.

The prolonged nature of the attack, utilizing resources of both the Israeli air force and navy, is consistent with a determined effort to sink the surveillance ship. Given that the ship's inflatable life rafts were machine-gunned, the orders must have been to make every effort to ensure none of the seamen survived. At the time, the Israeli government claimed their actions were a mistake, and inexplicably the Johnson Administration and Congress were willing to accept that explanation at face value. However, the facts of the incident, supported by voice recordings of Israeli pilots and air controllers, are not even remotely consistent with the action being accidental.

Without a doubt, the *USS Liberty* should have sunk. It is a miracle and testament to the heroic actions of her Captain and crew that she remained afloat. The surviving crew and immediate families were sworn to secrecy by the U.S. government under penalty of a long prison sentence. Reporters were kept away from the stricken ship, and within a few months the incident was mostly swept under the carpet. The Israeli government issued an apology and eventually paid minimal damages to the U.S. government for loss of property and to the families of the deceased.

Yet 50 years after this tragedy, the central question—why?—has not been fully and satisfactorily answered. Many historians have speculated that the *Liberty* and her crew intercepted radio traffic concerning the imminent invasion of the Golan Heights, and that this information could not be allowed to reach Washington for fear President Johnson would pressure the Israeli government to cease hostilities aimed at expanding the conflict. But this explanation falls short of explaining why U.S. aid to the stricken ship was repeatedly recalled, and why the Johnson administration did not insist on prompt and meaningful compensation from Israel.

With a lack of transparency, conspiracy theories abound—trust in our government is eroded. The explanation offered in *Hunting Savage* is of my own imagination, but it seems to explain the facts better than any official explanation put forward over the past 50 years. The American public, as well as the survivors of the *USS Liberty* and their families, deserve to know the complete truth; there can be no legitimate reason for failing to come clean on this.

ABOUT THE AUTHOR

DAVE EDLUND IS THE *USA TODAY* bestselling author of the award-winning Peter Savage series and a graduate of the University of Oregon with a doctoral degree in chemistry. He resides in Bend, Oregon, with his wife, son, and four dogs (Lucy Liu, Murphy, Tenshi, and Diesel). Raised in the California Central Valley, he completed his undergraduate studies at California State University Sacramento. In addition to authoring several technical articles and books on alternative energy, he is an inventor on 97 U.S. patents. An avid outdoorsman and shooter, Edlund has hunted North America for big game ranging from wild boar to moose to bear. He has traveled extensively throughout China, Japan, Europe, and North America.

THE PETER SAVAGE SERIES

BY DAVE EDLUND

More to come!

Follow Dave Edlund at www.PeterSavageNovels.com, tweet a
message to @DaveEdlund, or leave a comment or fascinating
link at the author's official Facebook Page:

www.facebook.com/PeterSavageNovels.